THE CINEMA OF LOST

DREAMS

Also by Alli Sinclair

Burning Fields
Midnight Serenade
Under the Spanish Stars
Under the Parisian Sky

Novellas
Dreaming of Spain

THE CINEMA OF LOST

DREAMS

Alli Sinclair

LYRICAL PRESS
Kensington Publishing Corp.
www.kensingtonbooks.com

LYRICAL PRESS BOOKS are published by

Kensington Publishing Corp.
119 West 40th Street
New York, NY 10018

All Kensington titles, imprints, and distributed lines are available at special quantity discounts for bulk purchases for sales promotion, premiums, fundraising, educational, or institutional use.

Special book excerpts or customized printings can also be created to fit specific needs. For details, write or phone the office of the Kensington Sales Manager: Kensington Publishing Corp., 119 West 40th Street, New York, NY 10018. Attn. Sales Department. Phone: 1-800-221-2647.

Lyrical Press and Lyrical Press logo Reg. U.S. Pat. & TM Off.

First Electronic Edition: November 2019
ISBN-13: 978-1-5161-0918-0 (ebook)
ISBN-10: 1-5161-0918-X (ebook)

First Print Edition: November 2019
ISBN-13: 978-1-5161-0919-7
ISBN-10: 1-5161-0919-8

Printed in the United States of America

For my brother, Dave

Chapter One

Claire Montgomery sank against the cushions of the rattan chair on the veranda of the Queenslander guesthouse. Her legs were weary, but her heart was full after a long day of filming. She gazed at the moon shining bright in the inky sky—the one constant in her hectic, nomadic life.

Closing her eyes, Claire allowed the symphony of cicadas to lull her as she inhaled the magnificent scent of the myrtle nearby. Soon she could reward herself with a beach vacation in Bali—a stark contrast to her chaotic life in Melbourne. Not that she'd been in her hometown often since entering the film industry. These days, she spent a vast amount of time flying or driving, scouring the countryside for the perfect location for whatever TV show or movie she was working on at the time. One day, she'd secure the role she'd dreamed about since she was a child—a documentary producer—although this had proved harder than expected.

Right now, though, she had to concentrate on the job she was hired to do, and so the long days of negotiating and troubleshooting whizzed by in a blur. She cherished this rare moment to get her mind and body ready for another day of filming *Little Cinema, Big Dreams,* a TV miniseries set in the 1930s that dramatized the life of architect Amelia Elliott. Getting permission to film in one of Amelia's renowned Art Deco cinemas had cemented Claire's position as location manager for Wattle Films. She'd just been promoted from location assistant and it felt like she'd finally taken one huge step up the rickety ladder she'd been clinging to the past three years.

She sipped her ice-cold glass of chardonnay. The taut muscles in her neck finally relaxed.

"Claire!"

She jerked forward. Wine sloshed out of her glass and onto the floorboards. Peering at the figure in the shadows, she spotted her longtime friend from film school, Phil Aitkens. He'd been living his dream of becoming a well-respected cameraman, and she loved that they were working together on *Little Cinema*.

Phil stood with his hands on his hips.

"What is it?" She put down the glass and rubbed her eye.

"You need to get your butt down here. Now!"

"Huh?"

"Nigel's on the warpath!"

"What for?" Claire grabbed her satchel and slung it across her body. *So much for a night off.* Clunking down the wooden stairs, she made her way to Phil. "What's happened?"

"You are never going to believe it." He took off, and she had to rush to keep up. "Actually, you probably will."

"James has been boozing and started a fight?"

"No, though it does have to do with our leading man."

"He's been caught with his pants down?" She laughed but stopped when she saw Phil's serious expression. "Who with? And why is Nigel in on it?"

"Given that Nigel is the director and James is the actor, Nigel gets to stick his nose in whenever he wants. Especially when James gets caught having sex with Annalise, the cinema owner's just-turned-eighteen-year-old daughter."

The tension that had slipped from her shoulders returned. "Oh no."

"Oh no, indeed. And the ten-year age difference doesn't help."

Claire kept pace with Phil as they hurried toward the cinema. Even a block away she could hear a commotion of deep voices, and a high-pitched female one screeching indecipherably.

As she drew closer, Claire noticed James slip away from the small cluster of mayhem and disappear into a dark alleyway.

Tony Karter, the location assistant, stepped in front of her. "Nice mess, Montgomery."

"It'll be fixed." Claire went around him, then stopped. "Perhaps you'd like to offer a solution?"

Tony shrugged, and it took all her willpower not to explode. Ever since she'd gotten the promotion over Tony, he'd had it in for her. Being location manager was hard enough without having someone like Tony trying to undermine her every move.

Claire tried to shake off the negativity and approached Nigel, who clenched and unclenched his fists.

"Montgomery, you need to sort this out. He's threatening to pull out of the contract."

"The cinema owner?"

"Who else do you think? You need to get him back on board." He paused and peered at her over his glasses. "I don't need to tell you the significance of this, do I?"

Her jaw tightened. Negotiating came naturally to Claire, which is why she'd gotten the promotion. Already there'd been challenges in her new position, like making sure production staff didn't damage property and securing all the right permits with local municipalities. But dealing with the irate father of a daughter who had succumbed to the charms of an international playboy was not an everyday affair—thankfully. "Where's Robert?"

Nigel cocked his head in the direction of the cinema owner, Robert Dennis, whose arms flailed as he yelled, "This is a disgrace!" A few feet away, his daughter Annalise sobbed in the arms of her mother. Camille Ford, the actress playing the role of Amelia, looked on, her expression one of helplessness. Tony sidled up to Camille and whispered in her ear. They both looked at Claire.

Steeling herself, she approached Robert, who now stared at his feet.

"Robert," Claire said quietly. Then she cleared her throat and said a little louder, "Robert."

He looked up, his face creased with anger. "I trusted you."

"I'm sorry, I—"

"Save your apologies. It's over. I want everyone off my property and out of Ashton by the end of tomorrow."

"Robert, please—"

"Forget it." The streetlights reflected in his eyes. "She is eighteen. *Eighteen.* What does she know about the world? How could he do that to her?"

Since James had broken up with his fiancée six months ago, he'd left a trail of booze and women in his wake. His agent and Nigel had thought working in remote Queensland might put James on the straight and narrow. So much for those grand plans.

Robert rested his face in his hands.

"Robert, I absolutely understand why you'd be upset—"

"Don't give me your understanding, just get the hell out of here." His expression was set hard, his eyes unblinking.

She drew a long breath. This was the part of her job she dreaded. "I really don't want to remind you about the contract you signed—"

"I don't give a damn about the contract! You broke that contract when you let my daughter be dazzled and seduced by that playboy!"

"Mr. Dennis, if we can just talk about this, find a way—"

"I'm done talking." He turned and stormed past his wife and daughter. Annalise's mother followed him into the cinema while Annalise stood outside, her eyes puffy.

Claire turned to her. "Are you okay?"

"Everything's been blown out of proportion," Annalise said.

"Just give your dad time to cool off. Maybe he'll—"

"I'm done for," said Annalise. "Now he knows I'm not the virginal daughter he thought he had. He walked in when…" She gulped back a sob.

"All fathers want to think their girls are pure, even if their daughter is forty."

Annalise sniffed. "I've ruined everything."

"It's not your fault."

Annalise stared into the distance. "I'm not even his type."

"James's?"

"Yeah. We're so different yet…" She shrugged. "We work, you know? I've never met anyone like him."

"James is a great guy, but he's got a lot going on. I'm sure he wouldn't deliberately hurt or upset you. It's just—"

"He's been nothing but kind and sweet to me!" Annalise raised her voice, then softened it. "We're in love."

Claire wanted to wrap her arms around Annalise, the young girl with stars in her eyes. Her life was so very different from James's. She'd just finished school and was working in the cinema. James had been acting all over the world since he was fourteen. The pair were a complete mismatch, so how on Earth could they ever work as a couple? Claire prayed this wasn't a one-sided love affair because if it was, poor Annalise was about to get her heart trampled on.

"Annalise!" Robert stood in the doorway of the cinema. "In here! Now!"

She gave Claire a sad smile, then hightailed it inside. The door slammed shut and the lights under the marquee turned off, leaving most of the street in darkness.

Phil stood beside Claire and gently nudged her with his elbow. "Sorted?"

"About as sorted as a bag of pretzels."

* * * *

Claire gripped the steering wheel of the ute as she negotiated the winding road that took her out of Ashton and away from the small town's unease. The beauty of the cane fields, towering eucalyptus trees and rolling hills did nothing to allay her rising anxiety. She'd done her best to negotiate with Robert Dennis, but he'd refused to give in. He didn't care about the production company's legal team threatening him, as his pride and willingness to fight for his daughter's heart overrode everything else. Claire admired his resolve in trying to protect Annalise, but if he didn't rethink things, he'd end up with nothing but the shirt on his back. He was a good man with a lovely family who deserved to catch a break. His cinema had been on the verge of closing until the production company hired it. A legal battle and knowing about his daughter's torrid affair were the last things he needed.

Nigel and the team had rearranged the schedule and started shooting scenes outside Ashton, taking James far, far away from Annalise and her irate father.

She guided the vehicle north, hoping that each passing mile would lead her closer to a solution. But her belief that she could fix this problem dwindled dramatically as time wore on. If she couldn't get a yes from Robert, then Plan B had to come through. If it didn't, then...

Her mobile phone rang, and she jumped. Would she ever get used to being contactable on the road? Although it was convenient not having to find public phone booths every step of the way.

Pulling over to the side of the road, she answered.

"Hello?" She was met with intense crackling. "Hello?"

"It's me," Phil said through the noise. "Any luck?"

"I'm ten minutes away." Claire took a long swig from her drink bottle. "Please tell me you're ringing to say Robert's changed his mind."

Silence.

"Phil?"

A distant voice came down the line. "No chance."

She didn't know why she'd thought it would be any different. "How's Annalise?"

"She's fine. Furious with her father. Embarrassed." Phil faded in and out. "Swears that she seduced James and not the other way around. I have a feeling it was fifty-fifty."

"But she's okay? She's not traumatized?"

"She's fine, don't worry." Phil paused. "I hate to say it, but everything is—"

"Up to me, I know." The incessant headache she'd endured for the past twelve hours reminded her exactly how dire this situation was. "So, none of the location scouts have had any luck?"

Crackle. Crackle. Weren't these mobile phones supposed to make her job easier?

"Not a thing. It appears that the only other surviving cinema is the one in Starlight Creek."

"I'll call you once I find it. Hey," she said, "thanks for being such a great support."

"Why wouldn't I? You spend all your time helping everyone else, it's about time something went your way—I just hope it's in time. Good luck!"

"I'm going to need it."

* * * *

The scent of eucalyptus flowed through the open window as Claire drove past trees and sugarcane swaying in the gentle breeze. A flock of bright green parakeets squawked as they flew in changing formation, dipping and rising across the clear sky. Stoic wooden Queenslanders sat back from the road, their beauty reminding Claire why she loved this region so much. The hot and humid days were a stark contrast to Melbourne's dry summers and cold, wet winters.

She passed a beautiful old red-brick building that hinted at secrets behind its dark brown doors, while the next property had gigantic metal sheds that reflected the sun and dominated the landscape. A stench of burnt caramel filled the air as she crossed the rail tracks that brought cane from the farms to the mill.

Farther down the road was the Starlight Creek township sign. It leaned heavily to the left, its paint peeling. The numbers stating the population had been spray-painted over with *leave while you can*. Any other time Claire would have found it amusing, but the current pressure had quashed her ability to find anything humorous.

Her chest tightened, and the headache returned once more.

Slowing the vehicle down, she drove through the main street, surprised at how run-down most of the shops and buildings appeared. The haberdashery store's corrugated iron roof was rusted, and the materials in the window were faded floral prints. The newsagents had a Coca-Cola sign that looked like it was from the 1970s and the bakery needed a good slap of paint. She reached the end of the shops and did a U-turn, taking her time driving back in case she'd missed the cinema. Surely a cinema would stand out in a town like this. Where on earth was it? Had it been torn down like the others?

Bright colors caught her eye and she pulled over, taken by a rainbow of ribbons, spinning mobiles and lush plants in ceramic pots. Claire got out of the car and looked for traffic. The road was deserted. She quickly crossed over to the shop and was immediately drawn to a collection of metal sculptures of native animals and bas-relief murals.

Claire gently touched the gray, shiny metal, her fingers relishing the coolness.

"They are spectacular, no?" asked a short woman with thick black hair. She stepped out from behind the counter and stood next to Claire. The woman gently touched a life-size wallaby. "Such talent."

"They're incredible." Claire had spent many hours wandering through galleries and art shops throughout Australia when traveling for work, but these sculptures were like nothing she'd seen before. It was as if the pieces had a living spirit. She could spend hours studying each groove, every curve.... What on earth was she doing? Since when did she have time to dawdle? Turning to the woman, Claire said, "I'm hoping you can help me."

"Which one do you want?"

"Oh!" Claire looked longingly at the bas-relief of vines and butterflies. "Sorry, I don't have time to shop right now. I'm looking for the cinema."

"The Fitzpatrick cinema?"

"Maybe?" She'd tried to find it on the map, but the cinema was as elusive as the Tasmanian tiger.

"It's the only one in town, but it hasn't operated in years." The woman walked out the shop door and pointed down the street. "It's right on the edge of town. Go this way and it is on your right."

"But it's still standing?" Hope clawed to the surface.

"You'll need to see for yourself."

The woman went back into the shop and Claire stared down the street. In a few minutes she'd know the fate of the miniseries and, quite possibly, her career.

After jumping into the ute, Claire turned on the engine and reversed. She shifted gears, took a deep breath and headed down the street past more faded shops, some boarded up. Starlight Creek had an odd feeling, not quite a ghost town but certainly not buzzing with energy like Ashton. There were no mothers with prams nor elderly gentlemen with dogs, not even a group of kids hanging out on a street corner. Where was the sense of community?

The cinema came into view next to a dilapidated shoe shop and a closed barbershop. The cinema stood tall, all rounded corners and bold lines. The white and red paint had faded, and where the rendering had peeled away it revealed a whitish-gray stone. But even though the run-down facade was heartbreaking, Amelia Elliott's distinctive design of curves and stars was apparent.

Claire's shoulders slumped.

This was nothing like the photos of the cinema she'd found at the Historical Society. Admittedly, they had all been taken in the 1940s and 1950s, and it had been impossible to find any recent ones. Now she understood why. Who would want to photograph such an eyesore? Though the cinema did hold an air of…something. Charm? Grandeur?

Claire exited the vehicle and made her way to the entrance. Despite the run-down state of the cinema, she felt drawn in by the opaque glass doors, tarnished silver bars and old movie posters with curling edges in glass boxes. She instantly recognized *La Dolce Vita*, *Psycho* and *G.I. Blues*. Those movies were from the sixties. Had it really been that long since the cinema had operated? If that was the case, she was thankful it hadn't suffered at the hands of developers like the other cinemas Elliott designed. Though judging by the ramshackle facade, she didn't hold out much hope for the state of the interior.

Knocking on the door of a deserted cinema felt like a waste of time, but she did it regardless. There was no point in coming all this way only to fall at the last hurdle. When no one answered, she tried again. Her knocks echoed in the foyer. As much as she'd hoped someone would be there, she had to face the harsh reality that this place would not be her saving grace.

Claire gave the door one last burst of heavy knocking, then looked up at the blank marquee with missing bulbs. "Now what?"

"I don't know."

She spun to find a tall man, probably in his late twenties, with sandy hair. He walked toward her, his incredibly blue eyes framed by a veranda of dark lashes.

"You don't know what?" she asked.

"I don't know what is next for you." He had a friendly smile.

"I'm hoping someone will answer this door."

"Why? The cinema hasn't operated for years."

Claire glanced at the building. She felt sad for Amelia Elliott. "My powers of deduction have figured that out already." She held out her hand. "I'm Claire Montgomery."

The man took her hand in his and they shook.

"Luke Jackson," he said. "Are you an architectural student? It's been a while since we've had anyone visit. Not many people study Amelia Elliott's designs anymore, which is a shame, because she really did get the Art Deco movement going in Australia. And I believe she led quite the dramatic life. She even—" Luke's laugh was light and friendly. "I'm sorry. I'm quite passionate about artists like Elliott and I forget that not everyone sees things the way I do. Which architecture school are you with?"

"What? Oh, no, I'm not a student but I have been studying Amelia Elliott's designs, and her life. I'm actually involved in a TV miniseries about her." She waited for a reaction, but Luke Jackson just stood there, still as sugarcane on a windless day. "I was hoping to find the owner, to see if we could work out some arrangement to film here."

"No." His firm tone was a stark contrast to his pleasant demeanor only moments before.

"Pardon?"

"The owner would not be interested in any such thing."

"Do you own the place?" she asked.

"I don't, but I am very close with the owner. There is no way they would agree."

"But we're making a miniseries about one of the most influential women of her era. We *need* this cinema. It's a part of history, and it's the cornerstone of this entire production. If I could just talk with the owner and let them know they'll be rewarded handsomely and—"

Luke shifted on his feet then looked to the sky. Resting his gaze on her, he said with a firm tone, "I can unequivocally say you are wasting your time. I do not need to consult with the owner, because I already know the answer. Why do you think the cinema has been closed for so long?"

"I have no idea. Perhaps they ran out of money for upkeep? We can help with that. Please, if I can just have a few moments with them—"

"That won't happen."

Claire straightened her spine and lifted her chin. "I'm afraid you've mistaken me for someone who takes no for an answer."

"And I'm afraid you've mistaken me for someone who changes their mind easily."

"The decision isn't yours," she said.

"Nor yours. Now, please, I have things to do, and you're on private property."

Tension gripped Claire's shoulders and she willed her voice to remain calm. Although she wanted to break down in tears and beg, it wouldn't get her the result she needed. She had to take a moment to regroup, rethink her strategy and find out who this elusive owner was and track them down. She also needed to convince herself she was tougher than she felt.

Claire hitched the strap of her handbag over her shoulder. "Well, it's been...interesting meeting you, Luke Jackson." *It wasn't exactly a pleasure.* "I'll be seeing you."

"What?"

"I'll be seeing you, because I'll be back—and the answer will be yes."

Chapter Two

Claire sat at a table in the only café in Starlight Creek. Crowded House's "Locked Out" played in the background, and Claire tried not to roll her eyes at the irony.

She sipped the tepid coffee then used her fork to move the half-eaten carrot cake around the plate. She was at a loss as to how to handle this situation. Not once had she encountered someone who wasn't ecstatic about being involved in a TV production, so why was Luke Jackson so adamant in his refusal to even discuss it with the owners? And who on earth were these elusive owners?

Claire glanced over at the teenager in a hot pink uniform and white apron who looked like she'd walked off the set of a 1950s TV show. She was hunched over the counter, her attention solely on a glossy *Girlfriend* magazine. Occasionally, a chunk of blond hair fell in her eyes and she pushed it back. When Claire had asked earlier if she knew who owned the cinema, the girl had shrugged, blown a bubble with her gum and focused on the magazine once more.

Surely in a town this small everyone knew everyone? Although, from past experience, Claire had learned that arriving in a small town unannounced and asking questions didn't always get quick answers. Normally, she'd get the lay of the land by talking with locals before diving into requests for filming. Unfortunately, though, this project didn't allow for such luxuries.

The doorbell tinkled, and Claire looked up to find a woman breezing through the door. Her silver hair was swept up in a stylish French knot and her tailored tweed suit was immaculate. Her cheeks held a pink tinge and she wore a simple strand of pearls and matching earrings, giving the impression of a high-society matron. When she walked past, a tiny cloud of freesia perfume followed her. The lady took a seat at the corner table, placed her small patent leather handbag on the chair, along with her gloves, and sat with a straight back, hands clasped neatly on the table. The young girl behind the counter looked up, closed her magazine then quickly went about preparing a pot of tea and laying delicate china on a tray. She took a scone out of the cabinet and placed small bowls of jam and cream next to it.

Walking over to the older lady and setting the tray on the table, the girl asked, "How are you today, Miss Fitzpatrick?"

"I am doing very well, thank you, Laura. Has your sister recovered from her cold?"

"Yes, she's doing much better, thank you." Laura put the teapot, cup and saucer and scone on the table as the two women conversed about people Claire didn't know. When finished, Laura went back to the counter, the magazine back in her beautifully manicured hands.

A couple of flannel-shirted teenagers burst through the door laughing and chatting loudly, but when they caught sight of the older woman in the corner they turned down their volume and quietly went up to the counter to order milkshakes.

They sat near the older lady and said in unison, "Good morning, Miss Fitzpatrick."

"Good morning, young men. Harry, did you fix the step on the veranda so your mother doesn't break her neck?"

"Yes, Miss Fitzpatrick."

"Good to hear."

The boys commenced a hushed conversation between them.

Claire watched, entranced. The woman sipped her tea, closing her eyes every so often, as if lost in the ecstasy of the brew. It wouldn't be hard to imagine her having tea with the queen. Miss Fitzpatrick appeared to be the embodiment of a Country Women's Association lady from the 1950s, with her old-fashioned airs and graces. Claire glanced around the café, noticing its outdated decor and Laura in her uniform. Had Claire stepped into another era? Was Starlight Creek some kind of time machine?

"Excuse me," Claire said quietly.

The lady turned away from the window and smiled at Claire. "Yes, dear?"

"I'm sorry to interrupt, but I'm wondering if you could help me, please."

Miss Fitzpatrick patted the chair beside her and Claire gathered her things and went over to sit down.

Holding out her hand, she said, "I'm Claire Montgomery."

"And I am Hattie Fitzpatrick." The older lady wrapped her small, warm hands around Claire's. "What brings you to Starlight Creek, Claire Montgomery?"

Choosing her words wisely, Claire said, "I'm actually here on business and—"

The small room filled with the ear-screeching whir of the milkshake machine. Claire waited for it to finish. A moment later Laura took the milkshakes to where the boys sat. To give Laura more space, Claire moved her chair, but Laura stepped in the same direction. A second later Claire was covered in cold, sweet-smelling milk that dribbled down the back of her new linen shirt.

"Argh!" She jumped to her feet.

Laura shoved a towel toward Claire. "I'm so sorry."

"It's okay, really. It's just an accident." Claire quickly toweled off as much as she could, dreading what she would smell like in a few hours.

The boys snickered behind their hands and Hattie shot them a death stare. They quickly quieted, then one of them went behind the counter to get a mop and bucket to clean up the rest of the mess.

Hattie reached for her gloves and bag. "Do you have spare clothes in the car?"

"No. I'm on a day trip. I'm staying in Ashton." *Until we're kicked out.*

"Such a lovely place. A bit more modern than Starlight Creek."

"Just a little." Claire smiled, despite feeling like she had just swum in a bottle of milk.

"Oh, look at you. You can't drive back in that state. I don't live too far from here. Where is your car?"

"Across the road."

"Why don't you come to my place to clean up?"

"I'm fine, really." Although her dignity had taken a battering, as her bedraggled state was far from professional.

"Dear girl, soon you won't smell so fine. Please, let me help."

Hattie did have a point.

Claire got up and went to the counter to pay for her and Hattie, but Laura shook her head. "It was my fault. No charge for either of you."

"Are you sure?" asked Claire.

"Yep."

"Thank you." Claire put a tip in the jar, then grabbed her keys and bag. She opened the door for Hattie and they exited into the warm morning sun and crossed the road to the red ute.

"This is a very large vehicle. Isn't it difficult to drive?" asked Hattie.

"I'm stronger than I look." Claire shoved the key into the lock and opened the door for Hattie.

"Appearances can be deceptive." Hattie climbed in with great agility for someone her age.

"That's for sure." She got into the driver's seat and turned on the engine.

"I'm not too far from here. I enjoy coming to the café because it's a reasonable walk, which keeps me nice and fit." Hattie grinned. "And I don't feel guilty about my daily scone."

Claire joined in the laughter and steered the vehicle in the direction that Hattie had pointed. She got to the other side of town and slowed down the ute. "Which house?"

"Here we are!" Hattie pointed to the right and Claire nearly ran off the road.

"That's the cinema." Claire's voice was barely audible.

"Yes."

"It's deserted."

"Oh no!" Hattie's laugh sounded like fine crystal. "I live here."

"You do?" Claire concentrated on pulling into an empty space, but she could barely contain her joy.

Claire felt lighter as she walked around to open the door for Hattie, who led the way to the weather-beaten double doors. She unlocked one and motioned for Claire to follow.

Claire had expected the theater to smell musty, so she was pleasantly surprised when she was greeted with a hint of freesias, just like Hattie's perfume. Leaving the bright sunlight of Starlight Creek behind, Claire stepped across the threshold and into the foyer blanketed in darkness. She hesitated, fully anticipating Luke Jackson to leap out of the shadows and once more tell her no. Thankfully, the room remained silent.

Just as her sight adjusted, Hattie turned on the light and Claire squeezed her eyes shut. A moment later she pried them open, and when she did a small gasp escaped her lips.

Behind the dilapidated facade lay a whole new world of color and geometric designs, all beautifully maintained. Beneath her feet were black square tiles alternating with pristine white, and to the side was the kiosk and the bar, both made from dark wood and lined with silver stripes and filigree. Tilting her head upwards, Claire took in the magnificent dome, the circular plaster mold painted in gold with an ornate gray, white and black light fixture made of squares, triangles and oblongs.

"I see you are quite taken," said Hattie.

"That's an understatement," breathed Claire. "This is so very different from the outside."

Hattie smiled but didn't say any more. Instead, she crooked her finger and Claire followed, unable to take her eyes off the splendor before her. This would be so perfect for the miniseries, way better than the cinema in Ashton. Now she just needed to find a way—

"My living quarters are out the back," said Hattie as she opened the heavy wooden door and continued on her way. Claire happily trailed behind, still not able to fully comprehend the well-preserved beauty before her. Her feet lightly trod on gorgeous bright blue carpet with the same geometric design as the foyer. Continuing down the aisle, she studied the seats, the backs and sides made of dark wood with royal blue cushioning. She looked up and found the same blue painted on the ceiling, with little specks of silver.

"Those stars are beautiful," said Claire. "There's something magical about them."

"I'm glad you like them. My father always had a fascination with the universe. If he'd been born fifty years later, he'd have loved to work for NASA." She stopped and lightly ran her fingers across a chair. "Instead he lived in a small town and had big dreams that were never fulfilled."

"It's a shame more people don't get the chance to turn their dreams into reality."

"Sometimes reality is nothing like the dream."

Claire remained quiet and followed Hattie to the side of the stage, through a swing door and down a narrow hallway. They stepped into another room that served as a small apartment, with living room and kitchen in one.

Hattie pointed to a door to the right of the kitchen. "The bathroom is in there. I have spare towels in the cupboard under the sink. I'll see what I can rustle up for you to change into."

"Thank you so much, Miss Fitzpatrick, but really, I'll be fine." Claire ran her hand through her hair, but her fingers got caught in a milk-sodden knot. Ugh.

"Please, call me Hattie. And I am sure you are fine, my dear, but you will be more than fine after you freshen up." She raised her eyebrows, and Claire wanted to obey this fascinating woman. Most of all, though, Claire wanted to know why Hattie Fitzpatrick lived in the back of a run-down cinema.

"Thank you," Claire said as she opened the door. She stepped into a large, glistening bathroom. In the corner was a black claw-foot bathtub trimmed with gold. The black and white tiles matched the foyer, and the mirror hanging above the sink was the same Art Deco style as the rest of the decor. She peeled off her wet clothes then turned on the shower above the bath, stepped in and pulled the curtain across, immersing her body under the water. The stickiness ran down the drain while she collected her thoughts and tried to figure out how to best approach Hattie about the cinema.

A knock at the door brought her back into the moment. "I have some fresh clothes for you. They're likely to be big, but they'll do the trick. I've set them outside the door."

"Thank you!" Claire called, feeling odd about the whole situation. Going to a stranger's house to clean up after a sticky accident would never happen in Sydney or Melbourne, but she had to remember that she was in a small town and things were different. After the hustle and bustle of her regular life, this made for a lovely change.

She turned off the shower, toweled herself down and quietly opened the door enough to grab the clothes Hattie had left her—a black T-shirt and a pair of jeans. To her surprise, they were men's clothes. Claire dipped her hand into her messenger bag and pulled out a small toiletry kit with spare underwear, a toothbrush, toothpaste and deodorant—a habit she got into when she first started working as a location scout. Often, she'd go on a fact-finding mission and have to stay overnight unexpectedly, so, just like the traditional Scouts, Claire endeavored to always be prepared.

After donning the clothes, she rolled up the jeans, cinched in the waist with her own belt, which had miraculously escaped the milkshake waterfall, and adjusted the T-shirt. Claire hung the towel, shoved her dirty clothes in a plastic bag she kept handy, exited the bathroom and shut the door.

"Thank you so much, Hattie, I feel…" Her words fell away as she caught sight of one Mr. Luke Jackson sitting on a chair at the round dining table. He held a cup of tea in his hands, the steam snaking skyward. "Oh."

Luke put the cup on the table and stood, his chair scraping against the shiny tiles. He turned to Hattie. "This is the stray you brought home?"

"Excuse me?" Claire placed a hand on her hip.

"Now, Luke, there is no need for this behavior," said Hattie.

"She's the one who knocked on the door today. I told her we're not interested. And now she's in your house, using your shower and wearing *my* clothes?"

Claire looked down at the black T-shirt and jeans. She'd felt so comfortable in the oversize clothes, but now they felt too constrictive, like every last breath was being squeezed out of her. She did an about-face and turned the handle on the bathroom door. To hell with clean clothes.

"Claire, do not listen to my great-nephew. He has no manners, just like his father."

Claire drew a deep breath and faced Hattie and Luke. His lanky frame dwarfed his petite great-aunt, who looked at Claire with large, round eyes.

"Is it true you were here this morning?" Hattie's confident tone was gone.

"I was here, yes, but I didn't know this was your home."

Luke's eyes narrowed. "It's a ploy."

"I'll have you know, everything is aboveboard," Claire said indignantly. "In fact, I had actually started telling Hattie about why I was in Starlight Creek, but our conversation halted when a wayward milkshake landed on my head."

Luke smirked and Hattie flicked the tea towel against him. He flinched and rubbed his arm.

"If I could just explain—"

"I have everything I need to know," said Hattie. "I'm sorry, young lady, but the answer is no. We do not wish to be involved in film."

"But—"

"I am sure you are very good at your job and you will find somewhere else more suitable."

"That's the problem; this cinema is the centerpiece we've been looking for. We *need* this cinema." *Great negotiating, there, Montgomery.* "We had another location, but... Look, we'll make it worth your while."

"Money has nothing to do with it. People crawling all over my cinema and sticking their noses in places they shouldn't is the issue. I like you, Claire, but it doesn't mean I'll change my mind. You'll need to tell your people it is no from us."

Her shoulders slumped as panic rose. "But—"

"A *very firm* no from us."

"It's just that the miniseries is about Amelia Elliott and your cinema is so beautifully preserved on the inside and—"

"Nothing you say will change our mind." Hattie gripped the tea towel and looked out the window.

Although overwhelmed with the stomach-churning fear of failing at her first job since her promotion, Claire couldn't berate the poor lady into changing her mind. She squeezed her eyes shut, imagining the grief she'd receive from Nigel—not to mention Tony Karter's glee—when she returned empty-handed.

"I think it's best if you leave," Hattie said, her eyes still trained on the view of the stark alley behind the cinema.

Gathering her messenger bag and her milk-drenched clothes, Claire said, "Thank you so much for helping me out. I'll wash these clothes and mail them back to you."

"That's not necessary," said Luke.

She didn't argue, having already pushed things too far. She needed to return to Ashton and devise a plan—and quickly. If only she could figure out Hattie's sweet spot, the one thing that would guarantee she would say yes.

"What if we sent you on a vacation while we shoot? Where would you like to go? We'll set you up with business-class flights, five-star accommodation. That way you won't be bothered by filming."

"I need you to leave." Hattie's soft temperament had been replaced by a hard edge.

"You'd be helping us honor Amelia's legacy. Honestly, we won't—"

"Out." Luke pointed at the back door. His steely eyes held no sympathy.

Clutching the plastic bag against her chest, Claire had no other choice than to make a hasty exit. As she opened the door, she said quietly, "I'm sorry we couldn't make this happen, Miss Fitzpatrick. I would really have enjoyed working with you."

Chapter Three

1950 – Hollywood

Lena Lee gripped her light blue purse with both hands as she stood in front of Stage Seven at Fortitude Studios. Her gaze traveled the full height of the thirty-foot steel door, which today seemed darker, more daunting. She really should have been grateful to have a supporting role in a star-studded movie, but recently a malaise had descended upon her and she'd found it impossible to push aside.

"Cheer up, old gal." She smiled at her brother's favorite saying. How she missed her family.

"Miss Lee!"

She turned to find a thin boy of about sixteen running toward her. He took off his peaked cap and gasped for air. When he'd regained composure, he handed her a small, pale green envelope. "From Mr. Cooper."

"Thank you." She studied the thick linen paper, unsure why the head of the studio was sending her a missive. Itching to open it but realizing a pair of eyes were fixed on her, she looked up. "Is there something else?"

He wrung his hat in his hands and shuffled his feet. "It's... it's..."

The poor boy had turned the same shade of crimson as the dress she'd worn on set yesterday.

"Yes?" She hoped her tone sounded encouraging.

The boy offered a crooked smile. "You are as pretty in person as you are on the screen."

He took off as fast as his long legs could take him. Lena laughed and shook her head. This kid, in his adolescent awkwardness, had been so genuine, she couldn't help but be flattered. Lena may not have the beauty of Ingrid Bergman, the sultriness of Veronica Lake or the sass of Mae West, but what she did possess was an ability to relate to people on and off the screen, no matter their background.

Lena undid the envelope, trying not to damage her freshly painted pink fingernails. She pulled out the stiff paper, unfolded it and sucked in her breath.

Dear Miss Lee,
You are cordially invited
to celebrate the twentieth wedding anniversary
of Mr. Stuart and Mrs. Lesley Cooper
Saturday 11 March 1950

A squeal of delight escaped, then she clutched the invitation against her chest.

Oh no.

This couldn't be right. Why would they want her to attend? She was nothing more than a supporting actress.

"What's with you?" Yvonne Richardson, wardrobe assistant and good friend, stood beside Lena. When Lena had found herself without a place to live, Yvonne had taken her in, reassuring Lena that she'd never be homeless again. This act of kindness had shown Lena that Los Angeles did have a soul, she just needed to surround herself with the right people. Although that was a harder task than she'd anticipated.

"This." Lena held the invitation in front of Yvonne, who scanned it a couple of times.

Her grin was as large as her personality. "That's incredible!"

"It has to be a mistake."

"Mistake or not, you're going, right?"

"I don't know. I—"

"I know just the dress! Come on!" Yvonne shoved open the door and grabbed Lena's hand. "You don't have to be on set for a while, so we've got time."

Lena let Yvonne drag her into the studio and across the set of cobblestones, rose bushes and a large fountain. With only two days left to film, *Parisian Dreams* had been Lena's biggest role to date—not that a dozen lines and a few minutes' screen time counted for much when starlets like Jeanne Harris took enough limelight for ten people. Lena and Jeanne had arrived in Hollywood and started working at Fortitude Studios at the same time. They'd considered themselves friends then, but things changed once Jeanne became a leading lady and dropped Lena like she had the plague. Jeanne had the advantage of youth on her side, whereas Lena, at the grand old age of twenty-nine, was considered by the studio as "well past it" for an actress. For the past two years she'd clung to the few sparks in a sea of darkness, while Jeanne's career had taken off like a rocket on the Fourth of July. If Lena didn't find a way to break through soon, her contract would be cancelled and the life she'd worked so hard for would vanish. But as much as Lena would love to be where Jeanne was right now, she refused to turn into a cutthroat diva. There were limits, even if it meant a less lucrative career.

Lena and Yvonne wove between the lights and cameras, the studio quiet at this early hour. Lena often arrived on set before anyone else, as it was her chance to sit in silence and remember why she'd made so many sacrifices for her chance at the big time—and how many more she'd have to make.

They left the set and walked down narrow hallways that twisted and turned.

"What is this place?" Lena asked.

"You'll see."

"Are we supposed to be here?"

"No one's around, it's fine!" Yvonne's laugh didn't instill confidence in Lena.

"But we're only allowed on certain areas of the lot," Lena said.

"Why do you worry so much?"

They reached a door and Yvonne yanked it open. She started sorting through the rainbow of dresses that sparkled and shimmered with thousands of tiny crystals. Yvonne grabbed an emerald number and placed it against Lena's body.

"Oooh! That color looks gorgeous with your red hair! Try it on!"

"Oh no." Lena shook her head. "It's not mine."

"Some of these are Jeanne's." Yvonne winked.

"Then I'm definitely not touching them."

"Oh, come on! Look." Yvonne ran a hand across the dozens of costumes. "These dresses have been long forgotten. It's sad, really. We create these masterpieces, they're worn on set for a short time then they end up in the costume graveyard. Honestly, no one would notice if one was missing."

"And what if it's recognized?"

"I doubt it." Yvonne shoved a violet dress at her.

"No, no, no." Lena backed toward the door.

"No one would care if you borrowed it for the weekend."

"I can't."

"Just try it on. Please?"

Her friend batted her eyelashes and Lena gave a nervous laugh. She held out her hand for the dress and stood in front of the mirror. Draping the silky fabric across her body, Lena studied the intricate beading around the sweetheart neckline.

"It truly is a work of art." She sighed.

"Here." Yvonne placed a tiara on Lena's head, then curtsied. "At your service, Miss Lee."

The door slammed against the wall.

Lena jumped.

Yvonne cursed.

"What the hell is this?" boomed Lawrence Doherty, Lena's movie director. Just like Lena, he often arrived early, but Lawrence's habit was to meander across the lots, mentally preparing for the day ahead. Trust Lena to be caught out on the day Lawrence decided to mosey past a place she wasn't allowed.

"I… I…" Lena couldn't put the dress on the rack fast enough. She stood with her hands behind her back, feeling like a schoolgirl caught with her hands in the cookie jar.

"Lee, get on set now. And you." He rested a steely gaze on Yvonne. "You shouldn't be here without good reason." He pointed at the door and Lena scurried toward it, but stopped when he put his hand across the doorway.

"I'm sorry," she blurted. "I was just looking."

Lawrence lifted the tiara off her head and cocked an eyebrow.

She glanced at Yvonne, who pursed her lips as if trying to contain a laugh. What Lena wouldn't give to be as carefree as her best friend.

Making a hasty exit, Lena bolted toward the communal dressing room outside Stage Seven. A cold wind whipped around her legs. She glanced up. The sky had turned almost black.

Today would be a long one.

* * * *

Lena entered Roy's Diner, took off her coat and removed the scarf from her head. Outside, the rain pelted, dropping the temperature but upping the humidity. She didn't dare glance in the mirror, as she was in no mood to deal with her unruly red curls. Looking around the crowded room, she spotted Yvonne and her other best friend, George Barrett, in a booth. Making her way over, she sat next to Yvonne and let out a long sigh.

"Still gainfully employed?" asked George.

"You would know, as you're always up on the latest gossip," she said.

"Why, yes, that is correct."

When Lena had first met George, he was an intern in the screenwriter's office, fetching coffee and filing papers that would be forgotten in a week's time. It had been Lena's first day and she was hopelessly lost, scooting from one place to the next, petrified she'd be fired before lunch. She'd rounded a corner in a rush and crashed into George, sending his boss's script flying across the pavement. From the goodness of his heart, George had taken Lena under his wing, and they'd become steadfast friends. It had been a delight to watch George move up the ladder so quickly to become one of the studio's most sought-after screenwriters.

"How did it go?" asked Yvonne.

"It was the worst day of my life." Lena hung her head.

Yvonne placed her hand on Lena's. "It was my fault. I shouldn't have pushed you."

"It's all right, really," said Lena. "I shouldn't be so easily swayed. Besides, I've always wondered where those dresses went."

"Such a waste," said Yvonne.

Meryl, the waitress, appeared with a tray of hamburgers, milkshakes and a salad. She gave Lena a wink and handed her the salad and a shake.

"Extra banana in your shake today."

"Thanks?"

"Don't look so surprised, sweetheart. I could see the cloud of sadness following you through the door. Hopefully comfort food will make it all better."

"Thank you, Meryl." Lena took a sip. "It's delicious."

"You're welcome, honey." Meryl went back to the kitchen.

"So." George shoved a fry in his mouth. "Are you going?"

"What?"

"Going to the party?"

"No."

"Are you crazy?" George's high-pitched voice carried through the diner, causing other patrons to turn and stare. Leaning toward her, he whispered, "Are you crazy?"

"The invitation has to be a mistake," she said.

George's eyes met Yvonne's.

"What?" asked Lena.

Yvonne drew her lips into a tight line and George shook his head.

"What?" she said loudly.

Yvonne said between clenched teeth, "You have to tell her."

"Tell me what?"

George rolled his eyes. "Okay. But you cannot breathe a word."

"About *what?*" This was painful.

"I snuck your name onto the list," he said.

"What? That could get me fired!" A thin film of perspiration broke out on her body and her stomach muscles tensed. "I feel sick."

"No!" George reached over and grabbed her hand. "It's all right, don't worry. It was just one of those chance things. I had to deliver some scripts to Cooper, but he was out and so was his secretary. The list was on the desk and..." He shrugged.

Lena slapped her hand against her forehead. "Good grief, George. There's no way I can go under false pretenses."

"Your name is on the list now—"

"No," she said with force, then softened her tone. "Look, I really appreciate your intentions, but it's not right that I go."

"Hollywood's biggest directors and leading men will be there. It's a treasure trove of potential for you. What have you always told me?" he asked.

"*Carpe diem*—seize the day."

"Then do it." Yvonne's perfect red lips formed a large smile. "Do you want to be second fiddle? Haven't you always said your time to make it big is limited?"

Lena scrunched her napkin. "I'm not getting any younger, I know. But going to this party feels dishonest, and I don't want to win a role because I was in the right place but not invited."

"Well, Jeanne's never had a problem with gate-crashing parties to meet people who will further her career," said Yvonne.

"Jeanne and I are different people," said Lena.

"You two used to be peas in a pod," said Yvonne.

Lena concentrated on pushing the salad around the plate. "Just leave it be."

Yvonne looked at George.

Lena dropped her fork. "Seriously, you two! Why are you ganging up on me?"

Yvonne faced Lena. "You deserve just as much as Jeanne—and then some. You are a good person, and you should take advantage of the opportunity that has landed in your lap."

"An opportunity that was forged."

"Creatively added," George said.

Despite her somber mood, Lena laughed. "Thank you."

"For?"

"Thank you both for looking out for me."

Yvonne put her arm around Lena and pulled her close. "We're family."

"We are indeed."

Chapter Four

1950 – Hollywood

George held out his hand and helped Lena out of the car. Her friends had done a brilliant job convincing her she should attend the party, although now, dwarfed by Stuart Cooper's towering pink mansion, she doubted her decision. Since arriving in Hollywood three years prior, Lena had tried to get over feeling like an imposter and acknowledge that she was finally living her dream of being an actress. Some days it was harder to believe than others. Today was one such day.

Lena smoothed her mint-green dress and took a moment to calm her nerves. When she'd initially put it on at Yvonne's she'd loved the way it hugged her curves, but now she felt like a boa constrictor was slowly wrapping around her torso, suffocating her. Lena's ribs hurt, her head felt like a pincushion and her makeup felt three inches thick.

George offered his arm and she took it. He said, "Cary Grant would be envious of me right now."

"You are such a charmer." Her laugh was light, like the steps she took in the heels that pinched her feet.

"Yvonne did well to get you this ensemble." He tucked a stray curl behind her ear. "Look, I know you're not comfortable with this, but mark my words: you won't regret it."

"I've heard that before. Remember last New Year's Eve when you tried to get us into the party at the Chateau Marmont?"

"That was so last year." George's gaze followed the length of her body. He let out a low whistle. "You do scrub up all right, don't you, Cinderella?"

She adjusted the thin strap on her shoulder. "Well, if Cinderella can gate-crash a ball, I guess I can go to a party under false pretenses."

"That's the spirit!" George slapped her on the buttocks and she punched him in the arm. "Come on, Cindy. There are some people I want you to meet."

They climbed the steps to the large double doors made of filigree iron and solid mahogany.

Lena stopped. She sucked in her breath.

"What's up?" asked George.

She shook her head. "I can't do it. It's wrong."

"Do you think everyone deserves to be at this party? Most are only here because they know the right people. They haven't earned their place. But you, my darling friend, deserve the chance to shine. You've been in Jeanne's shadow way too long."

"Is that so?" Jeanne Harris's voice came from behind them, more like a growl than a purr.

Lena tightened her grip on George's arm as Jeanne walked up and stood in front of them.

"Hello, Jeanne." Lena forced out the words.

Lena's once-friend ignored her and turned her attention to George. Her perfectly painted lips twisted into a half smile. "A word of advice, Mr. Barrett. There are many eyes and ears in this town who are more than willing to share information with me. Anyone who gets in my way or speaks badly of me will incur my full wrath. It would do you well to remember what happened to your old friend Oscar Connor after I discovered what he'd been saying."

George's body tensed under Lena's hand. Oscar had been George's secret lover until Jeanne had overheard Oscar calling her a diva, among other things. Although not as powerful as other stars—yet—Jeanne's skills of manipulation were second to none, and the right words in the right ears saw Oscar's job as director's assistant quickly disappear. Oscar's further efforts to gain employment in Hollywood had been met with myriad rejections, so he'd returned to Atlanta to work in his father's printing company. After George had lost the man he'd once shared his hopes and dreams with, he disappeared into a permanent cloud of romantic misery.

George drew himself up to his full height. "Jeanne, just because—"

"That's a really lovely dress, Jeanne. I like that shade of yellow on you," said Lena, almost choking on her words.

Jeanne narrowed her eyes and allowed the mink coat to fall slightly to show off her perfect milky-pale shoulders. "Just watch yourself, Barrett."

Jeanne stalked to the doors and a couple of butlers opened them for her, bowing as she breezed past in a sea of Dior and…whiskey?

Lena turned to George. "There's no way I'm going in now."

"Seriously?" George pointed in the direction Jeanne had sashayed. "You're going to let the likes of Jeanne Harris stop you?"

"Yes."

"Oh, please. That witch thinks she can walk over everyone to get what she wants."

"She's dangerous, George. Look at what she did to..." Lena didn't have the heart to finish the sentence.

"I will never forgive her for what she did to Oscar. And to me. And I darn well won't let her ruin your career because she feels so inclined. We are going in there, you will meet the right people and you will finish this evening not just with your foot in the door, but your whole curvy body and that very clever business brain." George fixed his eyes on her, daring her to argue.

"I'm still not convinced."

"You don't need to be," he said.

"I'm only doing this because I trust you, George Barrett." Lena hitched up her dress so she could navigate the stairs to the main doors and the steps that led down into the foyer. She stopped and looked around. Sparkling high above was a chandelier that appeared bigger than her kitchenette, the brilliant crystals shining like diamonds. Beneath her pinching heels was a magnificent marble floor with the Coopers' initials in the center. A marble horseshoe staircase snaked around both sides of the expanse, and an army of servants carrying drinks and hors d'oeuvres wove between women in ball gowns and tiaras and men in jet-black tuxedos and pristine white shirts. Some faces she recognized, many of them studio investors, other artists, musicians or journalists she'd read about or seen from afar.

In the middle of some men and women stood a man who had the group's full attention, their laughter raucous. He wore a red velvet suit that complemented his dark, slicked-back hair.

"Who's that?" she whispered.

"Reeves Garrity. He's worked in radio but, as you can see, it would be a waste to keep him behind the microphone." George grabbed two champagne glasses off a passing tray. He handed one to Lena, who couldn't take her eyes off this Hollywood newcomer. His height, broad shoulders, beautifully styled hair and strong jawline were the classic clichés of a movie star, though he didn't appear to have the arrogance—yet. Time would tell, however. Just look at what happened to Jeanne.

George said quietly, "You'd do well to stay away from him."

"I'm not... I..." Her cheeks flushed with heat.

"I know you, Miss Lee." He gave her a gentle nudge. "Although he is rather easy on the eye."

"Shh." Lena looked around, hoping no one had heard George. "Those things are fine to say to me in private, but you can't risk anyone else hearing you."

George's smile disappeared. "It's ridiculous, and it's wrong."

"Of course it is." She moved in close and said, "No matter how much you and I believe that people should love who they want, things won't change."

"Maybe one day."

Lena sipped the champagne. "Yes, maybe one day."

"What will happen one day?"

Lena turned around to find Lawrence Doherty, her director, standing behind them. How much of that conversation had he heard?

"Hello, Mr. Doherty. We were... uh..."

He held up his hand. "No need for formalities. So, Cooper deems you important enough to be here?"

"I..." Words! Where were the words? "I..."

"Lena Lee is very important," said George. "Have you ever heard her sing?"

"No." Lawrence looked at Lena like she'd come from the moon.

"She has the sweetness of a nightingale. Her voice will bring you to tears and make you feel like your broken heart will never mend."

Lawrence's smile seemed far from genuine. "She's just like every other actress in Hollywood. Sorry, Lena, but you just don't have that *je ne sais quoi* like Jeanne." He took a moment to study her face. "And aren't you a little more *mature* than Jeanne?"

Mortified that her age had been brought up in such a public place, Lena struggled to find a reply—but she couldn't let the comment go unacknowledged.

"Age is just a number," she said, praying she hadn't jumped across the line.

"Exactly," said George. "Besides, *mature* women have a natural elegance and grace that these young actresses can never imitate. Everyone knows Lena Lee is a star in the making."

"She is an excellent actress, I'll give her that," Lawrence said.

"Then why doesn't she get bigger roles?" asked George.

"Okay, that's enough!" Lena grabbed her friend's arm. "Let's leave Mr. Doherty in peace. I'm sure he has people telling him someone is a talented singer and the next big thing all the time."

"Prove it," Lawrence said.

"Pardon?"

"Prove you have what it takes." He pointed at the white grand piano in the next room. "Sing me a song."

"Uh…" *Oh no.* She'd hoped to keep a low profile, at least for the first couple of hours of the party. "Sure."

She straightened her spine and held her head high as she walked over to the piano, where a gentleman with gray hair had been playing classical tunes. Her heart raced as she approached the pianist. "Would you mind playing 'Over the Rainbow,' please? I've been asked to sing for our host."

He looked up and asked, "Which key?"

Lena eyed the main doors. If she took off her heels and pulled the dress up past her knees, she could run a lot faster…

"C," she finally answered.

A small crowd had gathered around the piano, and she recognized a lot of faces, many of whom she hadn't ever had the courage to speak with: director Henry Newman; scriptwriter Lloyd Ferrier; Charles Boyd, who was a devastatingly handsome leading man and the faithful husband of the elegant Cassandra Cleary; and eternal bachelor and rogue Gregory Silva.

"Ready?" asked the pianist. Lena nodded, terrified she'd landed herself in this situation. Well, George had, though she shouldn't have been surprised. George never played by the rules.

The pianist stretched his hands, then set to work, his fingers dancing across the keys in a flurry of creativity.

Her mouth was dry.

Her head was foggy.

Perspiration pooled at the base of her spine.

She swallowed hard.

The lump in her throat wouldn't dislodge.

She missed the opening notes.

People stared.

The pianist circled back to the beginning.

She opened her mouth, and at last her voice cooperated. She closed her eyes, losing herself in the music, feeling the words about longing, of wishing for something that may never be.

Looking up, she spied Reeves Garrity, who stood apart from the growing crowd. His eyes were fixed solely on her. Heat raced across her skin and she looked away.

A wave of anxiety tried to drown her, but she stood firm. The eyes and ears of Hollywood's elite were now on Lena, and one missed note could destroy her chances of being something more than a minor character.

The song's crescendo grew. She had to get that high note. It had never been a problem before, but the stakes were the highest they'd ever been.

Lena glanced at Reeves Garrity. He offered a slow, warm smile, and the confidence she'd been grappling with now raced through her with full force.

She hit the last note, her voice strong. Her heart connected to the music and her ears filled with applause and shouts of "Bravo!" George handed her a glass of champagne and she was swarmed by men and women congratulating her on such a beautiful rendition of Judy Garland's most famous song. Lena thanked each person, unable to comprehend what she'd just done. She mouthed "thank you" to George, who leaned against the piano, a smug I-told-you-so smile on his face. Lena looked over to where Reeves Garrity had been standing, but he'd disappeared.

"Well then," said Lawrence as he shooed the well-wishers away. "You and I need to talk. Monday, ten o'clock."

Lena looked at Lawrence. Her words wouldn't connect with her brain.

"What do you have to say?" he asked, his tone one of amusement.

"Thank you?" Why didn't she have the self-assurance Jeanne had? Even before she'd become a starlet, Jeanne had the amazing ability to convince even the most powerful people that she was someone important, someone who should be noticed, someone who was going places.

"Don't be late." Lawrence shoved his lit cigar in his mouth and walked into the foyer to talk with a group of men with pockets deeper than the South China Sea.

"That was wonderful, Miss…?" Stuart Cooper appeared beside her.

Where had he come from?

"Miss Lee. Lena Lee," she said.

"Miss Lena Lee." He let the words roll around his mouth. "That's a very Hollywood name."

"Thank you."

"And that was a mighty fine performance you just gave. Here." He reached into his pocket and pulled out a business card. "Call my office and we'll set up a screen test. I'd like you to join my studio. Can you act?"

"I'm…" How could she say this without making him look bad? "Thank you, but I already have a contract."

"You do? Who snapped you up?"

"Uh…Fortitude Studios."

"What?" His shocked expression appeared genuine. "Oh, Miss Lee, I sincerely apologize. Why have we not met before?"

"Probably because my roles to date haven't been very big."

"We need to do something about that. Which film are you working on now?"

"We've just wrapped up *Parisian Dreams* so I'm waiting to hear what's next. I'm meeting with Lawrence Doherty on Monday."

"Good, good. I'll have a word with Lawrence. Perhaps we can find you a singing role."

She tried to contain the excitement that threatened to spill out. "Thank you. I would be forever grateful."

"Wonderful. Ah!" His attention diverted to an older couple, and he saluted Lena as he walked away.

Lena's feet felt like they were cemented to the floor. Stuart Cooper had just made an effort to talk to her. It didn't matter that he'd had no idea who she was; with so many actors and actresses swarming the studio lots it would be impossible for him to know everyone.

Jeanne stood on the stairs, surrounded by a group of male admirers. Her fake laugh stabbed the air as she flicked her blond locks then narrowed her eyes when she spotted Lena.

A desperate need for fresh air overcame Lena, and she made her way through the crowd and slipped out a side door. She found herself in a small courtyard surrounded by lush, perfectly manicured hedges. Taking a seat on an elaborately carved marble bench, Lena let out a long breath. She glanced at her shaking hands on her lap.

"You have the voice of an angel," came a deep baritone.

Lena looked up to find Reeves Garrity casually leaning against the doorframe. In a few swift steps, he was in front of her.

He held out his hand. "I'm—"

"Reeves Garrity," she said, then chastised herself for sounding like a fan.

His laugh was warm. "I do hope that is all you know about me."

"I know you worked in radio and you're currently filming your first role—as a leading man, no less."

"I don't know whether I should be flattered and continue talking, or if I should run away because you know more about me than I do about you. One thing I do know, however, is you have a beautiful voice. Where did you learn to sing like that?"

"My mother says I was singing before I spoke."

"I can believe it. So, tell me, mysterious nightingale, what is your name?"

"Lena Lee."

"Miss Lee, I am very impressed with your talent. Can you dance?"

"Yes. And I can act," she added, finally finding some confidence.

"A triple threat." Reeves looked around, making sure no one was near. He whispered, "I'll let you in on a secret. I'm not a very good actor."

"But you're with one of the biggest studios in Hollywood! Surely they wouldn't hire you if you couldn't act."

He gave a crooked smile.

"Well, I guess that's never stopped anyone before." How many times had she witnessed actors making messes of their roles yet managing to hold on to their jobs because of what they looked like, or who they knew?

Then again, the studios had a plethora of behind-the-scenes people working magic to ensure the stars shone bright and the movies were a success so they could recoup the money already invested in the actors' careers. Nothing was ever as it seemed.

"People deserve to hear your beautiful voice, and"—His slow smile made her hold her breath—"see your gorgeous red hair, and those alluring green eyes."

Lena burst out laughing.

"What's so funny?"

A small snort escaped her. "If you're going to survive in this industry, you need to have better come-on lines."

"It wasn't a come-on line." He sounded disappointed.

"You're serious? Really?" Lena controlled her laughter, feeling bad for this Reeves Garrity, who seemed greener than the fields of her hometown. "I'm sorry for laughing. This industry is full of people saying what they can to get ahead. Call me cynical, but I've been around long enough not to trust anyone, especially if they're saying something nice about me."

"That's rather sad."

Lena crossed her legs at the ankles. "It's just the way it is. Although… it shouldn't be, should it?"

"No, it shouldn't. I hope you believe me when I tell you that I find you intriguing and I'd like—"

"Reeves!" Jeanne breezed over, the skirt of her yellow dress billowing behind her. She reached for his hands and ignored Lena. "I have someone you should meet."

"Let me finish talking with Miss Lee first."

"It's fine, you should go and mingle," Lena said, surprised at her disappointment.

Reeves took her hand and gently placed his lips on her skin. A shiver ran up her arm and down her spine. "Miss Lee, it has been a pleasure."

"The pleasure was all mine."

Reeves held out his arm and Jeanne rested her hand on his. As they walked into the house, Jeanne glanced back at Lena and smirked.

Under her breath, Lena said, "Good luck, Reeves Garrity, because you're going to need it."

Chapter Five

Claire sat in the front seat of the ute, head against the steering wheel. Sugarcane lined the narrow road, and in some strange way it cocooned her from the rest of the world, which Claire needed to hide from right now. When she'd started the drive back to Ashton, the ill-fated discussion with Hattie and Luke had been on a loop in her head, and it had caused a medium-sized headache to morph into something close to a migraine. She dreaded having the tough conversation with Nigel. Fear clawed at her chest, making it hard to catch her breath.

Claire wiped the thin film of perspiration from her forehead. How on earth could she deliver news that would surely destroy her career? She tried to figure out what Tony would do. He certainly wouldn't take no for an answer. He'd harangue Hattie into signing on the dotted line, even if it meant he had to camp out in front of the cinema to get the signature. Claire had no doubt Tony was biding his time in Ashton, waiting for her to make a misstep. Every other person who worked for locations had morals, but somehow Tony could leave his at the door—and get away with it. She was especially disgusted with his latest effort on an action film. She was certain he'd bribed someone to film the car chase in that beautiful park that had originally been off-limits. If the producers had been aware of his underhanded ways then...

"If only I could work like that," she mumbled, then tilted back her head and stared at the roof of the cabin. "Not going to happen."

A yellow Holden whizzed past, its panels battered and rusted. The sandy-haired man sat behind the steering wheel, his eyes on the road ahead.

"Bingo!" She started the vehicle again. Feeling like Nancy Drew, Claire kept far enough behind so Luke Jackson wouldn't see her. Being accused of buttering up Hattie had hurt Claire, but she had to give Luke and his great-aunt the benefit of the doubt. After all, her motives looked less than stellar after she'd received a no from Luke and a short time later was showering in Hattie's bathroom and wearing Luke's clothes. He'd made it very clear that she should leave town and stop bothering them. Following him would make her look like a stalker. But what other options did she have? Going back to see Hattie bordered on harassment, and that's the last thing she wanted to do to that very sweet lady. All Claire needed was to get Luke on board. If she did that, she had a feeling Hattie would agree to the deal. Besides, facing a cranky great-nephew was way better than telling her boss she'd failed on the most important job she'd ever been given.

Luke turned right down a gravel road, the red brake lights on his car casting a hazy glow through the dust. She panicked, afraid he'd caught her, so she pressed hard on the pedal and drove on, pulling over a few hundred feet further up the road.

Her phone rang and she steeled herself before answering, "Claire speaking."

"Any luck?" asked Phil.

Her shoulders relaxed. "Thank god."

"Thank god you've sorted it?"

"Thank god you're not Nigel calling."

"Yeah, well, somehow I've become his secretary. What's the scoop?" The phone crackled, then cut out. It rang again. Claire stared at it. She could just pretend she was out of range...but ignoring Phil's call would only delay the inevitable, so she answered once more.

"Jeez, Montgomery. Your head is going to be on the chopping block."

"I'm aware of this. What does Nigel expect?"

"He'll send Tony, or he might go there himself if you don't—"

"No, no way. Nigel or Tony barging into town and making demands is not going to cut it."

"You need to get a yes."

"I know, all right?" she said harshly, then softened her tone. "I'm sorry. I'm feeling the stress right now."

"You need to work through it. And find a miracle while you're at it. The good news is we're already filming outside of Ashton, like we'd planned."

"Robert isn't going to renege on pulling his contract?"

"I've never seen anyone so angry."

"Do you blame him?" she asked.

"Of course not." Phil's voice faded and Claire struggled to hear. "I feel for him, actually. Unfortunately, this complication is only going to get worse with legalities."

"Maybe if I talked to him again—"

"He made it very clear he would not speak to you. Ever."

"He blames me for what happened? What did he expect?"

"He expected someone to make sure James kept his pants zipped around his teenage daughter. And it doesn't help that she's threatening to run away with him."

"Run away with James? Oh, that poor girl. I hope someone's talking some sense into her."

"Leila's talking with Annalise, don't worry."

"Thank god." Leila, the on-set hair stylist and Phil's wife, was a great listener and could make most people see reason. Claire had lost count of the number of times she'd holed herself up in Leila and Phil's apartment for guidance in her personal and professional life. "Would it do any good for Leila to talk to Robert?"

"She tried, but even she couldn't sweet-talk him."

"Crap." Claire didn't conceal her groan of frustration. "Why couldn't James have kept it in his pants?"

"He was a liability from the start. Listen." Phil sounded like he was talking under water. "Tony's doing a really good job here with logistics, and he's just waiting to pounce. If you don't get those cinema owners on board…"

"Okay. The charm dial has been wound to overdrive. I'm pulling out all stops." She hung up and started the engine.

Checking for traffic, she did a U-turn and turned onto the gravel road where Luke had driven. Sugarcane fields lay on either side and she reveled in the beauty. Although she couldn't put her finger on it, there was something very romantic about cane fields—if she blanked out the cane toads, snakes, foxes and who-knows-what living in the thick foliage. Maybe one day she'd do a documentary about the sugarcane industry. Though that had been done before. Just like every other idea she'd come up with in the past two years. Finding an original concept that could get a production company excited was as challenging as James Lloyd not having sex for a week.

As she steered the vehicle up the road, she came across a small farmhouse surrounded by sugarcane. Its wraparound veranda, cream weatherboards and bright white window frames gave it a homely and welcoming feel— quite the opposite of the vibe she'd received from Luke. In front of the shed to the right of the house was Luke's battered car, but he wasn't in sight.

Gathering courage, Claire parked on the side of the road at the beginning of the driveway and got out. Driving onto his property felt invasive, and the less she irritated him, the better.

Hitching her bag onto her shoulder, Claire took a deep breath and traipsed up the driveway, gravel crunching under her feet. Despite the heat of the day, the setting sun had given the air a distinct chill. She grabbed her cardigan out of her bag as she studied the bright red front door. It was the perfect shade—not too bright, not too dark. The kind of red that invited one to knock on the door and know that the owner of the house would already have tea ready and fresh bread out of the oven.

Her knuckles hovered a moment before she let out a long breath and knocked.

Nothing.

She tried again, this time with more force.

Again, nothing.

With déjà vu haunting her, Claire knocked one last time. Where could he be? She'd seen him drive toward the house. His vehicle was out front. She turned and took in the surroundings. Pot plants of various shapes and sizes hung from the eaves and sat in an orderly line at the edge of the veranda. Green, rolling hills faded into the distance, the late afternoon sun casting a warm orange and red glow. Not far from where she stood was a huge wooden shed painted the same red as the front door of the house. Wandering across the gravel, Claire reached the door of the shed and knocked, hoping her luck had taken an upward swing. No answer again, but she spied a light through a crack in the sliding door. Slowly opening the door, she called out, "Hello?"

Silence once more.

Sliding the door open further, she stepped in and looked around. Along one side of the wall lay neatly stacked sheets of metal and poles in varying lengths, and at the back of the shed hung a tidy assortment of tools. On the right were half a dozen machines, and in the middle of the room were at least a dozen sculptures in different states of completion. One in particular drew her attention. Hesitating for only a second, she went over and examined the artwork. It was almost six feet high and the metal had been bent and soldered to represent a vine twisting toward the sky. Unfurled leaves sprouted at intervals from the thick stem, and upon those were butterflies, a couple of birds and flowers in bloom. The metal wasn't as shiny as the others in the workshop, but the piece was captivating. Before her was a moment frozen in time, and soon the birds and butterflies would take flight, the flowers would close for the evening and the light breeze would whisper to the vines and leaves.

This artwork was very similar to what she'd seen in town.

Oh...

"So beautiful," whispered Claire, unable to resist reaching out to touch the artwork. She expected it to be cold, but it felt warm, almost soft.

"What are you doing in here?"

Claire froze. *Shit.* Grimacing, she turned and faced the last man on earth she needed to—or wanted to—upset. "I'm sorry. I know I shouldn't have touched it—"

"You shouldn't be in here." Luke pointed at the door and she quickly exited the shed. He pulled the door across, slammed it shut and clicked a large padlock into place.

"I'm really sorry. I didn't mean to snoop. I was looking for you, but I got distracted." She studied his set jaw. "I apologize. I have no excuse. Though the sculptures are absolutely breathtaking. Are you the one who makes the artwork for sale at the shop in town?"

He answered with a glare. What was wrong with her? Had she left her people skills in Melbourne?

"How did you find me?" He folded his arms.

Claire closed her eyes for a brief moment and wondered what she'd been thinking. Nothing she said would sound good and she suspected Luke Jackson had a most excellent bullshit detector.

"I followed you." Her eyes met his, then she quickly looked away.

"Why?" She looked back, expecting his face to be creased in anger, but instead he appeared puzzled. He asked, "Why do you want this so badly? Do you get a bonus?"

"I get nothing out of this, except the chance to keep my job." He didn't need to know that securing the cinema would lead her closer to her dreams. Why would he care? Especially after she'd just admitted to stalking him and had been caught in his personal space. "I'm really sorry about how this has all played out. I assure you, I'm not normally a pushy person. It's just that there's so much riding on this. But I don't want to trouble you or your great-aunt in the process."

"It's too late for that." Luke folded his arms tighter against his chest.

"I really hope it's not. Maybe if we start again I can better explain why this is so important." She waited for a reply. He didn't say a word, and she took it as her cue to keep going. "The cinema your great-aunt owns is of huge historical significance. By allowing us to film the miniseries inside,

Miss Fitzpatrick would play a big role in preserving the legacy of Amelia Elliott. Surely she understands the importance of that."

"My great-aunt is well and truly aware how important the cinema is to architectural and Art Deco history. The problem is, other people don't understand the importance of her wishes for privacy."

"It wouldn't be for long, and she'd be really well paid."

Luke looked to the heavens and let out a sigh. "Why can't you understand that no matter what you say or do, the answer will always be no? If you don't leave her alone, I'll need to take things further."

Claire shoved her hands in her pockets. Never before had she met such resistance from a property owner. Normally they fell over themselves to get involved in a movie shoot, not just for the money, but for the thrill of seeing their property on-screen.

"Please leave now, Miss Montgomery." Luke pointed toward the road.

"I'm sorry if my request has caused undue stress," she said, all the while wishing she could find the magic words that would change his mind. Claire didn't like that Luke spoke on behalf of his great-aunt when she seemed more than capable of speaking for herself, but something in Claire's gut told her there was more here than met the eye.

Reluctantly, she made her way down the driveway, opened the door to her vehicle and got in. Starting the engine, she drove down the hill, watching Luke Jackson in her side mirror. He stood in front of the shed, hands on hips. Claire wondered how long he'd stand guard.

She turned her attention to the road ahead, taking the bends with care and trying to figure out what other disaster lay around the corner.

* * * *

Once again Claire found herself at the café in town, nursing a coffee and another piece of carrot cake. Discovering the café was still open, at this hour, had been a godsend. If only they sold alcohol.

Laura, the girl who had been working earlier, was nowhere in sight, and instead an older version of her was behind the counter, keenly polishing cutlery and every conceivable surface. Claire sat in the far corner of the empty café, well away from the large window that overlooked the street.

Today had been such a mess, and she chided herself for the way she'd handled things. Over the course of her career she'd been thrown challenges from all directions, so why was this cinema such a struggle?

Claire rested her head in her hands and groaned.

"Is it that bad?"

She looked up to find the woman standing next to the table. Her kind eyes made Claire tear up, and she fought to keep her voice calm.

"There's a lot worse going on in the world, I know," Claire said. "Though currently, in my world, it's bad, and it's about to get a whole lot worse." She hadn't been able to shake the image of facing a furious Nigel.

"Carrot cake isn't helping?"

"Nothing will, I'm afraid."

"What's the problem?" The woman sat down opposite her, and the concern in her eyes made Claire want to spill everything—so she did.

Claire let it all out while the woman remained silent, occasionally nodding. With every word that tumbled from Claire's lips the angst lifted a fraction. By the time she was done, the heaviness suffocating her had eased and the thumping headache had abated.

She let out a small laugh. "Oh man, I must have really needed to get that off my chest. Thank you."

"I am happy to help, although I'm not sure how useful I've been." She wiped the table with the damp cloth, then set about neatly arranging the sugar packets in the small wooden box. "The thing is…"

Claire waited for the woman to say something, but nothing came. Aware of her tumultuous relationship with patience, Claire forced herself to remain silent.

"Oh!" The woman laughed then held out her hand. "I have such bad manners. I'm Scarlet."

"I'm Claire." She happily shook Scarlet's hand, which was small and warm, much like Hattie Fitzpatrick's.

"Well, Claire, I'm afraid to say I don't like your chances." Scarlet rubbed at a spot on the table. "An Amelia Elliott biographer came here a while ago. He arrived with a professional photographer and Hattie was happy to help him out. She granted him access to her cinema, to the architectural plans that Elliott had drawn up… Basically, he was given free rein. The problem is, he abused that trust, and he was thrown out."

"Oh?" Claire shuffled forward on her chair. "That would explain a lot. What did he do?"

"No one really knows for sure. Whatever he did, it was enough to piss off Hattie and Luke." Scarlet's grin was contagious. "He's rather good-looking, huh?"

Claire adjusted her position on the chair. "He's not bad on the eye."

"He helps her a lot, especially with the cinema. You've seen it, right? If she repaired it, it could open again. Videos haven't killed cinemas as much as we thought they would."

"True."

"Although, I don't know why she persists in keeping it. She could have sold it a dozen times over. There's always someone wanting to buy it and renovate."

"There must be a reason she's desperate to hold on to it."

"Maybe." Scarlet shrugged. "My little sister Laura and I moved here a few years ago, so we don't know the full story. No one ever talks about it, no matter how drunk I've gotten Luke at the bar."

"Laura who works here?"

"She's the only Laura in Starlight Creek, as far as I know, and believe me, everyone knows everyone here."

"Everyone knows everyone, but they keep secrets from each other?"

Scarlet stood and collected the dishes off the table. "Starlight Creek is odd. I've never experienced a place like this. It's like there are two parallel worlds we're living in. There's the superficial one that you see, and there's a whole other layer that goes on behind closed doors, where secrets are whispered in hushed voices."

"Sounds like *The Twilight Zone.*"

Scarlet tilted her head to the side. "I don't know what it is, but Laura and I still haven't cracked the surface. I don't know if we ever will."

"What keeps you in Starlight Creek then?"

The smile went all the way to Scarlet's eyes. "We're surrounded by green hills, blue skies, sun and beautiful sugarcane. Why on earth would we live anywhere else?"

"Hmm. You do have a point."

"How long are you here for?"

"I'm supposed to be going back to Ashton tonight." Claire dreaded her meeting with Nigel and the rest of the production team.

"But?"

"There's no but."

"I have amazing powers of intuition. There is a but, I can sense it." Scarlet's cheeky wink made Claire wish she could spend more time in this friendly woman's company.

"I promise you, there is no but. I wish there were, *but* there isn't." Claire laughed, and Scarlet joined in.

"What are you going to do?"

Claire slumped against the chair, her shoulder blades uncomfortable against the hard wood. "I have absolutely no idea."

Chapter Six

Claire sat in the driver's seat, shining the light from her torch onto the neatly written letter she'd spent the last hour penning. A mountain of crumpled up paper was next to her on the passenger seat.

Folding the letter and placing it into an envelope Scarlet had given her, Claire got out of the car and crossed the road. The moon shone on the deserted street while she picked her way past potholes to avoid the indignity of tripping and sprawling face-first onto the ground.

Standing in front of the cinema, she turned the envelope in her hands and sighed. So much rode on the words on these pages.

Claire crouched down and shoved it under the door, then leaned her forehead against the cool glass. She took a few deep breaths.

She went back to the car, turned on the engine and replayed Nigel's phone message in her head: *Come and see me the second you arrive in Ashton. I don't care what time it is, you find me.*

Steering the car onto the road, she navigated through the dark and tried to prepare for the inevitable fireworks.

* * * *

The drive to Ashton felt like four hours instead of forty minutes. Although her grandma had always told her not to borrow problems from the future, Claire's mind couldn't stop playing out the scenario where Nigel would lose his cool and she'd be out of a job. She loved that he was a stickler for authenticity, and it made absolute sense to film Amelia Elliott's story in a cinema that had catapulted her to fame, but maybe Nigel was asking the impossible. Maybe she was, too. This was Nigel's dream. Claire's dream. The people at Wattle Films' dream. And it certainly was Amelia's family's dream. How could Claire ever expect Hattie or Luke to comprehend the importance of a dream that wasn't theirs?

She shook her head. The letter she'd left Hattie was useless.

Nearing Ashton, Claire steered the ute onto the field designated for production vehicles. She parked, got out and stared up at the inky sky. A powder spray of stars twinkled above, their innocence spellbinding.

Her bag sounded with the annoying Nokia ringtone, and she pulled out the phone.

"I'm already here, Nigel."

"Who's Nigel?"

"Who's this?"

"Is that Claire Montgomery?"

"Yes?" she answered slowly.

"This is Hattie Fitzpatrick. I'm wondering if we could meet tomorrow at nine o'clock?"

Claire's mouth hung open.

"Claire?"

"Oh! Yes, yes, of course we can meet. Where would you prefer?"

"How about the café? This time we'll try to keep you dry."

* * * *

Claire sat in the café and checked her watch for the tenth time in as many minutes. After meeting with Nigel the night before, she was able to dull his roar to a grumble after she'd told him about her upcoming meeting with Hattie. The night had been a restless one, with Claire tossing and turning, so she'd risen early, taken a walk through the beautiful rainforest nearby and sat by the river while she contemplated Hattie's change of heart. Whatever the reason for Hattie calling, Claire was grateful.

"More coffee?" Scarlet asked as she approached Claire.

"I think I'm good for now, thank you." Claire eyed the carrot cake but decided against it. The knots in her belly made it impossible to stomach anything other than coffee. It had been that way since Hattie had called.

"What's brought you back? When you said goodbye yesterday, I thought it was for good."

"I'm meeting Hattie Fitzpatrick this morning."

Scarlet's eyes widened. "Oh! You've found a way to film here?"

"I'd like to think this meeting is encouraging, but I've had enough experience to know things aren't always what they seem."

"Ain't that the truth." Scarlet set to work wiping down the already clean surface of Claire's table. "I often wonder if we're supposed to jump through a series of hoops to prove we really want something. And even then, the universe will only hand us what we need."

"Which is sometimes not what we want."

"Exactly!" Scarlet sat across from her. Claire loved Scarlet's easygoing nature. "Take my sister, Laura, for example."

"Okay."

"We moved here because we needed to, not because we wanted to." Scarlet scrubbed at a small stain that looked embedded into the wooden surface.

"How so?"

"We lost our parents when we were young. I was nineteen, and Laura thirteen."

"I'm so sorry."

Scarlet shrugged. "It's life, unfortunately. Or death, I guess. The thing is, I was the party girl, always looking for a good time, never at home, constantly giving my parents lip, all that typical teenage-angst stuff. Then we lost them in a car accident."

"That's horrible."

"It was. We don't have any other family, apart from a grandmother in England, so it was up to me to make sure we had a roof over our heads and food on the table. I had to change my life dramatically, and even though I resented it at the time, I now realize it was the best thing for me. If I'd continued on the way I was I could easily have ended up down the party-girl rabbit hole, never to surface again."

"I think a lot of us have teetered on the edge of that particular hole."

"I guess. Overnight I had to become mother and father, as well as big sister to a kid who had just become a teenager. I had no idea what I was doing, but I owed it to my parents to look after my little sister. We were living in Brisbane at the time, but it got too expensive. Plus, Laura was moving in crowds that weren't good for her. So we sold the house with the mortgage and packed up and moved to Starlight Creek. We could afford a house here, the school is good and I easily found work."

"Do you like it here?"

Scarlet sat back, her expression serious. "I do, actually. Originally, it was a plan of desperation. Starlight Creek is so very different from Brisbane, but that's not a bad thing. Laura seems settled. She's getting really good grades in school, likes her part-time job here…on paper it looks fantastic."

"But?"

"Like I was saying yesterday, I still feel like an outsider. There's no sense of community in this town. Not like I expected, anyway."

"Why is that?"

"I think Starlight Creek used to be a close-knit community, but that's not the case anymore. Don't get me wrong, people are friendly, but there's none of that unity that you expect from small towns." Scarlet laughed. "Or maybe I read too many books or watch too many movies and my ideas about small towns are skewed."

The bell above the door rang and in walked Hattie, not a hair out of place, her suit immaculately pressed. Claire glanced at the clock on the wall. Nine o'clock, right on the dot.

Getting up to greet Hattie, Claire wasn't sure what to do. Born into a family where hugs and kisses were as natural as waking up in the morning, she often had to stop herself from reaching out and enveloping someone she barely knew in an embrace. Normally she could read if someone was a hugger or not, but with Hattie Fitzpatrick, Claire had no clue.

"Ah, Claire, it is lovely to see you." Hattie held out her hand and took Claire's with affection. They walked over to the table where Claire had been sitting, and a moment later Scarlet arrived with a pot of steaming tea and a cup and saucer with delicate blue and gold swirls. Hattie set about her ritual while Claire looked on, anxious to ask questions but forcing herself to remain silent. Hattie added one sugar to her masterpiece, closed her eyes as she had a long sip, put the cup down and fixed her gaze on Claire. "Thank you for waiting."

"It's no problem at all."

"I imagine you have myriad questions running around that young mind of yours, and I'll give you the chance to ask them. But first, I wish to address the letter you wrote me."

"Oh."

Hattie let out a light laugh. "My dear girl, you don't need to look so scared! In fact." She pulled out the neatly folded letter, opened it and laid it flat on the table. She donned her reading glasses and said, "There was so much to enjoy."

"Really?" Claire breathed a sigh of relief.

"You don't have a great deal of faith in yourself, do you?"

Claire paused. "I couldn't do this job if I wasn't confident. I need to believe in what I'm doing, introduce myself to new people, open myself up to being rejected…"

"Does that happen often?"

"Not until yesterday," she said quietly.

"Yes, well, that's another matter we need to discuss, but first let's address this correspondence you left in my foyer."

Claire shuffled forward. "What did you want to discuss?"

"Although these are only words on a page, I connected with every single one you wrote. There's so much emotion, so much heart. I tried to remember your voice as I read it but I'm afraid it escaped me. Please, will you read it out loud? I want to imprint your inflections and feelings in my memory. I know I will read this again and again."

"You will?"

"There goes the confidence again. Please." She passed the letter to Claire. "Humor an old woman, will you?"

This all felt very odd, but right now Claire was willing to climb onto a unicycle, recite the alphabet backwards and wear an orange leotard. She cleared her throat and began:

Dear Miss Fitzpatrick,

First of all, please allow me to apologize for the manner in which I behaved today. I should have been up front and told you why I was in town the second I realized the cinema was yours. It was never my intention to mislead you and I am very sorry if it came across this way. I enjoyed your company, and your compassion for my messy predicament was greatly appreciated. I was brought up to always be honest and respect other people's feelings, and I'm sad to think that I have wronged you in any way.

Secondly, I am desperate.

"I could see that," said Hattie.

Claire glanced up, trying to read Hattie's expression. Thankfully, there was no anger in her eyes. Claire returned to the words she'd slaved over:

I've worked extremely hard to put myself through university to obtain a degree in film production. While in school I worked two jobs, ate baked beans for breakfast, lunch and dinner, took on work experience where I ended up spending money, not earning, and even now I am constantly studying the craft of film. This has been a passion since my grandma first took me to see Gone with the Wind at a cinema that showed Hollywood classics. I fell in love with actresses like Vivien Leigh, Hedy Lamarr and Mae

West—all strong women on and off the screen. They taught me about self-respect, reaching for goals no matter how impossible they seem and having faith that hard work and passion will get you through.

Being a woman in the film industry can be tough, no matter if you're behind the camera or in front of it. Actually, the film industry is tough for everyone, but more so for women in roles that have been dominated by men. This is why the production I'm currently working on means so very much. Amelia Elliott was a woman with vision, who followed her dream even when naysayers told her it was a waste of time. Her imagination and persistence helped establish the Art Deco movement here in Australia. And even though her designs weren't in large cities where so many designers received accolades, she still managed to make her mark and leave a legacy for all aspiring female architects. Amelia's family has put a lot of money into this project, and one of the producers is her great-great-grandson. To see her story on screen is a huge deal to many people. The production company I'm working for has poured a lot of love and effort into this project, which I believe will help multiple generations understand what Amelia went through to achieve what she did in a world that didn't support women like her.

Although I'm no Amelia Elliott, I understand what it's like to have a dream and not receive encouragement from others. I come from a family of doctors and accountants and lawyers, all very noble professions, but none of these careers are for me. You see, my family have always instilled in me the belief that I should work hard and reach for my dreams, but what I didn't realize, until it was time to choose a career, was that the encouragement came with a caveat. My family had always thought I would be "one of them," so it was a shock when I told them I was going to work in film. Storytelling, whether fiction or documentary, has always been my passion and it took a lot of courage to follow my heart and go against my family's wishes. Finally, after all these years and all that I've achieved so far in my career, my family are behind me.

Working on this film could take my career to the next level and further prove to my family that listening to my heart was the right thing to do. But if I fail, there is a strong chance they will doubt me once more. I know families are supposed to support

*each other no matter what, but that's not always the case in real
life.*

*Please, I don't want you to think I'm pressuring you or
making you feel guilty for saying no; I am sure you have solid
reasons. I would just like you to understand the motives behind
my actions and why, frankly, I'm so desperate to make this
happen. I know we could build a set based on Amelia's designs,
but Amelia's great-great-grandson, as well as the director, are
adamant that we remain as authentic as possible. As I walked
through your beautiful cinema I felt layers of history all around
me—from Amelia's challenges in making her dream a reality, to
the thousands of people who have sat in this cinema watching
movies or news reels, pondering their own dreams, creating new
ones, discovering new love, rekindling old love or mourning
the love they never found or once had then lost. A purpose-built
set cannot capture these ghosts and long-forgotten feelings that
would influence how the actors play their roles. But your cinema
can.*

*Miss Fitzpatrick, I hope this letter helps you understand there
is not just one reason for filming in your cinema. In the end, the
decision is yours alone, but I do hope that this letter might at
least help you understand that my intentions were honorable.*

*Again, I apologize if I upset you, and I thank you for being so
very kind to me.*

Sincerely,
Claire Montgomery

"You know what this is?" Hattie asked.

Claire shook her head.

"This letter is a reflection of the struggle so many have had, or continue
to have, around the world. The world is full of unfulfilled dreams and..."
She sipped her tea. "If I have the power to make someone's dream come
true, then who am I to say no?"

Claire swallowed hard. "Are you saying what I think you are?"

"Would you like me to write it on a serviette, dear?" The cheeky sparkle
in Hattie's eyes made her even more endearing.

Claire wanted to jump up and envelop Hattie in a tight bear hug. Instead,
she offered the widest smile possible. "Thank you. Thank you so very
much." She wanted to believe this was a slam dunk, but there was still one
major hurdle. "I hate to bring this up, but—"

"Luke?"

"Yes."

"Bless him. He's a good lad, but can be a tad overprotective." Hattie tapped her fingers against the china cup.

"I gathered that."

"Don't worry about him. The cinema is mine, so the decision is mine. However, before I sign anything, I need to know the details."

"Of course."

"Why film so much of Amelia's story in my cinema? Surely her life outside those walls is more significant."

Claire settled against the chair, delighted by Hattie's interest. "When Amelia first started designing, she couldn't get any work because she used her first name. Back then no one thought a woman should have that kind of career, even though she was more than capable."

"Those were different times, although it hasn't changed in some regards."

Claire nodded, refraining from getting on her high horse. "She started using initials in front of her surname and, a little like Cyrano de Bergerac, she had her male assistant stand in as AJ Elliott."

"That doesn't fit in with what you wrote in the letter."

"Ah, it does, don't worry." Claire took a moment to get her history straight. "Although Amelia was confident in her designs, the attitude of her day was that women should be in the kitchen or hosting tea parties. She had to find a way around it, but soon came to the realization she was cheating herself, and other women, of the opportunity to show the world what they can do. One of her clients was behind in payments, so she set up camp in the cinema until the bill was settled. That cinema burned down years ago, but it was where she made the decision to publicly announce who she was and the work she did. It was also when she fell in love with her assistant."

"How wonderfully romantic! Although, wouldn't having a man by her side make her less…progressive?"

"Not at all! It was because of her newfound strength that she realized she could have anything men could—a career and marriage and, years later, children. That's the beauty of her story. She set out trying to work around society's expectations, but eventually realized that the world wouldn't change unless she did something about it."

"I would have loved to meet her."

"Me too."

"But why do you need so long to film in my cinema?"

"A one-day shoot only creates six or so minutes of TV screen time, and because the cinema is so significant, there are a lot of scenes that need to be shot there."

"I see." Hattie's serious tone made Claire hold her breath. "There is one major stipulation—I will not sign unless you are in charge of the goings-on at my cinema."

"I can assure you that everyone will treat your cinema with the utmost care."

"I won't agree if I don't think that will be the case. What is it you do, exactly?"

"My job?"

"Yes."

Hattie's interest encouraged Claire. "I look after the health and safety of the cast and crew, as well as ensure you're paid on time and your property is looked after. I also have to make sure all the permits are in place and..." She paused, a desire to lay it all on the table overtaking her. "I should tell you this is my first time in charge of locations."

Idiot! Why bring this up?

Hattie's mouth dropped open. "You've never done this before?"

"I've worked my way up through the ranks over the years. It's been a hard slog."

Hattie stared. "Why are you telling me this?"

"Because I want you to go into this with full disclosure."

"This could give me a good reason to say no," said Hattie.

Claire held her breath.

"But I like your honesty. It makes me think I can trust you."

"I won't let you down."

"Those words you wrote are heartfelt. And I can see you are a woman who grasps a challenge and runs with it." Hattie's eyes lit up. "You remind me of a young me."

"Really?" Claire wanted to unleash an avalanche of questions, but bit her lip.

"Believe it or not, I was a young girl with dreams once."

"I absolutely can believe it."

"So," said Hattie. "Let's talk details, and I will give you my final decision."

Chapter Seven

1950 – Hollywood

Lena sat in the chair, trying not to wriggle. The hair and makeup process had taken longer than expected.

"Just a little more…" Vanessa, the makeup artist and one of Lena's friends, painted the last of the red lipstick on Lena's lips. "There! You look gorgeous!"

"I don't feel gorgeous," muttered Lena.

"Well, we've fixed up those bags under your eyes. You look like you've had a full night's sleep now." Vanessa stood back and admired her work.

"I wish!" Lena got off the chair, removed the cape from around her neck and placed it on the counter.

"You really should try it."

"Try what?" Lena picked up the gold dress she was to wear for her role.

"Sleeping."

The laugh that fell from Lena's lips was deep and throaty. "I'll sleep when I die. Or when they cancel my contract."

"That's not going to happen!" Yvonne waltzed into the room and took the dress. She motioned for Lena to remove her robe and Yvonne held out the costume so Lena could step in. The neckline plunged way too low and the dress was the tightest she'd ever tried to squeeze into. Yvonne fussed about, eventually securing the zipper. "You're up for contract renewal soon, aren't you?"

"Yes," Lena sighed. "They've already got their pound of flesh out of me. I don't know how much more I have to give."

Yvonne and Vanessa exchanged looks.

"What?" asked Lena.

"You're going to need to give a whole lot more of yourself if the rumors are true," said Vanessa.

"What rumors?" asked Lena.

"Shh." Yvonne looked around, then whispered, "Apparently Jeanne Harris has got herself in hot water."

"That's nothing new," said Lena at her regular volume.

"Keep it down! This place has ears." Vanessa packed the makeup. "This time, Jeanne's predicament is worse."

"What's she done now?" Although the friendship between Jeanne and Lena had dissolved, Lena still cared what happened to her.

"Booze."

"A heap of people have a problem with booze in Hollywood," said Lena.

"And drugs."

"That too." Lena tried to adjust the dress, but it wouldn't budge. "This is not news, ladies. Jeanne had a problem with it before she became a star." She stopped what she was doing. "She's all right, isn't she?"

"She's functioning, if that's what you mean. Cooper has a minder with her twenty-four hours a day now," said Yvonne. "Look, I don't want to spread rumors, but Jeanne's sliding on a slope that is very slippery, and if Breen gets wind of it…"

"Joseph Breen?" Lena stood straight. "Just because he spends his life enforcing the Hays Code doesn't mean he has a say over individuals. His job is to censor movies, not be the moral police in people's personal lives, even if they are Hollywood stars. And don't get me started on this stupid censorship code. Imagine how different *Casablanca* would have been had Breen and his cronies not wielded their power over the director and scriptwriters. If Breen had let things be, then Ilsa and Rick would have ended up together."

"But they had an affair in the movie."

"Yes, I realize this, and adultery should never be condoned but…it was Ilsa and Rick! One of the greatest couples in history!" Lena looked at the ceiling and sighed. "What I wouldn't give to have a role like that."

"I would design your costumes," said Yvonne.

Vanessa picked up a hairbrush and waved it with a flourish. "And I would do hair and makeup!"

Lena looked down at her high heels and the fabric caressing her every curve. "You don't think this is too over-the-top?"

"You're playing a seductress! What do you expect to wear? A nun's habit?"

"Ha!" Lena patted her freshly curled hair. "It just feels odd playing such an...interesting role."

"This is a great chance to show Lawrence you can do anything. Sweet, sultry and everything in between," said Yvonne. "And you have more lines and screen time than ever before."

"True." Lena pulled her shoulders back. She glanced at the clock above the mirror and moved her neck from side to side, stretching her muscles. "Guess it's time."

"Go get 'em!" Yvonne said while Vanessa gave thumbs up followed by a large grin.

Lena went to open the door, but the stupid thing wouldn't budge. She rattled the handle a few times and the lock clicked open.

"That should really get fixed," said Yvonne.

"Yup." Lena stepped into the corridor and straightened her dress. After her singing debut at the Coopers' a few months earlier, she'd met with the director, Lawrence. He'd been suitably impressed by her performance— enough to give her a bigger role, but not enough for him to stick his neck out and offer her leading lady. That would never happen as long as Jeanne Harris remained everybody's darling, regardless of her shortcomings.

Oh, Jeanne. What had she gotten herself into now?

Lena made her way onto set, skillfully dodging the cables strewn across the floor, the low-hanging lights and the wooden supports at the back of scenery. She found Lawrence at the far end of the set, clipboard in hand as he spoke with George, who used a pencil to point to sections of the script.

Lena waited off to the side, reciting the next scene's lines in her head.

George glanced over, his eyes earnest.

A hollow feeling grew in her belly.

Lawrence rubbed the back of his neck. George walked toward her, slowing down as he drew near. He didn't look her in the eye, but said quietly, "We'll talk soon."

She held onto his arm. "What's going on?"

"I can't tell you. We'll catch up later." He hurried away and disappeared through the narrow gap of the huge set door.

"Lee." Lawrence beckoned her.

The high heels and tight fabric meant her walk was more of a sashay, but she didn't mind, given her role in this particular movie was that of seductress. She might as well embrace her character before the cameras started rolling.

"You're out."

"What?" Then she remembered who she was speaking with. "Pardon?"

"We've had one of Breen's men go through the script, and we're going to have to do some serious rewriting. That means no seductress."

"But she's a huge part of the storyline! I have two songs!"

Lawrence pushed out a long-suffering sigh. "I am aware of this."

"You could change the role, make my character less...free-spirited."

"Sorry, Lee. I know you were excited about this, and I was looking forward to seeing what you can do, but it's not going to happen. Not in this movie, anyway."

Hot tears welled in her eyes, and she concentrated on staring at the glittery heels that were already causing her feet to hurt. "Can't—"

"It's out of my hands now. Cooper could fight for it, but it's not worth it. Better to scratch one role than end up getting the whole movie canned."

"What about the Italian movies? American audiences love them, and they're not offended by risqué themes or partial nudity. How can foreign films like these be shown here yet we can't have one character—and not a lead role at that—who is sultry? Where's the fairness?" The words tumbled from her mouth even though she knew she should reel them back in. "You assured me we'd get the seductress past the censorship board."

"I guess I was wrong. It could be worse."

"How?"

"We could have filmed it, and you would have ended up on the cutting-room floor." Lawrence put his hand on her arm and she looked up. "I truly am sorry, Lena."

"Where—" She cleared her throat. "Where does that leave me?"

"I don't have any roles for you right now. But don't worry, you'll be paid for this project regardless."

"That's not the point," she mumbled.

"What can I do?" He threw his arms wide.

"Nothing. Thanks anyhow." She walked away, wishing she could think of something—anything—that would save her role, even if it was watered down. But it made sense to take out her role altogether in order to make the movie more "wholesome." She couldn't even call her agent to go to bat for her, as he'd holed himself up in some beach hut in Hawaii for an extended vacation.

By the time she got back to the dressing room Yvonne and Vanessa had left.

Lena slammed the door and kicked off her shoes. She struggled with the zipper, and as she thrashed from side to side she let out a few curse words.

"May I help?"

Lena spun to find Reeves Garrity standing in the doorway. "What are you doing in here? Get out!"

She reached for the door and slammed it shut, horrified. Lena wrestled herself out of the dress then put on her day clothes, not worrying about hair or makeup. All she wanted right now was to get off the lot and far, far away from this day.

Opening the door, she stepped out to find Reeves leaning against the wall, arms crossed, staring into space.

"I thought I told you to get out," she said.

"I did. You never said to go away."

"I am warning you, Reeves Garrity, you do not want to mess with me today."

"I'm really not. I just happened to be walking past and heard you cursing and—"

"So you opened the door?"

"The door was already wide open."

That stupid lock was unpredictable. Just like this life she'd thought she wanted. But did she, really? Or would she be better off returning to obscurity? Where her heart wouldn't be ripped out and stomped on in front of her peers? She could be back at home and married with children right now, yet she persisted in chasing a dream that may never materialize.

A lump formed in her throat and hot tears welled in her eyes.

"Lena?" Reeves's expression wasn't one of pity. There was deep concern that made her feel vulnerable yet warm at the same time. "Lena? Are you all right?"

She bit her trembling lip.

"Come on, let's get out of here."

Lena nodded, not trusting herself to speak. Although anger and disappointment had been her initial reactions, a deep-seated fear of never being good enough, of never catching a break, now overtook her and she hated feeling so exposed. Especially in front of someone whose career was on an upward trajectory.

Reeves walked beside her, his long gait shortened to meet hers. He towered above her, like a strong sentinel, and, as much as she didn't want to admit it, she enjoyed the feeling of strength and protection he exuded.

"My car's near Stage Eight," said Reeves.

"I'd prefer to walk a bit, if that's all right."

"It is definitely all right."

They exited the gates and headed left onto the main road. She squinted at the glaring blue sky as cars whizzed by, the sun more intense than usual. The thin wool suit she wore now felt too hot, even though it was a cool spring day.

"Would you like a coffee? Perhaps a soda?" asked Reeves.

"Shouldn't you be on set? Aren't you filming with Jeanne?" The questions tumbled out before she could hold them back. "Sorry."

Reeves's laugh sounded kind. "Don't be sorry. We've finished filming. I was on my way to look at your movie."

"It's not my movie," she said, and all the disappointment and anger rose once more.

"What do you mean?"

"I had a role—my biggest yet—but they've scrapped it because of censorship."

"I'm so sorry, Lena." His sincerity touched her.

"It's not your fault. It's the industry, and neither you nor I have any control over it."

"Let's skip the coffee and go to the bar. What do you think?"

"I think that's an excellent plan."

Chapter Eight

1950 – Hollywood

Lena and Reeves sat in a booth at Lonnie's Bar, nursing a couple of whiskeys. A basket of fries sat untouched between them.

Reeves drummed his fingers on the table. "What are you going to do?"

All Lena could offer was a shrug. She sipped the whiskey. It burned her throat, but she didn't care. "I know I should let this movie go. There's nothing more I can do about it. I just need to concentrate on what's next."

"What is next?"

"I have no idea!" Lena let out a loud laugh followed by a snort. "Should I be worried?"

It was Reeves's turn to shrug.

"I should be worried but...I'm not." She leaned toward him. "Is that insane?"

"I don't know you well enough to know if you're insane—"

"I asked if my thoughts were insane, not me." She followed that with a wry smile.

"I didn't mean..." he stammered.

"I'm joking."

"Ah, I get it," he said, not too convincingly.

They fell into silence, the quiet chatter of patrons in the bar keeping them company. Lena traced her fingers across the scratched surface of the wooden parquetry table, suddenly self-conscious in the presence of someone she barely knew—and she'd already said too much. She was usually more wary about opening up to strangers, yet here she was, sitting in a bar at lunchtime, drinking whiskey with a man she didn't know if she could trust.

"I probably should go." Lena grabbed her bag.

"Please don't."

"Why?"

"I like your company."

"You do?"

He tilted his head. "Why do you sound so surprised?"

"In this town, people are only friendly when they need something."

"Actually, I do need something."

She should have known better. Lena stood. "I don't have anything to give, sorry."

"You've already given it."

"Huh?"

"Please." He gestured for her to sit, and she did, intrigued. "I've been in Los Angeles for some time and as much as I am loving it, there are aspects that are not so appealing."

"Like?"

"Like the lack of good company."

"You looked pretty happy to have Jeanne Harris on your arm last time I saw you."

He cleared his throat and looked at his drink. "I have to be seen with Jeanne."

"Why?" she asked, then quickly followed it with, "Oh, because of her adventures?"

Reeves pursed his lips but couldn't contain the smile. "You could call them that."

"She's as wild as the Atlantic Ocean in winter."

"I am beginning to see this. My agent—who happens to be Jeanne's— also thinks that my presence may have a calming effect on her."

"And in return you get exposure in the press." She leaned back and crossed her arms. "That's a pretty good deal for you."

Reeves rested his elbows on the table. "It sounds great in theory but..."

"Jeanne."

"Exactly." He sipped his drink. "I shouldn't be talking out of school."

"If anyone knows what Jeanne's like, it's me."

"What's the story with you two?"

"When I first moved to Los Angeles, Jeanne and I roomed together and became steadfast friends. But when Jeanne started getting attention in the right circles, she didn't want to be associated with the little people anymore, and she dropped me like the proverbial hot potato. In her effort to become a huge star, she's forgotten the days when we'd share a can of soup as our only meal and how scared we were living in this new city without any idea of what the future held."

Reeves fiddled with his empty whiskey glass. "I'm sorry she treated you like that."

"Hollywood has a habit of changing people. Friendships rarely last," she said.

"I doubt you've changed much from the time you arrived. You seem very down-to-earth."

"I like to think I am, but who's to say? This is a cutthroat business and sometimes we have to do things we'd rather not." She paused. "How long have you been here?"

Reeves glanced sideways and took some time before replying, "I've been here long enough to realize that people like you are breaths of fresh air."

She waited for more, but nothing was forthcoming. "And?"

"And?"

Good grief. It was like extracting teeth. "And what is your background? Where do you come from? Have you always wanted to be an actor? What are your plans?"

Reeves held up his hand and laughed. "You like to ask questions, don't you?"

Smiling, she said, "I guess I do."

"I suspect it will take some time to answer everything. How about you join me for dinner this evening?"

All the playful banter came to a screeching halt. "I'm not available."

"Tomorrow night?"

"Sorry. I can't."

"The next evening?"

She shook her head.

"When *can* we have dinner?"

Lena stood once more, this time determined to leave. "We can't. Ever."

* * * *

After her hasty exit from the bar, Lena caught the bus. She concentrated on the familiar scenery whizzing past—Kirk's Car Garage, Curly's Dime Store, Kozlowski Sports—but it became a blurred mess as she tried to hold back tears. She had no idea if they were tears of frustration, disappointment, sadness or anger. Perhaps a combination of them all.

Refusing Reeves's offer of dinner wasn't sitting right. He had been so very kind to her on a day that had turned from wonderful to horrendous in a matter of hours. But Lena couldn't accept his invitation even though he craved company. She wasn't ready for an innocent dinner date.

The bus pulled up to her stop and she alighted. The doors slammed shut and a haze of pollution spewed onto the street as the bus took off. Across the road, she could see her bedroom window in the apartment she shared with Yvonne. It was tiny, but it was a space she loved—her sanctuary from the craziness of the world.

Lena looked through the windows of Roy's Diner. The lights around the sign had a few blown bulbs yet to be replaced. Inside the diner, Meryl bustled from table to table, her energy never waning no matter how long the shift. A sudden longing for motherly company overcame Lena and she opened the door. The bell tinkled as Lena entered, and warmth enveloped her.

"Miss Lena Lee!" Meryl's smile quickly vanished and she walked over and put her hand on Lena's shoulder. "Honey? What's wrong?"

The tears she'd managed to hold back now came out in a steady stream. Meryl guided Lena to a booth, sat down next to her and put her arm around Lena's shaking body. Roy arrived a moment later with a banana milkshake, gave it to Meryl and promptly disappeared.

Meryl put the shake in front of Lena. "This will help you feel better."

Lena's bottom lip trembled as she tried to force the words past the lump in her throat. "Nothing will make me feel better. It's horrible. Just so, so horrible."

"What is, honey?"

The kindness in Meryl's voice and the caring in her eyes made it harder, but Lena had to get the words out because if she didn't, she feared she'd explode with the intensity of her confusion.

"My role got cut today and I have nothing coming up. Then Reeves Garrity was really nice to me."

"Someone being nice to you is horrible?"

"Yes. No. Oh, I don't know!" She rested her forehead on the table. Meryl's gentle touch on Lena's back helped her shoulders relax and she took a deep breath and sat up. Her eyes stung and felt swollen, but she didn't care. "I feel like every time I catch a break, something squashes it. This time, it's the censorship board."

"All studios have that problem."

"I know. It just feels personal because my big role has been ripped away. Then Reeves Garrity asked me to dinner."

"Oh." Meryl sat back. "I can see why that would upset you."

"Are you being sarcastic?"

"Lena, I know you don't want to hear this, but don't you think it's time you gave yourself a chance? If this Reeves Garrity wants to be nice to you, let him."

"I can't." She nearly choked on the words.

"Sweetheart, why are you punishing yourself? What happened with Charlie wasn't your fault. He wasn't a good person, and you suffered because of it. Not all men are the same."

Lena bit her lip.

"That's not all, is it?" asked Meryl.

Shaking her head, Lena said, "No."

"Home?"

"I miss my family so very much. I haven't lived with them for over a decade, but lately I've been thinking that my parents aren't getting any younger, and now I have nieces and nephews I've never even met." She sipped the milkshake and her nerves calmed a fraction.

"You know you have a different kind of family here." Meryl squeezed Lena's hand.

"I do, and I love you all dearly."

"Though it's not the same," said Meryl. "Would you ever go back?"

Lena shook her head. "Sadly, no. I'm too far down this road now. And I love my work. I really can't imagine doing anything else. No one in my family can relate to my life here, and I can't relate to their world—my old world—anymore."

"I truly believe that even though people are changed by experiences and circumstances, we stay the same in our hearts. And you, my dear girl, have a beautiful heart, and Hollywood can break people like you."

"I won't let it," she said, determination creeping in. "I'm strong."

"That you are, but you have your feet in both camps—strong and vulnerable."

Lena closed her eyes for a moment. "Why can't I be like Jeanne Harris? She doesn't care what people think, and that gets her everywhere. We started at the same studio at the same time, the same chorus line, yet…"

"Would you really like to be like Jeanne?"

"No."

"This is your story to write, no one else's." Meryl wrapped her arms around Lena and squeezed her tight. "And it's a story I love."

Lena rested her head on Meryl's shoulder. "Thank you."

"It's nothing. If I had a daughter, I imagine she'd be just like you. Now drink your shake before it gets warm."

* * * *

Lena spent all night tossing and turning, replaying the conversation with Meryl in her head. Every so often images of Reeves Garrity crowded in, with his large brown eyes, dark wavy hair and kind smile. Every time, she made a concerted effort to shake him from her thoughts.

She shuffled into the kitchenette, where Yvonne sat at the table, sipping freshly brewed coffee.

"Want one?" Yvonne held up her mug. "There's still some left in the pot."

"No thanks." Lena collapsed on the chair.

"You could pack my entire wardrobe in those bags under your eyes."

"Gee, thanks. Just what I needed to hear," mumbled Lena.

Yvonne reached over and grabbed Lena's hand. "That's what friends are for—to tell it like it is. How are you holding up?"

"If you're asking if I'm going to spend all day in the fetal position, no, I'm not."

"You could let yourself wallow for a while, you know," Yvonne said. "Not that I've ever seen you wallow."

"Wallowing is not my thing. Besides, I can't sit around and do nothing."

"You could try."

They burst into laughter and Lena snorted.

"Seriously, though, Lena, what are you going to do?"

"I'm going to go see Mr. Cooper today."

"What?" Coffee sprayed across the table, and Yvonne wiped it up with the sleeve of her dressing gown.

"I'm going to ask for a new role in another movie."

"You can't do that! They dictate who does what, and even though you are a very talented actress, you don't quite have the influence."

"But if you don't ask, you don't get," said Lena.

"No one gets anything unless Stuart Cooper says so. You are crazy to think he'd listen to anyone other than himself."

"I'm not asking to be cast in a lead, I just want to know if there are any roles that could replace the one I lost."

"Lena…" Yvonne looked at the ceiling, like she was asking God to give her patience. "It's going to come across like you're entitled."

"Really?" she asked, appalled. "That's the last thing I want!"

"You aren't like the entitled divas who swan around the studios, but you just can't go up and ask the head of the studio for a new role. It's not done."

"I know plenty of actors who have done it, though!"

"Because they are *men*. The rules are different. The only reason women are in movies is because sex sells," said Yvonne.

"That's not what Breen and the Hays Code think. They spend every waking hour saving people from their own lustful thoughts, or ensuring they don't become influenced to take drugs or become floozies or gangsters." Lena's voice was draped in sarcasm.

"The Hays Code people can rely all they like on their puritan ways, but the reality is that a beautiful woman with a curvy figure will get more men to a theater than Gregory Peck or Clark Gable. Even if the woman is in a suit, men will pay good money to watch her sashay across the screen," Yvonne said.

"Women have a lot more to offer than a pretty face or a perfect figure," said Lena.

Yvonne smiled. "You're preaching to the converted. I may spend my days draping women in expensive fabrics and precious jewels, but the fact that Breen and his cronies can dictate how women should behave does not go unnoticed." She threw her arms wide. "What are we supposed to do about it, though? Say no and end up on the street?"

Lena got up, walked over to the coffeepot and poured herself a cup. "I don't have the answers. I don't think anyone does."

"Maybe it's just the way of the world."

"It shouldn't be."

"No, it shouldn't, but if people in influential positions do nothing about it, how can anything change? It's a battle we'll never win, I'm afraid. We're at the mercy of the decision makers—who are men."

"And now I need to go and convince one to give me a role in a new movie."

Yvonne stood and wrapped her arms around Lena. "You do know this outrageous scheme is likely to get you fired, right?"

"That's a chance I'm willing to take."

Chapter Nine

1994 – Starlight Creek, Queensland

Claire exited the café, a new lightness in her step. For the past hour she'd spoken with Hattie about how an on-location shoot worked and the expected timeframe for filming. Given Nigel was currently shooting the outdoor scenes near Ashton, Claire had time to get legal to draw up a new contract, have Hattie ask her lawyer to review it and get the final signature. At this stage, nothing was set in concrete, so a dark cloud of worry still hung over Claire's head—what if Luke Jackson talked his great-aunt out of it?

Claire crossed the road to her car. Her phone rang loudly, like it was shouting at her. She whipped it from her handbag.

"Hey, Phil!"

"It's Nigel. Got an answer for me yet?"

"Actually, I do." *Thank goodness.*

"And?"

"And it's looking pretty good. Fantastic, in fact. She's a lovely lady and just needed to understand the importance of this production. I really like her."

"Liking her doesn't get me access to the cinema."

"Well, it helps, because now we have a rapport. She has some stipulations, which are totally understandable and very doable, but it's nice to have her on board. I'm meeting her in an hour to take some interior photographs, and I'll get them developed as soon as possible. I promise, you won't be disappointed."

"I hope not, because World War III is about to erupt."

"Robert?"

"Yes."

"How's Annalise?"

"She's been sent to her aunt's in Cairns until it blows over."

"But she's okay?"

"Yes, yes, she's totally fine. Angry with her folks, but what do you expect? Tony's been doing a good job here, but it's not the same as having you in charge. Listen, we're not far from finishing here, so your skates better be on. By the way, James has been warned about keeping his pants on."

"Easier said than done."

"Which is why you can be his minder."

"Pardon?" She wanted to scream "No freaking way!" but pushed it back down. "I work with locations. I have no experience with keeping actors in line."

"You're a people person, and you're smart. Plus, he likes you, but not enough to have sex with you."

Given that James jumped into bed with any female under thirty with a pulse, Nigel's comment was far from complimentary. "I'll have my hands full making sure Hattie's happy and the crew follow her wishes."

"I'll up your wage fifteen percent."

"Uh…thanks?" Claire hadn't given money a thought, but she was glad Nigel had offered it anyway. She'd put that extra cash in her production fund—a bank account she'd set up especially for making her "one day" production.

"So, it's sorted. You stay in Starlight Creek and get things started. I'll need a comprehensive ground plan, access points, etcetera. You know the drill. Now, break is over. Call me with a report ASAP."

"Sure."

"Montgomery, there's one more thing."

Uh-oh. "Yes?"

"Well done."

"Thank you! I won't let you—"

The line disconnected, and Claire did a little jump for joy. *Finally*, she was starting to get noticed. *One more step up the ladder!* Then she remembered her extra responsibility—James Lloyd, Casanova extraordinaire.

Keeping him in line would be a full-time job. She might as well give up on the idea of sleeping more than four hours a night. It would be worth it, though. Besides, she had that vacation in Bali to look forward to. All would be well in the end. Right?

Claire shoved the phone back in her messenger bag then fumbled around for her car keys, silently cursing the stupid bag for being so full. She put it on the hood and pulled out her hairbrush, spare underwear and deodorant, notebooks, pens in an array of colors and a small zippered bag that contained her three favorite lip glosses and one mascara. Her keys were nowhere to be found.

"Where are the stupid little mo—"

"What are you doing?"

The bag slipped off the hood and landed on the ground with a thud. A packet of mints split open and rolled under the vehicle while one of her notebooks tumbled out, pages flapping in the light breeze. Claire bent down to gather the wayward contents, but Luke beat her to it. They stood, and he handed over her possessions.

"Thank you," she said.

"No problem." Luke studied her intently. "Who are you harassing today?"

"I'll have you know, harassing is not in my job description." Finding an indignant tone was not difficult.

Luke raised an eyebrow.

"What?" Man, she really sounded defensive.

"I hear you met with my great-aunt."

"Yes, I did."

"She likes you."

"And I like her."

Luke rubbed his chin with his thumb and forefinger. "She better be right about trusting you."

"I cross my heart a thousand times that I will keep my word and make sure it is a positive experience for your great-aunt."

"She's not as strong as she seems. This cinema means the world to her. It's been in our family for generations."

"What's the family history with the cinema?"

"It's questions like this that will get her offside," said Luke. "Just do what you've both agreed on, and don't go asking personal questions. If you do, you'll lose her trust and your filming won't happen."

"All right." She liked that Luke had offered some advice. Maybe he wasn't so bad. And maybe, as she and Hattie got to know each other, information about the cinema's history would trickle out in conversation. Or not. Either way, Claire had just managed to do the next-to-impossible and source a site at the last minute. This was a defining moment in her career, and she should give herself a moment to celebrate. A wide grin broke free on her lips.

"You've got a nice smile." Luke's cheeks flushed red and heat rushed across Claire's face.

"I have?"

"For someone who can be so insistent, you don't have a lot of confidence in yourself, do you?"

Had he and Hattie been talking about her?

"I have confidence. I couldn't do this job without it." People who lacked confidence didn't have huge goals. And she had plenty. So why was she giving the impression that she didn't believe in herself?

"Maybe." He twirled his keys with his index finger. "That was an impressive letter."

"You read it?"

"Of course. My great-aunt called soon after she discovered it. It was eloquent. Inspiring. Sincere."

"I'm glad you thought so." She liked the turn this conversation had taken.

"It resonated with me on many levels."

"Like?"

Luke looked away. "Let's just say I know what it's like not to feel supported when pursuing something your heart longs for."

Visions of Luke's magnificent metal sculptures appeared in her mind. Could they be what he was talking about? No, impossible. After all, his art was in the shop, and seemed to be popular. Maybe there was something else...

"Right, well, I'm glad I ran into you. I guess I'll see you around," he said.

"I guess you will." She waved goodbye, and Luke crossed the road and entered the café. She watched him through the window, his tall, lean body lounging on the chair as he chatted with his great-aunt. The connection between them seemed unbreakable. Certainly, Luke's allusion to unsupported dreams couldn't have included Hattie. Who was it? His father? Mother? Were they still alive? He hadn't mentioned them...then again, Luke didn't seem like the type of person who told his life story to someone within the first five minutes of meeting them. She suspected his statement about not asking Hattie personal questions also pertained to him. Disappointment surfaced, because, whether she liked it or not, a sudden desire to know more about Luke Jackson resonated deep within her.

Oh, no, no, no.

Nope. She could not go there. But it wouldn't hurt to fantasize, just a little, right?

Claire rolled her eyes and scrounged around her bag again for the keys. She checked her pockets but had no luck.

Peering in through the window of her ute, she spied them sitting oh-so-innocently on the driver's seat.

"You have got to be kidding me." Sticking her hand in her bag once more, Claire fumbled around until she found the plastic strapping she kept for such occasions—which happened way more often than they should have. A mind that constantly buzzed with ideas interfered with everyday things, like remembering not to lock her keys in the ute.

Setting her bag down, Claire inserted the strapping at the right angle and slid it along slowly, waiting for it to gently touch the mechanism that would pop the lock. A faint click sounded and Claire quickly opened the door, clutched the keys and waved them in the air.

"Yes! Ha!" She did a spin of victory but stopped the second she caught sight of Luke and Hattie standing a couple of feet away. Claire dropped her hands by her side. "Oh, hi."

"Are you a criminal in your spare time?" asked Luke, his lips twitching.

"No...uh...breaking into your own vehicle isn't a crime, last time I checked." *Seriously, what crap timing.*

"Don't listen to him." Hattie gave Luke a nudge. "It's good to see you're more than capable of figuring out your own problems. A woman should be able to rely on herself. Why don't you come to my place now and you can get started?"

"That would be wonderful, thank you."

"Don't you have a doctor's appointment?" Luke asked his aunt.

"Oh, yes." Hattie tapped her head. "Sometimes my age catches up with me, but not often." She turned to Luke. "Why don't you open up, then Claire can start doing what she needs to do? I'll meet you there later."

"I can pick you up from the doctor's."

"No, no, the walk will do me good. It will give me a chance to clear my head."

Luke shrugged and gave Claire a look that seemed to say there's no point in arguing.

Hattie waved goodbye and walked a few doors down to enter a gray building with a faded pharmacy sign with the "ac" missing.

"Shall we go?" Luke started walking slowly, letting her catch up.

Walking afforded Claire the opportunity to take in the small details she'd missed while driving. For years Claire had trained herself to notice every element of landscapes and buildings, committing them to memory because she never knew when she'd need to call on them for a production. Whether it was the way the afternoon sun shone on a bougainvillea, the curve of a road through a valley or the intricate filigree on the banister of a staircase, she always looked for the beauty in things. Even run-down towns like Starlight Creek, which hadn't had a lick of paint since 1957, had their own charming stories to tell.

As Claire and Luke got closer to the cinema, a tingle of excitement started in her fingertips and ran up her arms. She loved nothing more than exploring a new site, mapping it out, using the logical side of her mind to maximize the space and minimize the shoot time, while also using her creative side to envision how everything would look on-screen. On-location sets were characters in their own right, and they could make or break a movie—the perfect setting could enhance a mood and give actors a better connection with the story.

Luke and Claire walked in silence. They arrived at the cinema, and she stopped and looked—really looked—at the faded exterior and peeling paint.

Luke opened the door, stepped into the dark foyer, flicked on the lights and motioned for her to enter. She hesitated, her head clouded in doubt, wondering if she'd dreamed the interior was better than it actually was.

Stepping across the threshold, she prayed she hadn't gotten it wrong.

Chapter Ten

1994 – Starlight Creek, Queensland

A wave of awe crashed over Claire as she took in the expanse of the foyer. The black and white tiles were just as pristine as she remembered, the wooden kiosk just as shiny, and the ornate chandelier hanging from the pressed metal ceiling still held every crystal.

"Wow." She breathed out slowly.

"Wow? But you've seen this before."

"I know. It's just…just…I have no words, really." She slowly walked in a circle, taking it all in.

A wry smile raced across Luke's lips. "I get it."

"You do?"

"I've grown up in this cinema, and sometimes I still find myself in awe. Check this out." Luke went behind the counter to the kiosk. He pressed a panel, and out popped a secret drawer. "They used this to store receipts until the end of the night."

"That is so cool!" Claire was as excited as a schoolgirl. "I'll have to tell Nigel about this."

Luke stood straight. "Nigel?"

"The director. He loves this sort of stuff. I bet we could use it in the miniseries."

Luke's body stiffened.

"You're really not on board with this, are you?" She knew she should shut up.

"I like the idea of our cinema being in a miniseries, but it's the behind-the-scenes stuff that worries me."

"Why?"

"My great-aunt." He brushed a speck of dust off the dark wood counter. "When I give my word, I mean it. I will not let your great-aunt down." "I believe you," he finally said, his voice sincere.

Her shoulders relaxed. "Excellent."

"Don't you need to take photos or something?" He was back to business, so she got her camera out of her bag, attached the flash and asked, "Do you mind if I walk around? I'll also need to take measurements."

"Go ahead."

She worked in the foyer, focusing her camera lens, getting the right light, sketching and jotting down measurements. Claire pulled out the shooting script, which she'd already made notes on.

"What's that for?" asked Luke.

"I'm just double-checking I've covered all the potential angles for scenes inside the cinema."

"Doesn't the director do that?"

"Yes, but part of my job is to relieve the director's logistical burdens. It's important for me to see things with a director's eye and the mind of a logistics operator. I have to think about where the crew and actors will stand—we normally mark the actors' positions with tape, but it won't mark your floor. Each actor has a specific color they stand on. I also look into the accessibility of power and water, where catering will set up and the health and safety of everyone—and everything—involved. I also have to time how long it takes to get the crew from one place to another, as well as put signs up on the roads and give the crew detailed maps so they arrive quickly and without confusion. Basically, when looking at a place to shoot, I have to consider every single angle of production."

"Interesting," said Luke.

"I'm glad you think so," said Claire, encouraged by Luke's curiosity. "My job means I live in the past, present *and* future."

"How?"

"Past because I oversee packing up a set and the logistics of getting everything from point A to point B. Present because I need to know what's happening while we're shooting, and because I'm a liaison between departments and property owners. And future because I'm looking at the next lot of locations and starting property negotiations while putting together information for the production team."

"When do you sleep?"

She let out a laugh. "Never!"

"Why the photos?"

"It's a storyboard for the production team, because they can't always see a property before they arrive. Normally I'd do this before I start negotiations with the property owner, but we're on a bit of a time limit."

"Hmm."

Claire continued photographing while Luke watched in silence. She couldn't tell if he was still interested or if he was having second thoughts. When she was done with the photography, she got out a tape measure, notepad and pen.

"Do you want me to hold the end of the tape measure?" he asked.

"That would be great, thanks." Luke's offer eased Claire's concerns.

They worked in the foyer, no words spoken except for the occasional direction or word of thanks. The whole time, though, Claire wanted to ask about the history of the theater, about his family's connection, where he got the inspiration behind the beautiful metal artwork and why he'd been so standoffish in the beginning.

Stop it!

She needed to concentrate. Every measurement had to be exact, because if she was off, it would mean wasting time trying to get gear in, resetting lighting design and camera angles and even figuring out the right number of crew for the space.

Claire eventually finished in the foyer and packed her gear into her bag. "Could we do the cinema itself now?"

"Sure."

They went into the cinema and, once again, the beauty floored her. She ran her fingers over the small gold rectangles used to secure the blue fabric on the seats. The light reflected off the curved wooden backs and armrests, highlighting the craftsmanship. "This is really something. Such a shame no one gets to see it anymore." She closed her eyes and bit her lip. "Sorry."

"It's fine," he said. "The public should have the chance to see it, and now they will."

"On screen. It's not quite the same, is it?" Backpedaling, she said, "But I'm sure it will show up brilliantly in the miniseries."

Claire saw a door at the side of the cinema she'd missed on her first visit. She took a step in its direction.

"That's off limits." Luke paused, as if testing her resolve. She remained silent, despite the urge to let a slew of questions fly. Luke smiled. "Nice to see you can keep your word about not asking questions."

"Of course I can!" Indignation set in, but she quickly quashed it. She reached for the camera, then closed her eyes and took a few deep breaths.

"Claire? What are you doing?"

"I'm waiting for the cinema to speak to me."

"Uh…"

She opened her eyes. "I'll admit, it does sound weird, but I am as sane as they come. I tend to do this when I'm in a beautiful place, because I want to get a feel for it." She shivered. "It's as if the souls of the people who used to come here are still present." Claire looked again at the blue velvet seats. "Like all their conversations, their laughter, tears, heartache and celebrations are still with us."

Luke stared at her.

"Don't mind me." Heat rushed across her face. "I'm not some weirdo or anything."

"Are you sure?" She liked the way his eyes crinkled when he smiled.

"Pretty sure. But"—she waggled a finger—"you never know."

Luke laughed, and the cinema instantly felt warmer. It was good to have him on her side, as it was one less stressor to deal with. *Ugh.* James Lloyd was already a massive headache, one she really didn't want to deal with, but if monitoring the movements of an actor meant she'd stay on Nigel's good side, she'd have to suck it up. There could be worse things, like Tony Karter muscling in on her job. She couldn't stomach the idea of going back to being the gopher of the production team. She'd worked too long and too hard to mess this chance up. It was now or never.

* * * *

Claire exited the Ashton news agency, the latest copy of *Queensland Country Life* rolled under her arm. She pulled her baseball cap over her eyes, not keen on being recognized by one of the locals. Then again, Ashton was so small that a stranger stuck out like a ballerina at a Nirvana concert.

The past forty-eight hours had been mayhem, and had required a lot of to-ing and fro-ing between Starlight Creek and Ashton, catching up with the legal team, long meetings with the crew and, of course, dealing with Tony and his attitude, along with making Nigel happy. All this had to be squeezed in between shooting the last of the outdoor scenes.

"Excuse me!"

Claire whipped around to find Annalise, the cinema owner's daughter, rushing up the street. She wore tight jeans, Doc Martens and a red-and-black checked flannel shirt. Right now, she looked eighteen, unlike in the outfits and hair and makeup she'd worn previously, which made her look at least six years older.

"Annalise! I thought you were on a…vacation."

"I'm supposed to still be away, but I heard about everyone moving to Starlight Creek and…well…" She reached into her back jeans pocket and pulled out a crumpled envelope. "Can you give this to James?"

Claire looked around, fearing glaring eyes would be watching her every move. "I'm sorry, I can't."

"But I *have* to get this to him! Please!"

"Annalise, I can't."

"But you're seeing him later today, right? When you get to Starlight Creek?"

"I am." Claire's heart went out to the poor girl. When was the last time Claire had been so taken by a man? "Your father would kill me, and so would my boss."

"But James and I are supposed to be together!"

"I understand that's how you're feeling right now—"

"I'm going to feel this way forever!" she yelled, oblivious to the butcher and his customer who had just stuck their heads out the door to see who was causing the commotion. "You have to help me!"

"Annalise, I want to help, but I can't. I'd be risking my job and—" This would be very hard to say. "James is a player. Deep down he's a nice guy, but he's not exactly been on the straight and narrow these past few months."

"He's told me that."

"And it doesn't worry you?"

She shook her head, her long, straight hair covering her face. Annalise pushed back her locks. "He said I'm different."

Now anger roiled through Claire—not at the starstruck teenager, but at James Lloyd, who should know better. Just wait until she saw him. "I agree. You are different from the women he normally dates, and that's why I'm concerned. The women he's usually with are…" How should she put this? "Actresses, models, women who have been around, who have thick skin. They're used to dating someone like James. You may think I'm sticking my nose in—"

"You are." Annalise crossed her arms.

Claire paused, wondering if she should continue. "I get the attraction to James, but life in the limelight isn't all it's cracked up to be, and people like James go from one shiny object to the next. I don't want to see you get hurt."

"My heart is already broken! My father made sure of that!"

Oh jeez. Robert. "Speaking of which…"

"He doesn't know. I'm only staying long enough to collect my things, then I'm going to be with James at Starlight Creek."

"Does James know this?"

Annalise pointed at the letter in Claire's hand. "He will when you give that to him."

"Oh." Claire stared at the innocent-looking envelope. She handed it back to Annalise, who crossed her arms once more. "I'm sorry."

"No one understands me!" yelled Annalise.

"Please, come with me." Claire put her hand under the teenager's elbow and steered her toward the deserted park on the other side of the road. They sat at a picnic bench under a jacaranda, while birds foraged on the grass and in the garden beds. "You know, I've been in your position. When I first started out in this industry I would get so starstruck I would almost faint any time a big-name actor acknowledged my existence. I tried dating a couple—"

"Who?" Annalise's eyes widened.

"It doesn't matter who."

"It does!"

"Fine," said Claire, knowing Annalise would stop listening if she didn't reveal names. "Steve Holt and Joey Reynolds."

"What?" Annalise grabbed Claire's arm. "Are you serious?"

"Deadly serious." She smiled. "It wasn't all bad. I liked the fancy dinners and expensive wine and beautiful presents, but there was a downside."

"What was it?" Annalise leaned forward.

"I was never going to be their number-one priority. A lot of actors live and breathe their work—which is why they get paid the dollars they do—but it means sacrificing many other things, including relationships."

"Other actors marry."

"Of course they do, and some of those partnerships are wonderfully loving and successful. It's a credit to the couples who manage to stay together with their lives under constant media scrutiny." Claire paused, not sure if she was crossing a line. "Are you sure this isn't a fling?"

"It's way more serious than that. James said so."

Damn James. He had this poor girl hook, line and sinker. "What exactly did he say?"

"He said he's sick of dating women who are plastic, who only want to be seen with him to advance their careers. He likes my down-to-earth view of the world, and that I'm not interested in all the glitz and glamour."

"He said all that?" Claire managed to hide the surprise in her voice.

"And he said he's never felt this way about someone before. That I am refreshing."

Claire wondered if they were talking about a different James. This was the second shoot they'd worked on together and, as much as she liked him, he'd never shown that side of himself. But even if Annalise was a mature eighteen-year-old and James a not-so-mature twenty-eight-year-old, ten years was still a big difference, especially given their life experiences. Claire liked to think James wouldn't take advantage of Annalise, and she prayed he hadn't been feeding her lines. If he was genuine, was it fair to keep these two apart?

Claire studied the pale green tiles of the fountain. "I can't be responsible for getting this letter into James's hands. I'd be hung, drawn and quartered if I got caught. I think what's best for now is to let James finish the miniseries. In a few weeks' time, when everything has settled down with your father, then maybe you and James can talk and reassess where you're both at." It wasn't the perfect solution, but it could work. With time, Annalise would see sense, and James would likely have moved on to the next bright new thing. And if he hadn't, maybe his interest in Annalise was genuine. Either way, time would tell.

"I don't want to wait."

"I tell you what." Claire grabbed a pen and paper out of her handbag, wrote down her number and passed it to Annalise. "This is how you can get hold of me while I'm in Starlight Creek."

"What's with all these numbers?"

"It's my mobile phone. If you ever need to talk—to me—I am here to listen. But I can't put you in direct contact with James for now. Do we have a deal?"

Annalise stared at the paper in her hand. "I guess so."

"Excellent." Claire stood. "I need to get going." She took a step, then stopped and turned. "Promise me one thing?"

"It depends…"

"Promise me you won't mope around, and that you'll get on with your life and make it as wonderful as possible. If it's meant to be, it will happen with James. Besides." Claire hitched her bag onto her shoulder. "Life's not just about falling in love with a man. There are so many other things we can fall in love with—ourselves, for starters."

"That sounds weird."

"It sounds weird, but it's not. If we spend time doing things that make us happy and learning about ourselves, learning to love ourselves, then people will be drawn to us."

"Is that what you do?"

"I try," said Claire. "I really must go, but don't worry. Things will work out the way they're supposed to."

"That's what I'm worried about," muttered Annalise.

Claire hurried across the road and over to the ute. She put the key in the lock and opened the door.

"You better not be encouraging her," came a voice that caused her body to instantly tense.

Claire steeled herself before turning to face Robert Dennis. "Definitely not."

"Good. I'll be glad to see you lot out of here. She's been corrupted enough already with promises that will never be fulfilled, and I'll be the one left to clean up the pieces."

"Mr. Dennis—"

He held up his hand. "I don't need to hear it."

The anger flashing in his eyes told her things hadn't changed since she last saw him.

Claire got in her ute. She rolled down the window and said in earnest, "It was really nice meeting you."

Robert rested his hand on her door, preventing her from reversing. He leaned so close she could smell the beer on his breath. "This is not the end of it. I will do my damned best to make sure this production fails."

Chapter Eleven

1950 – Hollywood

Lena stood before the doors that led to the main administration building of Fortitude Studios. The bluster that had propelled her here had dissipated the second her feet reached the welcome mat.

"This is a stupid idea," she muttered. She turned, slamming straight into a tall, muscular body. Lena looked up. "Oh!"

Reeves met her with a smile. "What's a stupid idea?"

"Nothing. Nothing at all."

Reeves stretched his arm past her and held open the door.

"I'm not going in," she said.

"It didn't look like that a few seconds ago. Changed your mind?"

"Yes. No. Maybe." Argh! Why did Reeves Garrity have this effect on her?

"Who were you planning to see?"

Jeez, he didn't let up. "No one."

"Hmm…" He tapped his finger against his chin. "A stupid idea that is about nothing and an appointment with no one."

"Exactly." She crossed her arms.

Reeves's smile was wide.

"What's so funny?" she huffed.

"I like the way your forehead creases when you're annoyed."

"Huh?" She made an effort to smooth her brow even though she was most definitely annoyed. "Listen, I have to go." She took a step away from the building.

"The door's this way." Reeves bowed like she was a princess.

"I'm not…" Why was she chickening out? This was her career, after all. Lena marched past Reeves and into the foyer. He followed.

"Thank you," she said.

"For?"

"For opening the door."

"It was my pleasure." Amusement sparkled in his eyes, then his expression turned serious. "How are you doing?"

"I'm fine."

"Really?" The way he asked made her feel like he could see right through her.

Lena fiddled with her gloves and purse. "Really."

"Hmm…"

"Well, see you around." She took a step toward the elevator, but he blocked her path.

"Yesterday you were far from fine. I may not know you very well, but what happened with your role had a marked effect on you. Now you're all sunshine and smiles. I suspect you are putting your acting skills to work."

"I'm taking it as a compliment that you can't tell if I'm being genuine or acting."

Reeves's shoulders dropped. "I would like to think you could be honest with me like you were yesterday. Or was that an act as well?"

"No," she said quickly. "You were very kind, and I appreciate it. I'm sorry for leaving so quickly but…" She could have invented a fib, but what was the point? Apparently, Reeves Garrity could see through her facade. That, or she had to go back to acting lessons. She didn't like either option. She rubbed her wrist. "But a lot of things have happened in my life that still affect me now."

"Things that stop you from having dinner with me?"

"Yes."

He blinked slowly. "I didn't actually expect that answer."

"I'm sorry, Reeves. I'm happy to be your acquaintance, but that's all it can be. Barring some close friends, I keep to myself. It's easier that way."

"So why are you in this business? Actors are open books."

"Not all of us are," she said.

"It's a fact, especially if you become a star. And I see that potential in you."

"Mae West manages to keep her life private."

"She's one of the few, and she's not with this studio. When you signed your contract, you pretty much signed your life—private and public—away."

"I don't need a legal lecture, thanks." Lena moved toward the elevator again, this time skillfully dodging Reeves.

He gave a wry smile and his index figure hovered above the buttons. "Which floor?"

"Eight."

"You're seeing Mr. Cooper?"

"Don't look so shocked. He's not a princess in an ivory tower."

"Why are you..." He shook his head. "It is none of my business."

Lena relaxed a little. "I do owe you an explanation, because you were so very sweet with me yesterday. You helped me when I really needed it. You really are quite the gentleman." She smiled. "But I didn't need rescuing, just so you're aware."

"I wouldn't dare!" He held up his hands in defense.

"Good, glad we have that sorted." She was willingly putting herself out on a limb, but something about Reeves Garrity encouraged her to do so—and it annoyed the heck out of her. "I'm going to ask Mr. Cooper for a new role."

"Whoa! Shouldn't your agent do that? Besides, he's not the one who makes those decisions—unless you're a big name."

"Which I am not, I get that. My agent is away, and I can't wait for him to return. I've met Mr. Cooper, and he seems like an approachable man."

"He's the head of the studio."

"He's human."

"Wow," said Reeves. "You really like to take chances, don't you?"

"Why would you say that?"

"Who goes to the head of the studio and asks for a role? I like you, Lena Lee, but you're crazy."

"My roommate said the same thing." She drew her brows together. Maybe this idea was too far out there. No actress she knew would ever do something this preposterous. But time wasn't on her side—directors like Lawrence already thought she was too old for a lead.

The elevator pinged, and the doors opened. She stared at the void, wondering what she was doing. Yvonne and Reeves did have a point, but... Lena straightened her spine. Hollywood would not be where her dreams went to die.

Lena stepped across the threshold.

She turned to see the doors close on Reeves, who waved and yelled, "Good luck."

She was going to need it.

* * * *

Lena adjusted her position on the creaky leather sofa once more. She'd been in the reception area of Stuart Cooper's office for over an hour. Behind a walled desk, the receptionist tapped away on her typewriter and answered phones.

She looked over her glasses at Lena. "It really would be best to leave a message for Mr. Cooper, or make an appointment."

"You said he doesn't have a spare appointment until next month."

"He is a busy man. Look, I have no idea how long this meeting will be. He's already half an hour behind schedule, and he has a lunch meeting shortly."

"I'm happy to wait all the same," said Lena. She wasn't convinced Stuart Cooper would get the message if she left one.

"Suit yourself." The woman returned to bashing the typewriter, her long nails clicking against the keys.

A while later, the heavy wooden door of Stuart Cooper's office opened. His large, round frame filled up most of the doorway as he patted the back of a man much shorter and leaner. The bespectacled visitor clutched a stack of papers against his chest. He reminded Lena of a frightened woodland creature.

"I'll send over the paperwork this afternoon." Stuart Cooper's voice boomed through the reception. "Good to meet you, Henry."

Henry nodded and headed toward the elevator. Stuart stopped for a moment to study Lena. When he smiled, it was kind.

"I know you from somewhere," he said.

"I'm Lena Lee. I was at your party." Lena stood and smoothed down her skirt. She prayed her sweaty palms didn't leave a mark on the material.

The secretary watched Lena, no doubt waiting for her boss to send her packing.

Mr. Cooper's puzzled expression sent a ripple of panic through her. *Oh no.* He didn't remember. She'd been banking on him recalling her performance, but now, with his stern expression, she realized exactly how wrong she'd been. Hollywood was full of actresses who were forgotten five minutes after they held the limelight in the palm of their perfectly manicured hands.

"Ah!" He held up his finger, his face lighting up. "You sang 'Over the Rainbow.' I told my wife that you reminded me of a nightingale."

"You did?" Her voice came out an octave higher than usual, and she made an effort to lower it. "You did?"

"Yes, yes. What are you doing here?"

"I…" *Take a breath, Lena.* "I was hoping I could have five minutes of your time, please."

"Hold all calls, Lorraine." His arm made a sweeping motion toward the office.

Trying to stop her body from trembling, she walked into the head of Fortitude Studios' office. She didn't need to look back to know that Lorraine was looking on with disapproval.

Mr. Cooper gestured for her to take a seat opposite his desk. She positioned herself on the edge of the chair and tucked her legs under, crossing them at the ankles, just like her grandmother had shown her when she was little. Gosh, she missed home.

"Now, Miss Lee, we do not have much time, so please get straight to the point. I gather this is not a social visit?" He tapped the edge of his cigarette on the desk, then placed it in his mouth and lit it. "Oh, I'm sorry. Would you like one?"

"No, thank you." A thin sheen of perspiration crept across her skin. She *had* to do this. "I'm hoping you can find a role for me."

"Don't you have one? Or are we paying you to do nothing?"

"I had a role. Until yesterday. I was cast in the movie with Lawrence Doherty, but my role got cut."

"Oh." A cloud of smoke swirled above him. "I heard about that. I didn't realize it was you."

"Mr. Doherty doesn't have anything for me and—"

"I know you can sing, and we wouldn't have hired you if you couldn't act. Show me."

"Pardon?"

"Show me you can act. Now."

"Uh…" Ever since arriving in Hollywood she'd prided herself on being prepared to perform at a moment's notice. No one knew when an opportunity would come their way, so having a scene ready to go was invaluable. But since being hired by Fortitude Studios Lena had slacked off, thinking she'd always have roles. Her mind scrambled to pull a scene—any scene—and act like her life depended on it.

She had nothing.

Mr. Cooper butted his cigarette and stood. "Time's up."

Lena's eyes grew glassy, and warm tears trickled down her face. "I know it means nothing to you, but for me, it's everything. All my life I've dreamed about this. Yet you reached into my soul, grabbed my heart and discarded it like a child's unwanted toy."

Lena got up and walked around the room, gesturing as she spoke. "I believed you when you said you loved me. That was just one more lie in a sea of untruths designed to misguide and misdirect me so you could get what you wanted.

"Did you ever care about me? This ruse you pulled, did you stop, even for a moment, and think about the impact of your betrayal? Where's your heart?" Lena gulped back the sobs. Stuart Cooper sat back down, his eyes not leaving hers. Her tone hardened. "You won't get away with this. For as long as I draw breath, I will take a stance against you and everything you stand for. You." She picked up the letter opener and wielded it like a knife near his nose. "You won't die today. That would be too easy. Oh no." She let out a long, guttural laugh. "You will suffer like a fly trapped in a web, and you will watch in horror as the spider slowly creeps toward you. The torment of knowing your death is inevitable will drive you insane. And I, like that spider, will revel in your pain."

She threw the letter opener on the desk, adrenaline rushing through her. "When it happens—and it will—you'll remember the betrayals and the lies and wish you were never born."

Lena unclenched her hands and looked at them. Half-moons of blood were on her palms. Her arms shook. Her breath came out fast. She looked up at Mr. Cooper, fearing what she'd see.

He stared at her, unmoving. The air was thick with anticipation. Or was it dread? Out of all the characters she could have played, why had she gone for a femme fatale rather than the sweet and sunny and likable characters this studio favored? She'd just lost the role of a femme fatale. What was she thinking?

A slow clap echoed in the office. It grew louder and faster and was punctuated with a deep laugh. "Well, well, Miss Lee. You are full of surprises. Who would have thought someone as innocent-looking as you would have the mettle to pull off an audition like that?"

"It was the first thing that came to mind."

When he got up, he seemed less gigantic than before. "It wasn't the kind of role I had in mind, but you've convinced me you are a very capable actress. The director who was here before wants an unknown to mold. I'll call to tell him I found her."

Chapter Twelve

Lena exited the sound stage. It had already been a long day filming, and it wasn't over yet. Even though she was busy, she took a moment to close her eyes and angle her face toward the sun. Warmth caressed her skin and she reveled in seeing daylight after what felt like weeks. She doubted she'd ever grow accustomed to getting up before daylight and returning home after sunset. Today was the first day she'd had a chance for a short break, while they reshot leading man Pierre's scene, which he managed to keep messing up.

"It's nice to see someone enjoying the sun. Others say it will age you," came a voice she hadn't heard in a long time.

Opening her eyes, she was met with the vision that was Reeves Garrity. Although dressed in an expensive navy-blue suit with his hair immaculately styled, he still held the same freshness as when they'd first met at Stuart Cooper's party the year before.

"Long time, no see." She looked at the hat in her hand but decided a few minutes of sunshine wouldn't cost her her career. Maybe…

"How have you been?" His voice sounded genuine, and memories of why she had taken a liking to Reeves Garrity came flooding back.

"Good. Busy. As you have been, I hear."

"You've been inquiring about me?" His lopsided smile set her off-kilter.

"No!" she said, a little too defensively. He didn't need to know she'd been watching his career—and relationship with Jeanne—with the eagle eye of a crazed fan. "It's a bit hard not to notice your name and face splashed across every single newspaper and magazine."

A flicker of…something flashed across his face. What was it? Apprehension? Embarrassment?

"It's mostly about Jeanne, who has a habit of dominating every conceivable form of publicity available," he said.

"Yet you seem to be inextricably linked to her. When are you getting married?" Lena grinned for good measure, hoping he understood the lighthearted ribbing.

"She wants…" He frowned, then relaxed. "Very funny. I see you have an *arrangement* with Pierre like I do with Jeanne."

"Let's not talk about them." She waved her hand to disperse any mention of Pierre Montreaux. "Do you have time for coffee?"

"As a matter of fact, I do." He offered his arm. She put hers in his and they started toward the small café near Reeves's sound stage.

As they walked across the lot, Lena grew nervous, like all eyes were on them. She extracted her arm from his.

"What's wrong?" he asked.

"Better to keep some distance. We don't want tongues wagging."

"Let them wag."

A small laugh escaped her lips. "Reeves Garrity, the rebel."

"Lena Lee, the rule breaker."

"What rule have I broken?" she asked.

"The rule that women should be quiet and do what they're told. That they shouldn't ask for what they want because that makes them a pushy diva."

"Is that how you see me?" she asked, stunned. Was this the true Reeves Garrity?

"Not at all! It's what certain people expect. I see you as someone who fights for what she believes in. The last time we saw each other, you were on your way to Stuart Cooper's office to demand he give you a new role."

"Demand? I asked nicely. He made me audition on the spot."

"And here you are, working your way to the top."

"Yes, here I am." Her steps felt lighter than they had in months. What was it about Reeves Garrity that made her feel like she could do anything?

"And here you are. How is fame? Anything like you expected?"

They sat at a small table in the far corner. Lena placed her purse on the red-and-white tablecloth. She shivered in the shade, surprised at how cold it was. Reeves took off his jacket and offered it to her.

"It's fine, really," she said.

"I'd rather have a conversation without the sound of chattering teeth."

She looked around at the actors and crew sitting at tables, engrossed in their own conversations, and she realized she was being paranoid for nothing. Her whole life felt like it was under the microscope these days. No wonder it tainted her view of the real world.

"All right, thank you." She put her arms through the sleeves and wrapped the fabric around her. An alluring, musky scent enveloped her.

Elsie, the waitress, appeared with two mugs. She carefully poured the steaming coffee.

"Good afternoon, Miss Lee. I haven't seen you here for some time." Elsie almost curtsied.

"Elsie, please, call me Lena. And yes, it's nice to be seeing you at the café rather than you bringing my coffee to the sound stage. I almost forgot what daylight looked like!"

Elsie laughed and held up a finger. "I have something for you. I made it with the berries from my family's farm up north."

She disappeared, and a moment later came back with two small plates boasting thick slices of pie filled with raspberries and blueberries. Elsie placed one in front of Lena and the other in front of Reeves. "There's one for you, Mr. Garrity."

"Why, thank you, Elsie," he said. "And you can call me Reeves."

Elsie's face flushed red and she retreated back into the café.

Lena dug the fork into the pie, trying to block out the voices that told her the zipper on the dress she had to wear on set tomorrow might have an issue. It was already tighter than a rubber band. She took a bite and the zesty deliciousness of berries and crusty pastry danced across her taste buds. It was absolutely worth it.

"You have quite the effect on people," said Lena.

"Apparently I do." Reeves broke off a large chunk of pie and shoved it in his mouth. He chewed slowly. Eventually, he said, "Did you hear about Geraldine Donnolly?"

"No." Lena sipped the black coffee, prepared just how she liked it— strong and syrupy. "I only met Geraldine once, at one of Cary Grant's soirees. Isn't she with Robin Studios? Ooh." Lena leaned forward. "Has she signed somewhere else?"

Reeves shook his head. "I thought the Hollywood grapevine would be faster. She's been subpoenaed to testify at the House Un-American Activities Committee."

"HUAC? Why?"

"Remember last year, when the *Red Channels* pamphlet was published?"

"The one that named some film industry professionals as communists or sympathizers?"

"Yes." He nodded.

"That was terrible." Lena looked around in case anyone was listening to their conversation. With the goings-on in Hollywood and the "Reds under the Beds" scare, she shouldn't trust anyone. Her intuition told her she shouldn't worry about Reeves, but any talk of communism these days was always a risk. "There were a lot of innocent people on that list. You can't tell me that out of those one hundred and fifty-one people, every one of them was disseminating communist propaganda through their scripts, music, acting or directing."

"HUAC likes to think otherwise. Though it's not illegal to be part of the Communist Party," he said.

"It shouldn't be legal to blacklist people based on their beliefs—proven or otherwise."

"Agreed." Reeves crooked his finger for her to move closer. Quietly, he said, "Did you know England has strong ties to communism? It's not just the Russians and Chinese."

"What?"

"Karl Marx and Friedrich Engels used to meet in Cheetham's Library in Manchester."

"No way," she whispered.

"It's true. The British industrial revolution and poor conditions of the workers inspired Marx and Engels to find a way for those without voices to be heard. That's why they wrote *The Communist Manifesto*, which was published in London in 1848."

"I had no idea. So all this panic about communists is not new?" She sat back, surprised.

"Not at all."

Lena bit her lip, unsure about her next question. "Reeves?"

"Yes?"

"You're not…"

"A communist?" He laughed. "The only thing I am committed to these days is my career."

"What happened to Geraldine?" Lena asked, afraid of the answer.

"It's more to do with her screenwriter husband, Walter, but she's suffered the fallout."

Reeves leaned toward her once more, and Lena started to worry people would think they were whispering sweet nothings. Though better they believe that than hear this dangerous conversation.

Reeves put his fork down. "This new round of investigations from HUAC is better organized—they're getting around the legalities of questioning people and their alliances. Walter was dropped by his studio, as they didn't want any trouble, or to have any of their writers under scrutiny."

"And Geraldine was fired because of guilt by association."

"Exactly."

"That is so unfair." Lena looked at the pie, but her appetite had disappeared. "When will this craziness stop? We have the Hays Code dictating what we can and can't do on-screen, now there's the worry about communists warping audiences' minds with subliminal messages."

"I can't see it changing." Reeves concentrated on stirring his coffee. "What can we do? We just need to keep our heads down and noses clean."

"Hmm."

"Hmm?"

"Hmm, you're right," she said. "I'm not saying I'm for communism, but I am for people's rights to support who they want. And I'm also for people being able to decide if a movie or book is suitable for them. Why should a handful of men in suits shape our culture? What will happen in future generations? Will there be any creativity left if the government and right-wing groups dictate what is acceptable? Where does it stop?"

Lena looked up and noticed a trio of men were staring at her and Reeves. She pulled her lips tight and clutched the fork in her hand.

"You're here?" A loud, high-pitched voice had Lena quickly turning around. Jeanne Harris stalked over to the table.

Great.

Reeves got to his feet and gestured for Jeanne to sit. She looked at the seat next to Lena like it was piled high with manure.

Reeves checked his watch. "Perhaps you'd like to join us for coffee and pie?"

"Pie?" Jeanne laughed. "No, thank you. We should leave and go through the script."

"I'm not ready."

A well-placed hand on her hip said plenty.

"I'll be over to your dressing room when I've finished talking with Miss Lee. You and I both had an early start this morning, why don't you have a rest before we start working again?"

"I'll see you in thirty." Her eyes fixed on Reeves's jacket draped around Lena's shoulders. Jeanne flinched, then spun on her heel and flounced between the tables. Every set of eyes in the small café stayed on the starlet until she was out of view.

"I'm sorry," Reeves said.

"Don't be, everyone knows what she's like."

"It's no excuse."

"No, it isn't, but people are who they are." Lena tapped her finger against the cup of cold coffee. "Perhaps you should go."

"I probably should. It's not worth the angst I'll have to endure otherwise." Lena laughed. "I can only imagine."

She gathered her purse and Reeves stood to pull out her chair. His nearness unnerved her, and her hands grew sticky as she fumbled in her purse for money. Reeves beat her to it, leaving a generous stack of notes on the table.

"I asked you for coffee, please, let me pay." She swapped the notes and handed his back.

"No, no. A gentleman always pays."

"A gentleman will end up broke."

"Not for as long as I'm leading man with Jeanne."

"Good point."

They fell into step with each other, and a question she had been trying to suppress grew so large it threatened to explode out of her.

"Say it," said Reeves.

"Is it that obvious?"

His cheeky smile warmed her heart but frustrated her at the same time. Was it good that he could sense what was going on in her mind?

"All right," she said, feeling brave. "What's the true story with you and Jeanne? You don't exactly look like the world's happiest couple."

Reeves clasped his hands behind his back, his eyes glued to his shiny black shoes.

"Sorry," she said quickly. "It's none of my business."

Reeves stopped and turned toward her, his dark eyes searching hers. "If things were different I would date you in a heartbeat."

"That wasn't what I was angling—"

"I understand, but I want you to know that in another place and another time I would be honored to take you on a date—endless dates."

Lena scrambled for something to say. Was she ever going to get over the way Charlie had manipulated her?

Warm fingers brushed hers and she closed her eyes. What would it be like to be held in Reeves's arms? To kiss his lips?

"Lena?"

"Yes?"

"I said thank you for the coffee and pie."

"Oh? Oh! Sure. No problem."

"One more thing." He kissed her on the cheek, and she inhaled his musky cologne.

"What was that for?" Her voice had turned husky.

"To thank you for being the most interesting person I know." With that, Reeves walked toward Jeanne's dressing room.

Lena stood rooted to the ground. If only she and Reeves had met in different circumstances....

* * * *

Pierre's arm snaked behind her neck. His baby-soft fingers caressed her skin; his blue eyes looked longingly into hers.

"I have loved you from the moment we met." His French accent wrapped around every word. "You are my love. My life. There is nothing else in this world I need."

Lena struggled out of his hold and stepped away. "You can't have what isn't yours. I am not some possession you can pick up and discard at your whim."

"You love me. I know it. I can see it in your eyes."

Lena turned her head away. "You only see what you want."

"I...I...Damn it!" yelled Pierre.

"Cut! Cut!" Henry lunged forward, waving his arms like a madman. "How many takes do we need? What is wrong with you, Montreaux?"

"It's not me, it's Lena. She's not into this scene. I'm not *feeling* it from her."

"What?" she spat. "I'm not the one forgetting my lines."

Henry held up his hand. "All right, all right. Let's leave it here. We've done more than enough today, but that doesn't mean I don't expect this scene to be perfect first thing tomorrow morning," he said. "And Montreaux, learn your damn lines."

Henry could have saved his breath, as Pierre had already stalked off the set and disappeared. His dressing room door slammed shut and confirmed his whereabouts.

"Sorry, Henry," said Lena.

"It's all right, honestly. I had a feeling we'd pushed too far today. There's only so many hours we can eke out before exhaustion kicks in. Go on, go home. Enjoy what's left of the evening."

"You too." Lena waved and headed toward her dressing room. She entered and shut the door, pushing the footstool against it in case the lock didn't click into place—again. After stripping out of the teal dress and putting on her floral day dress, Lena wiped off the heavy makeup and applied a light smattering of her own. Finally, her skin felt like it could breathe again.

She picked up her purse and noticed Reeves's jacket on the coat hanger next to her costumes. She glanced at her watch. He could still be working.

She hung his jacket over her arm, exited the room and headed down the deserted corridor. A door opened and Pierre stepped out. He casually rested an arm on the wall, blocking her way.

"Where are you off to?" His accent wasn't as thick as when the cameras were rolling.

"I'm not on the clock anymore, so I am off to wherever I choose to go."

Pierre glanced at the jacket. "Whose is that?"

"A friend's. I'm returning it."

"Which friend?"

"Really, Pierre? You want to play the green-eyed monster? What about you standing me up last night? I didn't appreciate waiting in the restaurant while you did god-knows-what with the blonde in the parking lot."

"I—"

"Please, don't embarrass either of us by denying it. Our being together may have its advantages, but at times I do wonder if they are worth it." She moved to go, but his stance held firm. "Let me pass."

"You better not be messing around with someone at the studio."

"I'm not *messing around* with anyone. What kind of person do you think I am?" She held up her hand. "Don't even answer that. It's been a long day, and I want to go home."

"My driver will take you."

"I have my own car, thanks."

"Why do you insist on driving? You could have your own chauffeur."

"I like driving."

Pierre shook his head. "Sometimes I don't understand you."

"Most of the time I don't understand you." She stepped forward and removed his hand. "See you tomorrow, bright and early. Don't forget to learn those lines!"

Lena hurried away. Her ears rang as Pierre fired off a round of expletives.

Despite it being so late in the day, the Fortitude Studios lot was buzzing. Lights shone through the darkness, making it easy for Lena to get to where Reeves was shooting. She quietly entered the sound stage and stood in the shadows. A few crew members glanced over then returned to their duties. *You've seen one actress, you've seen them all.*

Jeanne and Reeves were near where Lena stood. They were at the base of a winding staircase built to look like solid marble. A chandelier sparkled above them, casting a brilliant glow on Jeanne's creamy skin. She wore a red velvet dress, perfectly suited to the period film they were making. The black morning suit Reeves wore made him deliciously handsome.

Lena rested her hand on her heart.

"Theodore, please, don't leave." Jeanne's southern accent was perfect, showing what a brilliant actress she was. As for a decent human being, that topic remained debatable. "Let the others fight."

"In all good conscience, I cannot send my men to war and not go myself." Reeves's southern accent rolled off his tongue with apparent ease. *Huh. Impressive.*

"What about me?" Jeanne gripped his arm, her large eyes pleading with his.

Lena held her breath. Would he leave her?

"My duty is to my country, but my heart"—He leaned in close, his lips near the diamonds dangling from her delicate ears—"will always be with you."

"Oh, Theodore."

He grabbed her arms tightly and their lips met. Even from this distance Lena's body picked up on the electricity zapping around the room. Reeves kissed Jeanne for what seemed like an eternity. That horrible, tiny feeling of envy grew within Lena and she averted her eyes. It disturbed her how easily she fell into the useless trap of jealousy.

Lawrence finally yelled cut and called it a day. The set went into a state of ordered chaos as everyone efficiently went about their jobs while Jeanne and Reeves headed to their dressing rooms on the far side of the building. Lost in the flurry of activity, Lena couldn't get Reeves's attention.

"Miss Lee, how nice of you to join us." Lawrence walked up, his smile large. "What brings you here?"

"I, uh." She really should have thought this through. Lena placed her hands behind her back, obscuring Reeves's jacket. "I'd heard amazing things about this movie, and I wanted to see for myself."

"Well, you can tell Henry we are moving along swimmingly."

"Henry?"

"Didn't he send you over here to spy?"

"What?" Lena laughed, then stopped when she took in Lawrence's serious expression. "Sorry. I thought you were…doesn't matter. No, Henry did not send me over to spy. Why would you think that?"

"If you haven't noticed, we are in direct competition."

"We're the same studio. As long as our movies are making money, Mr. Cooper is happy."

"That doesn't stop us from competing for Cooper's coffers."

"It will always be you first, Lawrence. After all, you have Jeanne."

"If you haven't noticed, Miss Lee, you are proving to be quite the threat."

Lena looked at her tan shoes. "I'm not threatening anyone."

"You need to give yourself more credit. Or not. This whole non-diva thing works to your advantage." He sighed and stared into the distance. "You were always so easy to work with."

"I don't think I've changed." How did that defensive tone sneak in?

"I doubt you have. Listen, I'd love to chat all day…" Lawrence signaled to a young man with a clipboard.

"Well, it was nice seeing you." Lena stepped away, heading for the exit. It was a silly idea to track down Reeves and give him his jacket back. She'd get one of the runners to deliver it tomorrow.

"Lena." She turned and faced her old director. "I'm sorry I ever doubted you."

"Pardon?"

"I thought you were just like every other starry-eyed actress on the lot, but you've proven to be quite the force. I hate to admit that I viewed your age as a handicap. I'm glad I was wrong. Keep the competition fierce." Lawrence winked, and she laughed.

She dodged the crew arranging the set for the next day and made her way outside. The harsh lights from inside illuminated parts of the ground, and she started toward her car but stopped. This was ridiculous. Why should she care what people thought? Lena turned around and headed straight for Reeves's dressing room. She had every right to return his jacket without questions. Surely a woman could be friends with a man without suppositions and innuendo? To any sane person, yes, but going near Reeves would only provoke Jeanne if she saw. Though why should Lena let Jeanne dictate what she did? Surely those days were well and truly over?

Lena marched to the back of the studio and entered the side door. It was nice and quiet, with the majority of the activity out in the main part of the building. She made her way down the corridor, looking for Reeves's room. All she had to do was hand over the jacket. Simple.

Glass smashed behind the door Lena was passing. She read the name emblazoned on a huge golden star—*Jeanne Harris.*

More muffled screams and smashing glass came from behind the door. Lena raised her hand, ready to knock.

Should she?

The door swung open and Jeanne appeared in a slip, a strap hanging off one shoulder. She glowered at Lena, her face inches away.

"What the hell do you want?"

A wall of alcohol pushed Lena back. "I wanted to make sure you're okay."

"Me?" Her hollow laugh echoed down the corridor. "I am absolutely fine! I just don't appreciate you snooping in my business."

"Snooping? I heard glass breaking and... What would you have preferred me to do? Walk away?"

"Yes, as a matter of fact. Walk away. Walk far, far away so our paths never cross again."

"Given we work for the same movie studio, I would say us never seeing each other again is impossible."

"There are ways." Jeanne frowned. "What are you doing here, anyway? Who invited you?"

"I'm returning something that isn't mine."

"Damn right he isn't yours." Jeanne grabbed a bottle of clear liquid and took a long swig.

"Jeanne—"

"Put that down!" Reeves strode up and grabbed the bottle from Jeanne. She pulled back, dazed for a second, then fire flashed in her eyes.

"Give it back!" She reached for the bottle and lost her balance. Lena grabbed Jeanne's arm to help steady her, but Jeanne yanked it away.

"If Lawrence sees you boozing on set there'll be consequences. How many times do we have to go over this?"

"Oh, Reeves." Jeanne's laugh tinkled through the air. "You are such a joker."

"I am far from joking. Get dressed and go home." The seriousness in his tone had the desired effect, and Jeanne pushed the strap back on her shoulder and patted down her hair. Then she shoved her finger under Lena's nose. "This is not the end of our conversation."

The door slammed, and Lena stared at the golden star. "Wow."

"She's having a bad day."

"It seems she has a lot of those."

"Indeed." Reeves gestured that they should move away.

He walked with her to the exit while she struggled for something to say. Life would be so much simpler if it wasn't dictated by contracts and the expectations of adoring fans and bosses, especially about who she should date. Then again, she hadn't been that keen on starting any romantic relationships since Charlie, so fake-dating Pierre had seemed the perfect plan. In the two years she was with Charlie, he'd caused her three lifetimes of angst. It had knocked her confidence, and if they hadn't broken up she never would have found the courage to pursue her dream of acting in movies. In a very tiny way, she was almost thankful for the grief Charlie had caused her—although being accused of something she didn't do still hurt.

When the studio suggested she and Pierre could raise their profile by appearing to date off-screen, she'd been overjoyed at the opportunity to get her name out there. It certainly wasn't an uncommon charade to raise profiles; it had worked for countless others. Yet now, with more experience behind her, she realized how wrong she'd been to agree.

"I'm sorry she was so mean." Reeves opened the door and they stepped outside.

"I don't expect any different from her, I'm afraid. Jeanne and I haven't been friends for some time."

"She throws a lot of animosity at you. Surely it's not just because she thinks she's better than you?"

"I hope this doesn't sound conceited, but I think it's the opposite."

"Pardon?"

"Jeanne has always been insecure, but the bluster is a new thing. When we first met I helped her through a lot, as she wasn't coping with the endless rejections from studios and theaters."

"And this is the way she thanks you?"

Lena shrugged. "I can't change who she is and, honestly, I don't have the energy to worry about her attitude anymore."

"I admire you for that."

"Thanks," she said, a little embarrassed.

"So why did she turn against you if you were helping her out?"

"While we were trying out for studios, we were also doing theater work. I was gaining momentum, and I was offered two lead roles—one for a musical theater production and one for a play. I chose the musical, as it was a better boost to my resume."

"Did Jeanne try out for the same roles?"

"Yes, and when I said no to the play, she was offered the lead."

"She would have hated being second choice."

Lena concentrated on a dark corner of the lot. "She's never forgiven me for making her feel inferior. It really rattled her confidence, and it also brought out a vicious jealous streak I didn't know she had."

"But it wasn't your fault."

Turning to face him, she said, "I know, but Jeanne has never seen it that way. Ever since then, I've been a threat to her."

"What? She thinks you're going to waltz in and knock her off her pedestal? She's the one in the starring roles now, not you." Reeves stopped, his eyes wide. "I'm sorry, I didn't mean—"

"It's all right, really. Jeanne has done well, and I'm nowhere near the point of passing her star's trajectory." Lena grinned. "I'd like to one day, though."

Reeves's eyes locked on hers. "I have no doubt you will."

His intensity made her nervous, and she scrambled for another subject. She held up his jacket. "I thought you might need this."

"I was hoping you'd hold on to it. Then it would give me an excuse to spend time with you again."

"Reeves…"

"I know."

"So…"

"So…" Reeves echoed, his face hidden by the shadows.

"I better go." She handed him the jacket. His fingers wrapped around hers. Her breath caught in her throat.

He stepped toward her.

His strong arms pulled her against his masculine body.

She closed her eyes.

Their lips met.

Her body felt light.

Reluctantly, Lena inched away. "We can't."

"We just did."

"We can't anymore. What if someone saw us?"

"Do you think anyone at the studio actually believes Jeanne and I are together?"

"I don't know. But it's not the people at Fortitude who count, it's the public. You made your name on their belief that you and Jeanne are an item on- and off-screen. They love that, they lap it up like dogs drinking water on a hot summer's day."

Reeves stepped back like he'd been slapped in the face. "Is that what you really think? That I don't have enough talent to make it on my own?"

"That's not what I meant at all! What I was trying to say is that you got a boost, just like I did by being paired with Pierre. There's nothing wrong with forming a relationship that will help our careers."

"Wow." Reeves let out a low whistle.

"Reeves." She reached for his hand, but he moved it away. "You are very talented, there's no denying that. Jeanne just helped things along when she picked you as her new leading man. Pierre's profile has helped me."

He shook his head slowly, as if he was trying to process what she'd said. "I think it's time I went."

"Reeves…"

"It's probably best we don't spend any more time with each other. We don't want to ruin the *relationships* we have with other people, because it would destroy our careers. Imagine that."

As Reeves Garrity turned and walked away, Lena wondered why she'd opened her big mouth. She'd spent hours with Stuart Cooper negotiating her "relationship" with Pierre and how it would play out for their adoring fans. Both she and Pierre had agreed it would benefit them both—Pierre needed to tone down his reputation as a philanderer and she needed him to boost her image by dating a high-profile French actor. In hindsight, though, she doubted the sanity of such a decision.

Chapter Thirteen

1994 – Starlight Creek, Queensland

Claire pulled up in front of Hattie's cinema, still shaken by Robert Dennis's threat. She didn't blame him for being upset about her talking with Annalise. Most dads would be deeply concerned if their daughter dated a star with a playboy reputation like James's. A broken heart was inevitable. And no parent wants to see their child, no matter what age, shattered by love. Claire wanted to assume Robert's threat was empty, but the malice in his tone worried her.

She got out of the ute and went up to the door, excitement putting a bounce in her step. Claire knocked. The door opened, but instead of Hattie she was greeted by one Mr. Luke Jackson.

"Oh, hi!" She handed him a bag of muffins she'd picked up at Scarlet's café. "I've brought some sustenance."

"We might need it." He cocked his head toward the interior. "Guess we should get started."

Claire looked around. "Where's Hattie?"

"She wasn't sure she could handle the intensity of it all, so she's staying at my house until you're done here."

"Oh."

"You sound disappointed."

"I am a bit. I really like your great-aunt."

"She seems to be fond of you as well." Luke cleared his throat. "So, when do we meet the director?"

"He should be here shortly. There's a few more things to wrap up in Ashton."

"Is that business with the actor all sorted?"

"Yes?" She should have sounded more positive.

Luke studied her for a moment, his fingers tapping on the doorframe. "If it isn't, I need to know. There can't be any surprises, because my great-aunt won't cope."

"I get it, I really do." She hadn't spoken to James yet, but he'd been informed about her shadowing him the second they hit Starlight Creek. Apparently he hadn't objected, which rang alarm bells. "Right, then. Let's get started."

For the next four hours Luke worked under Claire's guidance, preparing the place for the arrival of the crew. The chatter with Luke remained superficial—weather, favorite bands growing up, favorite sport.

"What about your favorite movie?" she asked as they moved unneeded chairs to the shed behind the cinema.

Luke put a chair down next to the shed door. "I'm not really into them."

"What?" She laughed, then stopped when she took in the seriousness of his expression.

"But your family owns a *cinema*."

"Doesn't mean I have to watch movies. Between the sugarcane farm and my art, I don't have time for anything else."

"I guess not."

"What about you? Do you have a favorite movie?" He seemed to ask because he felt he should, not because he wanted to.

"I love the Hollywood classics. You know, *Singin' in the Rain, Gentlemen Prefer Blondes, A Star is Born.*" She laughed. "I could go on and on, though I guess that's lost on you."

Luke shrugged. "Guess it is."

"I would love to have been a fly on the cinema wall back in the day. Imagine the dramas that would have gone on."

"I really need to get this finished so I can get back to my place and check on my aunt."

"Sure, sure." She felt uneasy that he shut her down, but they needed to get on with the job.

Luke disappeared into the shed, taking the last of the chairs.

"This is it?" Nigel's booming voice had her spinning to face him.

"Yes," she said quickly.

"I know you said we had some work to do but good god, those photos did not tell the true story."

"Nigel." She opened her eyes wide to give him the please-shut-up signal as Luke exited the shed. If he'd heard Nigel, he certainly wasn't letting on. "Nigel Christenson, I'd like you to meet Luke Jackson. His great-aunt owns this cinema."

Nigel stuck out his hand and he and Luke shook. "A pleasure to meet you, Luke. I really appreciate you accommodating us at the last minute. Claire will be here twenty-four seven to ensure everything runs smoothly." He paused then laughed, as if realizing his mistake. "And, of course, filming at your cinema will run as smooth as silk. Especially with Claire looking over things!"

"Yes, yes," she said. "I'll be here day and night to answer any questions you may have. I'll be guarding the cinema like it's my own."

Oops. That was probably too far.

Luke stared at her. "Why the need to be guarded? From whom?"

"Nothing. No one. I just meant that I'll be checking that everyone will be very careful."

Sheesh. Was she making it worse?

Nigel stepped in. "The crew will be here early tomorrow, so if you have any questions during filming, Claire's your gal."

"How about we show Nigel the interior?" she asked Luke.

"Sure. This way." He waved his hand for Nigel and Claire to follow and they went through the back door into Hattie's kitchen. Despite Hattie having left, her kitchen still held the same warmth Claire had experienced the first time she was there. Well, until Claire had been asked to leave.

They entered the main area of the cinema.

"My god." Nigel looked around, his mouth open. "This is incredible. The exterior photos made it look better than real life but the interior…well, the interior photos definitely did not do it justice."

"It is the most beautiful thing I've ever seen," she said, trying not to let pride inflate her head.

Nigel moved around, inspecting chairs, walls, squinting his eyes and turning his head at various angles. He continued for some time.

"Does he always do this?" whispered Luke.

"Yeah," she said. "He needs to get a good feel for the place. He's imagining where the crew will be positioned and how the equipment will fit in, where the actors will stand and how they'll move around. Basically, he's playing the scenes out in his head."

"Like what you did before?" asked Luke. "Does everyone in your industry imagine things in their head?"

"What are you talking about?"

Alli Sinclair

He laughed. "Remember in your letter to my great-aunt when you mentioned ghosts and how the history of this place will have a big influence on the actors?"

"Huh? Oh!" She smiled. "You probably think we're a tad strange."

"No stranger than other types of artists."

"Like metal sculptors?" she joked, but his face had turned serious. "Sorry."

"It's all right. It's just a sore spot."

"Okay," she said, not game enough to push harder. If Luke wanted to tell her, he would. Though she doubted that would ever happen. One minute he was familiar with her, then the next an invisible wall shot up, shutting down any chance of getting to know him. It would have been nice, though, as there was something very interesting about Luke Jackson, and it wasn't just his gorgeous blue eyes.

Nigel strode up to them. "You have done one hell of a job finding this place."

"Thanks." There was so much more she wanted to add, but it wasn't the time or place, especially in front of Luke. When the moment was right, Claire would meet with Nigel and discuss her future. Surely this coup would get her the backing she needed to work toward her own production?

Stop counting chickens.

"Right, well I have a pile to get through and so do you, Montgomery. I'll see you at five tomorrow morning."

"Okay."

Nigel made his way out of the cinema and through to the back alley.

"It's his already," said Luke.

"No, he's just one of those people who doesn't have time for courtesies, like waiting to be shown out. You have my word that he'll treat this cinema with the utmost care and respect."

"I'm counting on you."

"You have nothing to fear," she said, then Robert Dennis's words crashed in on her: *This is not the end of it. And I will do my damned best to make sure this production fails.*

* * * *

Claire had woken in the small bedroom above the Starlight Creek pub at four every morning for the past couple of days. She was always on location before anyone else arrived. The crew had set up, ensuring everything was in place.

Today's shoot had gone well. Everyone had adhered to Nigel's strict instructions about keeping the place intact—he'd threatened death by gaffer tape should anyone damage a thing. He needn't have worried, though, as the crew were reliable and respectful, just as Claire had expected.

She stood at the back of the cinema going through the call sheet for the following day while visions of collapsing into an exhausted heap on her bed ran through her head.

"You've done a great job finding this place."

Claire looked up to find Camille, the leading lady, in jeans and a white shirt. Her hair and makeup were still very much 1930s.

"Thanks."

"You know, I was skeptical before we got here, but you've proven me wrong," said Camille.

"Oh?" How was she supposed to react to this?

"Sorry," said Camille. "That sounded rude. What I mean to say is that when I saw the photos I thought it looked like any other Art Deco cinema. But now, actually being in this space, there's a certain...feel." She looked around. "Like it's filled with special energy. Kind of like there's a piece of Amelia here with us."

"Exactly!" said Claire. "That's how I felt, and I was hoping you'd experience the same. We're not quite channeling Amelia, but at least feeling her presence."

Camille looked around and smiled. "Yeah. It certainly makes my job a lot easier. I've never felt more like Amelia than I do when filming in this cinema."

Tony walked up, and Camille waved a hasty goodbye and exited.

"I'm done," Tony said.

"Seriously?"

"I've done everything you asked." Tony's words sounded measured, like he was trying to contain his annoyance.

"That's great." Claire made sure she sounded genuine. "You can go if you want. I'll lock up."

Tony regarded her for a moment. "Like I said yesterday, that's my job."

Claire wondered if they were going to have this conversation every day, because it would get very old, very fast. "I appreciate you wanting to do so, but like we've discussed, the owner gave specific instructions that I be the one to open and close the cinema every day."

"So you're taking over my job now? Stealing the location manager role isn't enough?"

"Tony." She willed herself to remain calm. "I never stole the job of location manager. I was hired because they felt I was the best fit for this particular production. My history of renovating Art Deco houses with my family put me in good stead." Why did she feel the need to justify herself?

"Yeah, well, I see the way you're so close with Nigel."

Claire stared at Tony, not quite believing her ears and totally unimpressed with what he was implying. "Would you say that if I was a man?"

"This is bloody bullshit." Tony stalked off, leaving Claire with her mouth hanging open.

"You'll catch flies." Phil sidled up to her.

Still in shock, she turned to Phil. "Did you hear what Tony just said?"

"Nope."

"He thinks I got the job because of...you know..."

"What? He thinks you slept with Nigel?" Phil did a cruddy job of controlling his laughter. "Tony's an idiot."

"Yeah," she said, a small wave of melancholy hitting her. "I've worked my butt off to get this far, and it hurts when someone implies I've gained my position through less than savory ways. Men don't have this issue."

"No, they don't," said Phil. "I'm sorry you have to deal with this shit, Claire."

"I can't have him undermining me."

"You could get him fired."

Claire looked at Tony. "He has a baby."

"He doesn't treat you with respect."

"I know." She studied the gold buttons on the rows of chairs in front of her. "I'd love to fire him."

"Why don't you?"

Claire puffed out her cheeks. "I can't get rid of him because I haven't got time to replace him. Besides, we haven't got much longer to shoot, and he is actually really good at his job when he's not being a chauvinist pig."

"This industry gossip travels the grapevine rather fast. Word about his behavior could get out after we're done here." Phil gave a crooked smile.

"Hmm..."

"Now," said Phil, "moving on to a much nicer topic, when are you going to use your winning streak and talk to the production company?"

"About what? I haven't got anything in the pipeline. Well, I did, but they've rejected all my ideas. In fact, every production company I've spoken with has pooh-poohed them or yawned. My ideas for a documentary aren't that bad, are they?"

Phil shoved his hands in his pockets.

"They are?" *Wow. That hurt.*

"It's not that they're bad ideas, it's just that they're not…fantastic."

"Gee, tell me what you really think." .

"You know how tough this biz is. If you can't get the people with the purse strings excited, then you've lost the battle. Take this miniseries, for example."

"What do you mean?"

"Well, it's not a documentary, but it is based on the life of someone real. Someone who created magic in the 1930s yet wasn't really recognized for her brilliance at the time—because she was a woman."

"A very chauvinistic era," she said.

"Do you think much has changed?"

"Nope." Tony was a classic example. She leaned against the wall and tilted her head backwards. "God. How am I supposed to get any project off the ground? Sex shouldn't make a difference if the idea's good enough."

"Sex makes all the difference." Phil laughed.

"Very funny, not that sex. Sex as in gender."

"I know what you mean. Seriously, though, Amelia Elliott was a trailblazer in her day. All you need to do is find a topic like her and you'd be sorted."

"All the trailblazers have already had documentaries made about them." She tried not to sound dejected, but it was hard not to.

Phil squeezed her shoulder. "Your time will come."

"Thanks." Somehow, she needed to channel Phil's positive outlook. "I better get this place sorted, eh?"

"Need a hand?"

"Nah, I'm good. Go and rest."

Phil saluted her as he walked toward the door and chatted with the last of the crew. When they left, silence fell in the cinema and Claire sat in the back row, feeling more tired than normal. The encounter with Tony, the stress of ensuring everything was running to plan and constantly monitoring the crew and cast had started taking its toll.

Her stomach grumbled.

She stood, about to start the end-of-day check. Claire set about her ritual, wishing she'd finished up early enough to go visit Hattie. She wanted to assure her that everything was going well.

With only one door left to lock, Claire collected her bag and slung it over her shoulder.

"Slacking off, eh?"

Claire couldn't make out the identity of the dark figure standing at the back of the cinema.

"Who's there?" She wasn't scared, but she was certainly cautious.

The figure moved toward her and her muscles tensed, ready for flight or fight.

The aroma of chicken soup filled her nostrils.

"Thought you might like something to eat." Luke stepped out of the shadows and her shoulders relaxed. "Why do you look so afraid?"

"Because I'm not used to people stalking me."

"Stalking?" He laughed. "Nope, no stalking here. My great-aunt thought you might like some dinner. We'd heard about the crazy hours everyone is working."

"You did?"

"Why are you surprised?" he asked.

"I guess I shouldn't be."

"The miniseries is the only conversation around here at the moment." He walked toward her and handed over a basket that contained the soup and a couple of bread rolls. Hattie had even packed a red cotton serviette and silverware.

"I hope they're saying nice things." She sat and motioned for Luke to do the same.

"So far." He settled against the plush seat and placed his arms on the backrest.

She lifted the lid. "This smells amazing."

"Hattie's specialty."

"I can understand why." She unwrapped the serviette and realized there were two spoons. Claire offered one to Luke.

"No thanks. I've already had my fill, but you go ahead."

"Thank you." She hadn't realized how hungry she was until Luke showed up. If she were by herself she would have scarfed it but, given the present company, she took her time spooning in the delicious goodness.

They sat in companionable silence as Claire polished off the soup and rolls. As she was placing it all back in the basket she discovered another, smaller container.

"What's this?"

"Your favorite." Luke's secretive smile had her ripping off the lid.

"Carrot cake! How did she know?"

"You may not have noticed, but Starlight Creek is a rather small community."

"Scarlet blabbed." Claire broke the cake in half and offered a piece to Luke.

"No, I'm good. I'm Hattie's official taste-tester, and this definitely gets full marks."

"Ha!" Claire took a bite. Butter and cinnamon danced across her tongue. "Oh my god."

"Not bad, eh?"

"Not bad at all." She swallowed and broke off another piece. "Thank you."

"For what?"

"For giving me a chance to prove myself," she said.

"I didn't have much of a say."

"True." Claire smiled. "Hattie is a woman who knows what she wants."

"Yep."

Silence wrapped around them once more.

"I really like Starlight Creek," she finally said.

Luke shifted in his seat to face her. "What do you like about it?"

"I love the sugarcane fields, and the hazy blue of the mountains. I love the quiet—that is *so* refreshing, though silence actually keeps me awake."

"Really?"

"Yep. The sounds of the city are white noise for me. I live in Melbourne, and the traffic is constantly in the background, keeping me company when my mind is going a million miles an hour at three in the morning." She stopped and wondered if she was saying too much. Did he really want to know these things?

"What keeps you awake at that hour?"

"Stuff," she said, then realized her comment was shutting him down when he appeared genuinely interested. "I've got lots of projects I'd like to work on, but none have come to fruition yet."

"Ah. I don't have traffic keeping me awake. I have frogs."

"Frogs?"

"Frogs in the pond outside my window." His gentle smile was such a contrast to the expression he'd worn when they'd first met. "What kind of projects do you think about?"

"It's almost a case of what don't I think about. I don't plan on doing locations forever."

"I thought you enjoyed it."

"I love it, but it's not the be-all and end-all. It's just that I've got lots of dreams, and I'm not sure which idea is going to be the one that leads me down the road I want to travel."

Luke didn't say anything for a long time.

"Sometimes dreams aren't all they're cracked up to be." Luke stood and collected the basket. "I'll walk you back to yours."

Chapter Fourteen

1994 – Starlight Creek, Queensland

The next day, Claire stood at the side of the foyer as they filmed the last scene of a very long day. Camille looked resplendent in a mauve 1930s-style dress with a matching hat and feather. She swanned around the foyer, her smile bright, her laugh light. James, in the role of Amelia's assistant-turned-lover, looked as handsome as ever in his gray suit and pristine white shirt. Claire could certainly understand why he had a legion of adoring fans.

It had been a few days since Claire had seen Annalise and so far, so good. Robert Dennis had also kept his distance, and it appeared his threat was just him blowing off steam—that, or he was gathering his army.

Since her run-in with Tony yesterday, he'd gone about his business, not causing a stir. Claire had stashed their conversation in her memory bank, hoping she wouldn't have to drag it out again.

"Cut! Print!" Nigel walked toward Camille and James. "Nicely done, you two. Right, we're finished for today. Everyone back on set tomorrow at seven."

Camille and James quickly got involved in a heavy discussion, which resulted in Camille storming out the door. James looked at Claire then made his way over.

"I hope you're not upsetting Camille," she joked.

"She's always finding something to be pissed off about," he grumbled.

"She's far from a diva." A cloud seemed to hang over his head. "Are you all right?"

"I haven't heard from Annalise."

"Pardon?" These were not words she'd expected to hear from one of Australia's most enthusiastic Casanovas.

"She said she'd get in contact with me once things cooled down, but I haven't heard from her."

Claire studied James. Maybe she'd got it all wrong. Maybe *everyone* had got it wrong, and James and Annalise were the real deal.

Claire debated her next move. If she told James she'd refused to deliver a letter from Annalise, he'd lose all trust in Claire. And that wouldn't help with her second job of ensuring he didn't get himself into trouble with the locals. Yet if this thing between Annalise and James was the real deal, who was she to stand in the way of love?

Robert Dennis.

"Maybe she's letting her father cool down." She hoped this would buy some time. "I'm sure she'll contact you eventually."

James rubbed his forehead. "I hate this."

"What?"

"I hate this feeling of missing someone." He looked up and laughed. "I guess this is love, eh?"

"I wouldn't know."

"You've never been in love?" He looked at her, his expression puzzled.

"Nope." She didn't like this topic; it was way too close to home.

"Never?"

"Maybe?"

"If you aren't sure then it hasn't happened, because when you are in love, it is the most soul-destroying thing on earth."

Claire looked at James. Who was this person? What had happened to James Lloyd, International Playboy 1990–1994? "If it's soul-destroying, then I'm not sure that's the kind of love you want."

James sighed. "God, she's sexy."

Ah. There was the James of old. "Annalise is beautiful, there's no doubting that. How's about we concentrate on getting this miniseries done and we can worry about our love lives, or lack thereof, afterward?"

Claire hated putting Cupid on hold, and as much as she wanted to tell James about Annalise's letter, she couldn't risk him getting back in contact with her. At least not while they were shooting. One bad move and Robert Dennis could find a way to make the production topple like a house of cards. She had no doubt that was well within his capabilities.

"Yeah, I guess you're right." James's pout morphed into a broad smile. "If it's meant to be, it's meant to be."

"That's rather philosophical of you."

"I'm reading *The Road Less Traveled* by M. Scott Peck. It's inspiring. He talks about love requiring courage, and that it can be risky. That's true about me and Annalise."

Claire tried to act nonchalant, though she couldn't quite believe that she and James were having this conversation. "I had no idea you liked those types of books."

"I've only just started." He leaned against the bar. "Annalise introduced me to them."

"Really?" Her voice came out high and she forced it down an octave. "It sounds like Annalise was a good influence on you."

"She was. Is. Will be."

Guilt welled up in her. This was an impossible situation, but who was she to dictate whether two consenting adults could be together? Sure, she was supposed to keep an eye on James, but where was the line? Ugh. This was all too hard. She needed to sleep on it and talk to Nigel. Maybe he'd change his mind. Although she doubted it.

"Right, well, I better get sorted around here," she said. "See you tomorrow."

James waved and walked out of the foyer while Claire got to work helping the rest of the crew pack up and get everything ready for the morning. The crew left eventually and she started on her last task of the day: disposing of the leftover food and paper plates. The muscles in her legs and arms hurt, her back ached, and weariness had taken over. These long days were wearing her down, and the only thing that got her through was the vision of sandy beaches and clear blue waters. Although, the heat of northern Queensland made her sweat so much that she wondered whether Antarctica would be a better choice for a vacation.

"I thought I would find you here."

Claire dropped the plates onto the table, and remnants of half-eaten sandwiches scattered everywhere. "Jesus!"

"Sorry." Luke helped pile the plates.

"It's okay, really," Claire said. "What brings you here?"

"Food."

"Pardon?" She dumped the plates in a nearby bin.

"I have a delivery for you." He pointed at the picnic basket resting against the bar.

"A Hattie special?" She couldn't hide her enthusiasm.

"Yep." Luke grabbed the picnic basket and set it on the table. He pulled out a couple of containers and opened the lids. A beautiful green salad of cherry tomatoes, spring onion, almonds, with the delightful aroma of lemon filled the air. Her stomach rumbled when she spied the homemade lamingtons and quiche.

"Your aunt is amazing."

Luke pulled out a couple of plates and some cutlery. He dished out the salad and quiche and sat on the chair opposite. "I hope you don't mind me joining you?"

"Not at all! It's nice to have company." Although she'd prefer if the company didn't turn on and off like a leaky tap.

They ate in silence, and Claire began to wonder why Luke had bothered staying.

"Hattie was wondering when you have a day off." He didn't look up from his food.

"We have a slightly earlier finish tomorrow."

"Would you like to come over for dinner?"

"That would be lovely," she said slowly, not quite sure if the invitation was solely from Hattie. It disconcerted her that she hoped Luke also wanted her company.

He put down his knife and fork and looked directly at her. "What do you like to do for fun?"

"Fun?" Claire rested her utensils on the now-empty plate. "It may come as no surprise."

"Darts?"

She laughed. "No."

"Kickboxing?"

"No."

"Oh! I know!" He waved his arms in the air. "Skydiving!"

"Ha! No!" She liked this lighthearted side of Luke Jackson. "I love watching old Hollywood movies."

"Really?" He feigned surprise.

"Who would've thought, eh?"

"You know we have some Hollywood classics in storage here," he said.

"You don't say!"

Luke stood and offered his hand. Loving this chivalrous gesture, she put hers in his. It felt odd, but very satisfying, that their hands melded together so perfectly.

They went into the cinema and headed toward a door that led to a smaller hallway. She glanced back at the other door that remained off-limits. What was in that room?

Luke turned on the light and she squinted from the brightness.

"Sorry about that."

"No worries."

Luke opened a door and climbed a ladder. He motioned for her to do the same. A little uneasy with the steepness, she held on to the rails and made her way to the top.

"Wow." She looked down on the cinema, which seemed much smaller from this height. "This is the projection room?"

"Yep." Luke was on his knees looking through a pile of large round silver reel containers. He focused on the job and Claire walked around the small booth, careful not to touch anything.

"This is amazing. Time has preserved everything beautifully," she said. "How come you have so many reels? Aren't they expensive? I thought cinemas only hired a movie for a short while, then it went to the next cinema."

"I see you've done your research." Luke's voice sounded muffled as he hunted around for whatever he was looking for. "My great-great-grandfather—Hattie's father—bought a heap at auction before he passed away. He got them for a steal."

"I'm impressed."

Luke jerked back, then hit his head on the shelf. "Damn it!"

"Are you okay?" She bent down, and he edged away.

"I'm fine, fine." He rubbed his head, then returned to searching. Eventually, he pulled out several reels that looked just like all the others. "Aha!"

Luke pulled the cover off the projector and set about threading the film through the machine and checking everything was in place. Claire studied his every move. For someone who didn't like movies, he certainly knew his way around the projection room.

"Sorted." He stood back and looked at his handiwork. "Right, so you need to get back downstairs and I'll get this started."

"What are we watching?" She couldn't help herself.

"You like the classics, right?"

She nodded.

"I'm taking a wild guess, but I'm going to put on one that you're bound to like—I hope."

"Am I that easy to read?" She laughed.

"I am flying blind, but every so often I'll take a risk."

"There's nothing wrong with a calculated risk," she said.

"I'm not so sure about that." He turned on the projector and shooed her out the door. "I'll be down in a tick."

Claire tentatively went down the ladder, through the narrow hallway and back into the cinema. The screen flickered to life and the speakers crackled. It felt odd to be in the cinema without the buzz of the film set, to be actually watching a movie—like a cinema was designed for.

The second the movie started, she laughed. "No way!"

"Yes way." Luke sat beside her.

"How did you know *Some Like It Hot* is one of my all-time favorites?"

Luke looked ahead, like he wasn't sure how to answer. Or he was too embarrassed.

How sweet.

"Seriously, this is in my top five favorite movies of all time." She settled into the comfy seat. "All we need is popcorn."

"Back in a mo." Luke disappeared into Hattie's kitchen. He returned not long after with a bag of chips. "Will these do?"

"Sure will!"

Luke opened the chips and offered her some. She reached in and grabbed a couple, surprised by how quickly she'd switched from work mode to chill-out mode. Usually on set she lived and breathed work, often falling into a heap at the end of the project. Sitting in an old cinema, watching one of her favorite movies, with a handsome and fascinating man beside her, certainly rated high on excellent ways to end a long day.

The movie started, and Claire instantly felt her muscles relaxing. The pain in her back subsided. And the brewing headache faded. On the screen, Tony Curtis and Jack Lemmon were escaping the mafia after witnessing a murder, and to remain alive they had to transform themselves into women and join an all-girl orchestra.

When she burst out laughing at Tony and Jack trying to walk in heels at the train station, Luke joined in. The vast expanse of the cinema now cocooned them, like they were in a bubble that blocked the world outside. It wouldn't last, she knew that, but it was nice to be in the moment and not have to worry about scheduling, constantly checking the time and moving props and people around.

"Back in a second." Luke disappeared into the projection room for a few minutes then returned. "Had to change the reel."

"How do you know when?"

"It's a talent." He grinned.

Marilyn Monroe appeared on the screen sashaying down the train platform, then later playing the ukulele for the all-girl orchestra.

When she introduced herself as Sugar Kane, Luke snorted. "Really?"

"Ha! I never thought of that. Sugar Kane and we're in sugarcane country."

"Kind of weird, but funny."

"It is a bit," she said. "Marilyn was on her downward spiral when this movie was made. She was constantly late and messed up lines. One line took forty-seven takes before she got it right."

"She had quite the tragic life."

"Indeed," Claire said.

They returned their attention to the film, and Claire reveled in the fact that Luke seemed to be enjoying himself—nothing like a pair of men dressed up as women to lighten the mood.

They watched in companionable silence punctuated every so often with laughter and Luke ducking off to change the reels. Toward the end of the movie, Jack Lemmon jumped into a speedboat with the billionaire who says he wants to marry him, thinking he's a her. When Jack finally admits he's a man, the billionaire shrugs, adding that no one is perfect.

Luke's laughter was music to her ears. Any tension between them had lifted.

"Can you imagine what audiences would have thought when they saw this in 1959?" she asked.

"It's a wonder the Hays Code let it be released," said Luke.

Claire looked at him, perplexed. "You know about that?"

Luke shrugged. "I may not have watched many movies in my lifetime, but I do know a bit about their history." He shifted to face her. "I'd like to know more about this one, though."

"You would?"

Luke laughed. "Don't sound so surprised."

"But you said you don't like movies."

"I don't like the movie industry. There is a slight difference."

"Our production hasn't changed your mind?"

"Too early to tell," he muttered. "Tell me more about *Some Like It Hot*."

Claire couldn't contain her nerdy excitement. "The Hays Code was still in existence—it ended in 1969—but this movie was a big middle finger to the censors. The filmmakers didn't bother getting approval from the censorship board, which was rather gutsy, given this was in the conservative era of Eisenhower. And—" She paused to see if she'd lost Luke, but he appeared entranced. "The Catholic church wasn't impressed with this movie, especially since it's packed full of sexual language and innuendo."

"I'm surprised it didn't end up on the cutting-room floor."

"Yeah, it's a wonder. Most of the public loved it, and so did the Academy, because it was nominated for six Academy Awards, and it won an Oscar for costume design."

"I can see why. Lemmon and Curtis managed to pull it off somehow."

"They certainly did. This movie has been voted by many experts as the greatest comedy of all time." She paused, slightly embarrassed. "Sorry, I'm a bit of a movie nerd."

"I don't mind. I like to hear what you have to say."

"Okay." She took a breath, pleased Luke hadn't fallen asleep yet. "This movie really tested society, because it challenged morality and made people wonder whether the Hays Code was necessary. *Some Like It Hot*, in its own way, examines misogyny and female objectification, and does it so well. Tony Curtis and Jack Lemmon get an understanding of what women go through on a daily basis, having to deal with sexual advances and being judged on their looks, even when they aren't the prettiest girls in the room."

"Yeah, Jack and Tony aren't exactly the belles of the ball."

"Definitely not!" She smiled. "Especially when you put them next to a bombshell like Marilyn Monroe." Claire sighed. "They don't make them like they used to. Isn't she beautiful?"

"Certainly is."

Claire looked over to find Luke's eyes on her. The movie music finished and the reel in the projector room *flick-flicked* as it spun.

Luke gently touched her hair, his hand slowly caressing her face.

She held her breath.

Luke moved toward her, his lips dangerously close to hers.

She closed her eyes, dipping under a wave of lust, and when their lips met, any doubts she'd had about Luke Jackson disappeared into the ether.

Chapter Fifteen

1952 – Hollywood

Lena sat in the back of the limousine as they drove down her old street. She missed the little apartment she'd once shared with Yvonne, but after her monumental and rapid success, she'd been encouraged by the studio to buy her own house to "fit in with the public's expectations of a starlet." Waking up every morning, she still couldn't believe she owned a piece of Beverly Hills—and a beautiful one at that.

She sighed.

"What's wrong?" Pierre Montreaux placed his hand on her knee and she gently moved it away.

"Nothing." Lena returned to staring out the window. She should have been excited, but nerves had taken over the moment she'd donned the ochre gown Yvonne had chosen for her. Opening nights were always fraught with angst.

The limousine turned the corner and they entered a street lined with people waving and cheering. Spotlights angled skyward moved across the darkness and flashes from the photographers' cameras went off like fireworks.

The car rolled to a stop in front of the movie theater and Pierre said to the driver, "Go around the block one more time."

"Why?" Lena asked as the limousine pulled away from the curb and continued down the road.

"We need to give them a grand entrance, *oui*?"

"Being late is bad manners."

"No one minds waiting for the leading man and leading lady."

Lena rolled her eyes. "Just because you have a fake French accent doesn't mean you can be arrogant. I see through you, even if no one else does."

"Ah, my little rose, just because *you* have a fake accent doesn't mean you can play the innocent card. I see through *you.*"

Lena gripped the edge of the seat so hard her fingers ached. "My accent is one hundred percent genuine."

"Genuinely fake. You're no New Yorker. But who cares. The public believe what they want, and if they want to believe I'm French, then I'm all for it. My exoticness adds extra zeroes on to my paycheck." His smirk annoyed the heck out of her. "Not bad for a small-town kid from outside Calgary."

"You'll be found out one day. Then what will happen?"

"I've spent enough years crafting my persona, just like you. Nothing's real in Hollywood. It's a world built on make-believe, and you're a fool to think otherwise."

The limousine turned onto the street once more.

"Gee, I'm so glad we had this conversation," she said, ruing the day she and Pierre Montreaux had been paired as the "next big thing." Since she'd given her best performance in Stuart Cooper's office, Lena's career had taken off so fast her head was still spinning. If she had to suffer the company of a man like Pierre (whatever his real name was), then so be it. She'd achieved her dream despite the studio's initial concern about her *maturity.*

Another sigh threatened to leave her lips, but this time she held it in.

The limousine pulled up and Pierre turned to her. "Ready, *ma cheri?*"

Pierre exited and walked around to her side of the car. He opened the door and she held out her hand. When she stood, a roar from the crowd pounded in her ears. Adrenaline pumped through her veins and all the anxiety about whether this film would succeed or not fell away—for now, at least. She should take in the moment, breathe, and revel in the fact that a little over two years ago she'd been dropped from a movie before the filming had even started. Now she was one of the most popular actresses in Tinseltown.

Pierre placed his arm around Lena and guided her down the red carpet. She wanted to shake him off but she held back. Every few feet they stopped to pose for the cameras, a sea of flashing lights blinding her. She smiled into the brightness, unable to make out the faces calling their names. One voice, though, sounded familiar, and she peered into the crowd.

Stepping away from Pierre, Lena moved toward the mass of bodies. People waved and she signed autographs, surreptitiously searching for the owner of the voice.

"Lena!"

She looked up to find the face of someone she hadn't seen for years— Dotty Peters, the sister of Lena's ex-boyfriend, Charlie. *Oh no.* Lena dropped the pen and paper on the red carpet. An assistant quickly scooped it up and handed it to Lena, who finished signing and handed it back to her fan. Lena made her way over to Pierre.

"Let's go in," she whispered.

"Why the hurry?"

"I'm cold." The lies came out easier than they used to. Though acting was a form of lying, wasn't it? Pretending to be someone you're not? Was it acceptable if the lying moved from on-screen to off-screen? Was it really that bad? Although, if it wasn't, Lena wouldn't spend her days petrified of her past coming back to haunt her. And now a flash of her old life was only twenty feet away. "We need to go."

Pierre threw her a sideways look, but he didn't argue. Perhaps he sensed the urgency in her tone. The fact that he didn't quiz her or refuse her wishes endeared him to her, as much as she hated to admit it.

Pierre and Lena waved at the crowd as they entered the foyer of the cinema. It was a little less packed than the red carpet. Lena had hoped she could catch her breath, but the sighting of Dotty Peters had upset her more than she'd anticipated. Lena wasn't so naive as to think people from her past wouldn't surface one day, especially given her level of fame now, but she never expected Dotty to be the one who would come out of the proverbial woodwork. The last time she'd seen Dotty, harsh and tearful words had flown between them.

This could not be good.

Lena pasted on the smile she saved for meeting and greeting essential people and tried to lose herself in the thrill of being the center of attention. It didn't work. All she could picture was Dotty and her brother Charlie, a man she'd rather forget.

Hollywood's elite swarmed around her and Pierre, as well as director Henry Newman.

"This is your third movie with Henry, is that right?" asked social pages writer Gertrude Ackerman.

"Yes. We have two more planned over the next year," said Lena, her eyes searching the room. For whom, she had no idea. Dotty would be caught in the throng outside. Hopefully she'd give up and go home, but Lena suspected that may not be the case.

"I absolutely loved you in *These City Walls*," continued Gertrude, who grasped Lena's arm. "Oh! You are even more beautiful in person! And you're just as sweet as the roles you play."

"Thank you," Lena said, wondering when the bell would ring to signal the movie was about to start. The opportunity to enjoy this evening had evaporated the moment she saw Dotty.

"Well, well, the star of the evening." Lawrence Doherty strode up and took her hand in his. "Look at you."

"And look at you," Lena said. "You scrub up all right."

"We both do." Lawrence laughed.

Ever since Lawrence had delivered the news of her role being cut, which had led to Lena getting snapped up by Henry Newman, the balance between Lawrence and Lena had changed dramatically. She was no longer at his mercy, having to take any role he flung at her, because Henry had made it abundantly clear—in her contract—that Lena would act solely for him. And she didn't mind at all.

"When's your contract up?" asked Lawrence, a sly smile gracing his mustached lips.

"Henry will punch you in the nose if he hears you."

"I'm serious, though. If you ever want to do a movie with me..." His awkward smile reminded her of a nervous schoolboy.

"Thank you, Lawrence, but I think you have your hands busy with Jeanne and Reeves. They seem to be the magic pair for you these days."

Lawrence averted his gaze and took a long swig of whiskey.

"What's wrong?" she asked.

Lawrence finished his drink, put the glass on the tray of the waiter passing by and grabbed another, which he downed in seconds.

"Lawrence?"

"You haven't heard, have you?"

"Haven't heard what?"

The laugh that fell from Lawrence's lips sounded hollow. "Jeanne tore up the set this morning."

"What?" Lena had hoped things had calmed down, as she hadn't heard much about Jeanne's behavior lately.

"She's out of control."

"I thought she'd been seeing someone to help with her little...problem."

"She was, then she thought she was above seeing a doctor." Lawrence's sigh sounded despondent. "I just don't know what to do. We're already behind on production."

"Oh, Lawrence, I'm so sorry."

He shrugged. "It's not your fault."

"But Jeanne and I were friends once. Maybe if I talked to her…"

"Good luck with that. Reeves has tried his darndest, but to no avail. It's a sad state of affairs, Lena. The movie's in jeopardy at best, and at worst, our careers are on a knife-edge—mine, Jeanne's and Reeves's."

"But her behavior isn't yours or Reeves's fault." Reeves. Wow. It had been such a long time since they'd seen each other. Even though they worked for the same studio, they rarely crossed paths. It would be so nice to see him again.

"Look," continued Lawrence, "I was an idiot for not seeing who you were. Who you could become. I should have fought harder against the Hays Code."

"It wouldn't have made a difference. They are a force to be reckoned with. I don't know how many times Henry has gone to bat about a trivial matter Breen and his men have taken offense to. Oh, look," she said. "Here comes Henry. Well, hello!"

Henry couldn't get across the room fast enough, and Lawrence gave her a grateful smile for the warning. Although she had left Lawrence's movie under less-than-favorable circumstances, it had opened up an opportunity she wouldn't have had otherwise. No way could she ever harbor bitter feelings toward the man who had inadvertently opened a door for her.

"Lovely to see you, Lena." Henry kissed her on the cheek, then turned his attention to Lawrence. "How are you, old man?"

"I'm good, good." Lawrence scanned the room. "Please excuse me, I've just seen someone I *need* to catch up with."

Henry's gaze didn't leave Lawrence as he disappeared into the crowd. Henry turned his attention to Lena.

"What?" she asked.

"You know the deal."

"Of course I do, Henry. And you should know me well enough to realize that my word is my word."

"And we have a contract." He laughed, then studied the drink in his hand. "I'm aware I get possessive, and it's not right—you are a person, not a commodity." He looked up and grinned. "Ready for the great unveiling? It's our best work to date."

Lena spotted the film critic Frederick Schulz talking to colleagues on the opposite side of the room.

Henry squeezed her shoulder. "Don't be nervous. They'll love you."

The bell chimed steadily and the lights dimmed, just like during stage productions—one of Stuart Cooper's touches. Pierre arrived by her side and offered his arm, and they walked up to the front of the movie theater. Stuart Cooper stood on the stage, watching everyone filter in and take their seats on the plum-colored velvet. Henry climbed the stage too, and Lena and Pierre took their places in the front row.

For the next ten minutes Stuart and Henry spoke about the movie, which was titled *Hidden Motives*, Pierre and Lena and the supporting cast. The audience grew restless, and what was once a silent room, bar the talking of Stuart and Henry, had now become filled with coughs and quiet murmuring.

"Come on! Show us the movie!" a voice yelled from the back row and everyone laughed, including Stuart.

"I'm glad to see we have some eager beavers. So, without further ado..." He saluted the projectionist hidden in the box at the back of the theater. The movie sputtered into action and Lena squeezed her eyes shut.

"It will be over soon," whispered Pierre. She appreciated his understanding, though it was only a *short* matter of time before he said something to offend or annoy her again. What a shame she wasn't paired up with Reeves Garrity, but Jeanne had hand-picked him from the start. Although if the rumors were true...

Lena concentrated on the movie, cringing every time she saw her face on the screen. Although she was more than happy to act in front of the camera and have her photo taken for magazines, Lena didn't enjoy hearing her voice or seeing her face on a sixty-foot screen. It was all so...strange.

When World War II had broken out, all she'd ever heard were stories of men dying, women and children being bombed, countries torn apart. She'd watched families in her hometown lose their sons, and women had undertaken nontraditional jobs to help the war effort while they balanced being mothers and wives to absent husbands. War had clawed its way into everyone's lives—no one was safe from its clutches. The only escape, for a few precious hours a week, was the movie theater. There, Lena would lose herself in another world, imagining what it would be like to be held in Cary Grant's arms, to dance with Fred Astaire, to sing with Gene Kelly.... Never in a million years could she have imagined that she would one day be staring at her face on a silver screen.

The audience around her laughed when they should have, sighed and cried at the right moments and seemed entranced by the romantic scenes, which strictly adhered to the rules Breen and his men monitored. Romantic movies always ran the risk of breaking the Hays Code, which slithered its tentacles into every movie produced in the USA, but Harry had found a way to take scenes right to the edge before the censorship board wielded its shiny scissors. Sometimes Henry pushed too far, and entire scenes were cut, but he'd managed to keep the movie from being banned.

On screen, Lena and Pierre were in each other's arms, cheek to cheek. When they kissed, it lasted for the maximum three seconds allowed by the Hays Code. Henry, being Henry, dangled his toes over the line by having Lena and Pierre kiss for two and a half seconds, briefly talk, then kiss for two more. The result was sexual tension the audience lapped up. Although the scene looked romantic, Lena's neck had developed a crick that had plagued her for days afterward. Still, the final shot was perfection, and she admired Henry's vision. As the image faded, the room filled with applause and a few whistles.

Stuart walked onto the stage and motioned for the audience to quiet. "I am sure you will agree with me that this film is magnificent. Now, it's up to you to spread the word so I can afford to go to the Bahamas for my vacation this year."

Everyone laughed, and Lena shook her head.

"Come on, time to schmooze again." Pierre offered his hand and she stood, smiling her thanks.

"Remind me why we do this?" she asked.

"Because if you failed at this gig, what would you be doing?"

Dotty Peters's face flashed before her, and a hollowness grew in Lena's chest. No way could Lena return to that old life of working in a bar between modeling and acting jobs. She plastered on her best smile and looked around the room. "Let's do it."

Chapter Sixteen

1952 – Hollywood

The flashing lights, sparkling diamonds and silk dresses of the night before had faded into a distant dream. Lena sat in the makeup chair in her dressing room, waiting for Vanessa and Yvonne to arrive and work their magic, just like they'd done every day since she'd first set foot in Fortitude Studios three years ago.

Lena let out a sigh.

"What's that about?" asked Yvonne as she flounced through the dressing room door as fresh as a cool sea breeze. Vanessa followed behind.

"See these?" Lena pointed to the bags under her eyes. "They will be your greatest challenge yet."

"Ha!" Vanessa unpacked her box of tricks. "You know me, I always rise to a challenge."

"You seriously have your work cut out for you." Lena stifled a yawn.

"Did you get any sleep last night? Or did you party until the wee hours?"

"I got home from schmoozing at three o'clock."

"They really do work you like a Trojan. No resting on the laurels of your last film, huh?"

"Nope," said Lena.

Yvonne sorted through the nearby clothes rack while Vanessa scooped out some goop and started applying it to Lena's face. Lena's skin instantly felt like it was suffocating, but in the mirror she could already see the red blotches disappearing.

"You looked amazing last night," said Yvonne.

"With a lot of thanks to you and Vanessa." Lena reached for Yvonne's hand, then Vanessa's. "I really mean it. Thank you."

"For what?" asked Yvonne.

"For everything," Lena said. "You two are my dearest friends, and you've always been there for me."

Vanessa gave an uneasy laugh. "What's got into you?"

Lena's eyes stung with hot tears. "Lack of sleep, I guess."

Vanessa waved her hand, the signal for Lena to close her eyes while eyeshadow, mascara and eyeliner were applied. When Vanessa was done, Lena opened her eyes.

Vanessa concentrated on choosing the right color lipstick while Yvonne took out the turquoise dress with tiny yellow and white flowers. She hung it on the hook next to the dressing table and rested her gaze on Lena. "What's with that look?"

"Nothing." Lena wished she could hide her true feelings better.

"You said 'nothing' too quick." Yvonne pulled out a pair of yellow heels.

Lena coughed. "We don't have much time before I'm due on set."

"That's an excuse." Vanessa dusted Lena's face with powder. "Close your eyes again and we'll do your fakeys." Vanessa picked up eyelashes and started applying the glue.

"Come on, Lena, what's going on?" asked Yvonne.

"Noth—"

"Lena." Vanessa's deep tone told Lena she wasn't getting out of it this easy.

"I don't know, I've just…I don't know how to explain."

"Well, you have at least fifteen minutes before we're done here, so get that brain to work with your mouth. But not while I'm doing your lips, okay?"

Lena laughed despite feeling so maudlin. Up until now she'd been trying to ignore the unease, but it had been tugging at her skirt like a persistent three-year-old. She had to give her friends something. "I think it's because so much has happened in a short time. I signed on as a chorus and bit-part girl with huge dreams of becoming a starlet, though in the back of my mind I always told myself the chances of hitting the big time were extremely remote. Especially since I started in this game so much later than others."

"Yet here you are," said Vanessa.

"Yet here I am. Don't get me wrong, I love what I do and I'm so very grateful, but there's something missing. Something feels off."

"A decent man?" asked Yvonne, who motioned for her to get up off the chair now that Vanessa had finished. She placed a scarf over Lena's head and slid the dress on, then took off the scarf and adjusted the costume, pulling it here, tugging it there then cinching it all up with the zip and buttons at the back.

"Pierre Montreaux is a very decent man, thank you very much," said Lena.

Vanessa and Yvonne exchanged a look.

"What?" Lena threw her arms wide.

"You can say what you like, but we don't think so," Vanessa said.

"Pierre is a very fine man." Lena let indignation ride on her words.

"You protest too much," said Yvonne. "Besides, I've never heard you say you're in love with him."

"Why would I? That's my business."

"Your business became everyone's business the day you signed on."

"I know."

"So?" asked Yvonne.

"So, what?"

"So, tell us you love Pierre. That he's the man you've dreamed about your entire life. That you don't mind that his ego is bigger than the state of Texas, and that you don't have a problem with the way he flirts with every single woman on the planet." Yvonne put her hands on her hips. "Tell us we're wrong."

Lena pursed her lips. "It's complicated."

"I don't see what's so complicated about it. You either love him or you don't."

"Yvonne..."

"Look, I may seem harsh to you, but I don't like standing by and watching one of my dearest friends get sucked into this crazy ruse. I've seen it before. You can't tell me that Stuart Cooper hasn't coerced you and Pierre into being the perfect couple on- and off-screen. The general public may buy it, but I don't."

"I'm sorry you feel that way," said Lena. "Humphrey Bogart and Lauren Bacall managed an on- and off-screen love affair. And what about Laurence Olivier and Vivien Leigh?"

"Olivier and Leigh were married to other people when they fell for each other," Yvonne said.

She did have a point, unfortunately. Lena straightened her spine. "They fell in love on-screen and that flowed into real life. They were a powerful couple on film and off. Audiences loved that. True love is true love."

"Hmm." Vanessa got out the comb and tucked a few stray hairs into Lena's updo. As each minute ticked by, Lena's mood got worse. It was hard enough being expected to look glamorous and act and sing her best on three hours' sleep, so a lecture from two friends she valued made everything feel worse. She despised keeping the truth from them, but Stuart had put it in her contract that she could not breathe a word.

"There," said Vanessa. "More beautiful than Betty Grable."

"What about Jeanne Harris?" Lena let out a laugh, hoping to ease the tension in the room.

"Goes without saying. Come on." Yvonne straightened the seams on Lena's stockings. "We may have dropped the topic for now, but we're not letting you off the hook. We will get to the bottom of it."

"There's nothing to get to the bottom of."

Yvonne walked her toward the door. "We'll see."

* * * *

After warming up her vocal cords in the privacy of her dressing room, Lena walked onto the set to a round of applause. She moved toward the gigantic maple in the hanging garden and smiled awkwardly as actors and crew surrounded and congratulated her.

"Look at this!" Anna May Clifford, one of the chorus girls, shoved a newspaper in front of Lena's face. "They *loved* your new movie! Here." She ran her finger ran across the print. "It says, 'Once again, Pierre Montreaux and Lena Lee have delivered Oscar-worthy performances that will entrance and delight audiences across America. Mr. Montreux's near-perfect performance will have female moviegoers' hearts a-flutter, while Miss Lee's magnificent depiction of a woman who finally gets her man is enchanting and heartwarming. Her angelic voice soothes the ears and her beauty is a delight for the eyes.' Isn't that wonderful?"

"Yes." Lena forced a smile. Every movie was the same—Pierre the cad and Lena falling for him to make her life "complete." No one would listen to her pleas to tackle something with more substance. She said to Anna May, "Thank you for sharing the article with me."

"Enough chatting. Time for work! Places!" yelled Henry. He walked toward Lena and winked. "A good review's not a bad way to start the day."

"Not bad at all," she said, a lump in her throat. Shouldn't she be ecstatic?

"Where did you go last night?" Pierre's breath on the back of her neck made her shudder. She spun around to find him towering over her, his eyes steely.

"Where do you think?" She couldn't keep the sarcasm at bay.

"You left without saying goodbye. How did you get home?"

"If you're asking why I didn't leave in the limousine with you, it's because I was tired of seeing you openly make eyes at Sally Enfield. Really, Pierre, you need to watch yourself."

"Jealous, are we?"

"Of course not," she spat out. "I'm just saying that you need to watch what you do in public. It hurts *us*."

Pierre's gaze rested on the group of chorus girls in the corner. Even from this distance, Lena could see they were shivering in their tiny sequined outfits.

Lena took her place under the maple tree. The set designers had done a magnificent job. The leaves were so bright and green they looked like they'd been picked off a real tree, and the papier-mâché branches and trunk appeared authentic. Maybe they were.

"Ready, Miss Lee?" Henry asked.

"Yes, yes. Of course!" She lifted her chin, switching into business mode. Pierre stood to the side, waiting for his cue. Like the seasoned professional she was, Lena launched into her monologue, lamenting about how broken she was and how she could never fall in love again. What was to become of her? A woman on the shelf, craving affection from a man.

Her heart and head protested with every word that tumbled from her mouth. She felt like the world's biggest hypocrite, and a kernel of loathing grew in her belly.

"Cut!" yelled Henry. "I need more emotion, Lena—sadness, despair. Take it from the start."

Lena cleared her throat and smoothed down her dress. Every take cost money, and she had always prided herself on getting it right the first time, or, at worst, the second. Forcing herself to concentrate, she waited for Henry's signal then started again, trying to force her voice and facial expressions to match the mood.

"Cut!" Henry ran his hand through his hair. "Again!"

Once more, Lena tried, but her heart screamed even louder.

"Cut!" Henry strode over and said in a harsh whisper, "What's the problem?"

"I don't know." Her voice shook.

"I understand you're tired; we all are. Just get this right, then we can shoot the next two scenes and go home at a reasonable hour." Henry marched back to his position.

Closing her eyes and taking a deep breath, Lena willed her head to rule over her heart. *This is just a movie. The fate of the world does not rest on my shoulders.* This time, Lena gave it her all, and the words flowed freely.

The music started, and she broke into song, her dance moves smooth, her voice pitch perfect. By the time Pierre entered the scene, Lena had embraced her role, finally in control of her feelings.

He reached for her hand and their skin met.

Her voice caught in her throat.

Her step faltered.

"Cut!" Henry waved his arms about. "Lena!"

"I'm sorry!" She sounded as exasperated as she felt. "I really am!"

"Take a break. Pierre, let's get your scene done, then we'll go back to you and Lena once she's refreshed."

She went to her dressing room with guilt trailing her. She'd never messed up so badly before— why now?

She slumped in the chair in front of the mirror, leaned her elbows on the table and held her head in her hands. Her whole body ached. Her brain felt numb.

A woman's voice came from behind the door. "Miss Lee?"

"Yes?" She jumped upright, widened her eyes and blinked. One of her fake eyelashes fell onto the table and she scooped it up.

"Mr. Newman has asked me to tell you to be on set in ten minutes." The voice was quiet and gentle.

Getting up, Lena walked over and opened the door. Anna May stood in the hallway, her tiny frame covered in goosebumps.

"Come in." Lena motioned for Anna May to enter, then passed her dressing gown to the chorus girl. Anna May shook her head. "Please, take it. Your lips are blue," Lena said.

"I'm fine, really." Anna May grimaced and her body shuddered.

"You're freezing under that thin material."

Anna May finally accepted the dressing gown and wrapped it around her.

"How long have I been away?" asked Lena.

"Almost an hour."

"What?" The last thing she remembered was closing her eyes and burying her head in her hands—no wonder her wrists ached.

"Mr. Newman said he hopes you feel refreshed now." Anna May handed the dressing gown back and moved toward the door.

"Anna May," Lena said. "How are you doing?"

The young chorus girl turned to face her. "Fine, Miss Lee."

"How many hours do you and the other girls spend on set, or rehearsing the big musical numbers?"

"It depends. On average, though, I'd say around sixteen hours a day."

"How many days a week?"

"Six. Sometimes seven." Anna May frowned. "Why are you asking me this?"

"Because I was wondering if things had changed since I was in your position."

"I think it's always been this way. Sometimes we rush from one set to another, filming two different movies."

Lena turned to fix her eyelash in the mirror. Via the reflection, she looked at Anna May. "How about the men in the chorus?"

"What do you mean?"

"What kind of hours do they put in?"

"About the same, although there's usually more work for women."

"And they normally wear long pants and shirts, jackets and such, right?"

"Yes." Wariness spread across Anna May's face. "It's all right, though. It's nice weather here in Los Angeles, so we don't get cold very often. I just feel the cold when I'm tired."

"No wonder you're tired, with the hours you work." Lena finished fixing her eyelash and turned around, resting her buttocks on the table. "Do they still pay peanuts?"

Anna May glanced down the corridor then concentrated on her strappy dance shoes.

"I imagine it's still less than the men," said Lena.

Anna May shifted from foot to foot. She finally looked up. "It's just the way it is."

Lena had so much more to say, but she refrained from dragging Anna May into it. The poor girl had enough to deal with.

"It's been like that for a long time," Lena said. "Please tell Mr. Newman I'll be there in just a moment."

"Of course." Anna May took a step, then halted. "Miss Lee?"

"Yes?"

"Thank you for asking how I am. No one seems to know I exist around here. I'm just a girl who dances and sings in the background."

Lena gave a gentle smile. "You are so much more than that, Anna May. If you have dreams, pursue them, and don't let anyone deter you."

Anna May curtsied. "Thank you, Miss Lee."

"Anna May." Lena got up and rested a hand on the chorus girl's bony shoulder. "One day things will change, and you and every other woman in this industry will get the recognition you deserve. It's only a matter of time."

Chapter Seventeen

1994 – Starlight Creek, Queensland

The morning after *Some Like It Hot*, Claire felt rattled. She'd tossed and turned all night, images of Luke running through her mind. Nothing was as it seemed with Luke Jackson, and she found herself enjoying—craving—his company.

Claire jumped out of her single bed and opened the curtains. A few blocks away were the rolling sugarcane fields, framed by the hazy blue mountains in the background. She loved the way the sun rose peeking over the horizon, casting a glow across the valley that was accompanied with a chorus of singing birds—a peaceful moment before the busy day commenced.

There was something magical about Starlight Creek, and she wished she had more time to take it all in. Production was in full swing and she barely had time to breathe—although she had managed a moment to make out with Luke Jackson.

A sigh escaped her lips.

Given the dramas that had resulted from James and Annalise getting together, Claire was now consumed with guilt—and fear—over what had transpired with Luke. What if he got upset with her—for what, she wasn't sure—and talked Hattie into canceling the contract?

This thinking was ridiculous.

Last night, Luke's affection for her had shone through. They'd managed to stop before things went too far, but her body wanted to give in to his sensual touch, his breathtaking kisses. It had been a beautiful, romantic evening.

But this was dangerous ground she'd tiptoed onto, and it risked making her a hypocrite.

Claire readied herself for the day. By the time she arrived at the makeshift production office behind the cinema, Nigel was ensconced behind a wall of paperwork.

Claire knocked on the door. "Morning."

Nigel looked up and smiled. "Good morning." His face fell. "Everything okay?"

"There's something you need to know."

He motioned for her to come in and sit down, and she went through the conversations she'd had with Annalise and James. Nigel listened while scratching his head with his pencil.

"So, you see," Claire concluded, "we're playing with people's lives here."

"Celebrity comes with drawbacks."

"I get that, sure, but James seems to have changed, and I believe he really is in love with Annalise. We all know the media loves to make up all kinds of things about celebrities, especially if they have a rebellious reputation, but what happens when fact and fantasy are mixed up? I'm not saying that James is an angel—his long list of exes is proof of that—but what if his image as a playboy has been blown out of proportion? What would Robert Dennis think if James had a reputation for being the bookish type that stayed at home and played chess?"

"The outcome would have been vastly different," said Nigel.

"Exactly."

"Look, we can sit here all day and debate the gossip in the glossy mags, but the fact of the matter is I have to finish this series, and I cannot afford for anyone to get distracted. James can figure out his love life afterward."

"All right," she said. Nigel did have a point. It wasn't like they'd be filming for a year. The production would wrap up shortly and James and Annalise could figure out whether they were an item or if it was a fling.

Ugh.

None of this was her business. Aside from doing her job, Claire's biggest concern was making sure things didn't get weird between her and Luke. She just needed to keep her distance and finish the job she'd been hired to do. Although last night was very… *Stop it!*

"I'm off to get coffee. Want some?" she asked.

"There's some over there." Nigel pointed to the urn of boiling water and the jar of Nescafe sitting beside it.

"I'm from Melbourne," she said, which, in her mind, summed it all up. Having grown up in Carlton, she'd been surrounded by Italian friends who had educated her on the finer points of good coffee. And in Starlight Creek, there was only one place that came close to a decent brew.

She set off down the street to Scarlet's café, the air still cool before the heat of the day. When Claire arrived, she found the café closed.

Maybe Scarlet's alarm hadn't gone off? "Damn."

"Nice language," said a voice she recognized.

Claire spun to find James in a sweaty T-shirt and shorts.

"Have you been running?" She didn't mean to sound so surprised.

"Yes," he said, like it was his usual thing. He looked around, arms outstretched like Maria from *The Sound of Music*. "Isn't this amazing? If I'd known how beautiful this place was at this hour, I'd be up this time every day."

"I thought you were normally arriving home at this hour," she quipped, then realized she'd bought into the rumors in the glossy mags as well. Shame on her.

"I am a new me." He jutted out his chin.

"I can see. I'm pleased for you."

"This being fit thing is working. Check this out." He lifted his shirt and she caught an eyeful of a very taut six pack.

"Impressive," she said, not exactly comfortable with James showing her his body at 5:30 a.m.

"It keeps my mind off things."

"Oh?" The second she said it, she regretted it.

"I really miss Annalise."

Claire pulled her lips tight.

"What?" he asked.

"I'm going to get killed for this, but it's not anyone's business to tell you or Annalise what to do."

James rested against the telephone pole. The yellowy-orange of the rising sun shone behind him, highlighting his lanky physique, strong jawline and perfectly wavy hair that had women, and some men, gaga.

"What are you saying?" he asked.

"I'm saying that Annalise asked me to give you a letter, and I told her I couldn't. Robert Dennis saw me talking to her and he threatened to make sure the production fails."

"Bloody hell." James looked at the ground and shook his head. "He'd make an excellent father-in-law."

"Ha!" Claire stopped laughing when she caught his solemn expression. "Are you thinking about marrying her?"

"Why not?"

"But you've only just met, and your lives are so different and…I could go on for a while."

"I'm tired, Claire. I'm tired of this industry putting labels on people and expecting us to behave certain ways. I made my name being the playboy, but I'm done with it. I want a quiet life now."

"You're going to give up acting?"

He shook his head. "No way! But I'm going to lay low when I'm not doing the publicity rounds. I want to live in Ashton. With Annalise."

"Oh." She couldn't manage anything else.

"You think I'm crazy, don't you?"

"Actually, I don't. I get it." She'd enjoyed this trip to rural Queensland more than she'd expected, and it wasn't just because of one Mr. Luke Jackson. The incredible scenery of the sugarcane fields, the forests and the mountains and the possibility of a quieter life in Starlight Creek had struck a chord. It would be hard to leave. "Listen, James, I understand you wanting to be with Annalise and I really hope it works out for you—"

"It will."

She admired his unwavering self-assurance. "Though I do agree with Nigel that perhaps it would be best—"

"Nigel is in on this?"

Damn it. She should have been more careful. "Yeah, I'm sorry. I didn't know what to do. We can't risk Robert Dennis turning up and wrecking things."

"How would he do that?"

"You didn't see the fire in his eyes. He was ready to kill you with his bare hands—in front of witnesses."

"He was a bit upset, I guess."

Claire placed her hand on her hip.

"Fine," said James. "He was irate. I wouldn't blame him. If I had a daughter, I wouldn't want her with me."

"There's nothing wrong with you."

"You mean that?"

"Of course." Up until now, James had always been confident on- and off-screen, yet here he was, showing a more vulnerable side, and it had only surfaced since Ashton. "I like this new James, with the self-help books and willingness to get out and exercise. I also like this new James who seems to have discovered love."

"Yeah." He dragged the toe of his tennis shoe in the dirt. "Love's complicated."

"More than it needs to be, sometimes." She looked at her watch. *Oh shit.* "Right, I need to get back to Nigel, and you need to be on set soon. See you there."

"Hey, Claire."

"Yep?"

"Thank you," he said.

"For what?"

"For not judging me or having expectations about who I'm supposed to be. For just accepting who I am, warts and all."

"James, we all have different masks for different situations—work, home, with lovers, friends, alone. Everyone's a chameleon, whether we admit it or not."

"You're very perceptive."

"People are interesting creatures. Although I don't know if you can ever fully know someone."

"I guess that's why we're in the business we are—we get to play lots of different characters to try to unravel the mystery of what makes humans do the things we do."

"That's so true!" Wow. James really was full of surprises. She looked at her watch again. "I really need to go."

James stepped forward and wrapped his arms around her, holding her tight. The emotional warmth of his hug touched her heart, and she relaxed into his embrace.

Over his shoulder she saw a battered yellow car, with the bright blue eyes of Starlight Creek's resident artist staring at her as he drove past.

* * * *

The day went quickly as Claire rushed from one part of the set to the other. James seemed more focused than usual, and she figured it was because he was determined to wrap up and get back to his beloved Annalise. Logically, those two didn't work, but when it came to emotions, all rationality went out the window—for everyone except Claire. She'd yet to have a significant romantic relationship in her life. She'd always put it down to the nature of her job, with her traveling and working all over Australia and New Zealand. Or was there something else stopping her?

The day's shooting had finished, and Claire got to work preparing for the next day. As she did so, she kept an ear out for familiar footsteps that always came as soon as the rest of the crew had left.

Silence.

Well, they had finished early so maybe Luke was still on his way. Claire loved the baskets of Hattie's goodies she'd been receiving, though she loved the company of the delivery man more.

Claire checked the doors even though she knew they were locked. She'd developed her habit of triple-checking locks from an early age, having grown up in the crime-ridden inner city before it was trendy. The old grimy buildings of her childhood had been replaced by fashionable shops and chic cafés and pubs.

Claire shook her head. She doubted leaving anything unlocked in Starlight Creek would be an issue, but it wasn't worth the risk. You never knew who would wander through town and cause a problem.

Like Robert Dennis.

Pushing him out of her mind, she waited for Luke a little longer, then gave up and left the cinema, a tinge of disappointment surrounding her. Claire headed toward the pub where most of the cast and crew had gone to let off some steam. Through the open windows she could see Tony laughing with Camille and James, while Phil chattered intensely with a group from production. The pub staff were frantically busy behind the bar. Filming in small towns always brought money to the economy, and the townsfolk usually embraced the opportunity, which is why it had been a blow for Ashton when Robert Dennis had cancelled his contract. She wondered if the townsfolk would forgive him.

Determined to get him out of her head, Claire opted to stretch her legs and investigate the outer reaches of Starlight Creek. Before she got to the edge of town, however, she passed the news agency. Colin, the owner, was locking up.

"Good evening," Claire said cheerily.

He scowled and muttered as he shoved his keys in his trouser pocket.

"Pardon?" asked Claire.

The woman from the gift shop walked around the corner, her black curly hair perfectly in place. She clutched a large package against her chest and wore a bright smile. "Good evening, Claire! How is everything going with filming? It's so lovely to have you all in Starlight Creek."

Colin stared at her. "What are you talking about, Marcela? This town has fallen into disarray since this mob got here."

"Ridiculous," said Marcela. "This town has been falling apart for years. I don't blame the kids leaving and going to the city to study and work. Nothing ever happens here."

"That's because the kids have no respect for their parents. They don't want to get their hands dirty and do hard yakka on the land. A bunch of ungrateful and entitled swine, moving away and working in air-conditioned offices, pushing paper around a desk."

"Well, who'd want to stay in a town where grumpy old men can't be respectful to newcomers?"

"It's newcomers like these film people who plant ideas into kids' heads. They bring promises of an easy life in the big smoke. What will happen to this town if the next generation moves away? We'll be a ghost town, that's what. Forgotten. We might as well give up now."

"You just said the young people of this town have no respect and don't want to get their hands dirty." Marcela rolled her eyes. "Get a grip, Colin. The problems in Starlight Creek started long ago. Maybe if the townsfolk worked together, rather than spending all their energy arguing about trivial matters, we might bring some happiness back to this place. Lord knows it's been wallowing in the past for way too long. We need to make the town attractive—not just physically—to entice our young people back. Then we might have a future."

Claire had no idea whether she should interrupt or let the scene play out. Either way, this conversation unnerved her. It seemed Scarlet was right—Starlight Creek was a town divided.

Colin pointed a finger at her. "The sooner you lot leave, the better. Don't think we didn't hear what happened in Ashton."

"Oh." She needed to think—and quickly. "I assure you that was most unusual, and I am doing everything in my power to ensure everything runs smoothly in Starlight Creek."

"It better, because the last thing this town needs is more trouble." He stormed off, small clouds of dust swirling behind him.

Claire watched Colin disappear down a side street. This unprovoked confrontation had knocked the wind out of her.

Marcela rested her hand on Claire's arm. "Don't worry about him. He's got a chip on his shoulder the size of Mars."

"Why?"

"This town has been through so much. Farms are having a really tough time at the moment. They're earning a lot less, yet doing the same amount of work. A lot of young people don't want to continue the family tradition. They want to strike out on their own, which usually means moving away. Though it's not just that. There are townsfolk who prefer to live in the past. They think new technology or farming techniques aren't for them." Marcela adjusted the package she was holding. "There's been a push for green cane harvesting instead of traditional burning. Green cane harvesting helps with soil erosion, because the leaves and tops of the cane are left on the ground, which increases soil moisture and means they don't have to use so many nasty herbicides. It also reduces pollution. But there are stick-in-the-muds who get defensive and protest change before they know the full story."

"I know a lot of people like that."

"There are *way* too many. The thing is, though, I can't remember the last time the townsfolk got together. Hall dances died off years ago, and our lovely sense of community has disappeared. I have no idea how to get it back. Starlight Creek has bounced back so many times: from the losses during war, refusing to accept immigrants post-war...so many things, but whatever it was that pulled Starlight Creek through the hard times has vanished. And it breaks my heart."

"I'm so sorry," said Claire.

"Now, now. Don't you start feeling bad for us. Having your production here is a godsend. It's nice to have some fresh faces around. And"—she winked—"my gift shop is booming."

"I'm so glad." Claire smiled. "You have some beautiful items in there."

"Your lot have just about cleared me out. I've sold every one of my metal sculptures."

"Can't you order more from Luke? He must be pleased with the result."

"He's not making any more."

"Why not?"

"Family commitments, I believe." She looked at the ground and shook her head. "Such a shame. Such a wasted talent. Well." Marcela looked up, her demeanor changing. "Best be off and see what prints I've got to work on. I do framing on the side, you know."

"No, I didn't know, and I'll be sure to pay a visit to your shop before I go."

"Thank you, your support is much appreciated." She gave a knowing look. "It is returned tenfold, as far as I am concerned. The naysayers of this town need to move with the times and realize that change can be good."

Marcela waved goodbye and Claire continued on her way, crossing the tracks that took the trains to the sugar mill. The mill spewed out smoke, leaving a distinct stench in the air. Not pleasant, that's for sure. She doubted she'd have time to get used to it. Her time in Starlight Creek was nearly up, although a large part of her wished it wasn't.

Claire left the town behind, enjoying walking along the deserted road, sugarcane fields either side. She tried to quash her city-girl fears and not worry about rodents or reptiles attacking her. Her thoughts were irrational, but she'd been brought up in the inner city, not in the rural beauty of north Queensland.

The smell of the sugar mill now far behind, Claire reveled in the fresh air and the symphony of cicadas. Off in the distance, the river sparkled under the moon, and Claire slowed her pace, hoping her mind would do the same.

She loved this job and the opportunities it brought, but it wasn't enough. Her goals were lofty, but they weren't impossible. It was just a matter of figuring out how to get where she wanted to go—something easier said than done.

Claire kicked a stone and it skittered across the bitumen and into a fence post. She looked up.

At the top of the long driveway was a house with a red door. Beside it was a yellow car in front of a shed she knew all too well. What had her subconscious done?

Lights were on in the front rooms of the house, and she could see a bright-white glow streaming from under the shed door.

This was a bad idea. If Luke had wanted to see her tonight, he would have turned up with one of Hattie's meals. She wouldn't have cared if he turned up with a Vegemite sandwich. Delicious as Hattie's food was, it wasn't as delectable as Luke's company. For whatever reason, though, Luke had chosen not to see her.

Rolling her shoulders back, Claire marched up the driveway and knocked on the shed door.

"I'll be inside in a tick," came a muffled voice over metal banging against metal.

"It's not Hattie," she said.

The banging stopped.

"It's me, Claire."

"I'm busy."

"I just wanted to say hi." Oh no. Did she sound desperate? "Listen, I can come back another time."

"No." The shed door slid open. The bright light silhouetted Luke's body, the curve of his muscles showing through his light blue shirt. "It's all right, you're here now."

Surprised by the invitation, she followed Luke into his sanctuary. Last time she was here, he'd been quick to cover up his art and shut the door, yet now he was leading her between rows of half-finished work, sketches and colored stones and tiles scattered across work benches. Tempted to touch the shiny metal pieces, Clare shoved her hands in her pockets.

"How are you doing?" she asked.

"I'm good, thank you." Luke picked up a piece of cloth and started polishing a beautiful piece with birds and butterflies. Inlaid in the butterfly wings were turquoise and lilac stones.

"That is absolutely stunning."

"Thank you." He continued polishing.

"Luke."

Polish. Polish.

"Luke!"

He looked up. "Why are you yelling?"

"I was trying to get your attention."

He put the cloth down and rested his arms on the bench. He focused on her so intensely she grew self-conscious. "I'm sorry."

"For?"

"I'm sorry I didn't put my work down when you came in. This place is a little like white line fever."

"How so?"

He nodded toward the door. "Whenever I step across the threshold, I'm in my own world and it's all about design and art."

"It's your happy place."

He nodded.

"And you let me in? Last time I was here you practically shoved me out the door."

He cocked an eyebrow.

"Yeah," she said, "you had good reason. But why am I allowed in now?"

"You don't think you should be?"

"Yes. No. I mean, yes, I should be here." She really needed to work on her communication skills.

"The first time we met, I thought you were pushy."

"I was," she admitted.

"Regardless, the person I know now is very different."

"I'm the same person as before. Your perception of me has changed, that's all."

Luke stared at his hands lying flat on the bench. "I would like to get to know you better."

"And I'd like to do the same," said Claire.

"One thing, though."

Slowly, she said, "Yes?"

"James Lloyd."

"What about him? Oh. Oh!" She laughed. "I was counseling him this morning." She tilted her head to the side. "Are you jealous?"

"No." His voice was low.

"You don't need to be, he's just—"

"I don't entertain jealousy, it's a wasted emotion."

"Okay." *Wow.* She hadn't expected his reaction to be so...strong. "Well, even if you did entertain such a 'wasted emotion' there's no reason to be jealous. We're talking about James Lloyd here, the biggest..." She let the words fall away, remembering her conversation with James and his anxiety about labels. Casanova just didn't sit right.

"Biggest?"

"Biggest-hearted actor I know." It wasn't entirely a lie.

"I never would have guessed," he said. "So, there's no...?"

"Hanky-panky with James?" Her laugh turned into a snort. "God no! He's just a good guy who needs a friend."

"And that friend is you," he said.

"Exactly."

"Cool." Luke fiddled with a piece of wire. "I shouldn't jump to conclusions."

"Everyone does, especially about James. It's only natural that people feel the need to label people so they fit neatly into round holes. But most of us are square pegs, and don't fit neatly anywhere."

Luke studied her for a moment. "I'm not sure how that analogy works, but it does."

"I'm glad you know what I mean." Claire watched him dip a rag in liquid and start wiping down the butterflies. The metal grew shinier with each stroke. "Marcela said you weren't supplying her with any more sculptures. What are you doing with these?"

Luke put the rag down. "You were talking to Marcela about me?"

"She said she'd sold out of all the metal sculptures, and she wasn't getting any more in because you're busy with 'family commitments.'"

"She's right."

"Yet you're working on something rather breathtaking," she ventured.

"I just do these for me now, okay?" By the tone of his voice, it was far from okay. "If I had my way, I would spend all my days doing this." He rested his hand on a beautiful sculpture of a tropical fish.

"Why don't you?"

He picked up the rag and started polishing the fish. "Life doesn't work like that. I have responsibilities, and I can't discard them to follow my dreams."

"Why not?"

He stopped working and looked at her. "Imagine if everyone did that."

"The world would be a much happier place."

He kept rubbing the same spot. "I have a responsibility to my father to help out around here. He's getting old, and he needs to know that I can take over when he retires."

"Is that what you want to do?"

"It's not a matter of what I want to do; it's a matter of doing what is right, what is expected." Luke didn't look up from his work. "Too many young people are leaving for the city. This town will fall in a heap if some of us don't stay. Plus, I owe it to my dad."

"Hmm."

"You don't agree?" he asked.

"It's not exactly black and white, is it?" she said. "I believe in doing things we don't want to do, so we can appreciate it when we get the chance to do the things we love. But there has to be a balance. If we're miserable all the time, what's the point?"

"The point is that what doesn't kill you makes you stronger."

"That old line?" She laughed. "If you could do anything in the world right now, what would you do?"

"Anything?"

"Yep." She rested her hand on the bench.

"Anything at all?" He gave a lopsided smile.

"Yep." Good grief. This shed seemed to have its own little heat wave.

Luke stepped forward and placed his hand on her lower back.

Her breath caught in her throat.

Leaning in, he whispered in her ear, "Would you like me to tell you what I'd like to do?"

The shed door slid open and Claire jumped back like she was a fifteen-year-old caught behind the shelter shed.

Luke laughed. "Hi, Dad. This is Claire Montgomery, from the TV production company."

The tall, gray-haired man walked over to Claire and shook hands. His skin was rough, but the handshake was gentle.

"It's nice to meet you, Claire." If Luke's father had caught them about to get familiar, he certainly didn't let on.

"It's nice to meet you, Mr. Jackson."

"Please, call me Don."

"It's nice to meet you, Don," she said, a mixture of embarrassment and lust for Luke swirling inside her.

"Are you staying for dinner?" he asked. "Hattie's made roast."

"Oh, no, I couldn't stay. I really should be getting back," she said.

"Stay," said Luke. "Please."

"I hear you have a fan in my aunt," said Don. "I'm sure she'd love to see you."

"I'd love to see her as well," she said.

"I guess that's sorted!"

Don cast a frown at the artwork as he exited.

What now? The intimate moment had been interrupted and she had no idea how she and Luke could pick it up again. Had that chance gone forever?

Luke reached for her hand and winked. "I promise to tell you later what I would like to do."

Chapter Eighteen

1994 – Starlight Creek, Queensland

Luke led Claire out the door and toward his house, her hand still firmly in his. For someone who never had a problem striking up a conversation, words had finally escaped her. What was it about Luke that made her want to be with him every spare second she had?

It was all so pointless though. She'd be back in Melbourne again soon, looking for more work and jumping on a plane to who-knows-where for the next contract.

The wire door creaked open and Hattie came out and hurried down the stairs. Her energy defied her years. "It's so lovely to see you, Claire!"

Luke dropped Claire's hand and Hattie gave her a firm hug.

"Thank you so much for the meals you've been sending me," said Claire. "It's so nice to have home-cooked food."

"It is my pleasure, lovely lass." Hattie linked her arm with Claire's and they climbed the steps. "I hope you're hungry."

"I most definitely am."

They entered the house and walked down the long hallway. On both sides hung framed photos, black-and-white and sepia in color. As a location scout, Claire was used to noticing details in a glance, and as they traveled the length of the hall she took in images of multiple generations. One particular image, of a young woman with a 1970s hairstyle, crocheted cardigan and flared pants, caught her eye. Her head was tilted back and her mouth was open like the person behind the camera had told the funniest joke on earth.

"She's beautiful." Claire stopped and stared at the photo.

"Yes, she is," Hattie said.

There was something quite mesmerizing about this woman, and Claire wanted to know more. But Hattie's wistful tone and the way she gently urged Claire forward told her asking questions would be a mistake.

They reached the kitchen, where Don was already at the table, newspaper on his lap.

"Mmm, it smells amazing," said Claire. "Can I help?"

"No, no, it's all under control. Besides, I already have a helper." She nodded toward Luke, who was setting an extra place at the table.

"I really hope I'm not imposing."

"Not at all," said Hattie, motioning for Claire to sit.

On a large serving plate, Hattie piled peas, carrots, roast potatoes, pumpkin and a delicious-looking chicken. She poured gravy into a delicate bone china boat and Luke carried the plate over to the table, then sat opposite Claire. She averted her eyes, her heart still pounding from their near-kiss.

"Please, help yourself," said Hattie.

Claire dished small servings of everything on her plate and Luke, Hattie and Don went with generous sizes. The atmosphere wasn't formal, but she couldn't quite relax. It had been so long since she'd sat down for a family dinner. With her brothers working long hours and her semiretired parents traveling so often, months would go by before any of them got together for a family meal. Now, sitting with Luke and his dad and great-aunt, Claire realized how much she missed gatherings like this.

"Wine?" Don opened a bottle and filled Claire's glass.

She took a sip, enjoying the crispy, fruity flavors. "This is lovely."

"Great year," said Don, tucking into his meal. "Thanks for the dinner, Aunt Hattie."

"It's the least I can do for letting me stay. Now, Claire dear, how is it all going?"

"It's going wonderfully." She wasn't sure if Hattie meant the movie, or whether her cinema was being looked after. "You should come down and have a look some time. I'm sure they'd love to meet you, and I can show you what it's like on set."

"Thank you, but I don't want to get in the way. It's better they get everything filmed, then I can move back. I do miss the place."

"I can imagine," said Claire. "Although it's rather gorgeous here. How long have you lived on the farm, Don?"

"This farm's been in the family for four generations. Five once Luke takes over."

She didn't dare look at Luke.

Don continued. "Farming is in the Jackson blood. It's not easy, but it's what we Jackson men do. We've weathered some tough times, but that's the way it is." He slapped Luke on the back. "And with my helper here, we can get through anything."

Luke's smile was almost a grimace. Don seemed oblivious.

"So, Claire." Don cut a roast potato. "How long are you in town?"

"Until the end of filming, which is fairly soon."

"What's next?" he asked.

"I'm not entirely sure, but something will pop up."

"This isn't a permanent job?" asked Don.

"Dad, she doesn't need to be interrogated," said Luke.

"It's fine," she said. "It's permanent in that I usually have back-to-back work. Each project is different, and I get used to moving around to where the jobs are."

"You don't have a home?"

"I do, in Melbourne, but I'm rarely there. My friend rents from me, and when I'm in town I sleep in the spare bedroom." Luke was right, it did feel a little like an interrogation. Then again, she liked that Don was interested enough to ask questions.

"I couldn't imagine a transient life like that," said Don. "How do you expect to hold down a relationship? Have a family?"

"Donald!" said Hattie. "Leave the poor girl alone."

"Sorry." Don hung his head like he was in the principal's office. "I'm a bit of a traditionalist."

"A bit?" laughed Luke. "You would have been at home in the fifties, when women were tied to the kitchen sink."

"Now that's enough!" Hattie angled a finger at both men. "Claire did not come here to listen to you two carry on. Let's finish dinner in peace, and if you boys behave there might be dessert." She winked at Claire. "I may not have been a mother, but I know how to keep these two ratbags in line."

"It's a next-to-impossible task, I'm figuring," said Claire.

Luke and Don sniggered like naughty schoolboys and Hattie gave a dramatic sigh.

When everyone was finished, Claire offered to clear the plates.

"No, no," said Hattie. "The boys can do it. You and I can go outside and enjoy the fresh air."

Claire followed Hattie onto the veranda and sat next to her on the swing seat. The moon was high in the inky sky and the frogs sounded like they were right underneath them.

"I'm so glad you came by," said Hattie.

"So am I."

"That woman in the photo back there." Hattie cocked her head in the direction of the hallway. "That was Luke's mother."

"What happened...?" Claire stopped. "Sorry, it's none of my business."

"It's all right, really." Hattie patted Claire's hand. "You'd think after eighteen years it would get easier."

"Eighteen years?"

"Luke was only twelve when he lost her, the poor love. Most of the family had moved away from Starlight Creek by then, and it was only me and Don left to raise him."

"That's why you two are so close."

Hattie nodded. "I never thought I'd be a mother, but losing Stephanie allowed me that chance." She straightened her back. "I would have given all that up to have Stephanie with us, of course."

"Of course," said Claire. "Is Luke an only child?"

"No. Yes. Oh dear, it's so complicated."

"It's okay if you don't want to talk about it."

"No, no, it's good to get this out. Grief can't hold our hearts prisoner forever. It doesn't do anyone any good. Believe me, you don't get to this age and not experience the pain of losing someone you love." Hattie stared into the distance. "We have two choices—let the heartbreak suck us under the dark waves and drown us, or find a way to ride those waves and keep our heads above water, faces to the sun, our hearts remembering but not weighing us down."

"I can't even imagine how difficult it would have been for all of you," Claire said.

"You've never lost anyone?"

"No," said Claire. "I've been blessed."

"You have indeed, my lass. I hope you don't go through something so tragic for a long time." Hattie clasped her hands on her lap.

"I hope you don't mind me asking." Claire was tentative. "But what did you mean by it's complicated about Luke having a sibling?"

Hattie turned her head toward the screen door. The sounds of Luke and his dad chattering and washing dishes echoed down the hall.

Hattie whispered, "Stephanie had complications during childbirth. When Luke's little brother was born, he was very sick. We lost Stephanie, then a few days later we lost Scott."

Hot tears welled in Claire's eyes. She tried to swallow, but a huge lump had formed in her throat.

"It was a terrible, terrible time. After Luke was born, Don and Stephanie had trouble conceiving. In fact, they'd given up hope. Then out of the blue, almost eleven years later, Stephanie fell pregnant. You can imagine the joy everyone felt."

"Absolutely."

"The pregnancy had gone perfectly, the baby seemed to be thriving in the womb but, as we now know, nature isn't always predictable. So when she went into labor early, we were all surprised and totally unprepared."

"Oh no."

"Emergency medical treatment in Starlight Creek was a bit more rustic in the seventies. The doctor did what he could but…"

"I am so sorry," said Claire. "Though saying that just feels so inadequate."

"It was very hard to tell an excited twelve-year-old that he'd not only lost his little brother, but his mother as well."

Claire gulped back a sob. "I just don't know what to say."

"No one does, not even now. And it breaks my heart to see Luke and his father butting heads."

"They fight a lot? It looks like they get on reasonably well."

"Yes and no." Hattie looked around, like she expected someone to be hiding in the bushes. "Maybe I'm speaking out of turn, but I can see you and Luke have a thing for each other."

"We haven't known each other for long and—"

"Time has nothing to do with how we feel about someone. Sometimes you can meet a person and just know. You're a good influence on him. He's been a lot happier since you arrived."

"He practically yelled at me when we first met."

"He was just being protective of his old aunt."

The more she spoke to Hattie, the more the pieces of Luke's puzzle fit together—she hadn't realized it was so complicated.

Hattie smoothed down her skirt. "The thing is, Luke inherited his mother's artistic talents. His heart isn't in farming."

"Ah, so because Luke is the only child, Don wants—*needs*—his son to follow in his footsteps. Otherwise the sugarcane farm that's been in the family for generations will be no more," said Claire.

"Exactly."

"That's a tough spot to be in."

"For Luke, yes, but Don can't see the pressure he's putting on his son. Luke loves his father, and wouldn't do anything to hurt him."

"So he works on the farm and makes art on the side, instead of pursuing it full time."

"The art drives a wedge between them. His mother was a clay sculptor," Hattie whispered. "Seeing Luke's artistic talents reminds Don of Stephanie. He's never gotten over losing her."

Claire studied the mountains in the distance. No wonder Luke thought it impractical and self-indulgent to pursue one's dreams.

The door creaked open and Luke appeared with two mugs of tea. "A late evening refreshment for the ladies."

He passed Hattie a mug, then one to Claire.

"Thank you," she said, heartbroken with the knowledge of what Luke and his family had been through. How could she look at him now without showing her emotions? Claire had to process it all while Luke leaned innocently against the railing of the veranda.

All she wanted was to hold him in her arms.

Chapter Nineteen

1952 – Hollywood

On the empty sound stage, Lena collapsed on a folding chair in a dark corner. Now that everyone had left, the time to reflect gave her a sense of closure for the day and helped her prepare for the next one. Today's shoot had finally come together. Lena hadn't messed up her lines or tripped over air while dancing, and she'd managed not to break into a sweat whenever Pierre touched her. Anna May and all of the chorus girls had done beautiful work, and it was a joy to hear the voices come together and accompany Lena and Pierre on their duet.

She kicked off the yellow heels and wished someone would come to her rescue and carry her back to the dressing room.

Lena slapped her forehead. She was becoming the helpless heroines she depicted on-screen.

"Do you always smack yourself in the face?" Pierre sat on the chair next to her.

"Do you always sit down uninvited?"

"Touché." He put his hands behind his head. "Looks like we're getting closer to being Hollywood's hottest couple."

Lena looked away. She needed quiet time, but apparently Pierre had other ideas.

"Jeanne Harris and Reeves Garrity are the hottest couple," said Lena. "Anyway, it's not a competition."

"It is, according to the magazines *and* moviegoers. Why do you think Stuart Cooper keeps pushing our couple status?"

"I wish he wouldn't." Lena slid her feet back into the shoes. "It's all stupid."

"What?" Pierre looked incredulous.

"I seriously don't think us being a couple off-screen gets more people interested in us or our movies."

"My fans would say otherwise."

"How can all this be healthy, though? Men—and women—can be very successful without being tied to someone else."

Pierre let out a loud laugh and doubled over, clutching his side. "Oh, Lena. You do amuse me."

Tension gripped her shoulders and raced up her neck. "I am not here to amuse. I am voicing my concern that a woman is not considered successful in this industry unless she is attached to a man off-screen. Why are women seen as threats if they don't have a husband? Or, worse, people think there's something wrong with them, so no one will marry them."

Pierre snort-laughed then stopped. "You're serious? Happily married couples on-screen, happily married couples off-screen; this is how they want it. Good little Americans living the dream. You don't want to be responsible for tearing the fabric of our society, do you?"

Lena didn't answer.

"Anyway," he said, "I don't see what you're complaining about. You get paid plenty."

"Nowhere near as much as you," she grumbled.

Pierre shrugged and her annoyance grew. Turning to face him, she said, "I'd like to see how you'd feel if the shoe were on the other foot."

"Men will always earn more, and women will always be the sexy attractions."

"But why? Change can be good, you know."

"Yeah, yeah." Pierre crossed one leg over the other. "Well, changes are afoot."

"For women?"

"Ha! No." He lowered his voice, his eyes not leaving hers. "Just wait and see."

"What the hell does that mean?"

Pierre tut-tutted. "Such terrible language coming from those luscious lips."

Lena's tolerance level for Pierre plummeted dramatically. "Why do I have to wait and see?"

"It means what it means. No one is ever secure. Remember that."

She narrowed her eyes. "What are you angling at?"

"Nothing. You really should get off your high horse about women being paid equally. It's never going to happen."

Lena stood, hands by her sides, fists clenching so hard she could feel her nails digging into her palms. She stormed toward the stage door, then turned and glared at Pierre. "There is so much wrong with this industry, and it all begins with people like you."

* * * *

After her argument with Pierre, Lena had gone home and straight to bed. Her entire body ached from the long day, and her problems felt like they were weighing her down. The only way to fix this drained feeling was to sleep, but that had been as distant as the moon. She'd tossed. She'd turned. She'd cursed Pierre. Cursed the Hays Code, Hollywood, society... the list grew as the hours dragged on.

Hoping to get her mind off things, she dragged herself out of bed even though it was already mid-morning. Rubbing her eyes, Lena went to the bathroom, happy to finally have her first full-day break in months—no filming and no interviews. It was nice to get away from the journalists, who were never pleased about the studio's publicist giving strict instructions about what they could ask. Her publicist supplied interviewers with a list of questions from which they could choose. No deviation allowed. Some tried, of course, but Lena intended to keep her private life just that— private. Well, apart from her entanglement with Pierre. She had to give them something, and in the grand scheme of things, a romance with Pierre was the perfect trade-off. Focusing on her current love life left little room for her past to surface.

Dotty's and Charlie's faces flashed before her. Memories of shared happiness and the anticipation of unknown adventures twisted into fear and apprehension. Everything had changed so quickly. Lena clutched her stomach.

Refusing to let mistakes of the past dictate the present, Lena dressed in a casual light gray pantsuit and dark green wedge heels. A few minutes later she was in the car, traveling east toward Roy's Diner. If she didn't get a move on, she'd find a disgruntled George, who had no tolerance for tardiness—something she wished she could change but her life these days was filled to the brim; even on her days off there was always someone wanting something. At least all George wanted was company, and she was more than happy to oblige.

Lena parked on a side street and walked into the diner. The tinkle of the bell above the door reminded her of when she'd first entered this place

three years ago, alone and destitute. Amazing how things had changed in
what seemed a heartbeat.

"Well, well, well! What a sight for sore eyes!" Meryl bustled over and
Lena relaxed into her arms, realizing how much she missed this embrace.
Meryl pulled back and lightly pinched Lena's cheeks. "My goodness, there
is nothing of you! Come on." She led Lena to her once-regular booth. "I'll
make your favorite."

"Thanks, Meryl." Lena shuffled to the far side of the booth, happy to
be back in the only place she ever felt at home. "It's been too long."

"That it has. And I wanted to thank you for the tickets to your premiere.
Roy and I had a wonderful time. I felt like the queen!" Meryl fanned herself
like a royal. "I tried to say hello, but you were surrounded."

"I'm sorry about that. Premieres are crazy. Actually, the next few weeks
are. Today is my only day off, and I had to negotiate really hard for it."

"You deserve some rest, darling girl. And a banana milkshake. What
else?"

"I'm not really hungry."

Meryl's pencil hovered above her notepad.

"Really, I don't want anything else. Besides, I'm waiting for George."

"You got here before him?"

"I know!" Lena laughed. "A first time for everything!"

"Indeed. How about I get you a little something to tide you over until
he arrives?"

"Sure. Thank you," said Lena, aware that "No thank you" was not an
option.

Meryl went over to the counter and spoke to Roy, who was slaving over
the hot grill, as usual.

Lena rested against the padded seat and looked around the diner. The
lace curtains still framed the large windows adorned with a painted sign
boasting "The best fries and shakes on the block," which always made Lena
laugh, as the closest diner was six streets away. Bob from the hardware
store down the road sat at his usual table, his head buried in the betting
guide. Edith and Myrtle, the very sweet spinsters, were in their regular
corner, nursing a pot of tea that would have them sitting there for hours
as they gossiped about the clientele. The decor remained the same, with
orange salt and pepper shakers on the green Formica tables that were more
scratched than the last time she'd been here. The aroma of frying onions,
freshly brewed coffee and baked bread filled the air, and Lena inhaled
slowly, enjoying the smell of home.

Home.

A twinge of nostalgia threatened to spoil her mood and she refused to give in to it. Instead, she concentrated on the clock above the door and predicted how long it would take for George to turn up and how much glee she'd get from giving him a tongue-in-cheek lecture about tardiness.

Meryl arrived with the milkshake and a large plate of fries and pickles.

"Now, eat up. Don't they feed you at the studio?"

"I rarely have time to eat." Her stomach grumbled.

"Now you have no excuse. Enjoy!" Meryl left before Lena could protest.

She stared at the food and shake in front of her. When was the last time she had eaten something she wanted? Something that wasn't water-based, like celery or carrots? Lena picked up a fry and used it to push the others around the plate. Just being near them made her skin feel like it was coated in grease. But they smelled so good.

Lena quickly shoved the fry in her mouth, closed her eyes and chewed slowly, allowing the salty goodness to dance across her taste buds. Never in her life had a fry tasted so delicious. Opening her eyes, she stared at her plate, the willpower she'd been cultivating since working with Henry falling by the wayside. In her head she could hear Henry chastising her about the potential size of her derriere if she ate such food. And he'd be telling her this while stuffing his face with a burger.

Her gaze rested on the milkshake, and the image of Yvonne struggling to get the zipper up on Lena's latest gown crowded in on her. As much as she wanted this comfort food, she couldn't do it. Her career depended on it. Though it unsettled her that Meryl would be offended. Maybe if Lena had a few bites, then walked around the block a few hundred times...

Taking a bite of another fry, Lena savored the flavor.

Just one more.

Maybe another.

And another.

Or two.

Before she knew it, her plate was empty, and so was the milkshake glass.

Lena quickly looked around, but no one had paid attention—except for Meryl, who sauntered over and cleared the plates.

"How was it?"

"Good?" A pain in the center of her chest made her want to burp. "Actually, it was delicious."

"I'm glad to hear it." She piled the plates onto one arm, looked at the door and then back at Lena. "Still no George? Has he forgotten?"

"His memory is better than an elephant's. He remembered my agent's birthday, and they've only met once!"

"Hmm. Odd of him not to show."

"Yep." Lena's stomach felt like it was touching the edge of the table. She needed to lie down, but a long walk would be first on the agenda. And she knew just the place. Lena placed money on the table. "If George does turn up, can you let him know I was here, please? And get him to call me?"

"Sure thing, honey." Meryl put a pencil behind her ear and glanced at the table. "Lena, that's too much money."

"Gotta go! Bye!" She raced out the door. The generous tip was the least she could do for Meryl, who had always been there for her. Since her success, Lena had tried to give Meryl presents but she always refused, so it had surprised her when Meryl and her husband Roy finally accepted an invitation to Lena's opening night. Perhaps her persistence had paid off.

Adjusting her large hat to cover her face, Lena strolled down the street and tried to swat away the niggling voice in her head. Pierre happily ate what he wanted and no one criticized him. She was expected to have a tiny waist and slender legs, yet possess curvy buttocks and an ample bosom. Unfortunately, Mother Nature had designed it so that most women lost weight from their bust first. And who was Lena to argue with nature?

Ugh.

Hollywood could be so hypocritical.

Although the wedge heels were not designed for walking, Lena found herself covering quite a few blocks in a short time. The fresh air filled her lungs. She felt…free. Free from the watchful eyes of her bosses, other cast members, the crew. Right now, she was a normal person taking a Sunday stroll.

A couple with a small dog on a leash walked toward Lena and she kept her head down. Glancing behind her, Lena saw the couple had stopped to stare.

The woman shoved the leash at her husband and rushed over. "Lena Lee? Wow. You are so beautiful!" She looked around. "Are you filming around here?"

"No, just taking a walk."

"Oh?" The woman's eyes widened. "I never expected to see you in my neighborhood!"

Lena smiled.

"Can I just say, I loved you in *Parisian Dreams*. Actually, I love all your movies. You and Pierre Montreaux are perfect together! Tell me, is he as handsome off-screen as he is on?"

"Deidre, leave the poor woman alone." The husband arrived at his wife's side. "I'm sure she's got better things to do."

"No, it's fine," Lena lied. Even on a Sunday she couldn't take time off the professional clock.

The woman opened her handbag and searched inside. She pulled out a small notebook and a pen and thrust it at Lena. "Would you mind?"

"Of course not." Lena wrote a message to Deidre, signed it then handed it back.

"Thank you!" she squealed and clutched the notebook to her chest. Turning to her husband, she said, "Just wait until Clarissa hears about this!"

Her husband rolled his eyes. "I'm sorry for my wife's, uh, enthusiasm."

"It's all right, really."

"Come on, darling, let's leave Miss Lee to enjoy her walk in peace." The husband grabbed his wife's arm and they took off in the opposite direction.

Lena found herself smiling at the couple. How nice and uncomplicated their life must be.

She sighed.

She arrived at her car, got in and settled against the leather seat. She'd have been more than happy to get a secondhand vehicle, but the studio had insisted on giving her a brand new dark green Buick. She was used to tractors and rusting cars on the family farm, so driving the Buick never got old. She loved getting behind the wheel and navigating her way through Los Angeles. She appreciated a vehicle of this caliber, with its shiny exterior and immaculate interior. Lena often found herself peering under the hood, admiring the grand engineering that was so totally different from the farming machine engines that she'd learned to fix with odds and ends lying around the shed. She missed getting her hands greasy, but she certainly didn't miss her father telling her off for not "acting like a lady."

Lena reversed the car out of the spot, checking the rearview mirror. A red Nash-Healey sports car zipped behind her and she slammed on the brakes.

"Jesus!" Lena got out and stormed to the sports car, which had come to a sudden stop. The driver's face was obscured by the peak of his cap. She stood with one hand on her hip. "You are aware these roads are not part of a Formula One race?"

When he smiled, heat rushed across her face.

"You are aware vehicles have mirrors?" came the deep voice she didn't hear often enough.

"I'll have you know I checked my mirror."

"They are not there just for checking your lipstick."

If anyone else had said this, she would have taken offense, but she couldn't with Reeves. "Yes, well…maybe you need to slow down a little."

"I am more than capable of going slow, when it is required." His voice was almost a low growl.

Lena twisted her gloves in her hands and looked everywhere but at him. "It appears you have mastered the art of the double entendre."

"Maybe." His gorgeous lips lifted into his trademark smile.

Lena cursed her racing heart and went straight into acting mode, forcing herself to feign nonchalance. "Could you please move your vehicle?"

"What are you doing now?"

"Going home."

"Take a detour."

"Don't you have somewhere to be? Obviously you were in a hurry," she said.

"It can wait. Besides, I'd much rather have your company."

"Shouldn't you be with Jeanne? How's the romance?" She hated that kernel of jealousy.

"I think it would be safer if we left that subject alone." He got out and crossed his arms as he rested against the vehicle. "Why don't we talk about us?"

"There's no us," she said.

"Don't tell me you haven't thought about that moment in the parking lot all those months ago."

Lena chewed her lip, trying to get her thoughts straight. "Fine, there's unfinished business, and we need to talk about it."

"I would really like that." He looked around at the handful of people out walking their dogs or pushing children in strollers. "Perhaps somewhere less public?"

"How about we go to Cavendish Park?"

"I've no idea where that is," he said.

"Follow me."

Reeves patted the hood of his car. "What if we go for a spin in this shiny beast?"

"Sports cars don't impress me."

He gave a lopsided smile. "Then I have my work cut out."

"Yes, you do." Lena went to the passenger side, and Reeves ran around quickly to open the door. When she got in, she shifted on the seat so her skirt covered her knees, then reached into her handbag for the scarf she always kept handy—a habit she'd learned from Dotty. Her body tensed.

"Are you all right?" Reeves gave her a side glance as he gunned the engine and took off at a cracking speed.

"I'm fine!" she yelled above the mechanical roar while she hastily tied the scarf under her chin and tucked in the stray hair strands.

Instead of wallowing in things she couldn't change, Lena concentrated on guiding Reeves to the park. He took corners at an alarming speed, the car tilting in a way that had her holding her breath and gripping the sides of the seat. He zoomed between cars, the streets a blur.

"Slow down, Reeves!"

"You don't like it?" He gripped the steering wheel tightly as they veered into the lane next to them, narrowly missing a slow-moving truck.

"No!" she yelled, but he'd already slowed to a more respectable speed and her voice was louder than it needed to be.

"Sorry," he said.

"I'm not a fan of risking my life."

"I would never put you in danger."

"It felt like you were pushing us right to the edge."

Reeves concentrated on the road ahead, the vehicle purring happily. "I'm really sorry, Lena."

She pointed for him to turn a corner and they meandered down a quiet street lined with towering evergreens that formed a natural arch. The paths leading into the park were cobblestone, something rarely seen in LA, and a wall of various shades of green formed a natural fence at the edge of the park.

"Here?" Reeves nodded toward an empty parking space.

"Sure."

He maneuvered the car into the small spot, and when they stopped he held up his hand, then went around to the passenger side. Reeves pressed the button on the handle, but it didn't budge. Peering over the side of the door, she tried not to smile while Reeves wrestled with the lock and handle.

"Here, let me." She reached over and pressed the button, closing her eyes as she did so. Lena tuned in to the door's mechanism, sensing a slight jamming at the left side of the button. She took her nail file from her handbag and kneeled on her seat so she could get at the right angle. Inserting the pointy end of the file, she put pressure in the right spot, and a moment later the button popped out.

"What? How?" Reeves stood on the curb scratching his head. He lunged forward and opened the door. "Mademoiselle."

"Why thank you, kind sir." Lena placed her hand in Reeves's and plastered a smile on her trembling lips. She stepped onto the footpath and immediately withdrew her hand from his.

"That was impressive. You are definitely full of surprises, Miss Lee," Reeves said as they strolled toward the entrance of the park.

"I don't like being predictable."

His gentle laugh echoed off the trees. "You are far from predictable."

They meandered along the winding paths, a canopy of green above, rows of white lilies and purple sage beside the path. Silence enveloped them, and Lena snuck glances at her companion at every possible moment. Who was she? A teenager?

Breaking out of the lush tunnel, they arrived at a small square with a fountain in the middle. Water trickled down the intricately carved centerpiece as tiger-striped butterflies hovered above. Lena sat on the wrought iron seat and motioned for Reeves to do the same. He sat a comfortable distance away. That act alone warmed her heart.

Reeves looked around, his eyes wide. "This place is magnificent."

"It's my sanctuary away from the hustle and bustle of this crazy town."

A finch flew into the courtyard and perched on the fountain. The bird drank slowly, flapped its wings then flew up to the canopy and disappeared.

"The perfect place not to be recognized," said Reeves.

"Yes." Lena crossed her legs at the ankles.

He turned to face her. "How are you doing?"

"I'm good."

He tilted his head, his eyes not leaving hers. "How are you really doing?"

She gave a nervous laugh. "Truly, I'm good."

"You look tired."

"Well, yes, there's that."

Reeves regarded her for so long that she grew nervous. She concentrated on the purse on her lap.

"We work long hours," he said. "We're always in the public eye, and there's the constant threat of someone newer, younger, coming along and taking our roles. We spend more hours criticizing ourselves in the mirror than having meaningful conversations with people we enjoy." Reeves paused. "So Lena, I would really like to know how you are coping with everything." He took a deep breath, his gaze resting on the fountain. "I'm afraid to admit it, but there are days when I can't handle being under the glittery microscope."

Lena stared at Reeves, admiring his willingness to impart such personal information.

"Lena?"

She jerked, as if being pulled out of reverie. "Sorry! Sorry...I..."

"No, I'm sorry. We don't really know each other well, yet here I am, expecting you to tell me your deepest, darkest secrets." He shook his head and laughed. "See? This is what happens. I've watched every one of your movies—countless times—and I feel like I know you, but really all I know about you is what I've learned the few times we've seen each other—and what I see of you on the screen."

"The screen is all lies."

He paused, as if deciding what he should say next. "I've missed you."

She held her breath. "We can't do this."

Reeves stared at her with his dark eyes and she wanted nothing more than to kiss his lips and be held by his strong arms.

A couple of birds flew into view and landed on the side of the fountain.

"Look," they said in unison, their laughter creating a perfect harmony.

"You first," said Reeves.

"This is an impossible situation."

"I understand, although…" He shook his head. "Yes, it might be best if we find something else to talk about. Something that isn't about Hollywood."

"Anything?"

"Yes."

"How about…" Her voice trailed off as she grappled to find something that wasn't work related. "I can't think of anything."

"That's exactly what I mean! Work is our lives. We live and breathe it. It gets under our skin, invades our brain until we can't think of anything else to talk about."

"Oh." Lena slumped against the park bench. "That's rather depressing."

"It is."

"I always knew I had to give it my all, but now I'm starting to realize I've given everything." She ran her fingers through her loose curls. "How could I not have realized?"

"We all get caught up in this world. It's like a boa constrictor: once we're in, it coils slowly around us and wraps tightly until we're unable to breathe."

"And we die a slow and horrible death." She placed the back of her hand on her forehead and pretended to faint. Lena looked up at a grinning Reeves.

"We do like our drama."

"We do indeed. So…if we're not talking about movie-making, what will we talk about?" she asked.

"Well, I, for one, would like to know more about you—where you come from, what dreams you had when you were a child, what your family is like. I'm not sure how, but you've managed to keep all that under wraps."

Lena shifted on the seat, the wooden slats suddenly uncomfortable. She stared at the fountain, concentrating on one particular stream of water that had diverted from the steady flow.

"Lena?"

"That's boring," she said quickly.

"It's far from boring. I want to get to know you."

"Why? People only ever pay attention to my looks or what my status at the studio could do for their careers," she said, genuinely perplexed.

"In case you haven't noticed, Miss Lee, I have a great interest in you—in *you* as a person, not your career."

His eyes met hers and a desire to open up and tell him everything overcame her. She wanted him to know about what she'd endured when she was with Charlie Parker and how it skewed her view on relationships. She wanted to tell him about the heartbreaking way she and Dotty had ended their friendship and the reason she couldn't return to her hometown...but the wall she'd spent years building shot up once more. Reeves Garrity had to stay on the other side; it was the only way she could protect herself, protect her sanity.

Lena looked at her watch and stood. "I have to go."

Chapter Twenty

Reeves casually draped his arm over the back of the park bench. "You weren't in a hurry a few minutes ago."

"A lady can't change her mind?" Lena kept her tone light, even though a sudden weight had landed on her shoulders.

"I guess." He tilted his head to the side. "Please don't leave just yet."

Stay? Go? Both actions had implications. "I'll stay for a little longer *if* you tell me about you."

"Ha! You are an excellent negotiator." His warm laugh caressed her. "My upbringing was very straightforward. Born and raised in Santa Monica. Parents of Italian heritage—"

"Hence the tall, dark and handsome," she said, then felt embarrassed.

Reeves winked, and her skin prickled with heat—again. "Thank you for saying so. I'm not so naive; I know the main reason I'm Jeanne's leading man is because of my looks. In this industry we have to take what we can get. Though I like to think that I have proven myself a quality actor by now."

"I believe you have. You were amazing in your last role."

"You've been following my career?" He sounded surprised.

"Of course I have! I like being able to say, 'I knew him when.'"

Reeves laughed. "And I can say the same about you, too."

"You haven't finished telling me about you." She really needed to get the attention away from herself.

"I have a younger sister who has a brilliant brain but, unfortunately, is limited in what she can do for work."

"Women should be able to do anything they want." The conviction in her tone challenged him to say otherwise.

"I agree." He nodded. "And I tell her this all the time, but the world lacks role models for young women."

"What about Amelia Earhart? Hedy Lamarr? Madame Curie? Even Cleopatra!"

"Of course! Those women are inspirational. I'm sure there are plenty more just like them, but we don't hear about them often enough."

"You surprise me," she said.

"I do?"

"Here's a man who has the world at his feet, who can do anything, yet you're worrying about young women not having enough role models."

Reeves grinned. "What can I say?"

"Well, I can say thank you for not sticking your head in the sand. This world, especially Hollywood, doesn't give women enough credit for our intelligence."

"They are wrong."

"Yes, they are." She looked down and gave a half smile.

"What's funny?"

"Nothing's funny. I was just thinking that I rarely have these conversations. Pierre isn't exactly known for talking about anything or anyone other than himself."

"The same can be said of Jeanne." Reeves shifted a fraction closer to her. "I really want to get to know you, Lena, but you seem to make it impossible."

"No, I don't."

He wrapped his fingers around hers and she found herself buzzing from his touch. She knew she should pull away, but his warm, smooth skin made it impossible to resist.

He said quietly, "We've spent too long avoiding each other. Do you know how hard it's been to see you on the other side of the room, looking so divinely elegant? Do you know how hard it was not to go over and kiss your beautiful lips? Hold you in my arms?"

"Stop it. Please." She turned away.

"A day hasn't gone by that I haven't thought of you."

Lena faced him, and the moment their eyes met her resolve melted like ice cream on a hot summer's day. "I've thought about you every day as well. And...I need you to be honest with me."

"I promise."

"What is the real situation with you and Jeanne? Is it like me and Pierre?"

"It wasn't to begin with."

"Pardon?"

Reeves ran the palms of his hands down his thighs and rested his hands on his knees. "Initially, I fell for Jeanne. How could I not? She's beautiful, powerful. She commands attention when she walks into the room and her charisma on-screen..." He held up his hand and cleared his throat. "I'm digressing. The thing is, I was very green when I first started out, and when someone as influential as Jeanne picks you out of hundreds of budding actors, it's hard not to be in awe." He lowered his head, and a small laugh escaped his lips. "There goes my manliness."

"Getting sucked into someone's web doesn't make you less manly. Jeanne's charisma is strong enough to hypnotize anyone."

"I feel like a fool." He looked up, his eyes locking on hers. "She made me believe I was special, that I was one in a million. It felt like I was for the first little while but..." He shrugged. "I can see it was all a ruse to get me to do her dirty work. I was nothing but a whipping boy, and as soon as I realized it and started questioning her motives, I received flak—and lots of it."

"Was this around the time we, you know...kissed?"

"Just before. I'd had enough of her demands, and I wanted to break free."

"So you kissed me to get back at her?" The muscles in Lena's shoulders tensed.

"No!" His defensive tone rang through the air. "Far from it! I really like you. I want to spend more time with you, get to know you better."

Lena stared at the fountain, unsure how to react. If she'd first met Reeves under different circumstances...

He said, "I'm 'with' her for the sake of our careers, but I've told her countless times we are not an item behind closed doors. However, she refuses to believe that's the case."

"Jeanne has a habit of believing what she wants," said Lena. "This is such a crazy industry."

"Absolutely."

"And here I am pretending to date my leading man because that gives me more space in magazines and sells more tickets at the box office. Sometimes it really gets to me, this lie. It makes me feel like a snake-oil salesman."

"People believe what they want. Some probably do see through it, but they prefer to believe lies."

"Why are they so interested in what happens to actors and actresses outside the movies? Why is it so important for stars to have so-called perfect lives? Why can't we show we're human?"

"I have no idea." Reeves shrugged.

"Maybe it's because in movies we take them out of their own world, but it only lasts a couple of hours. Perhaps thinking stars have passionate love affairs off-screen builds their own hopes for a happy ever after."

"I've never thought of it that way, but now you mention it..." He shook his head. "What kind of world are we living in where people willingly buy into totally unrealistic fairy tales? What's wrong with the ups and downs of real life?"

"Sometimes real life is too painful. Movies and books and music can transport people, change their emotions, soothe their hurts, trigger memories of happier times or give them hope that their luck will change. That's not a bad thing."

"So, we're the happiness makers?" he asked.

"You could say that. Our job is to connect with people and their emotions, to entertain, to inspire. The trade-off is that we have to sacrifice some of our own happiness and freedom in order to do it."

"Sometimes I wonder if it's all worth it."

"Look at your car," she said.

"Pardon?"

"You have a gorgeous sports car that you never would have been able to afford two years ago."

"True."

"And you get to enjoy it whenever you want. I imagine you have a very nice house as well."

"I do. Though possessions aren't everything, Lena."

"No, they're not, but we have security. We can eat at expensive restaurants. We can pay our bills. We get to go to work every day and do something that makes us happy. How many people get to do that? This job is a privilege."

"It can be a ball and chain."

"Leave, then," she said.

"What?"

"Leave the industry if it's too much. Believe me, there have been days when I wanted to walk out of those studio gates, never to return. Maybe I'd give it all up if I had something better, but I don't." Lena bit her lip, chastising herself for being so uninhibited with her words.

"What would you do if you didn't act?"

"I have no idea." Her days of swimsuit modeling were firmly over, and she couldn't imagine ever returning to rural life. "The thing is, this job is all I have. If I have to fake a relationship with Pierre Montreaux to allow me the success I've worked so very hard for, then that's the price I pay."

"What about the chance at real love?"

"I've tried. It didn't work." Diving into that hole would only cause long-buried heartache to surface.

"So, in a perfect world, if you and I were far away from the prying eyes of Hollywood, you're saying we wouldn't have a chance?" The hope in Reeves's voice caused Lena to pause and really think through her answer. "Lena?"

"I..." Perhaps she should explain what happened with Charlie. That way, Reeves might better understand why it was so hard for her to ever consider loving someone again. She paused long enough to gather her strength. "I was in love once, and I was hurt badly. I was betrayed, blamed for things that weren't my fault and generally made to feel like I wasn't fit to be alive."

Reeves took a moment before he said, "I'm so sorry anyone made you feel like that."

An inkling of relief sparked within her. Maybe it was good for her to talk about it, but only a little. Most of those worms needed to stay in their can. "I was vulnerable. Very green. It was my first adult relationship, and I was blinded by love."

"We've all been there."

Lena looked at her perfectly manicured nails, wondering why she spent so much time on something so...vain. "The thing is, that relationship scared me, and I've not been able to have a meaningful one since."

"Fake-dating Montreaux is the perfect solution: you're off limits, and you don't have to give your heart."

Lena rested her elbows on her knees and held her head in her hands. "Lena?"

She sat up, hot tears filling her eyes. "I never realized I was doing this."

Reeves reached for her hand. His warm skin against hers caused a cascade of tears to slide down her face.

She removed her hand. "This is too complicated."

"Then we un-complicate it."

"We can't." She sat up straight. "It's obvious we have an attraction for each other, but our hands are tied. Don't you see? Wondering about what life would be like if we were together is a waste of time."

"I'm nothing like the man you were with." His voice was heavy with hurt.

"It's not...it's not just that. I'm talking about our careers. There's no point in imagining us being together, as you and I know it can't happen. Thinking about these things will only disappoint us. We can't have the best of both worlds."

"We could."

Her voice was barely above a whisper. "What we want and what we can have are often polar opposites." She looked at her watch. "I really do have to go now."

Reeves stood and held out his hand. She took it, and they walked in silence through the green archway to his car. He opened her door for her, then got behind the wheel. The engine revved to life, and a small part of Lena wished they could stay in the anonymity of the gardens. But she had to get back and rest—the bags under her eyes were not getting any smaller.

Reeves drove back to the studio slowly and parked his car next to hers. "Here we are."

"Thank you." Lena exited before Reeves could help. He stood in front of her, hands awkwardly at his sides.

"Thanks for the company," she finally said.

"Lena." Reeves moved from foot to foot. "I really liked our time together, and I was wondering—hoping—we could do this again?"

"As much as I would love to, we can't."

Reeves squeezed her hand and gave her a lingering kiss on the cheek.

She inhaled his musky cologne, reveled in his stubble brushing her skin. Closing her eyes, she willed herself to remain in control and not pull Reeves against her body, kiss him endlessly and forget the rest of the world.

He moved away, their eyes locked.

"Maybe one day." His voice was low.

"Maybe," she said, knowing it could never happen. Aside from the ghosts of her past with Charlie, the studios had way too much influence on their lives, and any friendship between them would be fraught with gossip and innuendo—which certainly wouldn't be without foundation.

Reeves waved and got in his car. He took off down the road and Lena watched until the vehicle zipped around the corner, a wave of loneliness and longing washing over her.

* * * *

Lena stood on the steps of George's apartment pressing the buzzer—again. She'd tried for a few minutes but didn't have any luck. Giving up, she wrote a note and popped it in his mailbox, hoping his no-show was just the result of a hangover. She turned, went down the steps and got into the car. There was no point in going home to rattle around the mansion, it would just depress her. So where to now?

The engine purred into action and she took off down the street, intent on enjoying the sunny afternoon. In an effort to take her mind off her conversation with Reeves, Lena navigated streets she'd never been down before, paying attention to the shops and houses, parks and schools. It occurred to her that in all her years in this large city, she'd never taken the time to be a sightseer. Then again, she'd never had a lot of time, even when she was starting out at the studio. The long hours were exhausting, and she'd certainly not had the means to buy a car.

Lena turned left and found herself on a familiar street.

Had her mind subconsciously directed her here? Was it that much of a habit?

She drove toward Fortitude Studios, intent on driving past, but she found herself pulling over, getting out of the car and looking through the bushes in front of the iron bars. It was Sunday, but the studio still buzzed with set builders and other tradespeople trying to get everything ready for the next scenes to be shot.

In the distance, she could see Stuart Cooper talking animatedly with another man in front of the main office. From where she stood she couldn't recognize who it was, but she didn't need to know. It was none of her business. Besides, it was her day off.

Oh.

Reeves was right. She lived and breathed this work so much that even on her first break in what felt like forever, she was standing at the gates of the studios looking in. What was wrong with her?

Appalled, she turned to head for the car but stopped when she recognized a face she hadn't seen for some time. "Nerida Curlewis!"

A woman in her mid-fifties with immaculate hair and makeup and a two-pack-a-day voice beamed at her. "It has been some time, Miss Lee. Dare I ask why you were lurking in the bushes? Who are you spying on?"

"No one!" She smoothed down her pantsuit.

"Nice outfit. A little different than the first time we met." Nerida rested a hand on her generous hips.

"Very funny. Back then I thought I was fashionable—"

"Since when is an oversize brown suit fashionable? Most casting directors would have thrown you out the door before you had a chance to audition. Lucky for you I stuck my nose in and convinced the studio to take you. I could see your potential, even back then."

"You know I've always appreciated you speaking up for me."

"And I've never regretted it. So, do you intend on hanging in the bushes all day, or would you like to get a cup of coffee? It's been a long time since we've chatted."

Lena glanced at her car. She desperately wanted to get in and speed off, though at the same time she wanted to take advantage of the opportunity to sit and talk with one of Hollywood's most powerful voices in publicity. Not only had Nerida reached the top of her game, she'd done it with style and integrity, ignoring the naysayers who fought to keep her down. Lena could learn a lot from this inspirational woman.

"What about a diner? There's one down the road," Lena said.

"I've got a heap of work to get through, so it would be easier if we have coffee in my office."

"Sure."

Lena left her car out front and rode into the studios with Nerida. They parked near the door of the main building, then took the elevator to Nerida's office. The bookshelves and her desk overflowed with newspapers and magazines, and she had to clear a pile from a chair so Lena could sit.

"Back in a moment." She left and came back with two mugs of coffee a few minutes later.

Lena gratefully took the coffee and sipped it. She placed the mug on the only spare corner of the desk. "How is everything? How are your great-nieces?"

"Good. Great, in fact! There will be a third in September."

"Gosh!"

"I know. Three under four. Mayhem for my nephew but joy for me!" Nerida studied her over the rim of her coffee cup. "So, how is it really going? Pierre can be a handful."

"Nothing I can't handle."

"I was never sure that you and he would be a good match on-screen, but Stuart had his ideas."

"He is a visionary, that's for sure." Lena crossed her legs.

"He is—to a degree. Although Cooper and the rest of the boys' club need to fight harder against the censorship board." She leaned against the high-backed chair. "If it were up to me, we'd have had this Hays Code knocked flat on its back by now."

"So you're not planning on taking over the studio?" joked Lena.

"I wish." Nerida leaned forward and rested her hands on the desk. "I may have been around this block a few times, but I've never had on blinders. Women getting paid the same as men—not just in this industry—is a long-term battle. I've done what I can, but it's time to pass the baton."

"You're not retiring, are you?"

Nerida let out a throaty laugh. "Not on your life! They'll be carrying me out in a wooden box."

"Well, I hope that doesn't happen for a very, very long time."

"I'm not getting any younger." Nerida rested her gaze on Lena. "Nor are you. But you've proved them wrong. An actress's age isn't a handicap. I knew you had it in you."

"Thank you." Age had been on her mind lately—was she leaving it too late to have children? Did she even want them?

"Lena?"

She looked up. "Sorry. I got caught up in a thought."

"About?"

"Children."

Nerida's mouth hung open. "Are you..."

"No!"

"Thank god, because if you and Pierre..."

"What would happen if I was?" Lena asked, though she already knew the answer.

"You could kiss your career goodbye. Imagine, an unmarried actress with child—the tabloids would have a field day. And, selfishly, it would be a nightmare for me to put out that particular fire."

"Yet there are actors who have broods of kids with women they barely know and no one bats an eyelid. No one says their career is over or sees them as less desirable."

"You're telling me what I already know," said Nerida. "No one should be made to choose between career and family."

"Agreed," Lena said. "So, any new talent of note?"

Nerida laughed and shook her head. "If you are asking if there is anyone who is going to threaten your rising star, then no, there is not. I'm still out there, getting as much publicity as I can for you, don't worry."

Lena's shoulders relaxed. "I guess I'm more insecure than I thought."

Nerida drank the last of her coffee and put the cup down. "I don't see why. You and Pierre are an excellent team. From what I hear around the trades, you two are rivaling the studio's biggest couple on- and off-screen."

"Jeanne and Reeves?"

Nerida nodded.

"I heard there was a—how shall we say this?—minor event on set a couple of days ago?"

"Minor?" Nerida said. "It was a major catastrophe! Shut down the entire set."

"That's not good."

"It's a disaster. In fact, that's why I'm in on a Sunday—trying to sort this mess out before the reporters twist it around even further."

Lena shifted forward. "Is she going to be okay?"

"Depends if you call going to rehab okay." Nerida rested her arm on a pile of scripts.

"Will she—"

"How about them Cubs?"

Lena smiled and nodded. "All right, I get it. Quit asking questions, Lena." Nerida winked. "You always were astute."

"She begs for a day off," a voice boomed behind her, "yet she's here taking up our head publicist's valuable time."

Lena swiveled to find Stuart Cooper filling most of the doorframe.

"Miss Lee, how about we leave Nerida to it and you come to my office and keep me company, seeing you're intent on never leaving this place?"

"Stuart," said Nerida, "I asked Lena in for a chat. It's not all work and no play."

"In my studio it is. I don't pay any of you to sit around and gabble. Miss Lee." He swept his hand in the direction of his office.

She grabbed her purse and got up. "Thank you for the coffee, Nerida."

"Anytime." She picked up a pencil and notepad.

Lena and Stuart Cooper crossed reception and went through the double office doors into Stuart's corner of the building, which was more the size of a small apartment than an office.

Stuart motioned for her to sit on the luxurious white leather chair and he took a seat behind his desk. "You perplex me, Miss Lee."

"Why?"

"You complain you haven't had a day off in ages, yet here you are."

"I know." She studied the gold clasp on her white purse. "I didn't plan on coming here but…" She shrugged.

"I've been meaning to talk to you, anyway. I believe your contract is up for renewal."

"Shouldn't you be talking about this with my agent first?"

"Middle-men. Pft!" He waved his hand and screwed up his face like he'd been overcome by a bad smell. "You're the one working for my studio. I want to hear what you have to say."

She was so ill-prepared for this. Where to start?

"Lena, it may be Sunday, but I don't have all day."

Her hands grew clammy and the purse started to slip on her lap. *Think, Lena. Think. What does your heart say? No, no. What does your head say?* She took a deep breath. "I am very grateful for what Fortitude Studios has done for me and my career. I—"

"This better not be a refusal to re-sign."

"Mr. Cooper, with all due respect, you asked me to discuss my contract with you and, I have to say, it is not as simple as signing a piece of paper." She paused, waiting for him to say something, but instead he leaned on his elbows and formed a steeple with his fingers. "I love Fortitude Studios. I love this industry. I love that I finally caught a break and have had the chance to work with very talented people."

"Enough with the platitudes, Miss Lee."

"All right." She took a deep breath, boldness taking hold. "The conditions for women in this industry are atrocious. The hours are long, the poor girls on the chorus lines are made to stand around for endless hours shivering in tiny little costumes when they're not on set. They rarely eat because they are worried about putting on an extra pound or smudging their lipstick. And as for those of us who make it through the ranks, we sell our souls to the studio, to the audiences, to the magazines and newspapers who make money reporting about every single thing we do—or don't do—and they don't have a problem printing lies if it will sell more copies."

"You knew this the minute you signed up."

"In my head, yes, but it was only supposition. I signed on as an actress who needed money to have a roof over her head. But I'm older and wiser now—and I know my days are numbered. I'm getting close to my all washedup date, and there are not enough decent roles for women of a certain age."

Stuart threw his arms wide. "What do you want? You chose this profession. No one forced you into it."

"I want fairness, Mr. Cooper. I want women to be paid equally to men." *If only Nerida could hear this conversation.*

"That will never happen."

"Why not?"

"Because that is not the real world. It doesn't matter if you or Jeanne Harris or Betty Grable have the qualities that pull audiences into movie theaters; men have always been paid more because it's the women who pay to see them in the movies."

"But it's the women's husbands and boyfriends who come along to see people like me or Jeanne or Betty. And the women aspire to be like us— they follow our fashions, our hairstyles, the way we talk. We take them from their everyday lives and entertain them for a couple of precious hours. People like me and Jeanne are their voices, and if we don't stand up for those who can't be heard, then what is the point of being in this position?"

"The point is that you make me money."

"With all due respect—"

"Anyone who starts with that is not about to show any respect. Be careful what you say, Miss Lee."

"Mr. Cooper—"

The door swung open and Nerida stood in the doorway, her face pale. "You are not going to like what I've just heard."

"What?" growled Stuart.

"Pierre Montreaux just signed with Moonlight Studios."

Chapter Twenty-one

1994 – Starlight Creek, Queensland

After dinner, Hattie and Don had retired for the evening, leaving Luke and Claire sitting outside on the swing. Luke's nearness shot her temperature skyward. If she leaned in just a fraction more…no. She could not go down this road in the middle of an important production.

"I really should get back. I have an early start tomorrow—again."

"Let me drive you." Luke stood and held out his hand to help her up. He didn't let go. "I wish you could stay in Starlight Creek longer."

"So do I." For the first time ever, Claire had started to question whether the transient nature of her work was something she could sustain forever. But she had goals. Dreams. And none of these could be achieved without widening her network of industry contacts, and the only way to do that was to work for as many producers and directors as possible. One day, one of these contacts could be the backer she needed to get her project off the ground. Whatever that project ended up being.

They walked down the steps to Luke's car. He opened the passenger door and she got in, smiling her thanks. His chivalry reminded her of the Hollywood classic movies she'd watched over the years.

Luke started the car and they drove toward Starlight Creek. The river sparkled under the moon, and the sugarcane remained eerily still. They drove in silence, Claire battling the urge to tell Luke about the conversation she'd had with Hattie. Though it was Luke's business, and if he wanted to share that information with her, he would.

They arrived at the hotel, now shrouded in darkness. She got out and Luke walked around to meet her, his body close to hers once more.

Looking deep into her eyes, he said, "Something's different. What is it?"

"Nothing." She bit her lip.

"That nothing is a definite something. What's changed?"

"Noth—"

Luke's raised eyebrow stopped her lie.

"Hattie told me about your mum and your little brother." She cringed as she blurted it out, but she couldn't lie.

His shoulders slumped. "Hattie should leave well enough alone."

"It's okay, really."

"No, it's not, because now I'm the guy who lost his mum and brother when I was a kid. You'll look at me with pity, you'll want to talk about it, try to counsel me, and it will deteriorate whatever relationship we've been building."

"Wow," she said. "I would have thought you'd have given me more credit than that."

"Experience has taught me otherwise."

"What happened?" she asked gently.

"I don't want my past to define who I am," he said.

"But it does—for all of us. Our past shapes who we are today, who we are tomorrow."

"It's more to do with circumstance."

He had a slightly annoyed tone, but at least he was talking.

Taking a deep breath, she said, "I do what I do because of how I was brought up. I'm the youngest of four kids and I'm the only girl. My very practical family doesn't understand my need to be creative, and they think me traveling so much for work is insane. But they can see I love what I do, and that I'm happy. They can also see that it's the path that will eventually lead me to my dream work."

"Which is?"

"I want to make documentaries. I want to film people who will inspire, make others think, and to tell a part of history that's never been told before."

Luke frowned, his silence disconcerting.

"Oh. I'm sorry. I didn't mean to highlight that my family supports me and your dad doesn't, I meant—"

"It's okay." But his tone told her otherwise. "Look, we are who we are because of circumstance. If my mother hadn't died, then chances are my brother would be working with Dad and I'd be pursuing my own dream."

"Sculpting full time?"

"Not just that. I want so much more." He leaned against the pole. "Farming is tough, and it's getting tougher. My dad is more fragile than he looks, and my heart isn't in the business. Believe me, I've tried, and will continue to do so, but it's not who I am."

"Who are you, then?"

"I'm someone who wants to use art to help and motivate people—much like your documentaries. I— Look, it doesn't matter what I want, it's never going to happen."

"Please, tell me." She reached for his hand. Although he didn't relax into her hold straight away, he eventually did.

It took a moment before he spoke. "It's all pie in the sky."

"I'd really like to hear about it."

Luke cocked his head in the direction of the bench in the park across the road. They walked hand in hand, but when they sat Luke let go and kept some distance between them.

Once again, he took his time before speaking and she waited impatiently. Eventually he said, "In a perfect world, I'd love to build a retreat where people could come and experiment with their artistic side. I'd get in art therapists, painters, I'd teach sculpting with various mediums…lots of things for people to try and experience. I especially want to help kids who've been through something traumatic, whether it's illness, the loss of someone they love…anything that has made them grow up faster than they should.

"When I lost my mum, my only outlet was art, but my dad couldn't cope. Seeing me do the things my mum did only brought back memories of the wife and son he lost, so in the end I had to hide the only thing that gave me solace from my grief. It connected me to Mum, but my dad severed that connection, and eventually my art became a source of guilt."

"Oh, Luke. That's a really difficult position to be in."

He shrugged. "I've worked through it over the years, and now I'm at a point where I can pursue my art on the side, but I could never voice my true wishes to my dad. He'd never understand."

All this made so much more sense now.

"So," he continued, "I want to give people, especially kids, a way to express how they're feeling, because a lot of times words just don't cut it."

"That's so very true." Right now, Claire was struggling to put all her thoughts together, let alone find a way to express them.

"And"—Luke appeared to be on a roll now—"how can people not be inspired by this landscape?" He motioned toward the mountains and the sugarcane fields lit by the moon. "There's so much beauty here just waiting to be discovered and enjoyed, and I want city folk especially to take time to stop, breathe and immerse themselves in this land. In its magic. In its heart. Maybe then they'll discover what's in theirs."

Claire couldn't keep her eyes off Luke. As he spoke about his dream, his passion shone, and that, coupled with his blue eyes, perfect straight nose and sandy hair that brushed his shirt collar...

"It's a shame you can't find a way to do everything—your art, the retreat, helping your dad."

"Life isn't like that," he said. "No one can possibly get everything they want, no matter how hard they work. Dreams are usually just that—dreams."

She debated whether to say more, then remembered Luke saying he hated how people acted with him because of losing his mother at such a young age. "I don't see it that way at all."

"How do you see it?"

"Dreams get people up in the morning. They inspire us to strive harder, work harder, study harder. Dreams keep us going through those moments in life when we're stuck in a dark tunnel that we feel we'll never escape. Writers, inventors, scientists, musicians, painters, *sculptors*, all of them had dreams that they would one day write that book, invent a machine that helps people, find a cure, compose a song that will touch hearts, design a piece that is so beautiful it brings people to tears...these people started with a dream and made it a reality."

"Dreams are just dreams."

"I wish you could see it another way, Luke." She turned to face him. "Your dreams sound amazing, and I'm sure you could make them happen."

"Let's talk about something else," he said.

She stifled a yawn.

"Perhaps less talking and more sleeping," said Luke. "Come on."

He helped her up and they crossed the road to the pub and stood outside the door that led to the rooms upstairs.

"I don't mean to be pushy," she said.

"I know your heart is in the right place. It's just that you and I come from totally different backgrounds, so it's only natural we see things differently." Luke brushed her face with the back of his hand.

Claire closed her eyes.

Luke's fingers traced her jawline.

She held her breath and fixed her eyes on his.

His finger gently traced her mouth. "I've been wanting to kiss these lips all night."

"Then do it," she rasped.

* * * *

Claire rolled over to check the clock. Bright red numbers shone: 0130. Luke stirred and slung an arm over her naked torso. She rolled over to face him. He lay peacefully, eyes closed, a small smile on his lips—those gorgeous lips that had covered the terrain of her body only hours ago. And although she should be basking in the joy of being with Luke, a nagging voice wouldn't let her fully appreciate this moment.

Questions about whether this was a one-off or the start of something else bounced around her head. Fears of whether he would wake and think it was pity sex because she'd found out about his mum and brother. Stress about not getting enough sleep when she had a massive day of filming that started in a few hours.

"Ridiculous," she muttered and got out of bed, slipping on an oversized T-shirt. Standing in front of the window, Claire took in the view before her.

Shadowy mountains, a sparkling river, the expanse of sugarcane, and a town caught in its own time capsule. No wonder Luke didn't want to leave. No wonder she didn't want to, either.

Claire shook her head, trying to dispel the thought. In a short amount of time, Starlight Creek and its residents had gotten under her skin like no place before. And Luke Jackson had had the biggest impact of all.

"Can't sleep?"

Claire turned to find Luke still in bed, resting on one elbow. The sheet lay casually across his hip, just low enough that she could see the V leading down to…

She let out a deep breath.

"Insomnia and I have an interesting relationship." She moved over to the bed and under the covers. Her legs brushed his and a small shiver shot up her spine.

"So how do we get rid of this insomnia?" He drew her close, his warm body melding perfectly with hers.

With a smile in her voice, she said, "I have an idea."

* * * *

Claire woke more content than she'd been in years. She nestled into Luke's warm embrace, her gaze resting on the hint of sun peeking from behind the mountains.

"I probably should get going," Luke whispered in her ear.

"I probably should get to work." She left a lingering kiss on his lips.

Luke smiled but his eyes were sad.

"What's wrong?" she asked.

He sat up and leaned against the headboard. "I'm not one to sleep with girls coming through town, that's all."

"And I'm not one to sleep with men in the towns where I work. We've both done something we don't usually do. What's the problem?"

Luke's voice was low. "I've been here before."

"You just said—"

"What I mean is that I've had sex with women who visit Starlight Creek, but that was a long time ago. I had an experience that left me…let's just say that after that particular event I made it a rule not to sleep with women from out of town."

"Given the population of Starlight Creek, I'm thinking you don't have much choice of single women here," Claire said, then her mouth dropped open. "Unless you have a thing for Scarlet?"

"No, no. I don't have a *thing* for Scarlet."

"What then?" The more she got to know Luke, the more complicated he was. Did she really want to delve deeper into his pile of baggage?

Luke twisted his lips, as if debating whether he wanted to go down this road or not.

She said, "If you don't want to talk about it, that's fine. I don't want to push."

He ran his hand down her arm, leaving a trail of goosebumps on her skin. "Why do I feel compelled to tell you my deepest thoughts and fears?"

"I don't know." But she certainly understood, because Luke had the same effect on her.

"I just…" He rubbed his forehead. "I just don't know where to start."

"At the beginning?"

Luke closed his eyes. "I'm wary about this. Us. I don't know what it is, but all I know is I want more. And I'm not talking about sex, as mind-blowing as it was. I like your company. You make me laugh. You see the world in an entirely different way, and as much as it drives me crazy, it also forces me to expand my horizons. Living in a small town like Starlight Creek does isolate me and, yeah, I get to Brisbane or Cairns every so often, but it's not the same. It's like you've brought the world to me, and I just want to soak it all in, learn from it. And it scares the shit out of me."

"Why?"

"A few years ago, I got involved in the WWOOF program—you know, the one that gives travelers a chance to stay and work on a farm, and in return they get food and board?"

"My cousin did that in New Zealand," said Claire.

"It's a great program, and Dad and I loved it. We had people from all over the world—England, Scotland, the States, Canada, China, Argentina—a real blend of cultures and nationalities. The problem was, it caused a bit of a rift within the community."

"Why? Travelers would be spending money in the businesses here."

Luke nodded. "Exactly, but there were a few incidents where a traveler stole or vandalized something. One ran off with the schoolteacher, who was expecting his first baby with his then wife."

"Seriously? Is that why people like Colin are so wary of people from out of town?"

"The wife who was left behind was Colin's daughter."

"Oh," she said.

"The townsfolk in general never got over it," he said. "To be fair, though, the majority of travelers were fantastic, but there were just too many negative events that made Starlight Creek wary of strangers."

"But you don't feel that way about outsiders, right?"

Luke took a moment before speaking. "To a degree. The thing is, a French backpacker came to stay, and we hit it off straight away. I'll be honest and say that there was a steady stream of beautiful backpackers coming through the WWOOF program, but I wasn't in it to sleep my way around the world, I promise."

"I believe you." And she did.

"Eloise was her name." His voice faltered a fraction. "And she knocked me for a six. My friends and Dad and Hattie all warned me not to get too involved, but I refused to listen. I was swept away by her beauty and accent and I was blinded."

"We've all been there."

"The problem was," he said, "that up until then I'd never experienced anything like the relationship I had with Eloise." He took her hand. "If this is making you uncomfortable, I'll stop."

"It's fine, honest. It's not like I expected you to be a monk. We all have histories."

"Thanks for understanding." He let out a low whistle. "Wow, I had no idea how much I needed to talk about this."

"You've not spoken to anyone? Not even Hattie?"

He shook his head. "I've always been embarrassed by how I fell in love so hard and fast."

"You don't need to be."

"Thank you." Luke paused. "So, Eloise told me everything I wanted to hear, and I believed her. She had me convinced we'd travel to Paris for our honeymoon, then return to the farm, where we'd raise a family. She told me she loved the land, that she felt she was born to be Australian, that her heart was here, with me, in Starlight Creek."

"But it wasn't?"

"When I proposed…" He looked at Claire, as if gauging her reaction. "Are you sure you're all right with this?"

As hard as it was to hear, she wanted, *needed*, to know more about this man who occupied so much time in her mind. "Please, go on."

"We'd only known each other for six weeks, but I felt so strongly that it was the right thing to do. The romantic in me wanted to believe I was right, though everyone told me I was wrong, that I should wait. She said yes, and I suggested we take our time before tying the knot, because I wanted to organize a wedding that would be memorable. But she didn't want to wait; she was happy to get hitched at the municipal offices."

"Why the rush?"

"That's what I wondered. It wasn't like her visa was going to expire; she had plenty of time left on it. I asked her for some time and I promised she wouldn't regret the surprise wedding I had planned. I wanted to create a gazebo out of metal that combined Australian flora and fauna with French designs—a marrying of two cultures."

"Oh, that sounds beautiful. You are definitely a romantic," she said.

"I used to be," he said quickly. "But she killed that when she ran away to marry a singer in a rock band."

"What?"

"Eloise went to Cairns for the weekend with some friends, saw a few bands and had sex with this guy in the back of a van."

"Classy."

"He was on a national tour, and she decided to follow him. They got married two weeks later in Brisbane."

"Are you serious?" she said loudly. "Who does that? Who would give you up?" Claire steeled herself, embarrassed by her outburst. "I mean, I…" *Montgomery, get it together!*

Luke laughed. "Thank you for being so indignant on my behalf, but it's okay, really. The whole point of telling you this is so you'll understand where I'm coming from. This thing you and I have scares the bejesus out of me, because I don't want to be in the same place I was before."

"I have an Aussie passport," she joked, then worried he might take her flippancy the wrong way.

"Well, I'm glad for that." He winked.

"What happened between her and this rocker who is even more impulsive than you?"

"Last I heard, she left him five weeks after she got her citizenship."

"Nice," said Claire.

"Yeah."

"Looks like you dodged a bullet."

"Yep."

Quietly, she said, "Still hurts, though, huh?"

"My brain tells me it was never love, but…"

"The heart is always going to win out."

"Yep." Luke's wide blue eyes looked into hers. "What about you?"

"Me? As in what's the biggest heartbreak I've ever had?"

"Only if you want to share."

Claire stared out the window. How to answer this? "I've never been in love."

"What?" Luke seemed way more surprised than she'd expected him to be.

"I've been in lust, infatuated, early stages of love, but not the gut-wrenching, world-out-of-control love."

"Wow," he said.

"What?" She didn't care that she sounded so defensive.

"I would never have thought… Look, it doesn't matter what I think. I'm guessing the right person just never happened along."

"Oh, a few did." She didn't like that she sounded so matter-of-fact. "But my career always came first." She chewed her lip. "Though maybe…"

"Maybe?"

"Maybe I rejected relationships because the men I dated were used to being in charge, used to having people drop everything and cater to their every whim." She laughed. "So maybe that's why it never worked—I refuse to be bossed around." Claire scratched her head. "I don't understand how people can have it all."

"See? That's what I was saying before—it's impossible to have everything we want in life," said Luke.

"We can, I'm sure of it," she said. "I just don't know how to make it happen."

Chapter Twenty-two

1994 – Starlight Creek, Queensland

Luke snuck out of the hotel room before the sun had fully risen, leaving Claire to stare at the ceiling and wonder what on earth had happened. The night had rocked between sensual ecstasy and gut-wrenching emotion. She hated that perhaps Luke was right, that realizing one's dreams may not always be possible. Her entire life had been focused on creating goals and working toward them, dreaming big and doing everything in her power to make them happen. And, despite all the study, all the networking, all the long, arduous hours working on film and TV shows, she wasn't any closer to fulfilling her dreams. And she'd never allowed herself to be in love.

Was all the sacrifice worth it?

"Ugh." Claire got up and showered, grabbed a banana from the breakfast buffet downstairs and went to the cinema to open up and get things started. The morning whizzed by, the actors got their lines right first go, and Nigel's mood was the best it had been since this project started. Everything had fallen into place because she'd saved the production at the eleventh hour by securing use of Hattie's cinema. Even Tony had pulled himself back into line.

So why did she feel so empty?

Luke. Their conversations had shaken her. Shouldn't she be floating with all those wonderful endorphins her body produced during fabulous sex? Shouldn't she be spinning in circles of happiness with the forward movement of her career? Why did she feel like a weight had been placed on her shoulders and her feet were dragging?

She excused herself and went outside for some fresh air. Warmth wrapped around her and she welcomed the sun dancing across her skin. Taking a deep breath, she headed toward Scarlet's café, keen to stretch her legs.

"You're with the miniseries, right?" A guy in his early twenties appeared from between a couple of cars parked outside the news agency. He was short, with the broad shoulders of someone who worked physical labor. His Akubra hat covered most of his hair, but a few brown strands poked out from underneath. It looked like he hadn't shaved for a few days.

"Can I help?" she asked.

"I want to see that James Lloyd."

Claire took a moment before replying. Who was this guy? "James is currently filming."

"When will he be done?"

"It's hard to tell," she said, her senses on high alert.

"When?" he spat out.

"If you would like me to pass on a message, I'd be more than happy to do so." Like hell. This guy gave off some very angry vibes.

"I need to see him—in person."

"What's it about? Maybe I can help." She did her best to sound calm, but his aggressive attitude was not encouraging.

"Tell him to keep his goddamn dick away from my girlfriend."

"Pardon?"

"He fucked my girlfriend, and now she wants to run away with him." Rage and hurt was in every word.

"Who is your girlfriend?" she asked, but she already knew what the answer would be.

"Annalise Dennis."

Bingo.

"You know her?"

"Yes," she said. "Sorry, what's your name?"

"Brody."

"Brody…?"

"Brody Hall," he said, like he was speaking to a three-year-old.

"Brody," she said gently, "I do know Annalise and she's a lovely person."

"She's a whore."

Claire steeled herself, aware this situation could get out of control very quickly. "It's obvious you and Annalise have a lot to work through, and I'd suggest you concentrate on that rather than worrying about James."

"He had sex with her!" he yelled loud enough that two older ladies faltered as they walked past.

Brody closed in on Claire. She stood her ground. "I really think you need to discuss this with Annalise," she said.

"She won't talk to me, and I want the full story. And her father isn't helping."

"Robert?"

"You know him?"

"Yes." Claire looked him in the eyes but also managed to assess her nearest escape route if this guy got physical. "What do you mean Robert isn't helping?"

"I've been away, working in the mines, and I come back to a town that is talking about my girlfriend having sex with some arsehole who wears makeup."

"It's makeup for the screen." What on earth was she saying? "Brody, I'm really sorry, but you need to talk to Annalise about this."

"For fuck's sake!" He punched the pole so hard the veranda shook.

The news agent, Colin, raced out. "What's going on?"

"It's okay," she said, her body on full alert. "Brody and I are done talking."

"This is not the last of it," Brody growled. He got in his ute and sped off, leaving clouds of dust in his wake.

Claire gripped the pole, her chest tight.

"Are you really all right?" asked Colin.

"I will be." She took a deep breath and laughed. "Man, he was angry, huh?"

"Did he say it has to do with one of your actors?"

"It's nothing." She needed to warn Nigel about this.

"Like I said before, no good has come with you lot here." Colin shoved his finger under her nose and she took a step back. What was with all the testosterone today?

Claire straightened her spine. "This is an issue between Brody and his girlfriend."

"His girlfriend who had *relations* with *your* actor. Something has to be done about this. Too many people coming here upsetting our peace and quiet—noisy cars polluting our air, taking our parking spaces, we can't get into the pub for a beer because it's too crowded. Enough is enough." Colin marched into his shop and slammed the door. He turned the open sign to closed.

"He's right," said a woman with a young baby in a pram.

"Pardon?" Jeez, not another naysayer.

She rocked the pram and said loudly, "Too many strangers in our town. We don't want unsavory elements influencing our children."

"We've been here for a while without incident, I think we've proven ourselves respectful and decent." What did the Starlight Creek residents think the production team were—a rock band hell-bent on trashing the town?

"We'll be glad to see the back of all of you." The woman pushed the pram away with haste, mumbling as she went.

What was going on? The residents of Starlight Creek had been happy to have the production in town, to give a much-needed injection into the economy, and now, a handful of townsfolk were turning on them. Why?

Oh no. Had Robert Dennis got his claws in? *This is not the end of it. And I will do my damned best to make sure this production fails.* Those had been his exact words. Had he sent Brody in to do his dirty work? A jilted boyfriend was the perfect way to create a stir on set and turn the town against the production.

"Bloody hell," Claire muttered as she headed back to the cinema. Some fires needed putting out.

* * * *

Claire sat on the swing on Luke's veranda. It had been a long day fraught with the usual challenges on set, and also the added stress of Brody Hall showing up. The ordeal had left her unsettled, and there was only one place that brought her peace.

The screen door creaked open and Luke came out with a gin and tonic adorned with a slice of lime.

She happily took the glass, sipped from it and basked in the slight burn of alcohol. The tension faded, just a little. When he held her hand, her shoulders relaxed and her problems somehow felt like they could be solved.

"I wouldn't worry about Colin," said Luke. "He's all hot air with nothing better to do than whine. Although…"

"Although?"

"Although his brother is the mayor. They're close, and if Colin got in his ear…" Luke shook his head. "Don't worry. You guys are nearly finished, right?"

"Yes." Aside from outside influences, production had been going along very nicely. And it worried her.

Luke sipped his gin and tonic, his gaze concentrating on the fields before them. The sun had started its descent, and a light, warm breeze danced through the air.

"About our last conversation," he said.

She looked at him, waiting for him to continue, though he seemed to have stalled.

"What did you want to say?" she finally asked.

He put his drink on the small table in front of them. "I've been thinking, and my head tells me this is ridiculous, but my heart is telling me something else."

"About?" She could hardly speak.

"About you."

"Me?" she rasped.

"Why are you surprised? Or…are you not interested?"

"In you?" She instantly regretted the shocked tone. "Of course I'm interested, I wouldn't be here if I wasn't. But it's early, Luke, and with your commitments here and my work taking me everywhere—"

"I'm not asking you to move here, I just want us to keep in contact."

"As friends?"

"I would say we are more than that." His low voice stirred her body in the same way his touch did.

Luke stood and moved over to the edge of the veranda, his gaze fixed on the horizon. Claire closed her eyes, wishing she could give him what he wanted. Given their conversation about the French backpacker, he had put a lot on the line to even suggest they keep in contact.

She got up, went to Luke and rested her hand on his lower back and her head on his shoulder. Quietly, she said, "It's not that I don't want to be with you."

"I get it." He stepped away. "I should have known better."

"Known better than to tell me what you want?" she asked. "Don't ever be afraid to tell me what you're thinking, what you're feeling."

Luke gripped the railing. "It doesn't matter now. You're leaving. You'll get busy. We'll drift apart, despite our best intentions." Luke turned to face her. "It's life. What's that saying? Reason, season, lifetime?"

"Luke." Claire reached for his hand, but he didn't wrap his fingers around hers. "We barely know each other, but I want to learn all I can about you. I want to know your favorite color, your favorite band when you were a teenager, what you think about at three in the morning…. I want to know everything about Luke Jackson, and I can't do that if you don't give us a chance."

"You want this?"

"Of course I do!" She heard the words fall out of her mouth, surprised by their enthusiasm, petrified by their implication. How could she balance a long-distance romance while building her career? Yet here she was, envisioning a future with Luke against seemingly impossible odds. "What's changed?"

"What are you talking about?"

"Yesterday you told me that it's impossible to have everything we want in life. You said it with conviction. Yet your tune is very different today."

"Things happen," he mumbled, his eyes not meeting hers.

"What do you mean?"

"I'm tired." His shoulders dropped. "I'm tired of trying to be someone I'm not. And despite my best efforts to resist, you inspire me, Claire Montgomery."

"I do?"

"Of course! You're working your way toward achieving your dreams and I'm here, stuffing about, not doing anything concrete, not making a solid commitment. I love my father, and I do love this farm, but there is so much more to my life. I don't know how, but I'm going to make my dreams a reality."

"Oh, that's fantastic!" She threw her arms around his neck and gave him a quick kiss. "I'm so excited for you!"

His smile was lopsided. "I've got a long way to go and a lot to figure out, but I'll get there. And I wouldn't be doing it without you."

"I've done nothing."

"Are you serious?" He laughed. "You are the most inspirational person I've ever met, and I love you for it."

Claire's arms fell to her sides. "You…" She couldn't say it.

"Oh god," Luke said. "I don't mean *love* love, I mean… *Shit*. I don't know what I mean."

Claire snaked her hand around the back of his neck. "I don't know what I mean, either."

Their lips met and the worries of the day—and future—faded into the inky sky.

Chapter Twenty-three

1952 – Hollywood

Stuart Cooper slammed his fists on the wooden desk and shouted, "What the hell has happened with Montreaux?"

Lena grabbed her purse and stood. "I think it's best I leave."

"Better you stay. This concerns you," said Stuart.

Lena sat on the edge of the chair. Her chest felt hollow, like someone had just torn out her heart. How could Pierre do this?

Stuart put his head in his hands. "Jesus Christ. Surely your source is wrong."

"I wish they were," said Nerida.

"Goddamn it!" He waved his fist. "How the hell did the tabloids know before us? I thought he and his agent had this deal signed!"

"I believe his agent had been stalling."

"We offered him more money! Extra benefits! What more does he want?"

"Top billing. Looks like he's got it from Moonlight Studios," Nerida said matter-of-factly.

"Why didn't we give that to him?" Stuart's face was so red Lena worried he would have a heart attack.

"Because Jeanne ensured Reeves Garrity was our number one studio actor when she renewed her contract last year."

"Goddamn diva," he mumbled. "Why didn't Montreaux come to me before signing with them? Isn't there a clause stating he's with us in perpetuity?"

"Not quite. We—"

"Damn lawyers. The ungrateful bastard will regret doing this." Stuart's fist pounded the desk so hard his coffee cup bounced off the saucer. "This is the last thing we need! I'll call the lawyers. You figure out what we do about the gaping hole left by Jeanne."

"I'll give Ernie from casting a call. Get him in here," said Nerida.

"No, we're fixing this right now. You're the one who's going to be handling this publicity nightmare anyway. The last thing we need is for our studio to be the center of another scandal. First Jeanne, now Montreaux." He snapped a pencil. "This studio will be the death of me."

Nerida rubbed the back of her head. "Everyone is tied up on other projects, except..." She looked at Lena then Stuart. "Lena has some free time."

"No, I don't. I'm filming with Pierre in...oh."

Stuart lit a cigarette and sucked on it. "You could be Jeanne."

"Excuse me?" The last person she'd ever want to be compared to—or be—was Jeanne Harris.

Stuart tapped his cigarette against the ashtray. "I have no idea how long it will take Jeanne to dry out—if she ever does—and I can't have Reeves Garrity kicking around the studio twiddling his thumbs. Same goes for you, Lena. It makes perfect sense for you two to do this film. We've just started, so we could cut Jeanne and use you."

"We don't know if they have any on-screen chemistry," said Nerida.

"They'll find it," Stuart puffed. "They're both attractive and can actually act." He laughed and slapped the desk. "Why haven't we paired them before? They'll be perfect!"

"Because Lena works with Pierre and Jeanne works with Reeves. We've not separated them for a reason—audiences want the same couples in different roles. Although...maybe a change is good. We certainly can't go on the way we have, especially given the circumstances."

Lena shuffled on the chair. "I'm not so sure this is a good—"

"She's perfect," said Stuart, not taking his eyes off her. "When she did an on-the-spot audition for me she played the siren—just what we need for this role."

"But I've always played wholesome parts. That's what my fans expect, and they love me for it. Plus, Pierre and I play the quintessential couple with strong morals."

"So much for Montreaux and morals," spat out Stuart. "You're taking her place. For the next little while you'll be heartbroken in public, burying yourself in tubs of ice cream or whatever it is women do when they've been jilted, but behind the scenes we'll be getting you ready for your new role. You'll need to do your best acting and convince the public you are devastated." Stuart rested against his chair.

"I *am* devastated. And I'm also furious." With the amount of time they'd spent together every week, surely Pierre could have dropped a hint. Oh. He absolutely had. *Well, changes are afoot.* How could she not have picked that up? She'd been so wrapped up in her own concerns she'd missed Pierre's clues.

"Lena? Will you do it?"

"Do what?" She hated the way her voice had gone up an octave, but the rising panic was hard to quell.

"Will you play the role of the heartbroken lover?"

"About Pierre?" She took a deep breath and squared her shoulders. "No."

"What?" Stuart's eyes widened, and his jaw dropped.

Nerida gave a quick shake of her head.

"I'm done with misleading the public about an affair that never happened. I won't ever admit to it being a charade; don't worry, I'll protect the studio. And I am sad that Pierre's left—I actually enjoyed working with him, even though he drove me crazy at times. His betrayal upsets and angers me beyond words. However, I refuse to play the role of the heartbroken, jilted girlfriend whose life has fallen apart because she doesn't have a man. I'm going to show women everywhere that being single is not the end of the world. It is a chance to hold your head high and move on with things that make you happy, to continue with your own dreams."

Stuart put his elbow on the desk and rested his forehead in the palm of his hand. He muttered, "If it's not one thing, it's another."

"I wouldn't do this unless I felt strongly about it," she said, terrified she'd just leaped over the very fine line between being offered a new contract or not.

"Why?" Stuart threw his arms wide. "Why are you doing this to me?"

"Why?" she asked, incredulous. "This isn't about you, Mr. Cooper. It's about so many things, including the Hays Code, which has done its darndest to stamp out people's freedom to decide what they want to watch. It has stifled creativity and, to a certain degree, shaped the public's expectations about how actors should behave. The stories we tell in movies and the way actors' lives are presented in public can inspire—not just entertain—so why can't I show young women that heartache is not a tragedy?"

Stuart stared at the ceiling, as if begging for patience—or a lightning bolt to strike him dead. "This is not an opportunity for you to get on your soapbox."

Nerida covered her mouth and coughed. "She has a point."

"Not you, too," said Stuart.

"Think about it. Jeanne Harris has been the studio's leading woman for quite some time. She's had public brawls, been arrested, fallen in gutters, flirted openly with married men…you name it. Now she's in rehab, and even though we're trying to keep it under wraps it won't be long before it leaks. I hate to say it, but my female friends gave up on Jeanne Harris a while ago. The only reason they go to her movies is to watch Reeves Garrity. The role meant for Jeanne in *Monterey Nights* is a sassy one, and it's totally out of character for Lena, but she's just suffered a public breakup and is no longer part of one of Hollywood's up-and-coming couples. So…"

"So reinventing herself is a good thing?" asked Stuart.

"Of course it is!" said Nerida. "She will be doing the exact opposite of what people expect. Everyone loves surprises."

"I detest them." Stuart pushed away from the desk and paced the room, his hands clasped behind his back. "You really think this will work?"

"Absolutely!" Nerida's enthusiasm bolstered Lena's spirit.

Stuart reached for another cigarette, lit it, and offered one to Lena. She shook her head. Nerida grabbed one and lit it quickly. She inhaled deeply, and a smoky cloud wafted above her perfect coiffure.

Stuart rubbed his chin vigorously. "Fine. But"—he held up a finger—"this is not going to turn into some farce where women get all up in arms and block the studio driveway, demanding things."

"I promise you, it won't." If Pierre was going to do her dirty, she had every right to a win, no matter how small. "This will be done with dignity."

"Her fans will lap it up." Nerida leaned forward, her excitement palpable. "This could really turn things around—take the focus off both Jeanne and Pierre and turn the light onto Lena and Reeves."

"Oh no!" Lena said a little too loudly. "We are not becoming a fake couple."

"No, no, not what I meant at all," said Nerida. "Far from it. In fact, if you and Reeves became romantically entangled, it will look like you've had an affair behind Pierre's back and he left because of it. It would also be detrimental to Reeves if he were to start a romance while Jeanne was in rehab."

"So we're just two professionals doing our best for the studio," she said.

"Correct," said Nerida. She turned to Stuart. "Does that work for you?"

Stuart grunted, then followed it with a nod.

"Great!" Nerida stood.

Stuart's gaze traveled from Lena to Nerida. "Go on, get started. You've both got a lot of work ahead of you."

Lena followed Nerida out of the room and into her office.

"What happened back there?" Lena asked.

"A major change for the studio." She trawled through a pile of magazines and scripts.

"I'm worried this will push Jeanne over the edge." Lena sat on the chair and rubbed her temples.

"The best thing we can do right now is get on with making movies. Stuart will make sure Jeanne gets the help she needs. There's nothing you or I can do right now that will help her."

The throbbing in her temples grew worse. "I just can't believe…I have no words."

"Well, you're going to need to study these words in a hurry." Nerida handed over a script.

Lena stared at the script titled *Monterey Nights*. "How can Stuart put so much faith in me and Reeves when he's never seen us act together?"

"Stuart Cooper did not become head of the studio because he takes risks that won't pay off. Everything he does is for a reason, and he's always right."

"He can't always be right. He didn't see Pierre with his foot out the door."

"Fine, Stuart is right *most* of the time. We need the focus off Jeanne and Pierre now. Everything will work out, don't worry."

"The worry train has already left the station— it's just arrived in Panic City." She tried to keep the tone light, because if she let the seriousness of the situation—*situations*—affect her, she'd be paralyzed with fear.

"Just go home and start learning your lines. It's the best script I've seen in a long time. You will love it. Between you and me, I've always thought this role was better suited to you than Jeanne."

"So why didn't I get it?"

"Because Reeves Garrity is one hundred percent perfect in the role, and he is—*was* Jeanne's leading man. We'd never thought of pairing you and Reeves, but now that we are, I have absolutely no doubt this will work."

Lena stared at the script lying innocently on her lap. "Who's going to inform Mr. Garrity of his new leading lady?"

Nerida looked expectant. "You?"

She shook her head. "That's not my job."

"You do know him, though."

Lena prayed the heat rushing across her face didn't show on her skin. "Yes, we've met a few times."

"No problems?"

"What?" It came out quickly, and she wondered if she sounded too defensive. "Why would we have problems?"

"Personality clashes happen."

"Definitely no personality clash." *Far from it, in fact.*

"Good, good."

"Yes. Good," Lena said. What else could she say?

"Look, I'll talk to Reeves, and tomorrow we'll meet with Stuart to discuss how we'll approach it. The studio will need to plan this very carefully."

"Indeed."

"It will all work out brilliantly, Lena." Nerida's tone sounded motherly, and a pang of homesickness struck. It always shocked her when it came out of the blue.

"I hope so," Lena said, feeling as fragile as the vase on Nerida's desk.

Chapter Twenty-four

1994 – Starlight Creek, Queensland

Claire finished checking the foyer of Hattie's cinema, ecstatic to be at the end of another long day but sad that the shoot was almost finished. Soon she'd be supervising the packing up and ensuring everything made it back to the warehouses. She was going to dearly miss the spectacular sunrises and sunsets, the endless blue sky, the warm air wrapping around her skin and the fields of sugarcane that stretched as far as the eye could see. There was also one certain man she was going to miss most of all.

Claire ran her finger along the dark wood of the kiosk, wondering what would become of the cinema once the production left Starlight Creek. It would be such a shame for the cinema to close its doors once more, as the atmosphere had changed dramatically since it had been full of cast and crew: now it was full of happiness, electricity, connection and, dare she say, magic.

"I'm going to miss you," she whispered into the semidarkness. Although she was talking to the cinema, they were words she needed to practice for when she next saw Luke. All of this was too difficult. No way could she achieve her career goals while splitting time between who-knows-where and Starlight Creek. Damn it. Luke was right. It was impossible to have everything.

Sadness trailed her like a lost puppy as she made her way into the theater. Picking up scattered pieces of paper from the seats and floor, she made her way over to the bin at the back corner, near the pile of old movie reels the set designer had styled for the shoot.

Crash!

Claire jumped, and the papers dropped out of her hand, slowly floating onto the floor.

"Who's there?" she said firmly, adrenaline racing through her veins. She looked around for a weapon but could only find a can of Coke. What was she going to do, caffeinate the intruder to death?

Rustling came from a dark corner. Her body tensed—fight or flight?

Fight. This was Hattie's theater, and she'd made a solemn promise to make sure it was well looked after. If someone with less-than-desirable intentions had snuck in when she wasn't looking, then...

Oh no.

Robert Dennis.

Brody Hall.

"Come out now!" she demanded, her hands shaking. "I know you're in there!"

A moment later a lanky figure appeared from the shadows, his head hung low.

"James?" It came out as a choked laugh. "I left you at your house hours ago."

Since arriving in Starlight Creek James had been behaving himself, so Claire had only needed to keep one eye on him, not two. Or so she thought...

He shook his head. In his limp hand was a creased piece of paper.

"She doesn't want me." A cloud of alcohol followed his words. *Oh no.* What would Nigel say?

"Who? Annalise?" Claire put her hand under James's elbow and guided him to a seat. He flopped into a chair. She pointed at the letter. "May I?"

He slowly handed it over, and Claire moved the missive around until she caught the dim light above.

Dear James,

This is the hardest thing I have had to do. I know we made promises to each other about spending the rest of our lives as one, but it's not going to happen. Our lives are very different, and even though you promised to take me with you, I can't ever see me fitting in.

You told me about the star-studded parties, the glamour, the champagne, and I got swept up in it all, imagining myself at a new event every night with you.

Then reality hit. I don't love you. I thought I did and I was willing to give up my family for you. Then Brody came home from his mining work and I realized that the only thing I want to be is with him. Brody and I had broken up before he went to the mines, and I thought it was over but now that he's back, I can see he's changed. I was wrong to start anything with you.

I did love our time together. You are funny and sexy and everything a girl could want. But you're not Brody.

I'm sorry, James. I'm truly sorry and I hope you can understand that I never meant to lead you astray.

I hope one day you will forgive me. I wish you all the best. Thank you for everything.

Annalise
XOXOXO

Claire put the letter down. "Oh, James."

He braved a smile, although it fell flat.

She should ask him how the letter got into his hands, but right now it didn't matter. "You really liked her, huh?"

James let out a long breath, and once more the air grew thick with alcohol fumes. "She was unlike anyone I'd ever met. I thought she loved me. I thought…" He punched the back of the chair, and Claire refrained from telling him off. "She lied! What's wrong with me? Why can't I make a relationship work? Why doesn't anyone want to love me?"

She really felt for him.

"How about we get you back to your place? Sleep it off? Things will look better tomorrow."

"No, they won't," he slurred, his eyes half-closed.

Claire stood and tried to lift him, but he was dead weight. "Come on. Let's get some water into you."

"No." He crossed his arms and pouted like a three-year-old.

"Come on, act like the grown man you are." She hoped tough love would do the trick. "Annalise has gone back to her ex-boyfriend. It happens. And it sucks. But you have so much more to look forward to. You have a career that's skyrocketing, and a really nice family—"

"My mum still talks about that time you sent me home with the lemon meringues you made."

"It was her birthday. I wanted to do something nice, and you'd told me they were her favorite. Look." She tried to get back on track. "The point is that there are so many great things going on in your life, why do you want to bog yourself down in a relationship?" She caught her breath. Crap. This is exactly what she'd been contemplating.

"Because when you love someone they make your life better, not worse. They give it purpose." For someone who had been drinking heavily, James made a lot of sense.

"Some things just aren't meant to be." Jeez. Now she sounded like Luke. She nudged James's leg with her foot. "It's been a long day. We both need a decent sleep."

James used the armrests to steady himself as he got up, and Claire wedged her shoulder under his arm so he could rely on her for balance. The night had rolled into morning, and she cursed that she hadn't made it to Luke's. She'd make up for it tomorrow. Today. Gah! She really needed sleep.

Claire locked up as she left the cinema. She struggled down the street under James's drunken weight until they eventually made it to the small house that had been rented out just for him. He fumbled in his pocket for keys, finally pulling them out, but missing the keyhole every time he took aim.

"Here, let me." She propped him up against the wall and unlocked the door. Claire turned to say goodnight, but James had disappeared. Looking down, she spotted him slumped on the veranda. Pushing him gently in the shoulder, she said, "James."

"Huh?" He opened his eyes. "Claire? Claire!"

"Yes, I'm Claire. We need to get you inside." With the way Colin and the other townsfolk had been acting, the last thing she needed was for someone to see James drunk in public. She doubted anyone would be roaming the streets at this hour, but she wasn't going to risk it.

James somehow managed to get to a standing position again and she guided him down the long hall to where she guessed was the bedroom. She was relieved when she found it, as James's weight was taking a toll. He stumbled forward, taking her with him, and they landed on the bed.

Laughing, Claire untangled herself from his legs and arms. "Okay, Mr. Lloyd, time for night-night."

By the time she'd reached the doorway, James's snores filled the room.

She left the house, closing the door quietly behind her. Claire stepped onto the street and looked up to find Colin standing on his front porch on the opposite side of the road.

"Morning!" She waved cheerily, then wondered what she was doing. Everyone knew James Lloyd stayed in that house, and it wouldn't take long before Starlight Creek residents thought she and he were playing musical beds.

Crap.

She needed to see Luke before word got back to him. It wasn't that he'd believe such gossip, though better to be forewarned and axe those rumors.

Weariness wove with sadness as she traipsed back to the cinema. From across the road she stopped and admired the way the half-moon shone on the worn facade. When she'd first seen the cinema, she'd been taken aback by the state of disrepair. Peeling, fading paint, movie posters from decades ago, an air of melancholy surrounding the place. With Claire's knowledge of Amelia Elliott's incredible journey, from fighting to study architecture to becoming a legend in her own right, it had been depressing to arrive at Starlight Creek and see one of her creations in such terrible condition. It felt like a disservice to Amelia and her legacy. Though now, knowing Hattie and how much she had struggled to keep the place maintained, she now saw the theater as an unfortunate victim of progress.

Claire crossed the road and double-checked the door, even though she remembered locking it. Happy everything was secure, she turned to walk back to her room at the pub. She stopped. Her nose twitched.

Was that...smoke?

Holy shit.

She put her hand back on the handle, but it was stone cold. Maybe it was a house nearby, or the sugarcane mill?

Claire fumbled for the keys in her bag. She found them and tried to shove them in the keyhole, but her shaking hands made it difficult.

Oh no. Oh no. Oh no.

The door finally clicked open and Claire ran into the foyer, turned on the lights and looked around. No smoke. No fire. Perhaps she had a massive dose of paranoia. Besides, if there was a fire the lights wouldn't work. Would they?

She cautiously walked into the cinema and reached for the main light. Claire breathed a sigh of relief when it worked.

It flickered.

Then went dead.

The distinct stench of smoke filled the room. In the corner where she'd found James, red and orange flames licked the walls. Racing to the electrical fire extinguisher, she released the valve and aimed. It was a perfect bullseye, and she kept it steady.

It was too little, too late.

The hungry flames climbed the wall and Claire ran out of the cinema, through the foyer and onto the street. She bashed on the door of the nearest house.

"Fire!" Claire screamed.

A few seconds later the woman she'd seen with the young baby appeared at the door. She rubbed her eyes. "What?"

"Fire in the cinema!"

The woman's eyes widened, and she ran back inside and was straight on the phone. Minutes later, the Rural Fire Service truck arrived and a handful of men jumped out and set to work.

Claire stood a small distance away. Nausea swelled in her belly.

Claire remembered the mobile she'd been lugging around. With shaking hands, she reached into her bag.

Pushing the buttons of the phone number she'd memorized, Claire waited for an answer.

"Hello?" came a sleepy voice at the end of the line.

"Luke. You need to come to the cinema. Quickly."

Chapter Twenty-five

1952 – Hollywood

The next day Lena sat in Stuart's office, her lips dry, a lump in her throat. Nerida sat between her and Reeves, who had smiled as he entered the room, but they had yet to exchange words. She'd considered talking to him the night before, but she'd barely been able to comprehend the changes herself. All she needed was time but, given the tight schedule that had now landed in her lap, time was a luxury.

Lena stifled a yawn, wishing she'd had more than two hours of sleep.

"And that's it," said Stuart, wrapping up the meeting. "As far as you two are concerned, you've both put aside your personal heartache over Jeanne and Pierre and have now stepped up to the plate because you don't want to disappoint your fans."

"They'll buy that?" asked Reeves. "Are you sure no one will figure out where Jeanne is?"

"I'm not paying through the nose for someone to blab that she's in rehab. As far as everyone outside this room knows, she's had a minor health setback, but will recover and be shooting her next movie in no time." He looked at Lena. "I take it you've read the script."

"Yes," she said. "Although I wondered…"

"What?" Stuart didn't bother hiding his annoyance.

"In the past I've had a similar role, and it was blocked by the Hays Code."

Stuart lit a cigarette and offered one to Nerida. "It's already been vetted. We know it will pass."

"It will?" she asked, surprised.

"All you need to concern yourself with is learning your lines. We'll look after everything else."

She chanced a glance at Reeves, who focused outside the window behind their boss. "Actually, there's one more thing," said Lena.

"You better not be asking for the moon."

"Not at all." She took a moment to compose herself, mindful this could fall in a heap very quickly. Lena didn't like holding her boss's feet to the flame, but her reasons were entirely unselfish. "About the women at the studio, especially the chorus girls."

Stuart grunted.

"They have hard lives. They put in long hours, and they know the chance of them being discovered is miniscule but they always put in one hundred percent—for a pittance. Many of these girls are sharing small apartments with ten other people. They eat one meal a day. They sleep three to a bed. Something has to change."

"They chose this industry."

"Regardless, they should be paid fairly."

"They are."

"I've checked. The men in the chorus earn forty percent more than the women. Forty percent!"

Stuart looked at Reeves, who shifted in his chair.

Reeves rested his elbows on his knees. "She's right."

"Of course she's damn right, but it doesn't mean I can start yanking money out of the company account and giving everyone an instant pay raise! I'd be broke! They're hired for a job, they're offered a certain amount of money and they accept it or they don't."

"Obviously they're going to accept it," said Lena. "They don't really have a choice."

"There's always a choice." Stuart's face turned red and he clenched his fists. "What do you want me to do about it?"

"I want the women to be paid the same as the men. That's all."

"That's all?" He jumped up and started pacing. "That's *all*?"

"Yes."

"And I suppose you want to earn the same amount as Garrity?"

Although this hadn't been on her agenda, she certainly liked the idea. Before she lost the nerve, Lena said, "Yes."

Stuart pulled at the hair near his temples. "*You* are going to send me broke!"

"That's not my intention. All I'm asking is for fair pay for everyone."

"Good god." Stuart flopped onto his chair. "If you ever give up acting you'd be an excellent politician."

* * * *

Lena sat under a shady tree in Cavendish Park, her bare feet rubbing lightly against the grass. The scent of roses and purple sage hung in the air, and birds dipped between the overhanging trees above. She alternated between chewing on the end of the pencil and using it to mark up the script that had been her main focus for the past twenty-four hours.

Thoughts of Pierre and Jeanne occasionally popped into her head, and she reminded herself that Stuart had things under control. She prayed he wasn't feeding her a pile of manure. Though why would he? Certainly it would be in his best interests to keep her happy, given she was about to step into her biggest role to date—and he desperately needed her.

"Coffee?" Reeves sauntered over carrying a picnic basket, his broad shoulders perfectly filling out his gray suit. He sat down on her tartan blanket.

"Yes, thanks." She put down the script while he pulled out a thermos and two metal mugs.

"Cream?"

"Black, thanks."

He passed her the mug and she took a sip. The thick, black coffee sent a zing down her spine. "This is *so* good!"

"Cookie?" He proffered a plate of chocolate chip delights.

"Did you make these?"

"No, no. One of my fans delivers them to the studio every Tuesday."

"Are you serious?" she asked.

"Absolutely."

"She could poison you!" Lena picked up a cookie and examined it.

"I don't know many eighty-year-old ladies whose goal in life is to poison actors."

"She's eighty?" Lena took a bite and marveled at the combination of gooey chocolate and buttery cookie. "Mmmm. These are incredible."

"Mrs. Schultz makes some pretty mean cookies. You should try her cakes!"

"Is she trying to make you fat?" Lena wiped the crumbs from her mouth and eyed another cookie. *No, no. Don't do it. But oh...so good!*

"She lost her husband two years ago, and all her children and grandchildren are scattered around the country." Reeves offered her another one and she took it, refusing to give in to the guilt.

"She's adopted you?"

"In a way." He pulled out a copy of his script, switching to a businesslike manner. "That was an interesting play you made with Stuart."

"About equal pay?"

"Yep."

"You think I was wrong?" Lena stuffed the rest of the cookie in her mouth. She really would suffer for this later.

"No, not at all! Your timing was perfect. You had him over a barrel." She leaned back on her hands. "He wasn't happy."

"That's to be expected. You've made some actresses very happy, though."

"I honestly didn't think he'd agree," she said.

"Then why did you push it?"

"Because someone has to give these women a voice, and I'm in a position to do just that."

"Most people in your position wouldn't care."

"I do. Don't you?"

"Yes, yes. I would never have thought to leverage it the way you did, though. Looking out for others is a nice quality, Lena Lee."

She shrugged, not sure how to react to the compliment.

"So, will you buy another house?" he asked.

"Pardon?"

"With the extra money."

"I will, but I won't be living in it."

Reeves furrowed his brows. "Nothing is ever straightforward with you."

"You say that like it's a bad thing," she laughed. "The salary increase is not mine. Well, technically it is, but I'm not keeping it." She paused for dramatic effect. "I have a plan."

"Why am I not surprised?"

Lena couldn't contain her smile. "Some actresses are getting more money, but it's still not enough. I'm going to buy a house that has plenty of space, and I'll set it aside to help women who have just arrived in Hollywood. Some of the most depressing things when starting out in this business are the knock-backs and the time it takes to secure work. There's the constant worry of if you'll be able to afford the next meal or the roof over your head. I want to remove these worries and help educate women about how this industry works. I want them to feel safe, to make wise decisions based on what is right for them, not say yes to jobs to their detriment. That way they can give their best performance and, hopefully, find decent work. This house will be a safe place to stay until they're on their feet. It's the perfect chance for them to make friends and stay in the loop about which studio is auditioning for what role. The strength of women helping and looking out for each other can be a true force."

"Oh, yes," said Reeves. "When my sister and our female cousins get together there is a definite change in the air. It feels more...powerful."

"Exactly!" she said. "This town is hard enough, and women are vulnerable, especially those who don't have enough money for food or a bed to sleep in."

"This is a great thing you are doing," said Reeves.

"It's not about me, it really isn't. It's about being in a position to help others. Isn't that what life should be about?"

"Life is about many things and yes, looking out for others is something we should all do." Reeves studied the branches above, speckles of sunlight falling on his face. "Can I write you a check?"

"You want to help?"

"Of course. None of the women in my family would ever dream about this lifestyle, but if they did I would want them to have a safe house like yours to turn to. There are so many women in Hollywood, though. How can we possibly help them all?"

"It feels like a tiny ripple in a very large pond, but maybe we can get others on board." She stared at the blue sky peeking through the branches. "Is it wrong to dream this big?"

"Dreams are what got us here."

"True," she said. "Although I never set out to be an actress."

"You didn't?" Reeves's eagerness to hear more made her realize she could be swimming into dangerous territory. But she wanted to get to know him better, to learn more about his life, and the only way to do that was to share a little about herself—she just had to make sure she didn't give away too much.

"I left my small town to go to the big smoke to become a swimsuit model."

"I can see why."

"Stop." She punched him playfully in the arm. "I enjoyed the attention and money, but I quickly lost interest. When I was offered a part in a play in New York I jumped at the opportunity. Then I kept getting offered roles, and people were paying me to act. It was incredible. Movies were what I really wanted to get into, so I came to LA. Then the opportunity for a part in a musical came along, and even though it petrified me I got up and sang my heart out."

"Had you ever had lessons?"

"Not one. Where I come from singing lessons weren't possible. It's a farming community, and the last thing they care about is music or acting."

"Where are you from? I don't think you've mentioned it."

"Just a small, rural town, not even a dot on the map." She needed to guide the conversation away before he had a chance to ask more. "Apparently I'm a natural singer, and it propelled me into larger roles. The problem was, the roles were always insipid, women falling at the feet of men. It drove me crazy, but I needed the money."

"Ah, so this is the reason you don't want other actresses to have to take roles that don't appeal."

"Actually, no. I am a strong believer in trying lots of different roles, and hard work should be what gets you to the top. Acting outside of our comfort zone is a good thing, because it makes us more motivated and determined to pursue the things we do want. This place I'm buying for actresses is not a free ride, it's a safe haven. There are plenty of dubious characters under the guises of moviemakers or agents who are more than happy to take advantage of a woman, especially one who has just arrived in Los Angeles greener than Montana."

"This is going to cause a stir among the higher-ups."

"I don't care." She crossed her arms. "Someone has to look out for these women."

"So, it might as well be you."

"Might as well."

"You can count on me to help in any way I can," said Reeves.

"Thank you. You have no idea how much I appreciate it."

"You have no idea how much I appreciate being able to help. My acting career has been a lot easier than most, and I count that blessing every day. I have no idea what it's like to have to turn up to cattle calls and put myself in front of others for criticism. I've been lucky, so it only makes sense that I show some of my gratitude by helping others. Although..."

"Although?"

"Although throwing money at the problem doesn't sit right with me. I'll donate, I'm happy to do so, but what else can I do? Could I get my agent to set up auditions for actresses? Getting on his books would at least be a foot in the door, right?"

Lena's cheeks hurt from smiling. "Reeves Garrity, the actor with a beautiful sense of compassion."

"Lena Lee, the actress with a heart bigger than Texas."

A bout of shyness overtook her, and she picked up the script and stared at it. Even after this lovely conversation, there was still something that had to be said. If she didn't say it now, she never would. "Are we going to be okay?"

"What do you mean?"

"Things have been...interesting between us. And with all the drama unfolding with Pierre and Jeanne, I just want to make sure we'll be fine."

"We're professionals. We'll do this well."

"But..."

"But?"

"It doesn't matter." Maybe she had it all wrong. Perhaps Reeves didn't feel the attraction she did. Although he'd kissed her—twice. And he certainly didn't seem like the kind of man who kissed women on a whim. Well, she hoped not, anyway.

"Shall we start reading at the spot where they first meet?" He pointed to his script.

"Sure, sure." As she flicked the pages she was accosted by images of their very first meeting at Stuart Cooper's party. She'd been so green and hopeful; he'd been so handsome and spoken for.

"Remember when we met at Stuart's party?" asked Reeves.

A laugh escaped her lips. "I was just thinking about that. Could you ever have imagined we'd be here right now, working on the studio's biggest movie of the year?"

"Never. Although"—he reached for her hand and squeezed it—"I am so very glad that we're doing this together."

"What about Jeanne?" She withdrew her hand.

"According to her agent—and mine—she's doing better, though the road is going to be long. At this stage no one is allowed to see her, and the staff are well-trained in what they can and can't say, so there's no risk of Jeanne finding out about us doing this movie. There's no need to worry. Jeanne will be fine."

"I hope so."

He smiled slowly. "Why do you care so much about someone who treats you like she does?"

"Honestly, I find it very hard to forgive Jeanne's behavior toward me and others, but I can't see the point in holding on to negative feelings. They just make my life intolerable." Dotty and Charlie came to mind, and she wished Dotty could forgive her. Maybe one day…

"Wow."

"Wow what?"

"Wow, I have no idea how you've made it so far in this business and still manage to hold on to such strong empathy."

"My status doesn't mean I should lose any sense of justice or compassion." She didn't care that she sounded indignant.

Reeves held up his hand. "It's not a criticism! I love that you are who you are."

"You do?"

"Why so surprised? In case you hadn't noticed—"

"Yes, I've noticed, but we're keeping this professional. Come on." She waved the script under his nose, losing her nerve to start the talk they needed to have. "Let's get on with this, because I have a whole lot of catching up to do."

* * * *

Lena sat in a booth at the back of Roy's Diner, facing the far wall. She sipped on a banana milkshake while she patiently waited for her best friends. The bell above the door tingled, and she resisted the urge to turn around. So far she'd managed to avoid being recognized, and she wanted to keep it that way.

"Here you go." A handkerchief appeared in front of her face and she looked up to find George grinning. He sat opposite and raised his eyebrows. "Where are the tears?"

"Not funny," she whispered harshly.

"Yeah, where's the mound of ice cream?" asked Yvonne as she slid in beside Lena.

"Just let it be." She sipped on the milkshake.

"That Frenchman is a dirty double-crosser." Yvonne spoke to George across the table. "I always knew he couldn't be trusted. I bet he's not even French."

Lena choked and tried not to spit the milkshake across the table. "Can we just leave this subject alone? All I want is a few precious minutes to hang out with my good friends and be normal."

"You've chosen the wrong friends if you want normal," said George with a wink.

"Ha!" Lena laughed for the first time in what felt like forever. "Mr. Barrett, care to tell me where you were last Sunday?"

"Oh." He concentrated on fiddling with the sugar. "Sorry about that."

"If you had to cancel, I wouldn't have minded. I just wish you hadn't left me waiting." Although, if George had turned up she wouldn't have spent that lovely time with Reeves or headed to the studio and talked to Stuart. Would things have played out differently?

"I'm really sorry, Lena." George shifted on his seat. "Something came up."

"What's his name?" She laughed, but stopped when she noticed his serious expression.

"I'm still not over Oscar." Annoyance lined his voice. "Thanks to Jeanne Harris."

"She's not in any state to…" Lena drew her mouth into a tight line.

"To what?" asked George.

"Doesn't matter." Lena finished the milkshake and studied the menu, even though it never changed.

"If you must know," said George, "I had a last-minute meeting about a script I've written."

Lena put the menu down. "Who with?"

"I don't want to jinx it. Just know it was someone very influential."

"Ooh!" Lena reached for George's hands and squeezed them. "You better invite me to opening night, *then* I'll forgive you for standing me up."

George laughed, but he didn't sound like his usual self. "I should have called, but the meeting happened quickly."

"It's fine, really." She returned to the menu.

"The usual, ladies and gentleman?" Meryl arrived at the table, her smile as bright as her newly dyed hair.

"Blond looks great on you," said George.

"Oh? This?" Meryl patted her perfectly coiffured hairdo. "I needed a change."

"Sometimes that is the best thing." Yvonne fixed her eyes on Lena.

"I'll have the cheeseburger," said Lena, concentrating on Meryl.

"Pardon?" Meryl and Yvonne said in unison.

"What?" said George. "No salad?"

"I need a change." Lena deliberately echoed Meryl. "Anyone have a problem with that?"

"No! Not at all!" Yvonne looked at George with wide eyes.

Meryl took the rest of the orders and waltzed back to Roy, who buzzed around the kitchen like a bee in a bottle.

"There have been lots of changes with you, eh?" George cocked an eyebrow.

Lena threw her hands in the air. "It was never going to work with me and Pierre, all right? We're very different people and we only stayed together because—" She shut her mouth, wishing she hadn't opened it.

"Because?" asked Yvonne.

"Because it suited us for various reasons."

"I knew it!" George slapped his knee. "It was a sham! People have been betting on this forever."

"What? No, not a sham," she said with haste. As much as she wanted to tell them the truth, she couldn't betray Stuart Cooper and Fortitude Studios. Too much of her career rode on this. She didn't fear Pierre opening his mouth; the last thing he needed was more scandal—he'd caused a big enough one defecting to another studio. Even though she didn't want to admit it, she actually missed having him around. Lena sniffed.

"I'm sorry." Yvonne's eyes were earnest.

"Yeah, sorry," said George. "What are you going to do now?"

"There're a few things happening, but I can't talk about them just yet."

"You mean the movie you're doing with Reeves Garrity?" asked Yvonne.

"How did you...never mind. That studio leaks secrets like a sieve." Which is why she'd been surprised she and Pierre had managed to keep their fake relationship under wraps—minus her way-too-suspicious best friends.

Meryl arrived with the order and Yvonne and Lena tucked into their meals. George pushed a fry around his plate, making a trail with ketchup.

Lena put her burger down. "Are you all right?"

George looked up and forced a smile. "Yes, yes, fine. Just have a lot on my mind."

"Your next big movie!" Yvonne took a long sip from her water.

"Yeah, that's it." George's tone didn't hold much enthusiasm.

"If you'd like to talk about it, we're here," Lena said quietly.

"Talking is not going to fix it!" he yelled.

Lena studied her friend's face. The window to George's soul was small, and only occasionally did he allow anyone to peer inside. Today was not one of those days.

George shoved a fry in his mouth and Yvonne concentrated on heartily eating her soup. Lena looked from one friend to the other. A lump formed in her throat. These two people had supported her from the moment she'd met them. They'd always been there to celebrate her triumphs and catch her when she fell. She'd learned about their dreams, their lives past and present, yet the whole time she'd only given them enough snippets of her own life to make them think they truly knew her.

Guilt swirled in her belly.

What would they say if they knew the truth? That she'd cultivated a persona before she'd even arrived in Hollywood? That the small-town American girl wasn't everything she purported to be? That there was a moment in her history that was darker than the desert night?

The only person who knew some of the truth was Dotty, but Lena hadn't spotted her since her unexpected appearance in the crowd all that time ago. For weeks after, Lena had prepared for a surprise visit, but Dotty had never materialized. Maybe her paranoia was unjustified. It wouldn't be the first time she'd misread her old friend.

She closed her eyes. No one could ever know the full story of Lena Lee.

Chapter Twenty-six

1994 – Starlight Creek, Queensland

Instead of the happy atmosphere that usually abounded at the end of a production, the cast and crew stood in the town hall, their faces solemn, their mouths closed, as the police updated them. The fire in the cinema had been contained quickly, but the smoke damage was an issue. Everything stunk. The biggest problem, however, was the damage to Claire's relationship with Hattie. Although the fire hadn't been Claire's fault, she had promised Hattie she would guard the cinema with her life.

As James and Claire had been the last to leave, they were questioned, and it was long and arduous. They'd been interviewed separately, and when James had turned up he looked the worse for wear, with red eyes, disheveled hair and shirt half-tucked.

Claire now sat in the shade on the back steps of the town hall, her head still spinning.

"Your career's shot now," said Tony, looking down on her.

"Are you serious?" Claire stood so she was eye to eye with him. Her mouth fell open. "Was it you? Did you sabotage me?"

Tony laughed. "I don't need to sabotage you—you've done a good enough job yourself. I doubt you'll ever work in this industry again, so you can kiss being the boss of me goodbye."

"Tony, if you—" Claire stopped herself. She clenched her fists. As much as she wanted to rant and scream, she didn't need Nigel and team to witness her losing her cool. "Forget it."

"What?"

"You can't bait me. Go on." She flicked her hand in the direction of the street. "Go to the pub and start some rumors. They're not going to affect me in any way. Nigel knows the real me, and he knows this was not my fault."

"That's what you think." Tony marched off, leaving Claire bewildered. What more could be piled on this already cruddy day?

Claire sunk back onto the step. A few seconds later, James plonked beside her so hard the wood rattled underneath her. "I'm so sorry, Claire."

"About being so drunk? The fire? What?" she snapped, still rattled from her run-in with Tony. She couldn't bear to think about the impending conversation with Hattie. After Luke had arrived in a cloud of dust, he'd donned firefighting gear and disappeared into the cinema. She'd been surprised by his familiarity with the equipment, and later found out he was a volunteer. That was the last time she'd seen him.

"I'm sorry." James rubbed his head, as if trying to dispel a headache. "I have no idea what happened. I wish I could remember…"

"It wouldn't change anything," she said, not quite sure how she felt about James right now. The poor guy had had it rough, and she was sure that whatever had caused the fire was an accident, but now she had to face the wrath of Hattie and Luke. She was the one who'd made the deal with them, not James. And it had been her responsibility to keep James in line, not give him enough rope to go and get drunk. Whatever the fallout, she had to face it head on, even though she dreaded the final outcome.

"We'll figure it out." She squeezed his shoulder. "Will you be okay?"

He nodded. "I'm really sorry."

Claire stood and took a deep breath. "There's something I have to do."

* * * *

Claire had her feet firmly planted at the base of the stairs leading up to Luke's house. She'd been standing there a good five minutes, her legs like concrete.

"This is *not* going to fix things," she mumbled and clenched her fists, taking the steps slowly. When she reached the front door, she knocked.

No answer.

She knocked a little harder, then waited. Heavy footfalls echoed down the hallway. A second later, the door swung open and Don stood in front of her, his eyes red.

Claire opened her mouth. "I'm—"

"Forget it," he said, his tone cold. "You're too late."

"Too late? For what?"

"She's gone," he spat out.

"Pardon?"

"She's gone to hospital." Don spoke to her like English was her second language.

"Hospital? What's wrong with Hattie?"

Don sighed, his contempt obvious. "As soon as she heard about what happened she took a turn."

"Oh no." Claire wasn't sure her legs would hold her.

"Luke's gone with her while I hold the fort here."

"I'm so sorry." She seemed to be saying this a lot lately. Claire hitched her handbag back on her shoulder. "Which hospital?"

"Don't bother," said Don. "You've done enough damage."

"But the police say it was an accident. They're running tests now, but they're pretty sure it was an electrical fault. They also said—"

Don held up his hand. "We don't need to hear it. You promised Hattie you'd look after the place, and this is how her trust is repaid. Robert said you were trouble."

"Robert Dennis?" She nearly choked on the words.

"Yes."

"You know him?"

"He made himself known after your production moved in. Hattie and Luke convinced me to trust you. We should have known better." He looked at her car. "It's time you left."

Arguing would be futile, so she walked back to the ute, her chest hurting. How sick was Hattie?

She got in on the driver's side, her mind numb. Don was right. Claire had believed she was in control, that everything would be absolutely fine under her watch. She'd been an idiot to think just because she wanted something it would work out perfectly. It didn't matter that the fire wasn't her fault; she'd made a promise, and now it was broken, and Hattie had suffered because of it.

Claire got out the map and studied it, trying to figure out the closest hospital.

Oh, great. Ashton.

She threw the car into gear, drove down the gravel drive and turned right. "Last Goodbye" by Jeff Buckley came on the radio, and Claire punched the button to turn it off.

The road to Ashton felt longer than it actually was, as thoughts about Hattie's health flew through Claire's mind—and heart. She didn't doubt for a second that Luke would turn her away, but she had to try. She'd never forgive herself otherwise. Though what would she say if she did get to see Hattie? "Sorry" just wouldn't cut it.

Claire pulled to the side of the road. This was ridiculous. Showing up at the hospital could make things a million times worse than they already were. Perhaps she could write another letter? It had worked once. But would her new letter be passed on? Could it make things worse?

She thumped the steering wheel so hard a sharp pain reverberated up her hand and arm.

What to do?

Her phone rang, and she reached into her bag. "Hello?"

"You need to get back here. Now!" Nigel barked.

"On my way." Claire threw the phone on the passenger seat and hightailed it to Starlight Creek.

* * * *

Claire pulled up at the town hall in a state of anxiety. Phil ran toward her, opened the door and gave her a massive bear hug.

"What's going on?" She wrestled out of his grip.

"They're not so sure it was an electrical fault now."

"What?"

He ushered her up the stairs and to the doors of the hall. "They think there was foul play."

"No way." *As if things couldn't get worse.*

"James's drunkenness may have contributed, because he could have set something off. The police and firemen don't think it's as simple as it looks."

"Robert Dennis." She gritted her teeth.

"Who?"

"Robert Dennis and Brody Hall from Ashton. The disgruntled cinema owner and Annalise's ex, current, whatever, boyfriend."

"That's too obvious," said Phil.

"You'd think so, right? Especially after Robert threatened me and said he'd make sure this production fails."

"Did you tell anyone before this?" he asked.

"Only James." She covered her face with her hands. "Oh man. I thought I'd dealt with it."

"Apparently not."

Surely it couldn't have been Tony. He didn't hate her that much. Or did he? Claire inhaled slowly and let it out. "I better go see Nigel."

"Good luck." Phil squeezed her hand.

"Thanks." She refrained from adding, "I'm gonna need it." Claire went up the stairs and into the hall, which was now empty except for Nigel and the policeman she'd met earlier. They waved her over and she crossed the floorboards, feeling guilty—of what, she wasn't sure.

"Take a seat, Miss Montgomery," said the policeman.

She did so, hoping this might stop her shaking legs. "How can I help?"

"We've received information about some trouble with you at the center."

"Me?" She looked at Nigel whose expression was neutral. "If you're talking about Robert Dennis, then I can assure you everything has been aboveboard."

"What about the altercation in the street with Brody Hall? There are allegations you threatened him."

"Pardon?" she squeaked, then quickly cleared her throat. "Brody threatened *me*. He wanted to see James, and I suggested it wasn't a good idea and that he should work things out with Annalise."

"Colin Dawson from the news agency said it was a heated argument."

"If he thinks that's heated, he's never been to one of my family's Christmases," she muttered. "Look, I get that from an outsider's point of view it might have looked like a huge argument, but it wasn't. I was just trying to reason with him, because he wanted to blame everyone except himself for his failed relationship."

"Would he be angry enough to cause a fire in the cinema?" asked the policeman.

"I've no idea," she said. "He was furious, no doubt about it, but enough to cause damage and ruin the production? I really don't know. Besides, how would he get in? There wasn't any evidence of a break-in, was there? There was only one other person in the cinema that night…James. He was really drunk, and absolutely not capable of setting fire to anything," she added quickly. "He could barely string a sentence together."

"Colin saw you leave his house in the early hours," said Nigel.

"I took him home after I found him in the cinema." Claire leaned forward. "We've been over this already."

"We just want to be sure we've noted everything correctly," said the policeman.

She doubted that was the case. It felt more like they were trying to trip her up on a lie. The room suddenly felt smaller. "Do you have everything now?"

"Yes," said the policeman, exchanging a look with Nigel. "We'll be in touch."

Claire stood, her legs feeling like jelly. She hated having to prove her innocence. All these allegations did not bode well. Not just for her current situation, but for future employment. Any blemish on her record, any gossip in the industry, even unfounded, would destroy her career and any hope of realizing her dreams. Although all that paled with her concern for Hattie.

Chapter Twenty-seven

1952 – Hollywood

Lena steered the Buick toward the studio gate, and she had to slam on the brakes to avoid crashing into a large black Ford. Two men in ill-fitting suits leaned against the vehicle as they spoke with Barney, the security guard. A moment later, all eyes focused on her.

The taller of the two strode over and indicated she should roll her window down. She did so, but only a few inches.

"Miss Lena Lee?" His muscular build and scowling face were intimidating.

"Yes?"

"We'd like you to come with us."

"Excuse me?"

He handed her a card:

Ned Ramsay
Representative of the House Un-American Activities Committee

She forced herself to sound calm. "Why do you want to talk with me?"

"We have some questions we'd like you to answer."

Lena's clammy hands gripped the steering wheel and she took a moment before replying. "I'm sorry, now is not the right time. I have appointments today that can't be moved." Which was true, but she doubted they cared if her costume fitting was delayed. Their take-no-prisoners air did not instill confidence in her ability to fob them off until later.

"Miss Lee, we have already spoken with Mr. Cooper, and he has assured us that a delay of a few hours will not hinder."

"A few hours?"

He motioned for her to roll down the window all the way. She did so reluctantly.

"Yes. Now, if you can park your car and please come with us to our office—"

"If you want to talk with me, then we'll find an office in the administration building," she said.

"Miss Lee—"

"I am sure you can understand that in this industry time is money, and I do not want to waste it traveling to the other side of town." She managed a haughty tone and prayed it brooked no argument. Lena hated the idea of two men in suits interviewing her in an office in full view of the studio gossips, but she had no intention of leaving Fortitude Studios with two men she didn't know. "I will also need time to call my lawyer and wait for him to arrive."

"There will be no need for that."

"I'll decide if there's a need." Lena waved her hand at Barney to open the gates and let her in. As she drove past he mouthed "sorry," and she gave him a half smile, hoping he understood she didn't blame him. Her mind went into overdrive as she wound her way through the lots toward the main administration office. Why would HUAC want to speak with her? Had Pierre said something?

Dotty?

Oh no.

But that whole incident with Dotty's brother had nothing to do with the film industry. Argh! What did they want?

Lena looked in the rearview mirror. Ned Ramsay and his offsider were following close behind in their black beast of a car. A small laugh escaped her lips. Just like in the movies.

She pulled into the nearest vacant parking spot, and the HUAC vehicle came to a stop just outside the door. Apparently, they wielded enough power to park wherever they wanted.

The men followed her into the foyer and waited with her by the elevator. Her heart smashed against her chest. Waltzing into Stuart's office probably wasn't the best plan, but she needed someone looking out for her, especially as she'd heard about HUAC investigations going south very quickly.

The elevator pinged and they got in, the stale air suffocating. They ascended to the top floor, then she stepped out with the men right behind her. Lena walked straight toward Stuart Cooper's secretary, Lorraine, who pushed her glasses back on her face and buzzed her boss. "Mr. Cooper, Miss Lee is here with some men—"

The intercom clicked off, and a moment later Stuart Cooper's door flung open. "In here. Now."

Lena walked through the door and saw two of the studio's lawyers sitting at a small table near Stuart's desk. A small wave of relief swept through her. Whatever the issue was, Stuart could help her sort it out. Though, if he'd known they were looking for her, why hadn't he warned her?

Stuart took a seat on the other side of the desk. He motioned for the men to sit, but they shook their heads.

Stuart addressed them. "Miss Lee has many, many things to get done before we start filming tomorrow, so let's make this short and sweet."

"We are aware of this," said Ned Ramsay, his tone relaying that he couldn't care less about Lena or the studio's tight schedule.

"Well then?" asked Stuart.

"We'd prefer to talk to Miss Lee alone."

"That won't be possible." Stuart crossed his arms.

Ramsay exchanged looks with his companion, who gave a short nod. "All right. We have questions for you, anyway."

Stuart nonchalantly lit a cigarette. How could he be so calm when she felt like she'd explode from panic?

"Miss Lee." Ramsay turned to her. "I believe Mr. George Barrett is an acquaintance of yours?"

"George?" she rasped.

"Is he an acquaintance of yours?" Ramsay repeated, his tone one of annoyance.

"Yes. Why?"

"Is he now, or has he ever been, a member of the Communist Party of the United States?"

"What?" She looked at Stuart, who appeared as surprised as her.

"We need an answer, Miss Lee."

"That's none of your—"

"It absolutely is our business. Now please, answer the question."

"No, he's not." Not that she was aware of. How could you ever know someone fully if they chose to keep aspects of their life secret? It really wasn't that hard, if you were determined enough.

"Are you aware he is a homosexual?" Ramsay's face contorted as he said the last word.

"What does this have to do with being a communist?"

Ramsay powered on. "You are aware that homosexuality is a psychiatric disorder?"

"I don't believe it is, and I object to this line of questioning. I will not talk behind my friend's back."

"We don't care whether you're comfortable with this or not, Miss Lee. The fact of the matter is that we have reason to believe George Barrett is a communist."

"Because you think he's a homosexual?"

"It is a well-proven fact that homosexuals are susceptible to blackmail, and therefore targeted by communists to carry out their work."

"So says Senator McCarthy," she said. Ever since McCarthy had made his 1950 speech saying that homosexuals working for the foreign policy bureau were prime candidates for blackmail by the Soviets, people had hit the panic button and the fear had spread far and wide. Now *anyone* who was homosexual was considered a communist.

"We have a copy of the script he has been writing, and there are many aspects that are of great concern to HUAC."

"He's a writer. He makes things up. Just because I play the role of a murderess doesn't mean I go around killing people. Life does not imitate art." Stuart shot her a keep-your-mouth-shut look. She ignored it.

"And what about his…" Ramsay twisted his lips. "lover, Oscar Connor?"

"Oscar?" Lena nearly choked on the name. He and George had kept their relationship under wraps. Aside from Lena and Yvonne, the only other person who knew about Oscar was Jeanne.

Jeanne. Could she be at the bottom of this? Why would she target George? *Oh no.*

Jeanne knew very well that George and Lena were best friends. Jeanne had already caused trouble for George by getting Oscar fired. Though how could Jeanne stir the pot when she was in rehab, supposedly sheltered from the outside world? What if she'd gotten hold of the news about Lena taking on the role meant for Jeanne? What if—

"Miss Lee, answer the question." Ramsay's tone caused a ripple of fear through her.

"I can't answer that, as I was not privy to the inner workings of their relationship, if there was one."

"We have evidence there was."

"Why are you asking me then?" No wonder George had looked so concerned the other day. Had he known the witch-hunt was about to target him?

"We do not appreciate your blasé approach to our questions."

"I'm sorry," she said. "I just don't understand why you're involving me."

Ramsay and his companion exchanged looks once again.

"Miss Lee, are you now, or have you ever been, a member of the Communist Party of the United States?"

"What? No!"

"All right, we're done here." Stuart strode to the door and opened it. He glared at Ramsay. "This was only supposed to be about George Barrett. I do not appreciate you changing tack like this."

"We will question how we see fit," Ramsay said. "And as Miss Lee is so closely linked to George Barrett—"

"Out," said Stuart. "Until you have some hard evidence on Miss Lee, do not return. I suspect we will not see you again."

Ramsay walked toward the door, stopped and looked over his shoulder. "We'll see. We're very good at finding the truth under layers of lies."

* * * *

The remainder of the day had dragged for Lena as she navigated her emotions, which ranged from angry to alarmed. After the meeting with the men from HUAC, Lena had taken a detour to George's office but hadn't found him there. She'd discovered he'd been sent home the moment word got out that HUAC had him on their radar. As soon as her day had wrapped up, she drove to his apartment and knocked on the door.

No answer.

"George!" she yelled, her knocks echoing in the hallway behind his door. "Please, let me in."

She stopped knocking for a minute then resumed, her intuition telling her he was home.

"I'm not leaving until we talk. Don't make me start singing 'Mary Had a Little Lamb,' because I will." Everyone had a weak spot, and George's was the childhood song, which drove him crazy.

"Not impressed." The voice came from behind the door.

"You forced my hand." The door clicked open and she slipped through the gap and entered his apartment, which was blanketed in darkness. Her friend hid in the shadows, and even though she couldn't see his face clearly, she noted his disheveled hair and untucked shirt. She went to the windows and opened the blinds, the setting sun casting an orange glow throughout the space that served as kitchen, bedroom and living room.

"I guess you've heard." George collapsed on the sofa and Lena sat next to him and held his hand.

She squeezed his fingers. "How are you doing?"

He let go and bent forward, hiding his face in his hands. "I feel ill. I can't sleep."

"Is it bringing back memories of what happened to Oscar?"

George gave a sad nod. "It's history repeating itself."

"It doesn't need to be," she said gently.

"Of course it will. This scenario has played out dozens of times over the years. I'm tarred by the communist brush even though my love life has *nothing* to do with politics."

"What can I do to help?"

"Nothing." He shook his head. "I might as well leave Hollywood now. There's nothing left for me here."

"What are you talking about? You have plenty. Your best friend, for starters." She nudged him gently, trying to lift his mood.

"I'll miss you, truly, but my career is as good as dead."

"What about the...oh." The script that had so much potential had possibly been what landed him in hot water. "Was there something in the script that could have set them off?"

"Not that I could see. Who knows, maybe they're using it as an excuse." His sigh was long. "There's no fighting it. Look at what happened to the producers and screenwriters who refused to answer HUAC questions. They ended up in jail, then got blacklisted from Hollywood."

"The Hollywood Ten? That was years ago."

"Yeah, well, it can still happen today. Even if HUAC can't prove I'm a communist—and they can't—I'm guilty in their eyes anyway. They'll hound me for information on people I work with, then when I tell them no one I know is a communist, I'll be accused of refusing to assist in their investigations."

Lena closed her eyes for a moment. "I wish there was a way around this."

"There isn't."

"It's not like you to give up so easily."

"What do you want me to do?" He stood and threw his arms wide. "It's me against an organization that has been on a witch-hunt for years. They won't be happy until every person who disagrees with their belief system is out of this business. The Hollywood Blacklist might not be official, but it sure as hell exists."

"And the list is getting longer."

"Exactly." George looked at the ceiling before resting his gaze on her. "How are you?"

"I'm all right." She wasn't keen on telling him her news, but it was better he was forewarned. "They tried questioning me, but Stuart shut it down quickly."

"Who?"

"A guy called Ramsay, and some other man."

"From HUAC?" George kicked the sofa. "Goddamn it! Why are they dragging you into it?"

"Because it's common knowledge you and I are good friends."

"We need to break up," he said matter-of-factly.

"That's rather melodramatic, and not necessary."

"You can't mess with these people, Lena."

"I'm not messing with them, I'm just not giving them anything they ask for," she said.

"You don't want them adding you to the witch-hunt."

"They have no reason to." That part was true, though the last thing she wanted—or needed—was for her history to be dragged into the present.

"That's it then." George went to his wardrobe and pulled out his suitcase. He grabbed shirts and jackets off the hangers and packed like a madman.

Lena got up and grabbed his hands. "Running will make you look guilty."

"Staying will only cause more problems. I don't need to remind you what happened to Oscar."

"Okay, okay." She let go and stood back. Surely there was something she could do. What, though? "George."

He stopped packing and looked up. The circles under his eyes were as dark as his hair.

"Can you give me some time?"

"For what?"

"For me to sort this mess out."

"How?" The agitation in his voice was out of character.

"I…" She had absolutely no idea but wasn't willing to admit that. "I have contacts. Good lawyers. Let me talk to them and see what can be done."

"I can't afford a lawyer."

"I can."

"Hiring a lawyer makes me look guilty," he said.

"Hiring a lawyer means you have a fighting chance of getting HUAC to back off and leave you alone."

George sat on a chair. "I don't know."

"Please?"

"Okay." He stood and closed the suitcase. "But I'm not unpacking just yet."

Lena forced a smile, even though her mind screamed that all this could be too little, too late.

Chapter Twenty-eight

1952 – Hollywood

By the time Lena got home she was exhausted. She collapsed on one of the three sofas in her living room and looked around. The pale green walls brought freshness into the expanse, and the earthy tones of the large rug reminded her of the land she grew up on, which felt like a lifetime away.

A knock echoed through the foyer and into the living room. Lena got up, wrapping her cashmere cardigan firmly around her. As she walked toward the door she glanced at the clock. Eight thirty-seven. Only one person she knew would turn up at this hour.

Yanking open the door, she said, "George, what's…oh."

"Miss Lee." Reeves tipped his hat and offered a large bunch of irises. She took them but didn't invite him in. "What are you doing here?"

"I noticed you weren't your usual self today, and I got talking with Stuart—"

"He told you what happened?" So much for keeping everything quiet. If Reeves knew, who else did?

"Actually, they spoke to me as well."

Lena motioned for him to come in and they walked to the kitchen, where she opened and closed cupboards trying to find a vase. Her maid, Rita, had retired to her quarters at the far end of the house a couple of hours ago.

Reeves opened a cupboard door next to the sink and pulled out a crystal vase she didn't recognize. "Will this do?"

"How did you know it was there?"

He shrugged. "My mother keeps her vases next to the sink."

"Does everyone do that?" Lena tried to think if her mother did the same. The house was always full of roses from the garden, but they were never in vases, always empty milk bottles. Did her mother even own a vase?

Reeves ran the tap and she filled the vase with water, then unwrapped the flowers and arranged them inside it.

"Thank you."

"You are welcome." He sat on the stool next to the island bench. "I'm sorry for turning up so late."

"You could have called." Why was she being so...unemotional?

"I could have, but some things are better discussed in person."

For a fleeting moment she wondered if he was referring to her telephone being bugged, but she dismissed it as a wild idea.

"Thank you for your concern, but I'm okay."

Reeves raised an eyebrow, and she instantly felt guilty for lying through her teeth.

Her legs gave way and she sat on the stool next to him. "All right, I'm far from okay. All this is out of the blue, and now poor George is being accused of all kinds of crazy things."

"And you're being dragged into it."

"Yes," she said, "but it's not about me."

"Lena?"

"Hmm?"

"What can I do?" The sincerity in his eyes made her feel terrible. For the first time in years, she felt compelled to blurt out everything, but she couldn't. She was accustomed to holding it all in. How could she possibly let it out now?

"Thank you for the offer, but there's not much any of us can do right now. I've got my legal team helping George, but aside from that, we just have to sit tight. We've seen it before. HUAC starts spreading fear and doubt through the industry in the hope that we'll turn in our own. When we don't, they start scrounging for anything that will fit their agenda and justify their existence."

"You're not a fan, I take it."

Lena laughed, then stopped. She had to be more careful. "I am not a fan of witch-hunts."

"And there have been many in the past. I get it." He cocked his head in the direction of the stove. "Would you like me to make you some tea?"

"Sure. Thank you."

Reeves got up and worked his way around the kitchen while the kettle came to a boil. He was dressed casually, in trousers and a sports jacket. She liked the fluidity of his movements, his strong hands holding the delicate cups and saucers with care. She liked the way he poured the boiling water into the teapot, ensuring the tea-to-water ratio was perfect. She liked his enjoyment of the tea ritual, like it was a precious moment that needed to be savored.

Reeves brought over a tray laden with tea cups, a pot of brewing tea, milk, sugar and spoons. "How do you like it?"

"One sugar and a dash of milk. Thank you."

He handed her the cup and saucer and she took a tentative sip. "This is wonderful."

"My grandma is English."

"Ah." She reveled in the sweet, hot liquid. "Thank you for checking in on me."

"It's my pleasure." He put down his cup. "And I made sure the coast was clear upon my arrival."

"Thank you. So…the first scene went well today."

"It did." Reeves slowly pushed the cup and saucer away. "That's not why I'm here."

"I thought…" Her words fell away when her eyes connected with his. "Why are you here?"

"Because I'm concerned. I want to know how you're coping with the fallout about Montreaux."

"It's been a circus, as expected." She sighed. "Then again, when is it ever any different? We live in a fishbowl."

"True."

"Which is why it's impressive you made it here without being detected," she said.

"I borrowed my agent's car."

"He knows you're here?" Normally a male visitor at this hour wouldn't be a problem, though given the events with Pierre, she needed to be cautious.

"He knows better than to ask questions."

"Smart man," she said.

"Have you seen Montreaux?"

"Since he defected? No. And I'm not interested, either. I have no time for someone who finds betrayal as natural as crossing the road."

It had taken some time for her to recover from the initial shock of Pierre leaving, and when the full severity of the situation hit, it had been hard to take. Still was.

"You never suspected this could happen?"

"No." And that was what hurt—Pierre Montreaux hadn't cared enough to tell her his plans. "I thought we were in a partnership, but I was wrong. I'm not going to make that mistake again."

"The actions of one man don't represent the rest of the men on this planet."

"Though there are certain traits I have seen again and again." When had she become so cynical?

"I'm sorry you see it that way. I'd like to think I could change your mind." She looked away, scrambling for words that wouldn't come.

Reeves didn't restart the conversation and the air grew thick. He'd made an effort to visit her in person, yet now silence shrouded them, and she didn't know how to break it.

Eventually, he ran his fingers through his dark hair. "There's a conversation we never really finished."

"Not tonight, Reeves. Please."

"It's important."

"More important than HUAC harassing people?" she asked.

"In my eyes, it is."

She ran her fingers across the cool, smooth marble of the countertop. She could stop this conversation in its tracks, though a part of her wanted—*needed*—to get it out in the open. Although today had been a huge rollercoaster, she hoped this conversation wouldn't send her off the rails.

"Lena?"

"Fine. Okay."

Reeves's smile shouldn't have had such a marked effect on her. The crinkle lines around his eyes softened his entire face.

"Do you remember when we kissed?" he asked.

"Yes." This conversation was such a bad idea.

"Don't look so scared. You don't need to be concerned, I promise." He splayed his hands on the marble and stared at them for a moment. "The thing is, I shouldn't have kissed you."

"Gee, thanks."

"Don't get me wrong, I *really* wanted to kiss you then—and now—but I didn't realize how complicated things were. And I couldn't foresee the complications we have now."

"You and I aren't complicated. We're filming a movie together, that's it."

"Is it really that straightforward?" he asked.

"Yes." The lump in her throat made it hard to swallow.

"So, you don't want me to kiss you again? Ever?"

"You'll be kissing me in front of cameras soon." Visions of their clandestine kiss on the studio lot caused a thin film of perspiration to break out on her body.

Reeves laughed. "It's not the same."

"No, it's not. Although..." She bit her lip, debating her sanity. "Maybe we should do a practice kiss."

Reeves laughed then halted. "You're serious?"

"Why not? The crew and Henry need to see us fumble and whatnot."

"Fumble? Whatnot? How bad a kisser do you think I am?" He punctuated this with a wry smile.

"I'm not, I'm... Look, last time we kissed it was nice."

"Nice?"

"Wonderful, okay?" Why was this so painful?

"I thought so, too."

"And that's my point. We are supposed to be kissing for the first time, and I just think we should make it look like that."

"By practicing now?" He tilted his head to the side.

"Yes." She took in his confused expression and paused to get her thoughts straight. "I don't know about you, but that kiss was the most natural, comfortable thing I've done." What was she saying? She'd never told any man exactly how she felt. Yet here she was, about to let her thoughts and feelings flow out like water after a glacial melt.

"I felt the same way."

"So we need to make it look awkward. To, you know, fool everyone."

Reeves moved toward her. "I'm happy to practice awkward."

Her gaze rested on his lips, those beautiful lips she'd wanted to kiss again for what seemed an eternity.

"Awkward is good," she breathed, her pulse racing.

The second their lips met, any idea of practicing disappeared. Reeves wrapped his arms around Lena and her body melded against his. Hands explored curves. Kisses intensified. Breathing grew shallow.

"We need to stop." Reeves drew back, his dark eyes searching hers. "This is far from awkward."

She pulled him closer. "To hell with awkward."

* * * *

Lena woke the next morning and, with her eyes still closed, reached beside her. All her fingers found was a cool mattress. Sitting up with a start, she studied the crinkled sheets where Reeves had laid after their lovemaking. Those few precious hours they'd shared made her realize what she'd been missing with Pierre. Were the accolades and glamour and wealth worth the sacrifice of being in the arms of someone she cared about?

Lena got out of bed, went in the shower and turned up the hot water, enjoying the sting of the heat on her skin. Visions of a naked Reeves made her temperature soar, and she quickly twisted the taps to cold. Then she exited the shower and prepared for a day at the studio, a nervous energy rippling through her. How would she cope with seeing Reeves today?

It didn't bother her that Reeves had left without waking her. After all, sleep was a commodity neither of them had the luxury of enjoying, so it was a matter of taking it while they could. But, if she were entirely honest, she didn't want this to be a one-off. How could she, when she felt so physically and emotionally connected to him? The only other time she'd experienced that was with Charlie when they'd first started dating. She'd been sucked in so easily until his drinking started, then he started undermining her confidence...no. She could not let any thought of Charlie ruin this moment. She'd spent too long trying to get him out of her mind, and even after seeing his sister, Dotty, she'd struggled with erasing the anger and disappointment.

Lena sat on the stool in front of her dressing table. Maybe she should find Dotty and get this over with. Lena thought it was all said and done, but a small doubt had been nagging her ever since the HUAC men showed up. The last thing she needed was Dotty blabbing about Lena's past to strangers.

By the time Lena arrived at the studio, the place was buzzing and everyone was in full swing. She went directly to her dressing room, where she was met by Yvonne and Vanessa, who already had the day's makeup and costumes ready to go.

Yvonne made a point of looking at her watch.

"Yes, I'm sorry." Lena collapsed onto the chair in front of the well-lit mirror. "I'm only a few minutes late."

"You're never late." Vanessa troweled on the makeup.

"There's a first for everything," said Lena, closing her eyes while Vanessa worked her magic. Even though she couldn't see the expressions on her friends' faces, Lena suspected looks of surprise were being exchanged.

"Mmhmm." Vanessa worked more quickly than usual. She started on Lena's hair. "Slept through the alarm, did we?"

"Yes," said Lena, a little too hastily. They fell into silence while Vanessa worked on Lena.

"You're done!" Vanessa stepped back to admire her work. "You really don't need me. You're gorgeous without all the makeup and perfectly styled hair."

"Thank you." Lena got off the chair and Yvonne fussed with the dress.

"First kissing scene today, huh?"

"Yes."

"Nervous?" asked Vanessa.

"No."

"Liar." Yvonne laughed and adjusted the strap on Lena's shoulder. "You'll do great, especially with such a handsome and charming leading man. Makes for a nice change." Yvonne froze, her eyes wide. "Not that I meant Pierre wasn't charming or handsome. It's just that...uh..."

"It's okay, Yvonne," Lena said. "You've never been a fan. A lot of people weren't. His arrogance put many people off, but deep down he was actually a nice person."

"Nice people don't dump someone without telling them, then go to a new studio," said Vanessa.

"Look, what's done is done. I've moved on, and you ladies need to do the same." Lena bent down to check herself in the mirror. "Wow. That is some very red lipstick."

"Sirens wear red," said Vanessa. "No more soft pinks for you. You'll get used to it."

"I'm sure I will." Lena chose not to mention that the dress showed a bit too much cleavage for her liking. There was no point in upsetting Yvonne as well. If Henry had an issue with it, he would certainly let them know.

Lena walked toward the door, her balance uneasy in the ridiculously high heels.

"Go get 'em!" shouted Yvonne.

"Knock their socks off!" yelled Vanessa.

"To dream is to live." Lena quoted one of her lines as she stepped out the door and into an unknown future.

Chapter Twenty-nine

1994 – Starlight Creek, Queensland

Claire sat in her ute in front of Scarlet's café, unsure if she wanted to enter. Now that filming had finished, the cast, crew and the production had left Starlight Creek. Phil had taken off to Cairns for a couple of weeks' vacation and had done his best to convince Claire she should go with him. She ended up canceling her Bali trip, but not so she could meet Phil and Leila in Cairns. Claire's heart just wasn't in vacation mode, no matter the destination. When she'd told Phil that she might join them later, they all knew it wouldn't happen.

It had taken a few days for the team to pack up due to the ongoing arson investigation and Claire had laid low, doing her job and staying clear of the townsfolk. Although that wasn't difficult—apparently she had the plague. Every time someone saw her, they'd cross the street and avert their eyes.

After taking a deep breath and getting out of the ute, Claire opened the door to the café. The bell tinkled, and Laura looked up from flicking glossy pages.

"Oh, it's you." She went back to her magazine.

"Is Scarlet here?" Claire tried to ignore Laura's stink eye, but it was hard not to take it personally.

"Scarlet!" Laura yelled over her shoulder.

A few seconds later Scarlet appeared from the back, wiping her hands on a tea towel. "Oh, hey."

"Hey," said Claire, her voice shaking. Damn it. She'd thought she'd be fine.

"Coffee?"

Claire nodded and sat on the nearest chair. Laura alternated between reading the magazine and glaring at Claire until Scarlet shooed her into the back room. "I need you to sort those crates of soft drink."

Laura headed toward the door, but not before throwing Claire her best steely glare.

"I'm sorry about her." Scarlet arrived at the table with two cups of coffee.

"It's all right," said Claire, even though it wasn't. "Everyone is on the anti-Claire bandwagon these days."

"I'm not." Scarlet squeezed Claire's hand.

"Thank you, but you're the only one." Claire sighed. "How's Hattie?"

"Good, from what I hear. She's left the hospital and is staying with Luke and his dad. The turn gave her a fright, but according to the doctors she was bound to have a health scare sooner rather than later." She looked at Claire intensely. "And it had nothing to do with the news of the cinema. It was just bad timing."

"I don't believe that."

"When did you get your medical degree?" asked Scarlet.

"Very funny. So what does that mean? A health scare?"

"Turns out she hadn't been feeling well for some time and hadn't fully explained her symptoms to the doctor. Apparently she'd thought it would pass." Scarlet straightened the sugar packets in the container in front of her. "They're doing more tests, but she's not telling anyone the details."

"Oh."

"Hattie getting upset over the cinema probably saved her life. By her going in to get checked out, they can now work on improving her health."

"It doesn't make me feel any less guilty," Claire said.

Scarlet hesitated but finally said, "You really don't need to."

Claire bent her head forward. "I just don't know how to make it right. I made a promise to Hattie and I broke it."

"How long are you planning on beating yourself up about this?"

Scarlet's blunt question took her by surprise. "Until Hattie and Luke forgive me."

"Ah." Scarlet stirred her coffee. "Now we've come to the crux of it. How serious did it get between you and him?"

"What?" Claire asked.

"No need to be surprised. This town has eyes and ears."

"Well, the eyes and ears should know that I had nothing to do with that fire."

"It will all come out in the end." She put the spoon on the table. "So, how serious?"

"Between me and Luke?" Claire looked up at the ceiling, then back at the only friend she had in Starlight Creek. "There was potential but…"

"But?"

"But we're so different. I travel for work, he loves Starlight Creek. He doesn't think you can ever have it all, and I do."

"Prove it," challenged Scarlet.

"What?"

"Prove to him you can have it all. Have you had any bites on projects you've pitched?"

"Nope. Nothing."

"Well, you need to change that somehow." Scarlet made it sound so easy.

"I've been building my career for years and now, electrical fault or not, this disaster is going to have a massive impact on my employability." Not to mention Tony gunning for her.

"Why not create your own luck?"

"How?" asked Claire.

Scarlet laughed. "I don't know! That's something you have to figure out. When Laura and I moved here, I winged it big-time. I had no idea what was going to happen, but all I knew was that I had to try."

"I've been trying *forever*."

"Then try something different. Maybe it's your approach."

Claire twisted the serviette in her hands. "Sometimes it feels too hard."

"I never pegged you as a quitter."

"Huh?" She couldn't believe Scarlet was talking with her so frankly. And it hurt, because she'd just hit the bullseye.

Scarlet stood and collected the mugs. "Look, I've gotta get back to work. Feel free to linger here as long as you like."

"Thanks," said Claire.

Scarlet set about organizing the café while Claire stared out the window. What was she hanging around for? And all she needed to do was get in the ute and escape Starlight Creek. Yet she couldn't convince herself to do it. The only way to cut the tie that was holding her back was to confront it head-on.

Claire put money on the table and gathered up her keys and bag. "Thanks for the talk, Scarlet."

"Any time." She finished wrapping the slices of banana cake. "And Claire?"

"Yes?"

"You need to believe in yourself more."

Claire left Scarlet's café feeling more unsettled than ever. She got in her ute and started the engine, leaving it idling while she stared at the steering wheel like it was a crystal ball. She could just leave Starlight Creek. There were quite a few people who would be more than happy to see her go. But she wasn't brought up a quitter. Facing consequences, owning up to mistakes...that's who she was. Not some scaredy cat who skipped town because she was frightened.

She chucked the ute into gear and drove slowly through Starlight Creek. Although nothing had physically changed, the town seemed different. An air of division still clung to the bricks and mortar, but there was something else. What was it?

Claire crossed over the tracks leading to the mill and headed down the road that led her to the last place she wanted to be right now. But she had to do this. Somehow.

When she pulled up to Luke's, she parked on the side of the road like she had the first time she'd come here. It felt like a lifetime ago that she'd begged him to come around to her way of thinking, yet here she was, about to plead her case once more.

Was it really worth it?

Memories flooded in of Luke's blue eyes surrounded by smile lines, his warm touch, his engaging laugh, the way he reached for her hand, the excitement when he talked about helping young kids through art, the kisses that sent her mind and body into a flurry of desire....

Claire stood at the gate, one foot on the property and the other on the road. Stay? Go?

A car pulled up behind and she turned around to find Don and Hattie staring at her.

Claire waved and forced a smile, despite her desire to flee.

Hattie returned the wave. She rolled down the window. "Come up for tea."

Claire walked up the gravel driveway, following Don's car. The fact that he hadn't offered her a lift did not bode well.

By the time she got to the house, Hattie was sitting on the swing, her floral dress perfectly pressed and hair beautifully styled. For someone who had been so sick, she looked rather marvelous and bright. Inside the house she could hear crockery banging in the kitchen.

Hattie patted the cushion next to her and Claire took a seat.

"How are you doing?" Claire asked.

"As well as can be," said Hattie. "How are you?"

"I'm so very sorry." The tears that Claire had fought to keep at bay flowed, and she had lost the willpower to stop them.

"There, there." Hattie patted Claire's knee. "I know you didn't mean for it to happen."

"But it did," she sobbed. "And you trusted me!"

"Listen to me," Hattie said sternly.

Claire sucked in another sob.

"If there is anything I have learned in my years on this earth, it's no matter what our intentions are, things don't always pan out the way we expect. Life is way too short to hold grudges."

"But—"

"Now, now," said Hattie. "I can see you're hurting, and my great-nephew is not making it easier."

"He hates me, doesn't he?"

Hattie's laugh lifted Claire's spirits just a little. "He's more stubborn than a Mallee bull, but I promise that he doesn't hate you."

Claire managed a smile.

"The report came back this morning, and the police said it definitely was an electrical fire. It could have happened at any time."

"So it had nothing to do with the men from Ashton?"

Hattie shook her head.

"Thank goodness."

"Why?"

"Because so many bad things have happened because of me. I'm beginning to think I'm cursed."

"Nonsense," said Hattie. "Sweetheart, this is life. Things do not always go our way. We just have to pick up the pieces and get on with it."

"I know." Claire crossed her legs at the ankles. "Some days are harder than others."

"True."

Claire shifted so she could face Hattie. "How are you really doing? Will you get better?"

Hattie's smile appeared forced. "I'm not a spring chicken anymore, and whether we like it or not, our bodies defy our active minds. Don't get me wrong, it's a privilege getting old, especially when..." A breath caught in her throat.

"Especially when?"

"Especially when we've lost others way too early." Hattie sat straight. "My heart's not good, Claire. It's only a matter of time..."

"No," Claire said forcefully. "You've got plenty of years ahead of you."

"Oh, darling girl, I wish I did. I've had an interesting life, and although there are some years I'd rather forget, it was the path I traveled, regrets and all."

"What do you regret?"

"Ah." Hattie waggled her finger. "Some things are better left unsaid."

Claire didn't push the issue, especially now that she and Hattie were in a good place.

"I need to ask you something," said Claire.

"He'll be home shortly."

"That's not it." Although it was good to know she had some time up her sleeve before facing Luke. "I was wondering if you would mind giving me the keys to the cinema."

Hattie's lips drew into a thin line.

"Just for a day."

"I don't know, Claire."

"I absolutely understand your reluctance. If I were you, I'd say no as well. I desperately want you to trust me, but I also understand you have no reason to." Claire looked down at her lap and realized her fingers on both hands were crossed. "There's something I need to do before I go."

Hattie kept her eyes trained on the mountains in the distance, her body still. A minute ticked by and Claire worried that she'd gone too far.

"I don't think it's a good idea," Hattie said slowly.

"What if Luke came with me?"

"That would be his decision."

Claire's shoulders dropped. She didn't like her chances. "If I can convince Luke to come with me, can I please go to the cinema? Just one last time."

Hattie nodded, but she didn't appear to have faith in her decision.

The screen door opened and Don came out with a tea tray. He placed it on the table next to Hattie and poured her a cup. Not once did his eyes meet Claire's. She desperately wanted to apologize once more, but she suspected bringing it all up again would just make things worse, and possibly change Hattie's mind.

Don went back inside without making Claire a cup of tea, so she set about making her own.

"He thinks I'm a fool talking to you." Hattie sipped from her cup. "Angry or not, he still makes a good cuppa."

Claire laughed. "Thank you."

"For?"

"Giving me a chance."

"Sometimes a second chance is all we need." Hattie put down the cup. "I know it seems like the townsfolk are over-the-top with their attitudes, but you need to understand there is *a lot* of history behind their behavior. Not just one incident, but many."

"Oh."

"One day I'll explain in detail, but right now I need to rest." She put her hand on Claire's. "You're welcome to stay here until Luke arrives. I hope you will forgive me, but I need to retire."

"Of course." Claire stood and helped Hattie up. She walked with her to the door where they were met by Don, who took Hattie by the elbow and led her to her room.

Claire stood at the front door, unsure what to do. There was no point going into town, as getting cold-shouldered by everyone would only chip away at her sensibilities. Waiting in the car in this heat would be a death sentence. Maybe a walk around the property. That way she could stretch her legs and get some fresh air.

She headed toward the cane fields, a little wary about what creepy crawlies were lurking. Trying to shake off her city-girl paranoia, Claire found herself meandering along the narrow paths between the sugarcane that rose high above her head. There was something comforting in being surrounded by the cane, like it was protecting her, giving her a moment to break away from the world. She'd only ever experienced that on beaches, when the waves rolled onto the shore, the vast expanse of blue ocean and sky representing the possibilities of her future. Yet here, cocooned among the sugarcane with the sun dancing across her skin, Claire felt the same sense of calm. Control.

Oh.

That was it. Ever since taking this job with Nigel's miniseries, Claire's world had spun out of control. With the happenings in Ashton then Starlight Creek—things she could never have foreseen—her sense of control had been ripped away and, in its place, uncertainty had taken over, leaving her reeling. She'd always prided herself on dealing with anything thrown at her, but with so much in such a short time her confidence had wavered. Scarlet was right.

Claire followed a path that wound through the fields. The mountains in the distance kept her company, as did the birds that fluttered in and out of the sugarcane. It was easy to lose herself here, and the longer she stayed, the calmer she felt.

Arriving at the river, she sat under a tree and took off her shoes. When was the last time she'd sat quietly and let her mind rest? Since leaving school her life had been a whirlwind, jumping from one job to another, constantly putting out feelers and making new contacts, thinking months ahead so she'd have new work lined up. And in the little spare time she did have, she was researching ideas for documentaries that ended up being nixed by the powers that be. All she needed was one idea that people couldn't resist—though that seemed as likely as enrolling in the NASA space program.

Claire leaned against the tree, enjoying the shade cast by the thick leaves. She closed her eyes, breathed in the fresh air and concentrated on every muscle relaxing.

"You wanted to see me?"

Her body jerked and Claire opened her eyes. She rubbed her hand on her mouth, getting rid of the tell-tale dribble. How long had she been asleep?

"Yes," she croaked. Her body ached and her brain was fuzzy.

"What did you want?" Although Luke's tone was even, the underlying annoyance was obvious. So much for not hating her.

"I was hoping you might come to the cinema with me," she said, trying to keep her voice steady.

"No."

"Luke, I regret everything that happened, and I wish things could be different. The last thing I wanted was damage to the cinema, and I would never, ever have wanted Hattie to become ill because of it."

"The doctors said it could have happened at any time." He sounded a little less terse.

"I still can't help but feel responsible." Her shoulders slumped. "Everything's a mess."

Luke's expression softened but he didn't move toward her.

"I'm really sorry about everything." She stood and brushed down her jeans.

"Is that why you wanted to see me? To apologize?"

"Yes." She now worried her goal was too lofty. "I was also hoping you might be able to help me with something."

Luke shoved his hands in his pockets and looked at his feet. "I think you've done enough."

"I want to make it up to Hattie. To you." She reached for his hand, but both remained firmly in his pockets. Claire stepped back. "I get this is going to take time, but will you at least give it a go?"

Luke looked away, like the reeds beside the river were more interesting than her. "I don't know."

"How many times do I have to apologize? How many times do I have to remind you it was an electrical fault?"

"The electrical fault happened because the cinema hadn't been used in so long, and the wires couldn't cope with the strain." He shook his head. "It's all impossible."

"Nothing's impossible if you fully believe in it." She tilted her head to the side. "How are plans for the retreat coming along?"

"It's not going to happen."

"You're chicken."

"Pardon?"

"You're chicken. You're scared of your art retreat actually happening." Wow. That came out of the blue.

"No, I'm not."

"Oh yes, you are, because if it happens you'll have to admit that it absolutely is possible to have it all. And I think that scares you. You're afraid of being happy."

"I'm more than happy, thank you very much!" Luke's indignant tone echoed down the valley.

"Really? Because it doesn't appear that way. I get that you don't want to let your dad down, and I absolutely understand why you try to keep the art from him. That's kind and considerate and I admire you for that. But when will you get to do what you want? When will you finally realize your dreams?"

Luke stared into the distance, his jaw set hard. He breathed in heavily through his nostrils then turned to face her, his gaze steely. "All you talk about are dreams, yet you're doing nothing to see your own to fruition. You blame it on people not being on board, or not having the right subject, or the timing being wrong. When will you stop blaming everyone else and just make it happen?"

"I have tried!"

"You're looking in the wrong places," he said.

"I look everywhere! I read books, newspapers, talk to people from all backgrounds and experiences…. I'm constantly searching for the subject that will get my documentary career off the ground."

"You don't get it, do you?"

"What?" She threw her arms wide. "What don't I get?"

"You're not looking here." He pointed at his heart.

"What has that got to do with anything?" Man, he was frustrating.

"You are thinking with your head. Once you find a topic that connects with your heart, it will show."

Annoyance roiled through her, because he was right. *Ugh.*

"Or," he continued, appearing quite pleased with himself, "you do it yourself."

"That's impossible."

"Don't you have contacts who would work with you?"

"It costs money. A *lot* of money. And yes, I have contacts, but it would be like pushing a ball of manure up the hill with a stick. Filming a documentary is just a small part. There are wages and distribution and other production costs and—"

"And?"

"And it's way more complicated than you think."

"Then un-complicate it," he said.

"If I could, I would." Her tone sounded just as cranky as Luke's had a short time ago.

"To quote the words of one Miss Montgomery, 'Nothing's impossible if you fully believe in it.'"

"Yeah, well, maybe Miss Montgomery is full of shit." She kicked a stone that skittered into the river. "I didn't want to see you so we could argue."

"You wanted help?"

"Yes," she said, grateful they'd changed the subject. "I know the insurance is looking after the inside of the theater. And I know I can't possibly make it up to Hattie, but I at least want to try."

"How?"

"I'd like to renovate the outside. Give it a face-lift. The facade itself isn't in bad shape, it's just faded and needs some plastering here and there."

"Who's going to pay for this?"

"I'll supply the materials and the labor."

"You can't do it all by yourself."

"I could, though it would take forever. I do have another idea, but I need your help."

Chapter Thirty

1952 – Hollywood

Lena was keen to leave the dressing room after a long day of filming. Her solo number had gone off without a hitch, and she hadn't been distracted by Reeves—she hadn't seen him all day. He was busy being fitted and going over his solos. Tomorrow, though, would be a different story, and Lena had no idea how she would deal with it. She liked to think she could be cool, calm and collected, but it would be a challenge. Her desire for Reeves raged constantly within.

She walked across the lot to her car, surprised by the warmth of the evening. Normally it was cooler this time of year, but the balmy temperature made her want to go home and take a nice, relaxing dip in the pool. A martini would make the perfect accompaniment.

Lena started the car and steered toward the gate that opened on Barney's command. Turning up the music, Lena sang and let the wind rush through the open windows, her hair whipping about. She took the long way home, reveling in being just another person driving home from work. This act of normalcy always helped ground her. She'd never let herself become one of those demanding actresses. It wasn't in her nature, yet some people managed to play the role of diva with ease.

Jeanne.

Lena had managed subtle updates from Reeves, even though no one had seen her for weeks. According to Reeves's agent, Jeanne was improving, but there was still a long road to full recovery.

Guilt threatened to muscle in on Lena every time she thought about stepping into a role originally meant for Jeanne, but what could she do? It wasn't like she had caused Jeanne's downfall—she'd been working toward that on her own for years. Lena was just helping out the studio in their hour of need. Though, if she were entirely honest, that wasn't what troubled her the most. Her flirtation and attraction to Reeves was what really concerned her, because if Jeanne ever found out…it could be her undoing.

Eager to get home, Lena turned off the main road and wended her way up the hill toward her house. This business with Reeves had to stop. As much as she wanted to be with him, it could damage Jeanne beyond measure, and Lena was not willing to be party to someone's meltdown. Though why should she be responsible for Jeanne's problems? After all, they started well before Jeanne and Lena had met. Regardless, Lena's conscience entertained the guilt.

"Fool," she chastised herself.

Lena arrived at the gates of her house and waited for them to open. She put her foot on the accelerator, then slammed on the brakes when a dark figure stepped out of the shadows.

She would recognize that incredibly attractive physique anywhere.

"And you say I drive like a race car driver," Reeves said as he approached her.

"What are you doing here?"

"That's a nice greeting." He grinned then his expression turned serious. 'We need to talk.'

"There's nothing to talk about."

"I think there is." He cocked his head toward her house. "Do you mind if we discuss this inside?"

She motioned for him to get in the car. His nearness drove her crazy, and she despised not feeling in control of her emotions. Or her body. It was almost impossible to concentrate on the narrow driveway. How on earth would she complete this film with her sanity intact?

Lena pulled up to the front door. She got out and climbed the steps, her shaking hands gripping the keys. It took a couple of tries to get her key in the lock, especially since she could feel Reeves directly behind her. It would be so easy to turn around and kiss him with fervor…but what if Reeves had different ideas? *Enough!* The only way to find out was to lay it all on the table. But right now talking was the last thing she wanted to do….

The door finally clicked open. She put her purse on the stand and removed her hat and gloves. Reeves placed his hat on the hook beside hers, and for a fleeting moment she wondered what it would be like if they did this every night.

No!

"Drink?" she asked as they walked to her living room.

"Sure."

"Sit, please." Her formality seemed odd, though she had no idea how to act around Reeves right now. They were in uncharted territory, but they had to figure out the map quickly, because time was not on their side. Lena set about preparing martinis, eyeballing the ingredients and shaking them like an expert.

"You've done this a few times before," said Reeves.

"You calling me an alcoholic?" she joked. She suddenly stopped shaking the vessel. "Sorry, that was not entirely appropriate."

"It's okay. We're allowed to make jokes, and I know you didn't direct that at Jeanne. You're not that kind of person."

Lena quickly finished making the cocktails. She handed one to Reeves, who took a sip. "This is the best martini I've had in a long time. Where did you learn to make these?"

"I worked as a waitress in a cocktail bar, and the barman showed me." Lena sat on the chair opposite Reeves. She sipped her drink, resisting the urge to down it in one gulp. Martinis hadn't reminded her of Charlie in years, but now the memories hit her with full force. Had she deliberately forgotten?

She placed her drink on the coffee table.

"Lena." Reeves also put down his drink. "I don't want what happened between us to be a one-time thing."

"It should be, though." She hated saying it. "We're professionals, and our personal lives should be separate. Besides, how would it look to the public? Jeanne is in rehab, for goodness sake!"

"Jeanne and I stopped being an item a very long time ago."

"But the public still believes you're together. We can't do this, Reeves. If word ever got out about our tryst, it could kill our careers. The public are not that forgiving. Nor is HUAC."

"Why do you care so much about what people think? What about you?" He leaned forward, his eyes earnest. "What do you want?"

"I…" Her mouth felt dry, and she glanced at the martini.

"Try to imagine the rest of the world doesn't exist—no producers, no directors, no Jeanne, no Pierre, no journalists scrounging for fodder for their magazines and newspapers, no public eagerly devouring gossip. *What do you want?*"

She studied her hands in her lap, forcing herself to hold back tears.

"What does your heart tell you, Lena?" Reeves's question was quiet and sincere.

She took a long, deep breath. "I don't think anyone has ever asked me that."

"Say whatever you want, I'm not going to judge."

She closed her eyes, hoping the tears and tumultuous emotions would stay at bay. "I've worked so very hard to get where I am. I've sacrificed a lot. I miss my family desperately. I miss where I grew up. I've lost friends. I love what I do, but I hate being in the public spotlight, because everything I do and say is judged harshly and misconstrued. However, I love that I can live in a place like I do. I love that I'm now in a position to help struggling actresses. I greatly appreciate the luxuries this work has afforded me. But..." She paused, scared to admit it, but needing to. "In a world where people are flocking to be in my company all the time, I'm lonely."

Reeves reached across the table and gently took her hand. "You don't need to be."

She pulled away. "We have enough going on with the movie. We really shouldn't confuse things."

"It's already too late for that." His eyes were earnest. "I'm lonely, too. We don't need to be sailing different waters."

"Reeves." She tried to draw up courage to say it. "It's not just us. There's so much you don't know about me and..." How to say this? "And I don't know if I'm ready to share just yet."

"Did you murder someone?" He laughed.

"No!" she yelled. "Absolutely not!"

"Okay!" He held up his hand. "I was only joking."

"Sorry," Lena said quietly, kicking herself for her dramatic reaction. She averted her gaze. It was now or never. "I'm Australian."

"What?"

"I'm Australian." She said it louder, letting the Australian accent she'd hidden for years roll off her tongue. It felt good. Like a part of her had been freed.

"Why have you kept this a secret?"

Lena's mouth hung open. "You're not angry I've not told you before?"

"Why would I be angry? You clearly started this charade years ago—way before we met. I'm glad you're telling me now, though."

"Errol Flynn," she blurted out.

"Errol Flynn?"

"Yes, Errol Flynn, he of the swashbuckling movies," Lena said.

"I know who he is, but what does he have to do with you?"

"I can't entirely blame him—he put Australia on the map in Hollywood. I know lots of people love him because of his bad-boy ways, but there is a huge double standard when it comes to the way men and women behave. It's hard enough making it in this industry without everyone assuming that I have loose morals and drink too much because I'm Australian."

"People really say that?"

"Time and again."

"But we've had plenty of foreign actresses make it big here. Hedy Lamarr is Austrian, Marlene Dietrich is German, Greta Garbo is Swedish—"

"But none of them are Australian. Name one big-name Hollywood actress who is Australian."

"I can't."

"My point exactly. All the actresses you mentioned have gorgeous, exotic accents. Not mine."

"Your accent is as beautiful as you are."

"Casting directors don't think so." She crossed her legs. "Wow. I never knew letting all this out could feel so good."

"You've kept all this bottled up? No one has ever known the true you?"

Lena bit her lip, fearing she may have opened Pandora's box a little too wide. This was more than enough information for now. When the time was right, she'd reveal the rest.

"Never in a million years did I think you were from anywhere but here."

"I have a good ear, and acting comes naturally."

"Obviously." Reeves slid back on the chair and put his hands behind his head. "But it does make me wonder how else you've been practicing your acting skills."

"If you're referring to us, rest assured it is not an act." She was indignant.

"I never doubted that."

"I'm glad," she said.

"Does anyone else know?" he asked.

"My agent, and a couple of others, but that's it."

"Yvonne and George?"

"It doesn't matter who. The thing is, I'm trusting you with my career on this. I hope you don't prove me wrong."

"You have that little faith in me?" he asked.

"No, I… It's just that…oh!" She shook her head. "I've spent so long living this lie that I don't know how to be *me*. I don't even know who me is!"

Reeves knelt in front of her, his hand reaching for hers. "Then let's find out."

The moment their lips met, any worry of fallout from her revelation disappeared. Reeves left a trail of soft, warm kisses along her neck and collarbone, and her body gave in to the desires she'd tried to suppress. Maybe now, in the arms of the man she couldn't resist, Lena would finally find out who she truly was.

Chapter Thirty-one

1952 – Hollywood

Once more, Reeves left Lena's bed before the sun made an appearance. She touched her lips, lost in the memory of yet another night of ecstasy with the man she was falling for. *Had* fallen for. As much as she wanted to deny it, Reeves Garrity was under her skin.

Resistance was futile.

A shot of panic pierced the bliss. She'd just told Reeves one of her biggest secrets. If he ever chose to leak it, she would instantly lose credibility. He may have understood her reasons, but she doubted her adoring fans would. By now, she'd proven herself reliable and talented, regardless of nationality. But no one liked being misled. Fans were smart, and they knew reporters sometimes printed lies, but they'd still feel betrayed by a lie as big as this one. She'd worked too hard and too long for any wrenches to be thrown in the spokes.

Lena showered and dressed, then decided to skip breakfast. An uneasiness in her stomach made her nauseous, and she wished she could will it away. Regardless, she had to get on set and start the day.

Driving toward Fortitude Studios, Lena pondered how things would play out with Reeves today. She'd been petrified yesterday, but after yet another night of lovemaking, and their talk, she felt she could hide her affection for him on set. She could do this. She was a professional.

She was in love.

Lena sucked in her breath.

No. No, no, no. Absolutely not.

But…

She slowly let the air out of her lungs.

There was no denying it.

Her heart was his. As much as she could give it.

She turned onto the lot and waved at Barney, who opened the gates. After parking near the studio, she walked into her dressing room, expecting it to be deserted at this early hour.

"Enjoying my life, are we?"

Lena dropped her purse, and the contents spilled across the floor.

"Jeanne? What...how...what..."

"What am I doing here? I'm out for good behavior." Her laugh sounded hollow. "I'm gone for six weeks and you move in on my role. I am far from impressed."

"Jeanne." Lena tried to keep her voice steady. "They couldn't stop production; it would have been too costly."

"They'll lose money with you at the helm, anyway. Who wants to see you in place of me?"

She tried to push Jeanne's words aside. "What are you doing here?"

"Oh." She moved around the dressing room, touching everything like she owned it. "Just checking on things."

"I'm sure there'll be a new role for you soon."

Jeanne ran her finger along the top of a painting, then screwed up her nose. "Given they thought I would be on my *vacation* longer, there's nothing in the works."

"I'm sorry to hear that." And she was. It couldn't be easy finding out someone had replaced you in what was being billed as the movie of the year. "It's good you were able to come back from your vacation early."

"Ugh!" Jeanne threw her hands in the air. "Let's stop tiptoeing about. I've had my eye on you for a long time, and I've seen you using your wiles to get what you want."

"Excuse me?"

"You know exactly what I mean."

"I'm afraid I don't." Lena wasn't willing to let Jeanne win this without a fight.

"Your rise to fame was swift. One minute you're doing bit parts, the next you've got your own movie." She narrowed her eyes. "Don't tell me there weren't any back-room shenanigans. You cheated me out of that musical theater production all those years ago, don't think you can keep doing it."

"You can't be more wrong. Just because you—"

"Now, now. No need for mudslinging."

But that was exactly what Jeanne was up to.

"I hear your friend George Barrett is in a spot of bother."

"That's none of your business."

"I make it my business to know what's going on around here. I may have been away, but that doesn't mean I'm not apprised of the latest developments."

How long had Jeanne known about Lena taking on her role? Perhaps that was just the fire Jeanne needed in her belly to get herself out of rehab and back to Fortitude Studios.

"Such a shame George is a communist. Just like his ex-lover, Oscar. You know, they say like enjoys the company of like, and you and George are such good friends. I understand you've had a visit from the gentlemen of HUAC."

Lena clenched her fists as a band of pain spread around her head. "It's way too early in the morning to deal with this nonsense. I'm asking you to leave."

"I'm not going anywhere until you hear me out." Jeanne stepped forward, her face inches from Lena's. "You may be the studio's darling right now, but rest assured, your star will not shine for long."

Lena resisted the urge to step away. Instead, she held her ground. "Your empty threats don't scare me."

"They are far from empty."

"Hey, Lena, you're in— Oh. Hello, Jeanne." Yvonne entered. "You're looking well."

Jeanne twisted her dark pink lips and turned to Lena. "This conversation is not over."

She stormed out the door. Lena collapsed onto a nearby chair.

"Whoa!" Yvonne's eyes were wide. "Are you all right?"

"Yes, yes," said Lena. "I was caught off-guard, that's all."

"She's hard enough to deal with at your best, let alone a surprise visit. I guess it was only a matter of time before she confronted you."

"You knew she was out of rehab?"

"I'm sorry, Lena, I thought you knew."

"Good morning, ladies!" Vanessa swanned in and wrapped a cape around Lena, then stopped and cupped her hand under Lena's chin. "Gee. You really need to get some sleep."

"I've had a lot on my mind," she muttered.

"Looks like I have my work cut out for me. Best get to it!"

* * * *

Reeves grabbed Lena's hand and they danced up the stairs, a chorus of men and women singing around them. They glided across the set, their steps in sync, their voices blending beautifully. Never in her life had she felt so at ease in front of the cameras.

With one last twirl, Lena fell into Reeves's arms as he dipped her and planted a kiss on her cheek. The electricity that sizzled up her spine almost caused her legs to give way, but Reeves held her tightly.

"Beautiful," he whispered, and she had no idea if he meant the performance or her. Either way, she didn't mind.

"Cut! Print!" yelled Henry. "Absolutely perfect! Let's take a break."

Reeves helped her to a standing position while the cast filtered toward the makeshift canteen outside the sound stage. The crew went to re-set for the next scene.

Lena moved toward the canteen, but Reeves grabbed her hand. She turned to face him, his fingers gently squeezing hers. "I've missed you."

"We can't do this here." She removed her hand and stepped away.

"I can't stop thinking about you."

"Reeves, I…" She quickly closed her mouth when Jeanne stepped from behind a tree at the side of the set.

"I knew it." Her voice was low, fire shining in her eyes. She shoved a manicured finger under Lena's nose. "I knew I couldn't trust you."

"Jeanne—" Reeves started.

She held up her hand in front of his face. "I don't need to hear it. I've seen more than enough."

"No." Reeves stepped forward. "You need to hear this. You and I broke up a long time ago, and there was never going to be a reconciliation. We talked about this. We agreed to continue the charade, but that was all."

"You will change your mind once you get tired of that—"

"You and I are over," Reeves said, his tone serious.

Jeanne lifted her chin. "We will see about that."

She stalked toward the open door of the sound stage, then paused and turned to face the workers who were busy doing their jobs.

"Just so you know," she said, loud enough for the crew to stop what they were doing. "I'm back, and I will be starring in Lawrence Doherty's next project, which will be nothing like this second-rate rubbish you're filming here."

A few crew members exchanged looks. Perhaps Jeanne had been expecting a round of applause? Lena felt sorry for her, as delusion seemed to be clouding her judgment. Jeanne flounced out the door, and Lena stood rooted to the spot, not sure what to say or do.

Henry walked over to them. "Her ego needs its own zip code."

"Looks like she's recovered," said Reeves.

Henry rubbed the back of his neck. "Indeed. The timing couldn't be worse; we haven't finished, and she gets to see what she's missed out on."

"I thought she was supposed to be on vacation for weeks, possibly months," Reeves said.

"We all know it wasn't a vacation," said Henry. "I hope it's true that Stuart has her working with Lawrence again soon, because I don't want her hanging around here causing trouble."

"I'm sure Stuart has something up his sleeve. He's always got plans A and B ready to go," said Lena, hoping this was the case.

"We'll see," said Henry. "Right-o. Let's get started."

"Sure," Lena and Reeves said in unison, then laughed.

If Jeanne hadn't shown up, Lena could have claimed today as being close to perfect.

* * * *

"Wow," Anna May said to Lena. The young chorus girl walked around the first of eight bedrooms in the house Lena had recently purchased. Anna May picked up a book about the craft of acting and turned it over in her hands. She put it down, then smelled the spray of orange and red flowers in the vase next to the bed. "This is beautiful!"

Anna May left the room and Lena followed. Her cheeks ached from smiling. It had taken Lena less time than expected to find the right house and decorate it. Now a group of sixteen women, two to a room, could share and bond and support each other as they took their first steps in their Hollywood acting careers.

Anna May entered the second bedroom and opened the doors of the wardrobe. Inside were dresses and suits of all colors and sizes. She turned to Lena, her eyes wide.

"I called in a few favors," said Lena. "Other actresses have donated outfits, shoes, handbags, beauty products and the like to help with auditions. I remember one of the hardest things when auditioning was having the right clothes to wear, so hopefully these will make it easier."

"This is incredible." Anna May gently stroked a turquoise cashmere sweater. "I can't believe your generosity."

"It's not just me, plenty of people were willing to help. We've all been in your position, and we understand how hard it can be."

"But none of you had to do this."

"But we want to." As promised, Reeves had partially funded the house with the proviso that his donation remained anonymous. And as soon as Lena had put the call out to affluent actresses and actors for donations, she'd been surprised by the positive reactions. Clothes, beds, books, sofas... anything and everything that could possibly be needed by young women had been donated. Nearly every single woman Lena had approached thanked her for looking out for the new arrivals, then proceeded to tell Lena about their early days, when they'd felt powerless and at the mercy of people who wanted to take advantage of them. It had broken Lena's heart, but it had also reinforced why this project was so badly needed.

"Thank you," said Anna May, her elfin face still in shock.

"There is one thing, though," said Lena, "and feel free to say no."

Anna May's face fell. "What is it?"

Lena reached for Anna May's hand. "You've been in Los Angeles for some time now, and I suspect you are well-versed in the lay of the land. These girls are going to need someone to look up to, someone they can go to for advice."

"Like a big sister?"

"Yes, exactly. So," said Lena, praying she'd get the answer she desired, "I would like you and one of your friends with similar experience to be big sisters to these girls."

"Really?" Her mouth fell open, her eyes wide.

"You're perfect for the job. And I'll be available if you need me. Also," she said, "I've organized for some actresses, and myself, to give the house free acting, singing and dance lessons as our schedules allow."

"Really?" Anna May laughed. "Sorry, that's the only word I can think of. I'm quite shocked, to be honest."

"Why?"

"I just never thought anyone would care," said Anna May.

"There are plenty of people who care."

"Thank you. Thank you so much!" Anna May wrapped her arms around Lena, squeezed her hard then pulled away. "I will be the best big sister, just you wait!" Anna May's excitement was contagious. "Does this place have a name?"

"Why don't you name it?" said Lena, full of joy.

"What about Stepping Stones?"

"I love it! Stepping Stones it is."

Chapter Thirty-two

1952 – Hollywood

Lena stood in the study with the telephone pressed to her ear. She'd been expecting this phone call for hours and finally, after much hand-wringing, it had arrived.

"Thank you," she said, trying to take it all in. "I'll let George know."

Lena hung up and turned to face her best friend, who waited on the leather Chesterfield. She replaced her earring and sat next to him, taking his hands in hers.

"The lawyers haven't got any further." The words were hard for her to say.

George hung his head, his shoulders sagging.

"I'm sorry, George."

"I can't even begin to thank you for all the trouble you've gone to." He sniffed.

"You don't need to thank me. I just wish there was something more I could do for you. If our team can get one of the Hollywood Ten's lawyers on board, we might get more insight as to how to best fight this."

"But they lost."

"Their experience could help us figure out to do this time around."

"It's worth the chance." This was the first time George showed a glimmer of hope since HUAC had started sniffing around him.

"I think it's a chance worth taking," she said, still not entirely convinced. Given the severity of the outcome if it went the other way, everything was worth a try.

"You know your helping me could incriminate you," he said.

"I really don't care." Although she did care, *a lot*, especially since everything else in her life had fallen into place. "You're my best friend, and I would never desert you."

"If you did, I'd understand."

"Nonsense." She waved her hand dismissively. "We've always been there for each other, so why stop now?"

"Because you could end up being accused, and the studio could drop you, and your career would be dead in the water. Or you could end up in jail."

"I won't. You won't. Everything will work out." She wished she believed it with as much certainty as she'd said it.

The doorbell rang, and she got up to answer, having given Rita the night off to go to the movies with her friend. Anticipation raced through Lena knowing Reeves would be on the other side. She swung open the door. "Well it's about time you—oh."

She gripped the doorframe to steady herself.

"Good evening, Miss Lee," said Ned Ramsay.

Her small kernel of confidence deflated the second she saw the HUAC representative. She looked around for Ramsay's offsider and spotted him smoking a few feet away.

"You really should lock your gates," he said. "Anyone can let themselves in."

Lena stared at the entrance to her property. There was absolutely no way Rita would have left the gate unlocked—she was one of the most reliable people Lena knew.

"Mr. Ramsay." She straightened her spine. "It is very late, and I would prefer you visit another time, if you don't mind." All she could picture was George sitting in the study, waiting for her to return.

"As promised, we did some digging and—"

"Miss Lee!" Reeves jogged up the driveway, then took the flagstone steps two at a time. He waved a script in the air. "Please forgive me for being so late to our rehearsal."

Lena stared at Reeves.

"For our scene tomorrow." Reeves raised his eyebrows.

"Oh! Yes! I'm sorry, Mr. Garrity, I didn't realize the time. We have so much to get through, and the last thing we need is to have to keep filming the same scene because we can't get it right."

Reeves turned to Ramsay. "I am sure you can understand the urgency of the matter. Perhaps you could make an appointment with Miss Lee for tomorrow? After she's finished filming for the day?"

Ramsay narrowed his eyes and pursed his lips.

Reeves slid past Ramsay and into Lena's foyer. Ramsay stepped forward and Lena blocked his progress.

"If you call administration, they will be sure to give you a suitable time," she said, all the while hoping the tremble spreading throughout her body wasn't visible.

Ramsay mumbled something and took a step in the direction of the driveway. Lena let her body relax.

Ramsay turned to face her. "You can tell your friend George we will be talking with him tomorrow too."

"I'll tell him when I see him," she said.

"I suspect that will be when you go back inside."

Lena quickly shut the door and leaned against it. Her temples throbbed, and she found it hard to catch her breath.

Reeves put his hand under her elbow and guided her to the study, where George stood, his face pale.

"I'm so sorry." George passed her a glass of water as Reeves helped her to the sofa. "I'm so, so sorry."

Lena gulped the cool water. "He's been spying on us."

"I think I better go. I've caused enough trouble already." George collected his hat and jacket. "I'll call later."

"No, probably best you don't," she said. "Who knows what they've done." She cocked her head in the direction of the telephone. If HUAC made a habit of watching her house, who knew what else they were capable of.

George leaned down and pecked Lena on the cheek. He whispered, "I will make this up to you."

Lena grabbed his hand and squeezed it. "You don't need to. It's society that has it wrong, not you."

George ran his hand down her face. "I love you, my beautiful friend."

"I love you more." She grinned.

George waved over his shoulder as he let himself out of the house. The small room seemed larger than before, a definite chill hanging in the air.

"Thank you so much, Reeves." She breathed out slowly. "How did you come up with the script idea?"

"I figured I needed a cover to enter your house at this hour, in case photographers were around. I certainly hadn't expected to see HUAC on your doorstep. Just as well I thought ahead, huh?"

"Just as well, indeed."

Reeves sat down next to her, and she collapsed into his arms. Resting her head against his chest, she listened to his steadily beating heart, taking comfort in the strength and security she felt in his arms. Although she didn't need a man, she wanted this one with all her heart.

"I'm worried for you." Reeves moved so he could look her in the eyes.

"Why?"

"With HUAC sticking their noses in, and the country's paranoia about Reds under the beds, innocent people are being accused, and their names are being dragged through the mud. It's getting out of control, and you've been pulled into it."

"It's not George's fault."

"I understand, but it's not easy watching you get harassed for being friends with someone they've targeted."

"Being a friend means standing by someone through thick and thin," said Lena.

"Even if you could lose your career? Or worse?"

She moved back. "What are you saying? I should dump my best friend?"

"No, of course not! Maybe you should just…not spend so much time with him for a while. Every minute you're with him gives them ammunition."

"I cannot believe you said that." Lena stood and walked over to the mantelpiece. She picked up a framed photo and held it in front of Reeves. In the photo, George draped his arm around Lena's shoulders as they both smiled at the camera. Her hair was natural, her makeup understated. She looked so free. So unburdened by the complications of the life she now led. "George was one of my first friends in this business and he's been with me ever since, riding the rollercoaster. He needs me more than ever, and I'll be damned if I desert him now."

"Lena." Reeves motioned for her to sit next to him.

She shook her head.

"Please."

"I can't believe you think I'm the type of person who would leave their friend when they need help."

"I meant for you to not spend so much time with George at the moment," he said, his voice low, "not give up on him."

Lena put down the frame, then crossed her arms.

"I can understand your defensiveness."

"I'm not defensive!"

Reeves studied her intently.

"I think you should go," she said. "I'm not in the mood for company."

He stood, his eyes soft. "I do understand your loyalty to George, and I love that you are standing by him. Everyone needs a friend like you. I'm just concerned about the spotlight onto your private life when you've tried so hard to keep it in the dark."

"I haven't."

"Lena," said Reeves. "We've had long conversations, yet you've managed to keep the most intimate details of your life a secret."

"I told you, I'm Australian."

"And I appreciate you telling me. But I want to know the real Lena Lee. What makes you tick? What was your first pet's name? What was it like growing up in small-town Australia?"

Whether it was the exhaustion of Ramsay's visit, worry for George, or the energy it took to keep her true life at bay, Lena felt ready to bare her soul.

"I come from a small town in northern Queensland called Starlight Creek." Those first few words broke the last barrier. "My family owns a sugarcane farm. My father runs it, and my mother is in charge of the local cinema. People come from far and wide to see movies."

"Your movies?"

"Yes. But my family are the only ones who know it's me. I've changed a lot since I left Starlight Creek. With my hair and makeup done, I look very different from the country girl who left town at seventeen."

"I can't see how people couldn't recognize your natural beauty, even after all the layers of Hollywood."

She laughed, feeling lighter by the minute. "Thank you. Though I'm not a natural redhead, I'm blond."

"I did suspect that was the case."

"How...oh!" She looked away briefly, trying to compose herself. "Anyway, I grew up watching movies, and longed for a more glamorous life than the sugarcane fields. Don't get me wrong, Starlight Creek is the most beautiful place, and it's very dear to my heart, but I always felt like a fish out of water."

"How on earth did a girl from northern Queensland end up in Hollywood?"

"We're going to need a drink." Lena got up and prepared martinis. In a short moment she was back by Reeves's side, handing him the cocktail.

He took a sip. "This is yet another talent of yours. How did you end up working in a cocktail bar?"

"One step at a time, Mr. Reeves." She sipped her martini, the alcohol taking the edge off the nerves. Exposing herself like this made her vulnerable. Not even George knew the full story. Maybe she needed to reel herself in, but the freedom she now felt far outweighed the caution she'd clung to like a life raft in a stormy ocean. "I spent my childhood watching movies with my favorite actresses—Vivien Leigh, Katharine Hepburn, Bette Davis, Greta Garbo—all very strong and inspiring women."

"Like you." Reeves held her hand.

"You are the most excellent charmer," she said, her voice shaking. Why was she so nervous?

"I don't set out to charm," he said. "Please tell everything, I want to know all about you."

"So," she continued, measuring her words, "I dreamed about being an actress in Hollywood, but never in a million years thought it could happen. When I was seventeen I went to visit my cousin in Sydney and a photographer spotted me. Next thing I knew I had an agent and was modeling swimwear, which led to work for fashion magazines."

"Do you have any photos? I'd love to see a young—younger—Lena Lee."

"Nice save there," she joked. "Anyway, the American branch of one of the magazines saw my photos and asked me to come to the States. I didn't need much encouragement, so I got on a plane and found myself in New York, meeting modeling agents and eventually seeing my face on billboards."

"Impressive."

"It was an easy ride, which always made me wary."

"Very smart thinking." Reeves stroked the side of her face. "Beauty and brains."

Lena closed her eyes, reveling in his warm touch. Although she wanted to remain like this forever, she also wanted to continue with her story. *Needed* to continue. "Modeling paid the bills, but it didn't fulfill me. I despised being judged solely on my looks, and I knew the gravy train wouldn't last forever. A prettier, younger model could come along at any minute and take my place, then where would I be? I decided to invest in my future and took acting classes. I did a few small plays and musicals off-Broadway, but they didn't change the world. Certainly not mine. Though they did light a fire in my belly. I remember reading an article about Mae West being thirty-nine years old when she started in movies. It gave me hope. And I'd also remembered reading about her clever negotiation with the studio head."

"Ah, yes. Didn't she ask him how much he earned?"

"She did, and then she asked to be paid one thousand dollars more, because then she'd be the highest paid at the studio, which would secure her position."

"Very clever."

"Absolutely," said Lena. "With my sights set on making it in the movies, I arrived in Hollywood and realized no matter how much I wanted something, there were no guarantees I'd get it."

"Do you have what you want now?"

"Yes." Without a second thought, she leaned forward and kissed Reeves. His arms wrapped around her tightly, pulling her close, his musky cologne tingling her nose.

"Maybe we should continue this conversation upstairs," she whispered.

"Perhaps we've done enough talking for tonight."

* * * *

Lena lay in bed, enjoying the warm breeze dancing across her naked body. An orange glow filled the room, the darkness of the night a faded memory. Rolling over, she studied Reeves sleeping soundly. She ran a hand along his arm, across his chest and placed a finger on his lips.

His smile was slow and alluring. "Good morning."

"Good morning," she said. "I like that you're the first person I see when I wake up."

Reeves looked at her with his dark, hypnotizing eyes. If only they didn't have to be on set shortly....

"We could make this a permanent thing," he said.

"How?"

"Marry me."

"Pardon?"

"Marry me, Lena Lee. I love you."

"How can you love me when you still don't know everything about me?"

"My heart knows enough. I want to be with you forever. I want to whisk you away to a tropical paradise, you and me being ourselves, away from all the nonsense that drags us down, makes us full of self-doubt." He sat up. "Let's do it."

"Reeves…"

"I'm serious."

"Reeves." She sat up next to him. "I love that you want to do this. But it's not practical. We'd never work again if we left right now."

"We might never work again anyway."

Memories of last night's HUAC visit hit her like a punch in the gut. "Please, let's forget that. Let's just be in this moment, enjoy it for what it is."

"What is it?"

Lena placed her hand under his chin and kissed him slowly, longingly, with all the desire that surged through her. "I love you."

"So you'll marry me?"

There was only one answer.

"Yes, I will marry you, Reeves Garrity," she said with conviction.

Lena wondered how one of the biggest decisions of her life could be made in a split second. It was as if this moment had been brewing since the minute they met.

Reeves jumped out of bed and pulled on his shorts, then trousers. He grabbed his shirt and buttoned it, all the while bouncing around like an excited kid. "You have made me the happiest man on earth!"

"And I'm the happiest woman!" Lena laughed, got out of bed and put on her silk robe. She helped him with the buttons on his shirt. "There's just one thing."

Reeves stopped fidgeting. "Yes?"

"We should keep this between ourselves for now. With our lives under the microscope and Jeanne just out of rehab, I think it's better if we enjoy this alone—for now. I don't want it ruined."

"Sure." Reeves tugged at the belt on her robe. "Maybe we could be a little late today?"

She slapped him on the buttocks. "Out! We've got a movie to make!"

Chapter Thirty-three

Lena stood in her dressing room and pulled at the red silk dress that clung to every curve of her body.

"Cut it out!" Yvonne laughed. "If you're not careful you'll split it."

"That's what I'm afraid of! I don't know how I'm going to walk in it, let alone wrestle anyone."

"Oh, that's right, you've got a huge scene today." Yvonne waved to Vanessa, who rushed over and applied yet another coat of red lipstick to Lena's lips.

"There!" said Vanessa, admiring her handiwork. "No more talking, or else it'll wear off."

"I've got lines." Lena laughed.

"Keep it to a minimum until you're on set, then," said Vanessa.

"Ha! I'd like to see the day!" said Yvonne. "Although…"

"What?" Lena asked.

"You've been awfully relaxed this morning."

"I'm always like this before a big scene," Lena said.

"No, no. There's something different. What's up?"

"Nothing's up!" She really needed to calm herself.

"Aha!" Yvonne waggled a finger.

"Aha what?" Lena asked, happy she'd managed to sound less suspicious.

"You're in love."

"No, I'm not!"

"Who is it?" Vanessa moved closer.

"No one!"

"The lady doth protest too much."

Lena snorted at Yvonne's attempt at Shakespeare. "I'm just nervous about this scene. It's the most emotional and powerful one I've ever done, and I want to get it right."

Yvonne tilted her head.

"Come on." Vanessa put her hand on the small of Lena's back. "You're going to be late."

Lena walked out the door and straight into the last person she wanted to see.

"Jeanne." What was she doing here?

"I see you're dressed for the part. Harlot suits you." Jeanne's sweet tone didn't match her words.

"I need to be on set." Lena moved to go past, but Jeanne blocked her way.

She leaned in close, her hot breath sending shivers down Lena's spine. "I know your game, Lena, and I can play it way better than you ever could. I am watching."

Jeanne turned, stalked down the corridor and out of the building. An arctic breeze enveloped Lena and she shivered.

"Was that Jeanne?" Reeves sidled up beside her and placed a protective hand on the small of her back. "What did she say?"

"It doesn't matter." She shook her body, trying to free up the tense muscles. "She's just being Jeanne."

"That is never a good thing."

"Let's not worry about her now."

"We have much better things to think about." Reeves planted a kiss on her neck and whispered, "We can celebrate tonight."

"Shh." She pushed him away, but loved the attention all the same. "We're a secret, remember?"

"Yes, yes." He drew himself to his full height and in a louder voice said, "Miss Lee, shall I accompany you to the set?"

"Why yes," she said just as loudly. "That would be delightful."

They arrived on set and Henry hurried up to them. "We're not quite ready."

"That's okay," she said, relieved she could spend a little more time preparing. Seeing Jeanne had rattled her, and she needed a moment to get into the right frame of mind. She pointed at a chair in the far corner. "I'll wait over there."

"Sure, sure." Henry buzzed away, and Reeves went over to a table and poured himself a coffee while she took a seat.

Just breathe. Lena inhaled through her nostrils and exhaled through her mouth.

"Miss Lee."

She jumped and gripped the wooden arms of the chair.

"I'm sorry to startle you," said the young man with blue eyes and blond hair.

"It's all right, really." She willed her body to relax.

"I just wanted to introduce myself before we got started today."

"You're Alan?"

"Yes." He beamed. "I'm the man you're going to kill."

Lena laughed and held out her hand. "Nice to meet you, Alan. I'm sorry about killing you today."

"It is an honor to die at your hands." Laughter danced in his eyes. "I hope you don't mind me telling you how much I admire your work. I've followed your career for quite some time."

"Well, thank you, Alan. Your words are very kind." She spotted Henry waving her over. "I believe we're about to start."

Alan followed Lena over to Henry. "Ready?"

"As I'll ever be." Lena resisted the urge to adjust the dress once more. Yvonne had assured her this was perfect for the scene, though Lena was yet to be convinced, especially as her breasts felt like they were exploding over the low neckline.

Lena, Reeves and Alan talked with Henry about their motivations and the emotions they'd be portraying during the scene. Once everything had been covered, Henry got them ready for blocking. Lena always likened it to choreographing a dance, where Henry would get the actors into the right positions, making sure the camera angles and lighting were what he envisioned. She didn't know how he did it, but Henry always got the best from everyone.

"Right, rehearsal!" Henry yelled.

Reeves took his place at the side of the set, ready to enter when the time was right. Their eyes connected, and for a fleeting moment the world melted away. Their silent conversation said everything: *I love you.*

Lena smiled as she moved her head from side to side, trying to loosen the muscles in her neck. She rested her arm on the mantelpiece and waited for Alan to take his mark.

"Lena!" Yvonne came up to her.

"Off the set!" yelled Henry.

"She needs her purse!" Yvonne thrust the glossy red purse at her friend. "Your prop's in there."

Lena opened it and checked. "Thank you."

"Of course." Yvonne walked away, saying over her shoulder to Henry, "I was quick!"

Henry rolled his eyes. "Places! One rehearsal, that's all you're getting."

She waited for the countdown and the signal. Taking a calm breath, she began. "You cannot blackmail me."

Alan stepped forward, his long legs and arms not quite coordinated. "I will do what is required to get the results I want."

"No one will believe you," she said, getting into full swing. Channeling her inner vixen, Lena slowly walked toward Alan. The dress restricted her movement, and she found it difficult to sway her hips. It didn't help that her heels had started to pinch. With her face inches from Alan's, she said, "Your plan is already thwarted."

Alan grabbed her by the hair and pulled her body against his.

The door burst open and Reeves stormed through. He grabbed Alan and yanked him away.

"Get your hands off her!" shouted Reeves.

Alan's laugh was perfect. "She's the one with her hands on me."

Reeves looked at Lena, anger roiling in his eyes.

Boy, can he act.

"Is this true?" he demanded.

"No!" she shouted, her body tense. "He's trying to blackmail me, but he can't prove a thing."

"Oh, I can." Alan edged forward, then turned to Reeves. "You should know she—"

"Stop!" Lena grabbed the pistol out of her purse and held it with both hands, aiming it at Alan. "Enough! No more lies!"

Alan drew closer. "You're not going to use it. You don't have the courage."

"I do!" she yelled, her hands shaking. Lena clicked off the safety, just like she'd been shown by the weapons specialist. It was scary enough holding a fake pistol, how would a real one feel? "Not one step closer."

Alan moved forward, and Reeves jumped on him. The men tussled, rolling over the sofa onto the floor, just as it had been choreographed. Lena skirted around the men, her pistol aimed at Alan, who appeared a little too enthusiastic about this fight scene.

"Stop!" she yelled. "Or I'll shoot!"

Alan reached up and grabbed for the pistol, just like he was meant to, but he grabbed too hard. She lost her balance, the tight dress restricting her. She toppled toward the floor, her finger squeezing the trigger.

A loud bang resounded.

Her arm jerked back with force and she fell hard.

Lena dropped the pistol and lifted herself onto all fours. She used the sofa to stand unevenly, as she'd lost a shoe in the scuffle.

Alan lay slumped on top of Reeves, both men facing the ground. Neither man moved.

"Bravo!" said Henry. "Let's get this on film."

Alan stood and wiped his brow. "That was louder than I thought it would be."

"We have a great props department," said Lena. She looked over at Reeves, who still lay on the floor. "Get up, lazybones."

Reeves didn't move.

"Reeves." His name caught in her throat. She kneeled down, her dress ripping at the back. "Reeves?"

Lena shook him.

"Stop messing around." She shook him again, then saw a dark red liquid oozing across the floorboards. "Oh god! No!"

Chapter Thirty-four

1994 – Starlight Creek, Queensland

Claire shielded her eyes from the sun to look at the ladders and wooden planks in front of the cinema. Turning to Luke, she asked, "You're sure Hattie will be out of town for as long as this takes?"

"Yep. She hasn't seen her cousin in Brisbane for years, so they'll have lots to catch up on."

"She didn't figure out that you were trying to get rid of her?"

Luke laughed. "Absolutely she did, but she also knew arguing would be futile. For once, I had the upper hand."

"Bet that doesn't happen often," joked Claire.

"Nope, not at all." Luke eyed the plaster, paint and tools Claire had gathered. "Are you sure about this?"

"Absolutely." She grabbed a trowel and bucket of plaster. "My parents used to renovate houses when we were kids, and we'd get involved. And they specialized in Art Deco, so I'm more than familiar with what's needed to bring authenticity."

"Is this why you wanted to work on the miniseries?"

"Partly. Plus, the whole Amelia Elliott story is fascinating. Did you know she had to petition to attend architecture school because women weren't deemed suitable candidates?"

"I had no idea."

"She's such an inspiration. If they hadn't made a miniseries about her I would definitely have pushed to make a documentary." She climbed up the ladder and onto the wood plank, balancing the bucket in her hand.

"You've definitely done this before." He looked up at her.

"I help out on set when they need it." She got a steady foothold while Luke climbed the ladder.

"Higher than I'd thought," he said.

"It's kinda nice being up here. If anyone wants to lynch me, they'll have to climb the ladder."

Luke laughed. "They have a hard time letting go."

"Well, as soon as I'm done here, I'll leave and—"

"Don't."

"Don't what?" she asked.

Luke grabbed her hand. "Don't leave."

"Luke..." She pulled her hand free. "It's not fair to expect me to give up my life and dreams for a long-distance relationship. Although..." She got the trowel ready. "No. Forget it."

"You can't start something and not finish it."

She stood straight. "Well, we've started something, but we're going to have to finish it. I don't want it to end, I really don't. I love being with you—you're talented, you're caring and you're so goddamn sexy and I'm falling—have fallen—for you. And I'm petrified that if I stay here too much longer I'll never leave."

"We can find a way." Luke rubbed his temples. "I swore I would never get involved with anyone from outside Starlight Creek, and now look." He ran his fingers through her hair and she rested her cheek in his palm. "I'm doing everything I swore I wouldn't."

"Let's just concentrate on this for now." She pulled away and focused on plastering the gaps. Her hands shook, and her throat hurt from keeping her emotions inside. Quietly, she said, "I want us to enjoy the time we have together."

Luke didn't answer; he turned to the task at hand. Upset by his silence, she continued crafting the plasterwork. Up close, it wasn't anywhere near as bad as she'd expected. What a shame life wasn't like that.

The sun beat down and she could feel her skin burning even though she had on a long-sleeved T-shirt. She adjusted her hat, but it flipped off and landed on the edge of the ladder. Claire reached for it and noticed a small group of townsfolk had gathered below. There was the woman with the baby, and Marcela, a few others she'd met at the pub, and even Colin from the news agency had ventured onto the street. She waved, but only Marcela returned the gesture.

Luke stopped and looked at the silent group. He whispered to Claire, "You alienate people wherever you go."

Incensed, she opened her mouth, about to let fly, but shut it when she noticed his cheeky smile. She threw a rag at his head.

"What are you doing?" yelled Colin.

"He was being—"

"Not that." He waved his hand dismissively. "What are you doing to Hattie's cinema?"

"We're organizing a surprise," Claire yelled back.

"She is not going to like this!" Colin shouted.

"She will love it." Luke peered over the edge. "You're welcome to help us."

"Not with her at the helm." Colin stormed off and the rest followed behind.

Claire looked at Luke. "You were right."

"About what?"

"I've alienated just about everyone in Starlight Creek."

"Claire." He held her hand. "This town has been divided for as long as I can remember; it wasn't just the backpackers. I have no idea what started it, but Starlight Creek has always been a town in denial. We like to think we're a community but, as you've seen, we're far from it."

"It's odd," she said. "They accept Scarlet and Laura."

"Only to a degree," said Luke. "Starlight Creek is tough unless you've been here for generations. Even Hattie found it difficult to assimilate once she came back."

"Where was she?"

"She was in Sydney for some time." Luke wiped his forehead. "How about we take a break?"

"Sure." She climbed down the ladder, looking forward to getting out of the hot sun for a while. "I'll grab us something from Scarlet's."

"Thank you. I might go call Hattie and check she's settled in to her cousin's place."

Claire waved at Luke as he crossed the road to the phone booth. She'd gotten used to having a mobile phone with her and had lamented giving it back once production was over. Maybe one day she could afford her own.

She walked under the shade of the verandas, careful to avoid eye contact with Colin. Relieved at avoiding detection, she kept her head down, Scarlet's café in sight.

"Miss Montgomery."

Crap.

"Yes?" She used her sweetest voice and plastered on a smile before she turned to face Colin.

"Why are you doing that?"

"Repairing the facade of Hattie's cinema?"

He arched an eyebrow. "I don't see you doing anything else."

"The insurance is looking after the inside."

"Yes, well, I'm not talking about that." Colin closed his mouth, and she waited for him to say something else. But the silence dragged on, and she wondered how long this weird stand-off would last. "If you think renovating the front of the cinema is going to get you in the good books, it won't."

"To be honest, Colin, I don't care what you think. I'm doing this for a lady who has been very kind to me, even when I let her down. She could have chastised me and made me feel like I was the lowest person on earth—instead, she realized that my intentions were honorable and that I would give anything to take back what happened. But I can't." She was on a roll, and she couldn't stop. "So I am trying to bring sunshine to her life by doing something nice for her. It's not to win her over. It's not a bribe. It has nothing to do with anyone else in Starlight Creek except Hattie Fitzpatrick."

"You look pretty cozy with her great-nephew."

"It's none of your business," she said. "Aren't there are more serious issues around here than a miniseries being made?"

"You almost burned down the cinema."

Claire inhaled slowly. She counted to ten. It didn't work—she was still angry. "The problems in this town are not because of outsiders—they're because of you. *All* of you. And before you say anything, I am not perfect, that's for sure, but at least I have the guts to examine who I am and work on myself. This town is toxic. I have no idea why I once thought this was paradise."

Colin held his head in his hands and she immediately felt terrible.

"Colin, I'm so—"

"You're right."

"Pardon?" She'd never expected this.

"You're right, Miss Montgomery." He looked up, his eyes sad.

"You can call me Claire."

"Claire." He gave a small nod. "You are right. There's been in-fighting for generations, and it's poisoned our town. I've been aware of it for years, but just didn't want to admit it. We only bond over our mutual annoyance for outsiders."

"You do realize this is strange, right? If you'd given our production a chance, you might have found it interesting."

He didn't speak for quite some time.

"I need a favor, Miss—Claire."

"Sure," she said, then worried she'd just committed to something she'd regret.

"Can you write a list of everything you need to complete the work? Perhaps draw up a roster of times and jobs?"

"You're going to help?"

"We are all going to help. It's high time the townsfolk of Starlight Creek came together to build, not destroy."

* * * *

The next week passed in a whirlwind of activity. Once the cinema had been declared safe, everyone from Marcela to Colin to the checked-shirted teenagers lent a hand. Claire was in her element, coordinating everyone, and Luke gave sanding and painting lessons to those who needed them. Before long, the faded paintwork and chipped plaster transformed into an Art Deco pièce de résistance. The blue facade matched the sky, the yellow trims represented the sun and the broken marquee board had been replaced. The electrician worked on the lights after he'd rewired the damaged electrics.

The ladders had been taken down, and Claire stood back and admired their handiwork, not quite able to believe everything they'd achieved in such a short time. Even more incredible was the camaraderie that had evolved.

"Afternoon tea!" called Scarlet, who was trailed by Laura. They each carried a large tray filled with sandwiches, cakes and fruit.

"I'm off to get my camera," said Marcela as she headed to her shop at the other end of town.

The rest of the locals made their way over to the spread. Laura handed out serviettes, and when one of the teenagers reached for one, their fingers touched and lingered. The guy said something quietly, and Laura laughed then looked down, her face flushed.

"Young love?" Luke appeared beside her.

"Maybe," said Claire. "It's kind of sweet."

Luke's hand slid around her waist and pulled her close. In her ear, he whispered, "I can't wait to get you alone."

Claire closed her eyes and wished she could stop time. The last few days had been bliss, but they still had to finish *the* conversation. It wasn't going to be pretty.

"She's coming!" yelled Marcela, out of breath from running down the street.

"Hattie? But she's not supposed to be here until tomorrow," said Claire, disappointed. "We haven't got the letters up on the marquee yet."

Luke squeezed her shoulder. "This is going to be a big enough surprise for her."

"What if she doesn't like the colors? What if she wanted to keep it the same? After all, she hadn't had it painted. Oh no." She clapped her hand her over mouth. "What if she hates it?"

"Then I will take the blame," he said.

"No, no. This was my idea. I'll deal with the consequences." Claire tasted metal in her mouth and realized she'd bitten her lip so hard it was bleeding.

"She's here! She's here!" cried Marcela.

The taxi pulled around the corner and stopped outside the cinema. The door opened and Luke rushed over to help his great-aunt. She stood on the footpath, her eyes not leaving the cinema.

"Dad was going to get you from the station tomorrow," said Luke.

Hattie kept her eyes on the cinema, her expression not betraying a single emotion. "I'm here a day ahead of schedule, and your father has enough going on with the farm. I didn't want to trouble him."

Claire stood near enough to hear the conversation without being obvious. She held her breath, unsure what to do. Better to leave it to Luke.

"I see you have been busy," she finally said, her eyes transfixed.

"Not just me. I had many, many helpers." He waved Claire over. "This clever and kind human coordinated it all."

Claire stood next to Luke with apprehension. "This was a community effort."

"Claire came up with the idea." Luke held her hand.

"I…I just don't know what to say." It was impossible to tell from Hattie's tone or expression how she really felt. Hattie reached out for Luke's hand. "I need to sit."

Claire ran over to the table and picked up a folding chair. A group of eyes followed her every move, and she prayed this surprise wasn't too much for Hattie. Luke had assured Claire that Hattie would love it, but, watching Hattie's reaction, Claire was scared they'd misjudged the state of her health.

She put the folding chair under the shade and Hattie sat, her lips pursed. Claire handed her a glass of water. Luke's eyes met Claire's and she knew he was thinking the same.

Hattie took her time sipping. She finished the water and handed the glass to Luke.

"It's beautiful," Hattie said. "I'm lost for words." A sob escaped her lips, and Claire knelt down and reached for her hands.

"Really?"

Hattie nodded. "No one has ever done anything so special."

"This is the least we could do," said Claire. "It's a way to thank you for being such a wonderful, caring person, and it's also my way to say sorry. I never meant to let you down."

"Oh, dear girl." Hattie rested her shaking hand on Claire's head. "Your heartfelt words were enough. But this..." Her gaze traveled the building. "This is so very beautiful." She reached into her handbag, pulled out a handkerchief and dabbed her eyes.

"Everyone helped," said Claire. "Starlight Creek is quite the community."

"Excuse me." Hattie moved to stand, and Luke held her arm. "I need a moment."

She went inside the cinema's open door, her pace slightly slower than usual.

"Should you go in?" Claire asked Luke.

"No. Let her have a moment. She likes to be alone when she gets emotional."

Claire checked her watch. "Maybe we should call it a day."

"Good idea. I'll deal with it." Luke went across the road and spoke to the helpers. They nodded, polished off the food then started packing away the equipment.

Colin walked up to her. "That was an anticlimax."

"I guess so," she said. "It would have been nice to have the marquee finished."

"Ah, well, best-laid plans and all that."

"Yep. Thanks for your help. We can finish tomorrow."

"It is a pleasure...Claire." Colin's warm smile helped lift her spirits.

Luke returned and put his arm around her. She rested her head on his shoulder, committing this feeling to memory.

"Maybe I should go and check on her," he said.

"I'll pack up out here."

Luke kissed her on the forehead and went inside while Claire busied herself. He and Hattie must have been deep inside the cinema, as Claire couldn't hear a word, which was probably just as well. Her desire to eavesdrop was not something she was proud of.

"Claire." Luke appeared at the door, his expression serious.

She placed a paint tin on top of another. "What's wrong?"

"Come inside."

She followed Luke, her nerves on edge. In the foyer she hesitated, allowing her eyes to adjust to the darkness.

Luke's warm breath grazed her ear. "Come with me."

Claire walked into the cinema but couldn't find Hattie.

"Take a seat," said Luke.

She did so and looked around, intrigued but concerned. A moment later Hattie appeared with a metal canister.

"Are you sure?" asked Luke.

Hattie's voice faltered. "Yes."

Luke went over and took it from her. He whispered something in her ear and gave her a quick hug, then disappeared up to the projector room with the canister.

Claire stood and went over to Hattie. "You're not upset?"

Hattie patted her hand. "No, my darling girl."

They sat and Claire got comfortable. The aroma of freesias surrounded Claire and she inhaled subtly. The scent matched Hattie perfectly—sweet and strong.

Hattie leaned in close. "I wish we had popcorn."

Claire rummaged in her handbag. "Mints?"

Hattie popped one in her mouth and sucked on it slowly.

The screen flickered to life. Music blared through the speakers and Luke turned it down. In black and white, a man appeared on-screen, his dark hair framing a handsome face with a strong jaw.

"He's gorgeous," said Claire.

"Shh."

Claire pursed her lips, worried she'd broken a rule. The man in the movie was running through dark alleys, gunshots in the distance. He wove between cars on the main street and skillfully swerved around poles and bins. When he entered another alleyway, a door opened and the silhouette of a woman appeared.

"I thought you'd never get here," she said.

"I had a few things to take care of." He entered, and the scene changed to inside the house, where the man held the woman in his arms. The camera panned back to slowly reveal her face. Her lips were painted perfectly, her eyelashes long, her hair curled and pinned in an early 1950s style.

Claire couldn't keep her eyes off the woman. She looked familiar, though Claire couldn't figure out the actress's name. She'd seen dozens of Hollywood classics over the years, but had she seen this particular actress before?

Claire listened intently to the actress's voice. She sounded a little like… Hattie, even though the actress spoke with a strong American accent. Claire rested her elbows on her knees as the actress glided around the apartment, giving the actor a hard time.

"Is that Pierre Montreaux?" Claire asked, hoping she wouldn't get shushed again.

"Yes." Hattie sounded distant.

The camera closed in on the actress, the lens soft, accentuating her beauty.

"And is that Lena Lee?"

"Yes," said Hattie.

"Why are you showing me this?" Claire spun to face Luke's great-aunt. "Oh my god. Are you Lena Lee?"

Chapter Thirty-five

Hattie waved her hand in the air and the movie shut off. A few moments later, Luke joined Claire and his great-aunt in the cinema.

"Did you know about this?" Claire asked.

"Yes, but only for the last few years."

She couldn't quite get her head around this revelation. "When I first arrived here you pushed me away. You were super defensive about filming at the cinema, and you didn't want me to meet Hattie."

"Yeah, sorry about that."

"You were just trying to protect her. What were you afraid of, though? That someone would recognize her? What's wrong with someone finding out Hattie's a Hollywood star?"

Luke looked at Hattie, who said, "I've spent the best part of forty years trying to forget who I was. I have my reasons, and in due time I'll let you be privy to them, but for now, I need you to have an open mind."

"Of course," she said.

"My time in Hollywood feels like another life, and I guess it was. I'd become so good at being someone else that I eventually forgot the essence of me. And because of my ability to reinvent myself, when the time came to come back to Australia, I was able to slip into my old life, albeit a changed person."

"But people in Starlight Creek would have known about your life in Hollywood, right?"

"They did, but it was a tight-knit community back then. Just like Luke, they protected me from the outside world. As time has worn on, though, our little town has fragmented."

"Until this week," said Luke. "Funny how it took an outsider to bring us together again."

"Indeed," said Hattie. "Words cannot express my gratitude."

"It's the least I can do," said Claire.

"There's something else you can help with, but we'll come to that shortly. First, there are some things you need to know." Hattie told Claire about her early days in Starlight Creek, and how she came to be a swimsuit model, which eventually led her to Hollywood. Claire listened with fascination, taking in every word while closely watching Hattie's movements, listening to the nuances in her speech. As the story unfolded, Claire's empathy for this courageous woman grew.

"Then I fell for a man who meant the world to me," said Hattie. "But things happened—many things I regret, and some I had no control over— and one split second changed my entire life."

"What happened?" Claire asked.

"Ah, this is where you doing me a favor comes in."

"Oh?"

"I've been observing you, seeing the passion in your eyes and hearing it in your voice, about how much you want a project you can embrace." Hattie shifted in her seat. "I've spent too long keeping this secret, and the time has come for me to lay it on the table. Even Luke doesn't know about all of it."

"Why are you trusting me?" she asked.

"I trust you because you are a woman after my own heart," said Hattie. "You're trying to make the world a better place, but you haven't had a break. And I'm offering you one on a silver platter, my dear."

"You want me to make a documentary? I would love nothing more!" Her enthusiasm waned slightly. "Though it could take forever to get funding."

Hattie smiled. "I've lived a frugal life since coming back. I can pay for this project."

Claire swallowed hard. "Are you sure? This would be my first documentary. What if I don't do your story justice? What if—"

"Claire," Hattie said firmly. "I would not be asking you to do this if I didn't think you were the right person. Luke would not be in love with you if you didn't have a beautiful soul."

"What?" Claire looked at Luke, whose eyes were wide.

"Oh, please," Hattie said. "You two have been dancing around each other like you have all the time in the world. At your age, it probably feels like you do. Believe me, though, life can change in the blink of an eye, and the future you thought would always be there can be ripped away."

"Aunt Hattie, Claire and I are more than capable of figuring this out ourselves," Luke said.

"From what I can see, you're both off the mark, and you're both too stubborn." Hattie finished this with a firm nod.

Once again, Hattie had left Claire short on words.

"So," said Hattie. "I want you to make a documentary about me. This is not some grandiose affair to show off what I achieved, it's to set the record straight."

"Are you sure?" asked Luke.

"Darling, I've never told you everything, because it's been too painful, and I wanted to remain Hattie Fitzpatrick. That's why I sent Amelia Elliott's biographer packing. He started getting too interested in who I was, and he got way too close to uncovering the truth. But I'm ready now." Hattie concentrated on her clasped hands on her lap, then looked up. "When I was in Brisbane I went to a heart specialist."

"Why didn't you say anything?" asked Luke.

"Because I didn't want to worry anyone. Look, the short of it is that my old ticker isn't what it used to be, and I need to come to terms with the fact that it could give out at any moment. This is why seizing the day is so important." She gazed from Claire to Luke and back again. "I have kept this to myself long enough, and it's high time I cleared my name."

"Cleared your name?" asked Claire.

"Yes," Hattie said matter-of-factly. "Now, how quickly can we get started?"

Chapter Thirty-six

1994 – Starlight Creek, Queensland

In the cinema, Phil adjusted the lights on Hattie while she fussed with her dark green dress. The backdrop of Amelia Elliott's legacy was an apt setting for Hattie to tell her life story, and Claire still couldn't get her head around how fast things had happened. The second she'd contacted Phil, he was on his way to Starlight Creek with his best friend, sound man Rodney. Getting the project off the ground so quickly meant she and Luke hadn't had time to talk, but that would come—and she was frightened of how it might turn out.

Claire sat off camera, her questions at the ready. Knowing Hattie so well had helped her prepare for the interviews, and as Hattie talked about her life, Claire saw that the parallels with her own journey were uncanny. Both women had entered a world where they had to fight to be heard, and despite all the challenges, they were determined to succeed. Hattie's ability to negotiate a higher wage was impressive.

Hattie patted her hair into place.

"You look beautiful," said Claire.

Hattie gave a nervous laugh. "Bless you, lovely lass."

Claire placed the clipboard of questions on her lap. "Are you ready to continue? Remember, we can take a break anytime you want."

"No, talking about what happened is the reason we're doing this. Promise me one thing, though."

"Anything," said Claire.

"Keep filming—no matter what." Hattie's determination was admirable.

"All right." She wasn't so sure that was a good idea, but nothing would stop Claire from honoring this promise to Hattie.

"Right to go, Rod?" asked Phil. The sound man nodded, and Phil got behind the camera and used his fingers to count down from three.

Claire asked, "Hattie, after Reeves was shot, the grief must have been terrible, especially while under investigation for his death."

Tears welled up in Hattie's eyes.

"It was an extremely difficult time. I couldn't mourn the death of the man I loved with all my heart, and I was hounded by the police. I'd cooperated fully with the detectives, yet they seemed determined to drag me through the mud. And in Hollywood, mud sticks." Hattie nervously clutched a lace handkerchief. "When they arrested me two hours before his funeral, my entire world collapsed."

"Oh, Hattie, I'm so sorry."

"They were doing their job; I can see that now, but at the time I was livid. And distraught. Not only had I lost my soul mate, I was denied any chance of saying goodbye. I was a criminal in the eyes of the police and the public. Fortitude Studios dropped me like a hot potato, and I was left floundering on my own, except for my good friends Yvonne, Vanessa and George. Though they had to save their necks, as any association with me would kill their careers."

"They dumped you?"

"'Dump' is such a harsh word. No, they stood by me in silence, and I knew they had my back. I don't blame them. Hollywood is a small town, and in a time when people were getting banned for the smallest offenses, they couldn't risk it."

Claire paused, trying to take it all in. Hattie's life must have been miserable for so many years. Quietly, she asked, "Did you ever seek out your friends after you moved back to Starlight Creek?"

"I did with George, but I'll get to that momentarily. When I got back to Australia, I was determined to keep my nose clean and my head down. I said goodbye to Lena Lee as soon as I left Los Angeles, and I haven't looked back."

"How is it now, talking about your life as Lena?"

"It's hard. There're so many emotions swirling inside me right now. I had a good life for the first few years in Hollywood. It was tough, but the friends I made were incredible, and as my star rocketed skyward I managed to hold on to most of those friendships. They kept me grounded. But life has a funny way of turning things upside down when you least expect it." Hattie's laugh sounded hollow.

"What happened when they arrested you?" Claire asked gently. She studied Hattie, watching for any signs of physical distress. So far, so good.

Hattie closed her eyes, and when she opened them they were glassy. "I have no idea how long they held me in jail before my lawyer arrived. It could have been hours. It could have been a day. I'd lost all sense of time in that tiny concrete cell—my heart and mind were with Reeves as I imagined him being laid to rest. I'll never forgive them for making me miss my final goodbye." Her words were laced with bitterness, her usually relaxed jaw set hard. "To be honest, after his death, nothing held significance. If it wasn't for my friend George, and my lawyer, I probably would have gone to jail. I had no energy left to fight. I didn't think I could go on."

"What changed?"

Hattie focused on her hands for a time. Eventually, she looked up. "I realized Reeves would be heartbroken if I rotted in a jail for something I didn't do. Not fighting for my freedom would have been a disservice to his legacy, to our love." Hattie shifted in her chair and took a deep breath. "The biggest problem was that when Reeves was shot, the cameras weren't rolling. It was only a rehearsal. I'm sure it would have made a difference if they had seen my reaction on film. I may have been a good actress, but there was no way I could ever have faked my shock and grief."

Hattie shifted on her seat once more. "Even though I had won over the hearts of fans and brought in incredible amounts of money for the studio, loyalty meant nothing. It didn't help that real bullets were found in my dressing room, either."

"Oh no," said Claire. "How on earth did your name get cleared?"

"It wasn't for some time. Since it was a high-profile murder, every stone had to be turned over. That takes time. George and my lawyer did what they could, but the public were baying for blood, and circumstances meant it was mine. After all, I was the homewrecker older woman who tore Reeves Garrity and Jeanne Harris apart."

"Given what you've told me, it wasn't that way at all."

"It wasn't," said Hattie. "But because Reeves and I had snuck around like a pair of adulterers, we made ourselves look guilty." She let out a long sigh. "I would do things so very differently if I could go back."

"I think we all would."

Hattie's smile was sad. "You still can." She sat up straight, her voice businesslike once more. "All evidence pointed toward me. If I were a policeman, I would have thrown me in the slammer as well. The perpetrator was clever, oh so clever. I have to give them kudos for that."

Claire desperately wanted to hurry Hattie along to find out who'd done it, but she remained silent, waiting for the older woman to tell her story. This documentary wasn't about Claire; she was only a vehicle to help

Hattie finish business that should have been over years ago. And she was more than happy to help.

"So with a real gun in my hand and bullets in my purse, they were ready to throw away the key. Then George discovered the one thing that everybody had missed."

Claire leaned forward. "What was it?"

"Jeanne Harris was one smart cookie. She played the diva so beautifully, and she never really showed how intelligent she was. Even in the time that we were friends, I never realized how cunning she could be." Hattie inhaled slowly. "Turns out she was very good at making friends with my past."

"Oh?"

"Remember I told you about Dotty Parker, how I'd seen her at the premiere of one of my movies?"

"Yes."

"Well, I didn't hear from her after that, and I honestly thought all was well. But I should have known better. What came out later was that Dotty had come looking for me at the studios not long before that fateful day. She'd run into Jeanne, who'd been hanging around like a bad smell, and they got to talking and discovered their mutual dislike for me. Jeanne was still furious with me for taking Reeves, and Dotty had never gotten over the death of her brother, Charlie."

"The man you dated before you started working for the studio?"

"Yes, the one I met when working at the bar." Hattie ran a finger along the velvet armrest. "He was such a beautiful man. Funny. Handsome. We were quite the item. Even Dotty approved of us."

"What changed?"

"Charlie had another he was courting—booze. Of course, working in a place with such easy access didn't help. When he was sober, he was a lovely person, but that drink...oh, it really is the devil. He raised his hand to me a few times, and I quickly realized he was not someone I wanted to be with. Though breaking up with Charlie was harder than it should have been.

"He followed me. Harassed me at every turn, trying to berate me into seeing him again. When I mentioned his issues to Dotty, she refused to believe her brother could behave like that."

"She never saw him drunk?"

"He was a master of deception. Even when he hit me it was in places that could be covered up." Hattie swallowed hard. "The point is, he got drunk one night. I fought him off, and he stumbled back and fell down the stairs. I am sure he was dead before he hit the bottom."

"That's horrible." Hearing about all the traumas Hattie had gone through made Claire wonder how on earth she could be the sane, loving person she was today.

"It was. And I felt terrible. The police believed me—they had a record as long as your arm about Charlie's assaults on other women—but Dotty refused to."

"That's some serious sibling loyalty," said Claire.

"She never forgave me, even though it wasn't my fault. I tried to make it right, but Dotty wouldn't hear of it. So I left without a forwarding address, and not long after I was hired by Fortitude Studios."

"I don't quite understand the connection with Jeanne."

"It all comes together, don't worry." Hattie looked away, then focused on Claire again. "Jeanne and Dotty met at the studio, realized how much they despised me and set about formulating a plan."

"How could anyone do that to you?"

"I represented what they didn't have—I had the role meant for Jeanne, and I also had Reeves's heart, and in Dotty's eyes I took the life of her beloved brother. I'm assuming that once Jeanne heard about Charlie she figured I'd be easy to frame, that it meant I had a higher chance of landing in the clink."

"Wow."

"It was a very dark time in my life."

"I don't quite understand how shooting Reeves would help Jeanne get revenge."

"Ah." Hattie held up her finger. "That's where everything unraveled. My dress was too tight, and I fell when Alan, the novice actor, tripped. The bullet was meant for him."

"Why?"

"Because if I got arrested for shooting someone—anyone—then I'd be out of the way."

"But you didn't have any reason to shoot Alan. Hadn't you just met him?" Claire couldn't quite get her head around this very depressing story.

"Jeanne and Dotty were so intent on setting me up, I don't think they thought it through."

"What did George discover that pieced it all together?"

"No one was aware Jeanne was hiding and watching, waiting for me to pull the trigger on innocent Alan. When the gun went off and we realized Reeves had been hit, she ran from the sound studio. She collided with George on the way out, so we knew she was nearby when…" Hattie's eyes welled up once more.

"Oh, Hattie, I'm so sorry you went through all this. I'm so sorry for Reeves as well."

"I like to think I'm past it all, but I'm not. You never forget your grand love."

Claire nodded. After meeting Luke, she knew what Hattie meant.

"When George and Jeanne had run into each other, the contents of her purse spilled everywhere. He went to help, but she yelled at him and shoved everything back in. As she did so, George saw something shiny, but at the time he thought it was an earring."

"Was it...?"

"It didn't click with him at first, but after the police spoke to him a couple of days later, he started replaying that moment. Then he realized that the earring was likely a bullet. So the police went to Jeanne's house, interviewed her and found the bullet, which matched the others in the gun. No one knows why she kept it, but in this instance she did not think clearly. Thank goodness. It took some time, but they eventually got to the truth. Jeanne and Dotty may have teamed up for my downfall, but there was no loyalty between them. They both pointed fingers at each other and got what they deserved."

"Jail?"

"For some time, but Jeanne went away longer, as she was the one who exchanged the fake pistol for the real one."

Claire sat back, trying to take it all in. "It sounds like the plot of a classic Hollywood movie."

"It surely does." Hattie fell into silence and Claire let her be. Recounting such a torrid and heart-wrenching time would surely take a lot of energy. "I think of him every day."

"He sounds like a very special man."

Hattie's smile reached her eyes. "We weren't together very long, but they were some of the best days of my life. I loved him so."

"I can see," said Claire.

"There are some days I wished I'd stayed and ridden the tide. I was just getting started helping women in the industry. I wanted to use my voice to help them." Hattie reached for Claire's hand and held it gently. "You and I are cut from the same cloth, you know. We're determined, we play on our strengths but are smart enough to work on our weaknesses, and we want to change the paths of the women who come after us."

"You make it all sound so noble," said Claire.

"During my time in Hollywood I would never have said it was noble, but now, looking back on the lives I was able to change, I'm proud of

what I've achieved. Even if the end of my career brings me heartache."
Hattie stared into the distance, then shook her head, as if bringing herself
back to the present. "George and Anna May—the young actress I first
helped—kept up the home for actresses with the money from Reeves's
estate. Unbeknownst to all of us, he'd changed his will prior to his death.
Anna May became famous in her own right, so she banded with a few
other high-profile actresses to continue the legacy, and that network still
exists—at least half a dozen houses now, as I understand—and well-known
actresses still go there to give guidance and free acting lessons to those
just starting out."

"What a wonderful legacy."

Hattie sighed. "I wish I could have seen it all through. Anna May writes
often and tells me how it's all going and what the latest success stories are."

"What about George?"

Hattie dabbed her eyes with her handkerchief. "He passed away a few
years back. That's one of my biggest regrets, you know. I never saw him
after I left Los Angeles. We talked, and we wrote, but it just wasn't the
same. He was my dearest friend, and I miss him."

"Did he ever find love again?" She was met with a bright smile from
Hattie.

"He did. A young man from New York. A banker, of all people! An
interesting match, but George and Ethan were extremely happy, and for
that I am thankful. They still had to be secretive about their life together,
but at least George left this world in peace with his heart full."

"I'm so happy to hear this," said Claire. The way Hattie spoke about
them, with such detail and emotion, it was impossible not to feel like she
had met them herself. "Would you ever go back?"

"No." Hattie shook her head. "Too many ghosts."

"Ghosts can find us no matter where we are," said Claire.

"This is true."

"How hard was it to adjust back to life in Starlight Creek? After all,
you'd spent years going to glamorous parties and wearing designer gowns,
only to return to overalls and gum boots."

"It took me a very long time to be happy about living in Australia once
more. After all, I hadn't had any plans to leave Los Angeles, yet I found
myself hounded out of there clutching a fistful of broken dreams. I laid
low for a long time, living with my parents out on the sugarcane farm. My
mother still ran the cinema, but I never went near the place. Once they'd
died and I inherited it, I discovered reels of every movie I'd made, aside
from the one with Reeves, which was never finished." Hattie sighed. "That

was the best work I'd ever done. Our chemistry on and off the screen was incredible. But I digress." She rolled her shoulders back. "I inherited the cinema, and they'd even written into the will that I was welcome to sell it. Living on the farm had become difficult, because I was now a city girl trying to fit into country-girl shoes."

"I can relate."

Hattie laughed. "I think you're more country than you realize. Anyway, I needed some space to myself, and the cinema was the only place around here that afforded me that opportunity. Remember, I'd gone from a mansion in the heart of Hollywood to a tiny two-bedroom house on a farm. By the time my mother and father passed, the cinema had been closed for a few years."

"That's such a shame."

"It was," she said. "TV changed everything. The cinema used to be where everyone would gather with their families and discuss the latest goings-on in the town, but television fragmented that sense of community. Instead of chatting with friends between short films, people opted to stay home and watch TV. Don't get me wrong, I quite enjoy snuggling up on my own couch and watching a movie, but it's not the same as going to the cinema. Maybe that's where it all started going wrong."

"What did?"

"This town. Maybe this lack of community started when people exchanged a large screen for small." She shrugged. "Who knows. This is just the speculation of an old woman."

"It's a fair point," said Claire. "Do you think, though, that things are swinging around again? That movies will become social occasions? That they could bring a community together once more?"

"You could be on to something." Hattie tapped her fingers on the arm rest. "So anyway, I moved into the cinema, as it wasn't operating anymore. I originally thought it would be like living with ghosts, but somehow it was strangely comforting. Maybe being able to sit in the quiet and remember fonder times of my life as a starlet was what I needed. I'm sure it helped me come to terms with realizing that part of my life was over."

Claire hesitated, not sure about asking the next question. "I imagine painful memories would crowd in on the good."

"Yes," said Hattie. "I look at those early years living here as therapy. Mental health professionals might call me crazy, but it worked. I managed to face my demons. Well, most of them. In a way, this cinema became my crutch." She slowly looked around, taking in the expanse. "I don't know how I would have gotten through it without all this."

"Is that why you didn't sell?"

"When I first inherited it, I tried, but who wants to buy a cinema that's gone broke?"

"I've heard of people buying old churches and renovating them into bed and breakfasts."

"Pfft." Hattie waved her hand. "Those yuppies and their money."

Claire tried to contain her amusement.

"Oh, laugh all you like, but these young folk with money often don't have taste." Hattie rolled her eyes. "Will you listen to me? I sound like my grandmother! Ha!"

"Well, I, for one, think you have a very progressive view on the world."

"I like to think I do."

Claire looked at her extensive notes. "After the Hays Code was abolished in the late sixties, do you feel women in the industry have more opportunities for substantial roles?"

"To be honest, I'm not sure if we'll ever get to the point where women are valued as highly as men—at least on the payroll." Hattie rubbed her finger on her chin. "I wonder if the wheels I started turning would have sped up if I'd stayed in Hollywood."

"From what I understand, you made a very big difference in a very short time."

"I did." Hattie leaned her head against the back of the chair. "Maybe leaving was a mistake."

"Was there any way you could have stayed, though?"

"No. My time there was done. Besides." She leaned forward. "My heart wasn't in it anymore. How could it be? I'd lost the love of my life, my career, my dreams. There was nothing to salvage. Oh my." Hattie sat back. "That took more out of me than I'd expected."

"How do you feel?"

Hattie drew her brows together. "Good, I think."

"Maybe it will take some time."

"Yes, I suppose it will. So what now?" Hattie asked.

"We'll head back to Melbourne and edit everything we've filmed. We've already had interest from distributors."

"Already?"

"Yes," Claire said. "But it won't go out until you've approved it."

"Just show me when you're done. I know you will do this justice."

"Thank you." The words just didn't seem enough.

"You remind me so much of me when I was younger." Hattie's smile was slow and warm. "You're strong, independent, and want to change the world. I did—for a time. And I suspect you will as well—with longer-lasting effects, I hope."

"I'm not so sure you're right," said Claire.

"Why not?"

"You set up an organization to give women somewhere safe to live and skills they need. What have I done?"

"Oh, my dear girl! You are helping me put a matter to rest." Hattie picked at a fleck on her jacket. "You're helping me honor my Reeves. Honor those whose voices have been lost."

"There are so many lost voices."

"Exactly," said Hattie. "And it's high time they were heard. You can do this, Claire. You have the perfect medium to help, and you're talented and passionate."

Claire let Hattie's words wash over her. Everything she said made sense, and it spoke to her heart.

"Women," Claire said.

"Pardon?"

"Women's voices. That's what I need to do. I need to seek out women who are struggling to be heard, whose voices are suppressed for whatever reason, whether they were born into a world that silences them or have had their voices taken away." Claire sat forward, her body buzzing with energy. "This is it. This is what I'm supposed to do!"

Hattie grasped Claire's hand. "I couldn't think of anyone more perfect for the job."

Claire wrapped her arms around Hattie and squeezed her tight. "I don't know how to thank you!"

"You've thanked me by following your heart."

Chapter Thirty-seven

1995 – Starlight Creek, Queensland

Claire sat in the front row of Hattie's deserted cinema, hardly able to believe that six months had already passed. The TV miniseries that had originally brought Claire to Starlight Creek was well into the final stages of production, with the premiere scheduled in a couple of months. Tonight, though, was the opening night of another project—one very close to Claire's heart.

"When did you arrive?" A familiar voice echoed from the back of the cinema.

Claire spun around, happiness washing over her. "About three hours ago."

Hattie walked toward her, looking as elegant and spritely as Claire remembered. Hattie wrapped her arms around Claire, who relaxed into the hug.

Stepping back, Hattie said, "By the way, I wanted to thank you for the offer to watch the documentary before everyone else, but I'm truly happy to wait."

"Are you sure?"

"My dearest Claire, I have every faith in you. Why the self-doubt?"

"I don't know."

"Well, maybe seeing my great-nephew will cheer you up."

Claire's shoulders tensed. "We haven't spoken for a while."

"That's because you two are being ridiculous."

"No, we've both been busy. We tried, we really did, but the distance has made it next to impossible."

"I call BS."

"Hattie!"

Hattie shrugged. "If only you young ones would realize how pointless it is to let obstacles get in the way of true love."

"They're very real obstacles," she said, slightly miffed that Hattie was making it all sound trivial. "We really did try."

Between working on the documentary and picking up extra jobs with Nigel's company, Claire barely had time to eat or sleep, let alone maintain a long-distance relationship with Luke. She hated that something had to give, and doubly hated that it was Luke. But they'd promised each other neither would get in the way of the other's dreams. Although, from what she understood, Luke had done nothing to work toward his own goals. Had he fallen back into the trap of trying to please his father?

"How's he doing?" Claire asked gently.

"You'll have to ask him yourself when you see him tonight."

The butterflies in Claire's stomach fluttered. For weeks she'd convinced herself that she'd be fine seeing him, as they'd parted ways amicably. But now, in the heart of the town that had become her second home, Claire was hit by nerves and shyness. How on earth would she cope with seeing Luke? Especially when she thought about him every spare second she had?

"Is everything ready to go?" asked Hattie.

"Yes. Phil sends his apologies, as he's shooting a story in Papua New Guinea."

"Bless him. You are surrounded by such lovely people."

"I am." She stood. "I guess I better get ready."

"You can use my bathroom to shower and get dressed if you like."

"Are you sure? I don't mind going to the hotel."

"Nonsense. I like the idea that it's full circle." Hattie laughed at Claire's frown. "Don't you remember? The milkshake?"

"Ha! Yes! Oh wow, that feels like it happened ages ago."

"It certainly does." Hattie cocked her head toward the door. "Come on, let's go glam up."

* * * *

Opening night had every man, woman and child in Starlight Creek dressed in their finest. They mingled in the foyer of the cinema, as well as outside on the street, eating sausage rolls, sandwiches and delicious cakes, including lamingtons and strawberry tarts. Claire socialized, talking and laughing, happy to be back in the company of the townsfolk who once saw her as the devil incarnate.

"This is quite the crowd," said Colin, who looked smart in a light blue shirt and navy trousers.

"It's amazing," Claire said. "Thank you for coming."

"I wouldn't miss it for the world." Colin bit into a lamington. "You know, there's always been an air of mystery around Hattie. Those who knew her way back when are long gone, or have kept her secret close to their chest. I'm looking forward to learning more about her other life." He laughed. "To think we had a Hollywood starlet living in our midst!"

"Hattie is one inspiring woman." Claire tried to engage in the conversation, but the whole time she was on high alert, wondering when Luke would show.

The bell rang and the cinema lights dimmed then brightened.

"Please, excuse me." Claire went over to Hattie and threaded her arm through hers. "Are you ready?"

Hattie's lips drew into a tight line. Had she gotten cold feet?

The townsfolk swarmed into the cinema. Marcela, Scarlet and even Laura waved at Claire as they entered through the main door. Hattie stood rooted to the spot.

"Are you all right?"

"No." Hattie's body trembled.

"What can I do? Do you need a drink? To sit down? Shall we delay?" Perhaps it was all too much. After all, Hattie had bared her deepest emotional pain in front of the cameras, and now she was about to share it with everyone she knew.

"It's a mistake," Hattie muttered.

"What is?"

"I should have watched it first."

Claire looked around the deserted foyer, not sure what to do. As much as Claire wanted this premiere to go ahead, Hattie's feelings and well-being were way more important. If the townsfolk turned on Claire once more, so be it. "If you don't want me to show it, I won't."

Hattie stared at the closed doors leading into the cinema, her body stiff.

"Hattie?" Claire said gently. "What do you want to do?"

"I miss him." She sniffed. "I miss him more than I've ever expressed."

"Reeves?"

"I would have given up everything to have him alive. I've spent a lifetime keeping my hurt close to my chest. And now…" She choked on a sob. "Now I'm telling the world my innermost secrets. For what? Entertainment?"

"You did this because you wanted to honor Reeves by finishing your story. And to give voice to the young actresses who have suffered at the hands of the industry, remember?"

Hattie nodded, but her feet remained rooted to the black and white tiles.

"Can I help?" Luke strode in, his face flushed.

"Hattie's having second thoughts."

"Aunt Hattie?" Luke gently clasped her hands.

She didn't answer, and Claire feared this would be too much for her heart. She went to a nearby table and poured icy water into a glass, then handed it to Hattie, who took a few slow sips.

Luke's blue eyes looked into Claire's, and all the bravado she'd been clinging to fell by the wayside. Who was she fooling? Luke still had her heart.

"Claire is the most compassionate person we know." Luke addressed Hattie. "I would bet my life that she's done an absolutely amazing job with this documentary." Luke concentrated on his great-aunt, his eyes not straying to Claire. "Remember why you trust her. Why we both trust her."

Claire studied Luke's broad shoulders, the way his sandy hair skirted his collar, his tanned arms, his strong jaw. The soothing tone of his voice when he spoke to Hattie, and the kindness in his eyes were enough to bring tears to her own. God, she'd missed him.

Hattie blinked hard, like she was coming out of a daze. She patted Luke's hand. "I'm a silly old fool. What was I thinking? Come on." She looked at Claire. "Let's get this show on the road."

Luke glanced over Hattie's head at Claire and his expression said exactly what Claire was thinking—Hattie was faking this boldness. But wasn't everyone? Isn't that what Claire was doing now? Pretending she was absolutely fine seeing Luke again when inside she was a sad and crumpled mess?

Hattie held her chin high.

"I'll go and introduce the documentary first," said Claire. "Then I'll announce you and you can make your grand entrance." She looked at the closed doors. "I wish we had a red carpet for you."

"I don't need fanfare; I've got two of my favorite people by my side." With one hand she took Claire's hand and with the other, Luke's. "Let's do this."

Hattie squeezed Claire's hand, then let go as Claire entered the cinema alone, making her way to the small stage in front of the screen.

She took a deep breath, hoping it would calm her nerves. It didn't work. Clearing her throat, she said, "Ladies and gentlemen, boys and girls, thank you all for coming to the world premiere of *Lena Lee: The Woman Behind the Mystery*. This story was decades in the making, and we are very honored to have the star of the show here tonight. Everyone, please give a very big welcome to our beloved Hattie Fitzpatrick, also known as the talented and inspirational Lena Lee."

The audience burst into a round of enthusiastic applause as the doors to the back of the cinema opened. Bright light framed Hattie as she stood on the threshold. She didn't move forward, and once again Luke appeared at her side and held out his arm, which she took. With slight hesitation, they moved into the cinema and began the long walk to the front. As they passed each row, people stood and clapped, and some even cheered. Hattie's steps grew more self-assured, and by the time she reached the seat reserved especially for her, it was like she was walking on a cloud of confidence. She turned around, waved at the adoring audience, and motioned for them to sit down.

"Thank you." Her voice wavered slightly. "I do appreciate you taking time to come here. Please, enjoy." Hattie sat and rested her hands on her lap, her eyes trained on the blank screen.

Luke waved up at the projector room where his father was, and the screen flickered into action. Claire sat next to Hattie, while Luke took up the position on the other side of his great-aunt. As the music started, images of sugarcane blowing in the gentle breeze under a bright blue sky filled the screen. Nausea swelled in Claire's belly. She struggled to breathe. Here, in this moment, her dream was finally coming true, and she was scared out of her wits. What if Hattie didn't like it? What if the audience hated it? What if—

A tap on her shoulder brought her back into the cinema. She looked at Luke, who mouthed, "Are you okay?"

She shook her head. He motioned toward the back of the cinema. She shook her head again and followed it with a smile. Luke smiled back and returned his attention to the screen, where the camera was focused on Hattie with the sugarcane in the background. The image faded and an early photo of Hattie as a swimsuit model appeared on-screen. A loud wolf whistle filled the cinema, followed by some laughter. Hattie smiled broadly.

As the documentary progressed, Claire's nerves eased, though she kept sneaking glances at Hattie to gauge how it was all going. Thankfully, Hattie only seemed to express happiness mixed with nostalgic sadness for times long gone. Claire didn't know how she'd handle it if Hattie was angry or disappointed.

The documentary moved along, and as Hattie recounted her days in Hollywood and her rise to fame, the audience remained silent, hanging on every word. When an image of Reeves Garrity appeared on-screen, Hattie gasped and held her hand to her heart.

Claire leaned forward and whispered, "Are you all right?"

"Yes," Hattie rasped. "It's just been so long since I've seen a photo of him." Her eyes welled up and she dabbed them with her handkerchief. "Such a handsome man."

"Very handsome," whispered Claire.

Hattie remained transfixed by the documentary, her body unmoving. As the story of her love life with Reeves unfolded, a few gasps mixed with sobs filled the cinema. Her heartbreaking story of love found then lost, and then her blacklisting from Hollywood, appeared to touch people's hearts. Claire forced herself to look around at the audience and found dozens upon dozens of glassy eyes fixated on the screen. A couple of women openly cried. She glanced at Luke, whose eyes were directly on her. He smiled, and she couldn't help but do the same. Checking on Hattie once more, Claire found her staring straight ahead, her bottom lip trembling. Hattie grabbed Claire's hand and held it tight.

Hattie's face faded on the screen, and the credits slowly rolled up while Nigel's composer-wife's music floated through the speakers. Claire closed her eyes and braced herself. The silent audience unnerved her, because usually by now the cinema would be full of clapping and cheers.

A solitary, continuous clap started and in a few moments the room was full of whistles, clapping and shouting. "Bravo!" "Fabulous!" "Well done!"

Claire opened her eyes to find the entire cinema, including Hattie and Luke, on their feet, clapping wildly, their attention focused solely on Claire.

She got to her feet, using the armrest to steady herself. Turning to face the enthusiastic audience, she waved for them to stop and sit. They did so, but the excited chatter was barely contained.

"Thank you," said Claire. "You have no idea how much I appreciate your enthusiasm and support. If it wasn't for Hattie's willingness to share her story with us, we wouldn't have the documentary we do. Hattie." She reached for her hand. "I can't begin to express how grateful I am. Thank you for giving me this chance and for being so open and honest about your amazing life. I am honored to call you my friend."

Hattie patted Claire's hand.

"And now," said Claire, "please join us for post-screening celebrations!"

Hattie and Claire were instantly swarmed by people wanting to congratulate them—the love from people Claire barely knew warmed her heart. For the first time, Claire felt like part of the Starlight Creek community. After a while, the group dwindled and Claire stepped away, grateful to have a moment to herself. She quickly exited the cinema and headed over to the park to sit on the swing—just a few minutes of quiet to take it all in and breathe.

Claire pushed her toes into the ground. The swing took off and she swung her legs, her head back, eyes taking in the inky sky above. Stars twinkled and the moon shone on the town, highlighting Colin's news agency, the pub and the bakery. Since she'd left all those months ago, the entire town had enjoyed a lick of paint. Even the old Coca-Cola sign had been replaced by a mural painted by one of the talented teenagers. How could she say goodbye to Starlight Creek in a few days? Especially as she had no excuse to return, other than to visit Hattie?

"Well, they didn't lynch you."

Claire stopped swinging as Luke came over and sat on the swing next to her. "No, they didn't."

"In fact, they loved it."

"Really?" She gripped the swing chain so hard her hands hurt. Letting it go, she said, "I didn't realize I was so needy for everyone's approval."

"You've just realized your dream, Claire. It's only natural you're going to worry what people think. And from what I've been hearing, it's the best documentary a lot of them have ever seen."

"It's not exactly the world stage."

"True, but who knows where this will take you?" Luke slowly ran his hand down the side of her face. "I'm so proud of you."

Claire bristled and stood. "Don't."

"Don't what?"

"Don't think we can go back to this again. We've tried, it didn't work."

"Claire..."

"I'm serious, Luke." Even though she sounded confident in her decision, her heart yearned for the only man she'd ever loved.

"Stop," he said.

"What?"

"Stop pushing me away. We can make this happen."

"I want to, more than anything, but the distance is too great and you've barely returned my phone calls and—"

"My retreat opens next week."

"What?" she almost shrieked.

"I've been working crazy hours to make it happen."

"Luke!" She wrapped her arms around him and gave him a kiss, then quickly stepped away, embarrassed. "I'm sorry."

"Why?" He laughed. "I'm glad you're happy about this."

"Of course I am! This is your dream!" Excitement buzzed through her. "Oh my god. Your dream. You're actually doing it!"

"Thanks to you."

"How so?"

"After you left, I reassessed my entire life, especially what I wanted. You were off living your dream and I was…just thinking about it. Your belief in yourself inspired me."

"Belief in myself?" Claire laughed. "It's all bravado. Like my grandma always said, 'fake it until you make it.'"

"She really said that?"

"My grandma was before her time." When Claire looked into Luke's eyes, her resolve wavered and nerves made her want to flee. "I better go back to the party."

She turned, but Luke grabbed her hand. He gently pulled her toward him and she leaned against his chest, listening to his rapidly beating heart.

"I've missed you," he whispered into her hair.

She pursed her lips, too scared to say anything for fear the dam of hot tears would explode.

They stood in the park in silence, the sounds of merriment across the road. Claire nestled into his strong arms, wishing she could stay like this forever. Being in his company only reminded her what she'd walked away from, yet she couldn't give up on her dream now that things had started moving in the right direction. Damn it. Luke was right. There was no way anyone could have everything they wanted.

"Ah, here you are!" Hattie crossed the street and Claire and Luke broke apart. "When are you coming back to the party? People want to talk with the woman of the hour."

"That's you, Hattie, not me."

"Oh, my dear girl, without you I would never have been able to tell my story—Reeves's story. When are you going to realize how talented you are? You could get Marcel Marceau talking!" Hattie stopped and looked from Claire to Luke. "I'm sorry, I've interrupted something."

"No, no, it's okay," said Luke. "We were just reminiscing."

Luke's offhandedness made Claire wonder if she'd imagined the tender moment they'd just shared. Hattie turned and headed toward the cinema but stopped before she crossed the road, her eyes fixed on her building. Luke and Claire stood next to her.

"My, she is beautiful," sighed Hattie.

"She is," Claire said. "What's going to become of her now?"

Hattie looked at Luke.

"You tell her," said Hattie. "I better go mingle. And Claire?"

"Yes?"

"Thank you for everything. Your arrival in Starlight Creek has changed the lives of many, and you've helped this old duck finally remember her past and how much she's achieved." Hattie's grin was like a five-year-old's. "I'm going back to it. Toodle-oo!" With a wink at her great-nephew, Hattie crossed the road, leaving Claire and Luke in the darkness once more.

She turned to Luke. "What's happening with the cinema?"

"My artists' retreat isn't all that's happening."

"Pardon?"

"Hattie and I have decided to keep the cinema open, and we're going to specialize in Hollywood classics. In fact…" He smiled. "Hattie is going to lead the way by showing movies and talking about her time in Hollywood. We're already booked up every weekend for the next six months."

"Really?"

"And it wouldn't have happened without you."

"I'm sure in time you two would have—"

"Claire." Luke's tone was one of frustration.

"What?"

"You can't see it, can you?"

"What?"

Luke laughed. "Is that your favorite word?"

"Pardon?" She joined in his laughter.

Luke held her face in his hands, his gaze intense. "Please, stay."

"I can't. I ……" Her shoulders slumped. "We can't keep going around in circles!"

Claire looked at the cinema and all the townsfolk milling out front, camaraderie in their laughter and animated chatter. How very different Starlight Creek was from when she had first arrived. Once a town on the verge of collapse that had shunned newcomers for years, now it had a palpable energy and warmth that invited strangers in. Never in her life had she felt more at home.

"This could be my base," she said. "I'd have to travel a lot."

"I'd be here, waiting for your return."

"Are we really doing this?" She laughed. "Are you sure?"

"I've never been surer in my life."

Luke's lips met hers.

Home at last.

Luke moved back slightly, his lips kicking into a slow smile. "And Claire?"

"Yes?"

"You were right. It is absolutely possible to have everything you wish for. I've wished for you for a very long time."

"Then you have me." She rested her head against his shoulder, taking in the cinema that had changed so many lives. "Dreams really can come true."

THE END

Acknowledgments

Once again I am so very blessed to work with a wonderful group of people who love stories as much as I do.

A huge thank you to the talented and magnificent team at Kensington Publishing. It's an absolute delight working with all of you. Extra special thanks to my wonderful editor, Esi Sogah, whose passion for the written word shines through in everything she does. Esi, your fabulous feedback and encouragement is always greatly appreciated and your eye for detail is amazing.

A super big thank you to the brilliant Lucienne Diver of The Knight Agency. I adore working with you and your insight, support and enthusiasm is fabulous. Thank you so much for all that you do.

Stories like this can't happen without in-depth research and I've been so very fortunate to have had the help of a plethora of experts in the field of film and television. My heartfelt thanks goes to those who answered my myriad questions and allowed me to experience what life on set was really like: Pino Amenta, Sue Edwards, Yael Bergman, David Hart, Kevin Carlin, Kate Atkinson, Susie Porter, Kathy Chambers, Penny Moore, the cast and crew of *Trust Frank*, Marion "Maz" Farrelly, Denise Eriksen, the Australian Film Television and Radio School, and Women in Film and Television.

Of course, I need to thank my writing crew who think it is totally normal if I talk to myself or the characters in my head. Thank you to: Dave Sinclair, Angela Ackerman, Di Curran, Nicki Edwards, Delwyn Jenkins, Heidi Noroozy, Juliet Madison, Kariss Stone, Kerri Lane, Louise Ousby, Natalie Hatch, Lisa Ireland, Rachael Johns, Supriya Savkoor, T.M. Clark, Ros Ward, Tess Woods and Vanessa Carnevale for brainstorming and cracking the whip when needed.

Thank you so much to all the booksellers, book bloggers, librarians, journalists and every reader who promotes authors and their books. On behalf of every author, I extend a huge thank you because without you, our stories would not be make it out in this world.

A whole world of thank-yous to my extended family and nonwriting friends who don't mind when I'm a little distracted with my characters and plotting. This journey is so much sweeter with your unwavering support. Special thanks to Mum, Dave and my beloved Dad and Nanna (missing you always) for encouraging me to follow my dreams.

Thank you to my partner Garry and my gorgeous kids Rebecca and Nicholas: you are the sunshine in my life and your laughter the sparkle. Love you so very much!

This book is dedicated to my brother Dave who shares my passion for writing books as well as our love for Hollywood classic movies. I probably don't say it enough, but I'm so glad you're my brother, Dave. Love ya!

And a special thank you to you, dear reader, for choosing to spend time in *The Cinema of Lost Dreams*.

CPSIA information can be obtained
at www.ICGtesting.com
Printed in the USA
LVHW031509071119
636673LV00002B/156/P

9 781516 109197